LAC

CHIMERA
Part One

LACUNA

CHIMERA
Part One

Erin Hosfield

Elsewhen Press

LACUNA
First published in Great Britain by Elsewhen Press, 2024
An imprint of Alnpete Limited

Elsewhen Press, PO Box 757, Dartford, Kent DA2 7TQ
www.elsewhen.press
British Library Cataloguing in Publication Data.
A catalogue record for this book is available from the British Library.
ISBN 978-1-915304-43-8 Print edition
ISBN 978-1-915304-53-7 eBook edition

Designed and formatted by Elsewhen Press

LACUNA | ləˈkjuːnə |

(*n.*) *a blank space; a missing piece.*

✳ ✳ ✳ ✳ ✳ ✳ *ONE* ✳ ✳ ✳ ✳ ✳ ✳

"She says I worry too much," the woman says, the metal crochet hook glinting with her repetitive motions. It's purple, same as her handbag. "But I mean, as her mother it's hard *not* to. I don't want her to make the same mistakes I did."

I sigh as I pick at the pilled fabric covering my armrest. If only we had foresight when it comes to mistakes. You never know until it's too late, and then you're stuck with your choice. It's a concept I'm all too familiar with, but I don't want to say something so negative to a complete stranger, so I opt for advice instead.

"From what you've told me it seems she's both smart and capable, just don't be too hard on her when she *does* make a mistake. It's bound to happen."

"I know," she sighs. "I just want her to find her joy a lot faster than I did. The first step is landing a good job after she graduates. Her field is so competitive. What kinda work do you do?"

The train wheels clack loudly as we cross a bridge, the noise allowing me a pause before I answer. I'm still hung up on her comment about joy. I want to tell her that some people never find it, but I don't. Instead, I shift my eyes away from the purple hook to the streaked glass. It's raining, wet droplets hitting the dirty windows at a sharp angle. Scenery blurs past, the amorphous landscape of the past few hundred miles now sharp squares of tightly packed buildings. The cloudless blue skies had turned to gray haze somewhere within the past hour, and the dreariness is only making me drowsier. I'd planned on sleeping through the last leg of this trip, but the woman seated next to me insisted on conversation. It was nice for a while — having company, watching her effortlessly crochet a long string into a square of neat little rows. Listening to her tell me about how excited she is to visit her daughter alongside her worries about her future.

Lamenting our joint distaste for the obtrusive scents hanging in the air — diesel, sweat, and someone's overbearing perfume. Now she's asking questions. They're not too probing just yet, but they could become so at any moment. I used to be able to fend them off without a second thought, but it's times like these I wish I didn't have to. I'm tired of dodging casual inquiries, hiding behind lies. It's extraordinarily lonely.

"What do you do? For work?" She asks again. I'm still looking out the window, but I can feel her eyes on me. I'm covered in tattoos and wonder what occupation she's already made up for me in her head.

"Me? I'm a tattooist." It's truth, but I hope the follow up isn't to ask for how long. That I can't answer truthfully.

"Really?" She pauses to wind the yarn. "I figured you must've just known someone who did them. You do yours yourself?"

"I did a few on myself when I was learning, but otherwise no."

"My daughter has a tattoo," she continues, the crochet hook moving swiftly again. "You work in the city? Maybe you know where she got it."

"I wouldn't know, unfortunately. I'm only just moving there." I nod to the bags surrounding my feet. I hate moving, but it's necessary. I'm lucky jumping around isn't uncommon for someone in my line of work. I shove my hand into my pocket to feel for the keys that will unlock the next part of my life, making sure they're still there. They are, and I feel their jagged edges along with my dulled switchblade and a chewed piece of gum, sticky in its wrapper.

"Why anyone would want to live there is beyond me," she sighs, shaking her head. "Rainiest spot on this side of the continent. I'm glad my daughter wants to leave once she finishes university. I hope wherever she finds a good opportunity is a little sunnier — maybe even with a beach. I'd much rather visit somewhere like that. Why you moving? Have family there?"

That I can't answer with complete honesty. The truth is that I'm stuck in an endless cycle of not staying in one place for too many years and not getting too close to anyone. I ache to build a home and stay there, to trust someone enough to share my secret. I fantasize about a different life, but I'm trapped in this one, the result of my own immutable mistake. I can't tell her any of that, so I decide to answer with vague truth instead.

"No family, just work. I got one of those good opportunities you mentioned."

"You must *really* love your job," she laughs, nudging me with her elbow. "Or you just don't hate the rain as much as I do. Seriously — do you enjoy it? Your job?"

I smile back at her. Tattooing is the center of my universe, but maybe that's because it's all I have to love.

"Very much. It keeps me going."

"Good," she says. "I want that for her, too. Beach or no beach."

Before she can ask anything else, the crackly operator's voice announces the last stop before entering the city, and the train begins to slow. Passengers move to gather their belongings, and the woman winds up her yarn.

"Well, this is me," she says, wrapping the hook in the crocheted square and stuffing it into the pocket of her handbag. I'm trying to think of a proper farewell as she stands up, when she unexpectedly grasps my hand.

"It was really nice chatting — made the trip go so much faster," she says. She pauses, squeezing my hand gently. "Best of luck to you. I know you'll find it."

"Find what?"

She smiles. "Your joy."

She slings her handbag over her shoulder and gives me a little wave as she filters into the aisle. Her departure is sort of bittersweet. Even though I'm happy to be off the hook from answering any more questions, she's left me with a certain longing. I'd gotten to experience a glimpse of her life, and though I'd wanted to, I couldn't let her into mine. I hadn't even told her my name.

3

I pull my bags from the floor and set them beside me. The interaction with the woman was pleasant enough, but I'd prefer to spend the time I have left on this train in silence, and a small blockade should ensure I get it. I nestle further into the seat as I rub the condensation from the window. There it is, shimmering in the distance, the glittery lights of the city veining gray landscape like crystals in a geode. It's beautiful, and a swell of hope rises in my chest as I think of her parting words. Maybe she's right. Maybe this beginning will be different from the others. I can allow myself that belief, can't I?

I'm finally dozing off when I'm jolted by someone dropping heavily into the seat beside me. It's a large man, and he's moved my bags across the aisle. Two more men seat themselves in the row in front of us, their similar looking jackets leading me to believe they're traveling together. A quick glance tells me the rest of the car is empty, and I'm suddenly annoyed. Why did they have to crowd me in? There's plenty of space on this train. He looks like he might be considering engaging me in a conversation I want no part of, so I get to my feet.

"Oh, you're all right there, miss," he says. His size is a little intimidating, and I'm noticing his greasy skin and pockmarked cheeks. I don't like the way he's grinning at me. "No need to get up on my account."

I'm all out of politeness, but I offer him a thin lipped smile anyway. "I need to get my bags. Excuse me."

He doesn't move at all. It takes an effort to squeeze around him without crawling over his lap, and I grunt as I lurch into the aisle. So much for common courtesy.

"Come on — don't go," he says. "Keep us company."

When I glance over my shoulder he's right behind me, and the hair on the back of my neck stands up. Is he going to *follow* me? If he's this bold maybe I should relocate to another car altogether. Silently I pick up my bags and move down the walkway. Exiting and ignoring work best in these situations — never respond, never antagonize, just *go*. If I'm good at anything it's removing myself when necessary. Just as I reach the door I'm jerked to a stop — he's grabbed the strap on my bag. I whirl around to face him, and his smile sends a shiver through me.

"What's your hurry, love?"

He moves in close — so close I can smell his rotten breath. To my horror, he reaches up and tucks a strand of my hair behind my ear, his calloused fingers grazing my face. I recoil at his touch, and his grin quickly turns into an ugly sneer. In a flash he grabs a fistful of my hair, and before I can react I'm slammed against the glass.

"That how it's going to be, eh? I don't think so," he growls. Panicked, I slap the glass with my palm and call for help, but he laughs. "Go ahead. Scream your little head off. You see anyone on that car?"

I glance sideways and he's right — that car is empty too. Just my luck. Everyone must've gotten off on the last platform. He's got me pinned — meaty fist full of my hair, hot breath steaming my cheek. What do I do? He's strong, and there's no one here to help me. I try not to whimper as he grinds against me, and feel the sharp corner of the door latch press painfully into my thigh.

Wait — it's not the door latch.

It's my knife.

I've never used it as a weapon but I might have to now. I creep my hand into my pocket. He snakes his fingers into the waistband of my leggings, and when I writhe away he grabs hold, exposing my hip.

"What have we here? Tatted all over — wonder what else you've got under there for me."

I know what he's after, and it's only heightening my fear. I can't let this happen. I have to do something. He loosens his grip on my hair, and my heart races as I blindly sweep my arm up. The blade makes contact, and he roars as he steps back. It's the opportunity I need, and I'm through the door in an instant, quickly locking it behind me. He lunges for the latch, his hand pressed to his cheek, bright red blood oozing from between his fingers. His face — gods, I've cut his *face*. I turn on my heel and dash down the aisle, his booming voice behind me.

"I'll kill you, you bitch... I'll *FUCKING KILL YOU!*"

I'm almost to the back of the train when I hear the operator's voice again, and the vessel slows. The train stops and I leap onto the wet platform, nearly falling to my knees with the weight of my bag. I'd dropped the others in the scuffle, but I can't go back — the men are piling off a few cars up and they've already spotted me. I sprint to the end of the platform, pushing past people and running right into a few. I reach a stairwell and jump several steps to the landing, then bolt onto the street. I hear their voices behind me, so I keep running and don't look back.

I end up near a dark body of water with rows of docks. A harbor. I'm winded and can't keep running — I need to hide. My eyes land on dry ground beneath one of the docks, so I hop over the low wall and squeeze myself under the wooden planks. I freeze when I hear shoes slapping to a slow and cover my hand with my mouth. They're right above me.

"Where'd she go?"

"I don't see her. Let's try that way."

Some coughing, and phlegm splats on the dock."We can't chase her all fucking day. We're not even supposed to be here and he knows it."

"He's gonna be pissed."

"He'll deal. Come on — let's go. We gotta catch the next train."

The footsteps pick up and recede, finally trailing off into nothing. I think I'm safe, but I should wait a little longer to make sure they'd actually gone. My heart rate slowly returns to normal as I listen to water lapping against rock, and the sounds of the city echoing across the water. I inspect the bag I managed to save, fabric rustling as I zip it open. I hope everything is still where it should be. The others were stuffed with clothing and books that can be replaced, but there are things in this bag that cannot. I sigh in relief — all my equipment is inside, and that green glass bottle is intact. I sink back against the wall, cradling the bag in my arms. This better not set the theme for my time here. Moving again so soon isn't in the plan.

★ ★ ★ ★ ★ ★ TWO ★ ★ ★ ★ ★ ★

Despite the rocky entry, I'm determined to give this city a fair chance, and let hope resurface as I unlock the door to my new home. It's much smaller than I envisioned, the tiny two story building sandwiched between taller more modern looking structures. The second floor living space is one main room, containing only two windows and the tiniest kitchen I've ever seen. The washroom is a closet, barely big enough to turn around in. The ceilings are low, some of the lights don't work, and the baseboards are thick with too many coats of paint. A few pieces of furniture are scattered around — a table with a single chair, a floor lamp with a smudged shade, and thin mattress on two wooden pallets. The apartment is clean though, and despite its meager furnishings, I like it.

The studio below is equally small. A client barely fits let alone another artist, and I'm happy to not have to share my space with anyone for once. The former occupant is an old coworker I'd kept in contact with here and there, and she'd recently retired. Even though it caused me a fair amount of guilt, I'd had to continuously make excuses for why we couldn't meet in person, since I could never again let her see my face. She'd been kind and generous despite my avoidance, and had set me up with this place before she moved, leaving behind all her studio furniture and supply contacts. The lease would remain in her name, but I prefer it that way, and it'll give me five years to decide my next step. It's perfect. She'd been steadily busy, and my style of tattooing is in line with hers, so I slip into a new routine without much of a hitch.

I stay close to home, worried I'll run into the men from the train. I haven't seen them since, but I'm still on edge, and one of my new clients calls attention to it.

"Scared I might run?" she grins after I greet her, watching me double check the lock on the studio door.

"Lady who used to work here never did that. Do you have a stalker or something?"

I attempt to laugh it off. "Oh — no. Well… Sort of. The stalker, I mean."

She eyes me eagerly, hands clasped as she waits for me to elaborate on what I'm sure she thinks is a tidbit of entertaining gossip. A relationship gone sour, or an obsessed client, perhaps. I decide to give her an edited version of my train encounter so as not to let her down completely.

"Oh, *them*. That gang's a nasty lot." She shakes her head, casually dropping her coat on my table. "A real shame that happened, and on your first day here, too!"

She seems more disappointed than worried about what I revealed, and it makes me curious.

"You know of them? Who are they?"

"Everyone *knows of them*. Call themselves the Skulls — could've been a bit more creative with that, I think. They're bad news, but they don't come around much." She smiles reassuringly, jutting her chin toward the locked door. "I don't think you have much to worry about. Especially not in this part of town."

I want to feel relieved, but I'm not quite swayed.

"How do you know that?"

"Used to work at a bar uptown," she says. "Seedy as hell. When they'd show they'd only stay a couple of weeks tops. Stay out of places like that and you should be good." She shifts her gaze to the sketches I'd taped to the wall, clearly ready to move on. "I *love* these! Think you can pick up where she left off?"

Comforted by my client's reassurance, I begin cautiously venturing further, taking long walks through the rainy streets to see what this city has to offer. I like its dreary moodiness, misty clouds often obscuring the tops of the buildings, their sharp shapes reflected in oblong pools of standing water. There's life beneath the city's dismal grit, embedded in the structures like hidden treasures, and discovering them quickly becomes my favorite activity. A specialty grocer here, a quaint bookshop there, a smattering of warm and cozy hole in the wall restaurants. More secondhand stores than I can count, their eclectic wares piled haphazardly behind dirty fogged windows. There's an open air market that appears every weekend beneath the harbor bridge, the stalls disappearing as quickly as they came, come the work week. To my delight I encounter an actual gem — a little apothecary only a few yards from the market. Dried herbs and fragrant sundries line the narrow aisles next to elixirs and hand labeled remedies, and a mousy looking man with thick glasses smiles from behind the counter. He's kind, greeting me sweetly every time I visit, which becomes often. I love the feel of the place, and could circle it for hours taking it all in. I'd come across a handful of similar places throughout the course of my life, but none quite like it. I fill my bag with crisp bundles of yerba santa to scent my apartment, valerian root to help me sleep, a variety of incense sticks for the studio, and mint and lemongrass for my tea.

The weeks begin to blend together, turning into months. I spend my mornings wandering along the harbor, treating myself to takeaway coffee before opening my studio for the day. I cover the apartment walls with taped up drawings, fill the surfaces with knickknacks and books, and cycle through bouquets of flowers I buy at the market. I disappear into paperbacks while I do my laundry, and listen to the same songs on my thrifted stereo as I draw night after night. The newness of the city fades along with my hope, and that loneliness creeps in. As time progresses, it grows worse than ever before, and I begin to question everything. What's the point of living like this? Doomed to exist on the outskirts, watching the lives of others unfold? Always feeling empty, like something's missing? I have everything — or at least, I tell myself I do — but a void has taken up residence in my heart and I don't know how to fill it.

I picture it sometimes. It's an incomplete shape, like an

early draft of one of my drawings. A half circle waiting to be shaded in, a bud waiting to bloom into a flower. I try to find a way to fill it — I duck into bars, hoping that surrounding myself with others will make me feel less alone. Present the illusion that I'm part of something. All the ones I find are too full of the sort of people I dislike, leaving me more empty than before. Maybe there's no answer there — maybe this is just the way it's supposed to be. Me and that void and nothing else, until one day it sucks the rest of me in.

I stop going out and the depression rises, becoming an endless sea with me in the center. The interactions with clients keep me from floating too far, so I let them buoy me along as I drift in and out of their lives, imagining what it's like being them instead of me. I retain the hope that living vicariously through them might be enough, but it isn't. I long to feel like anything besides what I am — a shadow, lost in a perpetual daydream.

"So you really don't go out? *Ever*?" My client asks. He's young, with a kind face, and his name is Seth. He'd been telling me about his own spiraling depression, and I'd mentioned my hermit-like tendencies as an afterthought. I didn't really expect him to zero in on my response.

"Well, I... Guess I don't really see the point to it. That and I've yet to find somewhere I actually enjoy."

"I know what you mean, but if you hole yourself away you'll only feel worse. I can tell you that from experience. Here —" he says, struggling to reach into his back pocket. "I know a place you might like."

The machine continues to buzz as I sit back, waiting for him to locate what he's after. After a moment of searching he hands me a card.

"There's this club I went to the other week. You should try it out. I guarantee it'll lift your spirits."

I stop the machine and remove my gloves to accept it, his unfinished forearm of dark roses staring up at me. The card is black matte, with shiny characters spelling out an address.

"No name? It's not called anything?"

"If it has a name I don't know it. It's sort of a secret, so I think it might be more your speed. Less mainstream crowd." I set it down to resume shading in the last rose, and he winces. "Oof — this is really starting to hurt. How much longer?"

I finish his piece sans further interruptions, and after I've cleaned my table I pick up the card again. I've already decided it won't be worthwhile, so I toss it into the top drawer of my workbench.

He's not the only one to encourage me to broaden my horizons, and it becomes clear I need to do a better job of keeping my personal life to myself. I have another client ask me a series of questions I answer with too much honesty, and she scoffs when I tell her I'm not seeing anyone, nor am I interested in looking.

"You can't be serious." She raises an eyebrow. "You haven't been on so much as *one* date since you moved here? For a whole *year*?"

"Not a one." I'm amused by both her nosiness and her incredulousness. Especially since there's a little irony to the latter, as I'm halfway through covering up the name of a no longer significant other on her ankle. "I don't mind it. Really."

"Bullshit," she laughs. "It's not good to be by yourself for so long. Maybe you just haven't met the right person yet. Ooh — I know! I have this friend, and —"

"I'm perfectly fine, thank you." She's about to try and rope me into a setup, and I want no part of it. "Now what would you like for this flower? Purple or blue?"

It's a lie though — one of many I've constructed for myself. I'm not fine on my own, even though I've spent a long time as such. Regardless, relationships are dangerous territory, so it's better to skip them altogether. I don't need that sort of complication.

I long to have real friends too, and it's been an equally lengthy time since I've had any at all. It's easier to keep to myself; it lessens the amount of lies I have to fabricate.

I have to put on enough of a show for my clients, and I'm not sure it's worth continuing outside my work hours for the sake of a little company. It's an endless loop — the quiet honesty of solitude perpetuating my loneliness, and I don't know if I can break free of it.

Several weeks later I'm sitting in the same spot, listening to my client divulge her most recent romantic failure while I decorate her hip with a strand of curving green ivy. I nod sympathetically along with her story, trying to concentrate on my work while simultaneously playing my part. Her woes only compound my own, and together they form a heaviness in the pit of my stomach. It's a hopeless feeling, and I have to pour all my focus into giving her my best smile as I finish up. Her new adornment cheers her, and she hugs me after observing it in the mirror. I'm no stranger to hugs but this one brings me to tears, the simple gesture reminding me how much I long to be close to someone. I've successfully imparted her with a little positivity but I'm empty all over again after she's gone, and slowly clean my tray in silence.

As I'm putting my machines away I notice a loose screw, and sigh when I can't immediately find the tool I need to tighten it. I rummage through the top drawer but instead of the tool, there in the bottom is that black card, long forgotten. I pick it up and turn it over, the lettering shining under my work light. I catch a glimpse of myself in the long mirror next to my workbench as I shut the drawer. I look tired, my face a little gaunt. I turn the card over again and so does my reflection. It can't hurt to try, can it?

✳ ✳ ✳ ✳ ✳ ✳ *THREE* ✳ ✳ ✳ ✳ ✳ ✳

Neon lights pulse in a steady rhythm, illuminating the steps in pink and green as I ascend. I do the same thing each time I visit this club — pause at the top to take a deep breath, hoping it'll slow my heart. I tell myself it's because I'm out of shape, but the true reason lies just beyond the top step, behind the bar.

"There you are," he says, greeting me with his standard crooked smile as I slide into my chair. "The usual?"

I smile back. "Hi Rhys. Am I predictable now?"

"I prefer 'steady' in lieu of 'predictable'," he chuckles, watching me set my bag on the bar. "And I like steady."

He reaches for a glass on a high shelf as I dig in my bag for my cigarettes. It's a vice I'd quit on and off, but I see no reason to deny myself small pleasures at this point. Once I find them, I survey the scene as I wait for him to hand me an ashtray. It's quiet up here tonight, only one other patron at the end of the bar, though the dance floor below is in full swing. I had no idea what to expect the first time I came in, but it wasn't this. When I arrived at the address I wondered if I was in the right place, since the exterior didn't resemble any sort of venue at all. It looked like an abandoned warehouse, its corrugated siding rusted and dirty, and there was no sign, no lights, no line to get in. Just a double door. I almost didn't open it, but I'm glad I did. I liked what was behind it so much that I became a regular.

I prefer the bar on the upper level — it's calmer here, separated from the nightclub portion by a glass wall. The sleek modern accents give it an upscale feel, but the warm wooden bar top and leather chairs are cozy, and the electronic music is exactly my vibe. I like to sit in the corner where I can see everything while I sip my cocktail and draw or read. My low-key experience differs from that of the frenzied dancers below, but I enjoy watching. Sometimes I even join them for a little while, returning to my seat hoping the thin sheen of sweat I've accumulated won't be noticeable to the bartender. He's always working on the nights I visit, and his presence is mainly the reason for my repetitive attendance. I'd never disclose that even if I *had* someone to tell, since I can barely admit it to myself.

A glass ashtray appears in front of me along with my cocktail, and he waits for me to position my cigarette, matchbook in hand. He always offers to light it if he's available, and I always let him. I think it's a nice gesture — dated, but nice. He follows by lighting his own with the half burned match, the delicate paper clenched between his thin lips. They're hand rolled, never store bought, which seems a little pretentious even though I've come to know him as anything but.

I'm usually reserved, and prefer silence around strangers until I observe them long enough to calculate my words, but he felt nothing like a stranger when I met him. He was warm, and something about him seemed almost familiar. He's definitely familiar now, and I cautiously let my eyes drift over him as he wipes down the bar top, the cigarette clamped between his teeth.

He's always in a white button down rolled to the elbows, his jeans so weathered they're more pewter than black, their pocket edges tattered. His forearms are covered in tattoos, and there's another peeking out from beneath his collar — a missable detail to most, but I find it hard to overlook anything about him. He's tall, and a little on the lanky side of thin, though he's not graceless or awkward. He has tired circles beneath his dark eyes, but he's vibrant, never withdrawn. His face is angular — high cheekbones and aquiline nose, his sharp jaw edged with grayed sideburns stretching to meet the lines that form when he smiles. He's older than I — at least, he *looks* older — though it's difficult to pinpoint his actual age. The head of gray hair suggests he's more advanced in his years, but he doesn't move like it. He's not what most would consider conventionally attractive, but I'd never been drawn to those with that label anyway. Conventional or not, he's caught my attention. So much so that it's sometimes hard for me to make eye contact.

I shift my gaze just as he fixes his on me, heat creeping up the sides of my face. It happens every time, and has since the very first night.

**

"I've never seen someone so immersed in a book of botanicals before," he says, peering over his shoulder to watch me page through a musty smelling hardback. It's illustrations of local flora — I'd picked it up in a bookshop I liked to frequent, and brought it along so I have something to do. He smiles a little crooked smile as he wipes down the mirrored wall behind the bottles in wide circular motions.

"It's research." I run my thumb along the sketchy lines detailing the life cycle of a maidenhair fern. "Well... Sort of."

"Are you considering adopting one of these ferns?"

"No — it's more reference than research, actually. For drawing purposes." I earmark the book before closing it, and swig the last of my drink. He motions to the empty glass, and I pause as if I'm considering before nodding for another. I can tell he's waiting for me to elaborate while he fills the shaker with ice, but I say nothing.

"You're an artist, then?" he muses, reflected light from the shining container dancing across the bar. I smile shyly as my answer, and he smirks as he pours the liquid into a glass. "Possibly of the dermatological persuasion?"

"You've guessed right. What gave me away?"

He raises an eyebrow as he looks me over. Dark green foliage and wine colored blooms wind the length of my arms, cascading across my chest. His gaze is making me self-conscious, so I pull my sweater up a bit.

"An uncommon deduction. Usually people assume I look the way I do because I'm friends with a tattooist, not that the artist is, in fact, *me*."

He looks amused as he leans back against the shelves. "Well, I haven't. Besides —" He scratches behind his ear, the tip of a tattooed wing revealing itself beneath his white collar. "I like to think I've spent adequate time in the company of your fellow craftsmen to recognize you as one."

My eyes move over his forearm, watching the sinewy muscles flex. Dark twisting thorns and broad leaves cover his skin from elbow to wrist, with symbols dotted in between. I'm not close enough to see what they are, and don't want to ask. Instead, I nod towards his arm.

"It seems you certainly have." I open the book again, and smooth the creased corner. He leans across the bar to peer at the page.

"So what's your next client about to receive? One of these?"

"Maybe. I get requests, but mostly I draw in hopes someone will choose something I like, too."

"Ah, so you're a genuine fan, then," he grins, a crooked smile taking over his face.

It's hard not to smile back at him. I *am* a fan. I'm tempted to tell him I have both drawings and pictures of botanicals taped all over my apartment, but I don't.

"I mean, isn't it obvious? Just look at me."

"I *am* looking at you."

He is — he has been the whole time — and it's making me blush. It's not at all the sort of stare I find unwelcome, either. His eyes are dark and deep with a lively spark to them, and a certain softness I'm not accustomed to. The kind that makes my pulse quicken; a feeling I'd thought long dead. I don't know how to respond, but thankfully he doesn't wait for me to speak.

"I hope you don't mind my imposition," he says, resting his elbow on the bar as he nods towards my book. "Horticulture is an interest of mine too, so I can't help but be curious. How do you dictate your design?"

I don't mind it. His polite inquisition is pleasant — not

at all like the sort of questions I'm usually barraged with when unveiled as an artist. I'm happy to oblige him, so I explain my curation process — how I choose a leaf that turns just the right way, and which unfurling frond will translate best to skin.

***

"So?" He asks, snapping me out of my memory. "How was your week? Anything new and exciting?"

"Nothing out of the ordinary. I doubt I have anything to dazzle you with."

"I'll be the judge of that," he jokes, leaning his elbow on the bar. "Any projects to share with me? Have a plot line in one of those paperbacks you like that you're dying to pick apart?"

I smile as I tap my cigarette on the ashtray. We've established something like a routine, and he's become a bright spot in my otherwise mundane life. The time I spend with him usually involves him asking about my sketches before he moves on to ask more about me — my likes, my dislikes, my opinions — then following up with his own. I like the familiarity of his questions, and for once I don't feel the need to shy away from them. They're basic enough that I have yet to answer with a lie, and I get to learn a little about him as a bonus. We'd been ticking them off one by one — I'd discovered he'd traveled more than me, he prefers nonfiction while I like fiction, and we have overlapping tastes in music. Only partially when it comes to that — his admittance of a few of his guilty pleasures made me wrinkle my nose. I was also surprised to find out we share a mutual distaste for a staple of modern society. Neither of us watches television, which seems a rare thing nowadays.

I pick up my glass to take the first sip, its tart spiciness burning my tongue. I'm acutely aware of his eyes on me, and my heart speeds up again. I wonder what I'll learn about him tonight.

✶ ✶ ✶ ✶ ✶ ✶ *FOUR* ✶ ✶ ✶ ✶ ✶ ✶

I'm at war with myself.

I know I should keep my distance, but it feels impossible. The smile that appears on his face when he sees me approach the bar makes my heart beat a little faster, and I've started living for my nights with him. His addition is spurring forbidden daydreams, and I'm asking myself all new questions. Ones I shouldn't be considering.

"Sorry — I promise I'm not ignoring you," he says, hastily lining up glasses on the edge of the bar as he nods towards my empty one. He's busier tonight, and he seems annoyed about it. Almost like he'd rather it be quiet so we can have one of our easy conversations.

I glance at the group of girls crowding the end of the bar. "I can wait — I'm not your only task at the moment, and I'm not in any sort of hurry."

"While I do appreciate your easygoing nature, I'd prefer if you *were* my only task," he says, muddling clumps of bright green mint in the bottoms of the glasses. "That being said, I wouldn't label you a task at all. Just give me a few more minutes."

I blush deeply, and glance at the group again as he divvies out their drinks. They're all beautiful and dressed to the nines, meanwhile I hadn't even changed out of my work clothes. I was in too much of a rush to get here. My eyes move over their perfectly made up faces and shining hair as I try to smooth the rain frizzed strands of my own, frowning at a snag in my sweater. Am I being naïve? He couldn't possibly prefer chatting with me to being surrounded by beauty such as theirs, could he? No. He's just being polite. It's in his interest as a bartender to be friendly, and I'm reading into it too much. I shouldn't be reading into it at all.

"At last," he sighs, laughter wafting up the steps as the group descends. "Well *that* looks interesting."

I look down at my open sketchbook, the page covered in scribbles shaping a more intricate project. A client wishes their arm covered in a multitude of herbs and blooms, and it requires a bit of planning.

"Medicinal flora?" he asks, noticing the book peeking out of my bag. "May I?"

I hand it over and he pages through, stopping on one I'd marked. His dark eyes move over the illustrations as he smooths a strand of grayed hair over his ear. There are small beads of sweat on his temples near the creases edging his eyes, and I can't help but focus on the way he bites the corner of his lip as he reads. I'm imagining what it'd be like to place my hand on his fuzzy cheek and feel him rest it against my palm when he glances up.

I inhale sharply. I'd frozen as I stared at him, my pencil hovering over the sketchbook. I shift in the chair, embarrassed to have been caught, but he doesn't make note of it. Instead he tilts the book to me, opened to a long leafy stalk with a cluster of white flowers, the page haphazardly creased.

"Still no bookmark?" he asks, one eyebrow raised.

I smile sheepishly. He'd made it a point to comment on my folded pages more than once, but I like the gentle ribbing.

"No, and I doubt I'll be breaking myself of that habit any time soon."

He smirks, shifting his eyes back to the book. "Let's see... *Achillea millefolium —*"

"It's edible," I interrupt. "I've been reading as I go."

"Mmm," he says. "The flowers and leaves, yes, but one must be cautious — it can produce a psychoactive response if too much is ingested, as well as several other ill effects. It's more commonly used externally, as a coagulant."

"Where does it say that?" I reach for the book, and he hands it back. "I must've missed it."

"It doesn't," he smiles slyly. "Though it *should* if it claims to advertise itself as any sort of medical reference.

Listing half uses without proper warnings can be dangerous for those looking to implement them for healing. A milder example, but still. From the looks of it, what you've got there is quite useless for much else besides drawing reference."

"I know you're into horticulture, but I wasn't aware you're so well versed." I can't stop the sarcasm that creeps in. He's showing off, and I'm simultaneously impressed and amused.

"I have a multitude of volumes on the subject if you'd be interested," he says, watching me slide the book back into my bag. "Not useful for drawing, but very informative. Worlds more than this."

"Oh, you mean so I can educate myself as to not disgrace you with my ignorance?" I joke.

"No, no — that's not what I meant at all," he says quickly, scratching behind his ear. "Forgive me. I can come off as a little... supercilious, at times. One of my lesser qualities. You're not ignorant in the least. I find our conversations to be incredibly stimulating."

"Come on. I find that hard to believe," I laugh. I'm trying to play it off like I'm still joking, but I'm not. I hope he means it. He rests his elbow on the bar and leans forward.

"Believe it or not, I do."

There's a long pause. He's staring directly into my eyes and it's filling me with longing, so I focus on my drink instead.

"Well, if you're offering me something fascinating to read, I won't turn it down." I'm blushing yet again, and I want it to stop. "You might regret it, though — clearly I can be hard on literature. Old habits, and all."

He laughs. "I'm more than happy to let you ruin my books. In fact, I might even demand it."

I smile a little, but before I can say anything more I hear laughter growing as the group of girls returns. He greets them as they clamor for another round, our interaction ended for the time being.

21

I don't see him the following week, or the one after. One of my clients had brought a nasty virus along with them, incapacitating me for days on end. Instead of going out I spend the nights sniffling miserably in my dark apartment, consumed by my thoughts. I'm disappointed I won't see him, but I'm not sure he'll even notice I haven't shown up, even though I'd been doing so for weeks on end like clockwork. Disappointment grows into devastation, and his absence begins to pain me physically. In my fevered state I grow more and more woeful, realizing I'm definitely harboring something more than just a crush on him. I'm usually decent at closing myself off, but this is different. I'm drawn to him like a magnet — a moon trapped in his orbit. I lie curled on my small bed, sweaty and shivering, my only comfort stemming from the image of his crooked smile. I attempt to draw him from memory to console myself, but his resemblance in the penciled lines only makes my heart ache, so I crumple the pages. I shouldn't entertain this. I should keep my heart closed, and concentrate on my work instead of the buzzing elation I feel around him. My loneliness is only being exacerbated by this illness. It'll pass. I've got to stay guarded.

✶ ✶ ✶ ✶ ✶ ✶ FIVE ✶ ✶ ✶ ✶ ✶ ✶

Nothing passes. It only gets worse, and I fail miserably despite my efforts. I glance repeatedly at the clock while I stipple black into a gardenia flower on a client's calf, counting the minutes until it's time to close up. I shouldn't go to the bar at all, since my building anticipation is sign enough that I've let things go too far, but I've already dismissed reason. I finish the flower and wait for the girl to inspect in the mirror so I can bandage her, and my heart sinks when she asks if I can add a few more leaves. Instead of letting my face register my impatience, I smile and assure her I most certainly can, reluctantly pulling on fresh gloves as she climbs back onto the table.

I arrive much later than I intend, and the doormen nod as I rush past them to the stairs. My heart is racing — it's as if my body's taken over, rebelling against my better judgment. I'd nearly run through the streets in an effort to regain the lost time, and focus on regulating my breath as I saunter over to my chair.

"There you are," he says when I set my bag on the bar. "I worried I might've chased you away."

"I had a bit of a cold is what kept me. I was honestly wondering if you'd miss me."

I'd said it without thinking and cringe. I hope he didn't catch that.

"Well, I *did* miss you," he says, smiling softly. "Honestly."

I fumble through my bag in search of a cigarette as he begins preparing my cocktail. My face is on fire, and my heart feels like it's ready to leap from my chest. I have to stop this — I can't continue to perpetuate this charade. It's all in my head anyway. I press the cigarette between my lips as I chastise myself, and my cocktail appears alongside his hand holding a lit match. I let him light it, and my fingers tremble as I lift the cool glass, so I drink deeply hoping it'll calm my nerves.

"I've brought you something," he says, stooping behind the bar. "After last time I immediately perused my shelves for what I thought might interest you most."

He places a few worn hardcovers in front of me, the lettering beautifully embossed in the fabric binding. I trace the delicate words on one with my finger before putting it to my nose. It smells lovely, and I notice him watching me with a small smile on his face.

"I'm weird — I know." I set the book back on the bar. "I just really love the smell of old books. I think I heard somewhere that it has something to do with how the pages age."

"You'd be correct. The chemical breakdown of the paper is what gives it that pleasant fragrance, and I happen to be quite fond of it myself. It's the lignin present — a close cousin to vanillin."

I'm pleased I was right, and overjoyed at the fact that he'd remembered offering them to me at all. I imagine his fingers delicately turning the pages, absentmindedly chewing his lip as he reads. I won't be able to think of much else if I attempt to absorb the words, and can hardly do so even now.

"Thank you. I'll be careful with them — I promise."

"If they don't come back to me dog eared with pencil smudges, I'll be a little disappointed," he smiles, and I laugh.

"Well then, I'll treat them as if they were my own. They'll be ruined in no time."

"Good. Now, we've got some catching up to do, don't we? Tell me what I've missed."

I brief him on the mundane details of my time without him, all while simultaneously wrestling my inner monologue. I keep telling myself this is something to fill the time for him — our conversations — and not that he's actually interested in me. Gods. Why do I even *care* if he's interested or not? This should be just that for me. A way to fill my time. A pleasant reprieve after a long week of working and nothing more. The rational part of me is strong, but it struggles to overtake my imagination. I can't help but notice how he doesn't seem to pay this much attention to any of the other patrons, leaving me wondering if he's harboring any of the feelings I have and am so desperately trying to mask. Maybe it's not that at all. Maybe it's that I've actually made a friend, and have evolved that friendship into something it's not, as I've all but forgotten what real friendship actually feels like. *Could* it be something more? I catch him watching me far too often, and he goes out of his way to talk just to me. He even said he missed me — I didn't make that up.

Fantasy always loses to reality in the end. Even if I cast aside all rationality and grew brave enough to push this further, the possibility of how it might play out is enough to stifle my imagination. Gods forbid he ever find out what I'm hiding, but I doubt things would even go well enough for it to come to that. He'd probably be put off by my admission alone, and I can't bear picturing his expression changing if I asked him if this is something more. I'd definitely never show my face here again if he rejected me. I want to keep what I have — I want to be on the receiving end of those warm greetings and pleasant banter. If I ruin it, I'll just be left with that loneliness all over again. Never leaving home with nothing to look forward to. Crying myself to sleep night after night.

* * * * * * *SIX* * * * * * *

"Well, you're miles away today."

My client's voice snaps me back to reality. It's Claire — the same woman I'd tattooed months earlier, the covered up name needing another pass to fully obscure it. My cheeks grow hot as I realize I'd been silent for most of the time I'd been working on her, lost in a daydream. My thoughts keep drifting back to the last conversation I'd had with him, and how different it was from the others. Last time he'd hit me with a curveball, and I'd bared a piece of myself I'd never shared with anyone. I can't stop thinking about it, and I can't help but wonder just how many more layers of myself I'd allow him to peel back.

***

"Do you believe in the concept of... Soulmates?" He asks. "Twin flames, or whatnot?"

He's caught me off guard. I'd been casually eavesdropping on the conversation drifting from the other end of the bar, and I'd heard the couple refer to each other as such more than once. It's clear he has too. I watch him pile empty glasses in the sink as I replay his question.

"You'd like me to divulge my personal convictions?"

He smiles. "Humor me, if you will."

I take a long swig of my drink as I consider my words. Is this his roundabout way of asking me about my beliefs in general, since we've yet to cross over into the territory of spiritualism or religion? I don't know where he stands and I'd rather not risk offending him, but I'll have to take that chance.

"Well, what defines a soulmate anyway? Is it someone you're destined for? If that's the case, one would have to ultimately believe in destiny, right? And maybe even the higher power that controls it?"

"From a logical standpoint," he says, glassware clinking in the sink as he washes.

"Ironic." I pause to sip. "Since logic doesn't exactly go hand in hand with destiny or the gods."

He laughs softly. "Closing the gap between the logical and the unexplained can be a bridge too far at times."

"Well there's your answer. I've wasted enough time believing in those sorts of things, so I just… I don't anymore. Destiny. Soul mates. The whole lot."

"Mmm," he says, setting a clean glass aside. "I most certainly identify with that standpoint. I'm curious as to how you arrived there, if you wouldn't mind elaborating."

I spin my glass in slow circles as I stare at it. I spend a lot of time trying to convince myself that the course of my life has nothing to do with the intentions of a higher power and is solely the result of my choices. I only mostly believe it. What I believe for sure is that I'm destined to remain alone, and it ties back into those choices.

I sigh. "Sometimes… Sometimes I feel like I've been abandoned by the universe — the gods, whatever — and to reconcile that I've tried to choose logic. Realistically, there's no soulmate out there waiting to complete me. My existence can only be my own, since no one can ever truly share the human experience with another, and no one will ever be able to understand my soul on the deep level a term like that implies, so it's pointless to hope for."

"And you think no one could ever come close?"

I meet his gaze, and a tingling sensation rolls through me. I have the sudden innate sense that he could come *very* close. Close to knowing me — truly. Close to seeing me in a way I desperately want. I shift my eyes to my drink as I bite my lip. It's just another fantasy. One that'll never be real.

I nod towards the couple. "Maybe the stars can align for some, but for most it seems a cruel dream left unfulfilled — myself included. If we're speculating about destiny as a confirmed reality, I don't think mine involves finding that missing piece. I'm not destined to be whole. There's this... *void* somewhere inside me. I think it's always been there, and it reminds me of a —"

"A half circle?"

He pauses after he says it, water dripping from the soapy vessel in his hand. I clear my throat in an effort to dissolve my stunned expression. It's like he's read my mind.

"Exactly. You know... I've never told anyone that. I can't believe you understood what I meant."

He turns the water off. His expression is soft and serious, his dark eyes fixed on me. "Honestly, it's rare I hear something that resonates with me so profoundly. My convictions on the subject are weighted heavily on the side of the realistic, but occasionally —"

"You let your mind wander?"

He laughs quietly as he dries his hands, his eyes never leaving mine. "Indeed. It's been wandering plenty as of late."

My pulse elevates as I swig the last of my cocktail and carefully set the empty glass on the bar. This entire conversation has sent my own mind wandering right off the rails. Part of me feels raw and exposed, like he's seen something I should've kept to myself. Another part of me feels closer to him because of it, and because of what he's let me glimpse in return. I want to see more.

He picks up my glass, silently asking if I'd like a refill. I cross my arms and offer a half smile.

"I'm not sure. That particular concoction seems to lead me to say things I've never spoken aloud, so it depends heavily on the next subject."

His crooked smile appears as he leans on the bar. "In that case, I'm *definitely* pouring another."

***

I can barely keep the smile from my face as I recall it. That night we'd talked until well after closing, our words filling the space the club patrons left behind, and it was clear he didn't want me to go even when it was time. I'd connected with him in a way I hadn't ever connected with anyone, and it left me with a sense of giddiness I've felt all week.

"So?" Claire asks, a smirk on her lips. "Who is he? Or... she?"

"I'm not sure I follow." I'm playing dumb, but I'm embarrassed she's interpreted my distraction correctly.

"Oh, come on," she groans, resting her forearms on her bent knee. "Your head is in the clouds, and you're positively *glowing*. I'd know that look anywhere. You've finally met someone, haven't you?"

I shrug. "I've made a friend is all."

"Don't be coy," she laughs. "Admit it — you've fallen in love!"

My stomach flutters when she says it, and I realize it's true. I had indeed fallen for him. I thought I'd been taking adequate steps to prevent that very thing, but the evidence is clear, and she's seen right through me. My distraction has shifted — what's now on my mind is the realization that if *she* can tell, *he'll* certainly be able to. Does he know already? Am I more transparent than I thought?

"I don't think it's quite like that. He's... we're... just talking. That's the extent of it."

"He doesn't know how you feel, does he?" she says, smiling softly. "Well you need to *tell* him! Take a chance! You'll never know if you don't try. Why deny yourself the possibility for happiness?"

I can't delve into this anymore so I change the subject, and she blessedly takes the hint and refrains from pressing the issue while I finish her tattoo. Part of me wants to take her advice, but it's too risky. I can indulge my little daydreams all I want because they're safe. I have too much to hide, and the potential for things to end badly is weighted against me. I don't want the biting sting of reality to deflate what little pleasure I've gained from his company. It's best I keep it to myself.

Isn't it?

It's all I can think about at the bar that night. It's busier than usual, which grants me plenty of time to turn my thoughts over in my head. I'm thinking about the universe, wondering if its trying to send me a sign by interrupting our evening, giving me a chance to collect myself so I don't inadvertently spill my guts. Or maybe this is what I need to give me that final push and step into unknown territory. I can't be sure, and I don't know which path is the right one. Rationality and fantasy are at war yet again.

"My gods. If it keeps up like this I'll be here past dawn just to restock," he sighs. He's finally been granted a break, and nods towards my drink. "Would you like another?"

The level in my glass has sunk to near empty, but it's the third one and my head is starting to swim — I know I'm on the verge of destroying the next day if I continue. I nod for another anyway as it means I have a tangible reason to linger, so I swig the last sip. I lean my head on my fist as I watch him ready a new one, and it's only a moment until he glances up. This time his eyes land on me for a split second before darting away.

My heart skips a beat. There's something different about him tonight — he seems scattered and looks uncharacteristically nervous. It can't be because of the swell of business, as I'd seen him handle a full bar with calm fluidity many times over. Is it me? Has it become painfully obvious I'm head over heels for him? Is he uncomfortable and unsure how to address it? My chest grows tight, and heat licks at my face when he sets the glass in front of me. I'm trying to think of something to say when his eyes meet mine again, and his sideways smile appears.

"You've got a funny look on," he says. "Everything all right?"

I shrug. "Lots on my mind lately."

He raises an eyebrow, his smile fading. "Such as?"

I desperately want to tell him. Everything — all my hidden truths, starting with what I'm almost certain is obvious. His elbow is resting on the bar, his hand nearly touching mine. If it makes contact I'm afraid I'll blurt it out. I'm dangerously close already, so I pick up the cocktail and take a deep drink. There's acid in my throat after I swallow, and as my stomach churns I realize I've exceeded my limit. I'll have to cut this short, and though I don't want to it might be for the best.

"Work has been a little stressful," I lie as I dig though my bag to close out my tab. It's hard not to slur my words. "I have a lot on my plate right now, and I should really get back to it. Sorry — I think I have to go."

The disappointment on his face is almost enough to make me stay, but I can't for several reasons. The most prominent is the impact of the liquor on my empty stomach, with my longing for him at a close second. As I'm getting up to leave, he ignores a patron attempting to get his attention and leans towards me.

"Well, I hope the rest of your evening is productive," he says. He pauses, tapping his fingers on the glossy wood. "You know, I was... I was wondering if you..."

I freeze with my bag in my hand as I wait for him to finish, but he doesn't. Instead he shakes his head, and offers me a crooked smile.

"Ah... Will I see you next week then?"

"I wouldn't miss it. Goodnight, Rhys."

The room spins as I lie in my bed, scolding myself for not eating all day. I'm sad I'd ruined the night, but I'm also relieved I'd kept my mouth shut. What I should do now is concoct a strategy to distance myself — to ensure that it *stays* shut — but I'm thinking about him instead. I can't help but recall the look on his face when I left, and that question he hadn't asked. What was it? Will he ask it next week? His tone sounded hopeful, and I close my eyes as I replay his words in my head. I love the sound of his voice, and I begin to think about how much I love *how* he speaks. I'd overheard another patron comment on it even tonight — that at times he sounds so academically proper it's almost pretentious. It's yet another thing about him that feels familiar to me, and think it's lovely. He soothes me like no other, and my last thought is of him before I drift to sleep.

✶✶✶✶✶✶ SEVEN ✶✶✶✶✶✶

The evening unfolds as usual, and I close my studio and climb the narrow stairs to my apartment. I don't even bother telling myself to stay away from the bar anymore. Instead, I focus on readying myself to see him, and frown at the selection of clothing I own — all worn, all ink spattered. I wish I had it in me to dress up a bit more, but I'd always kept my style painfully simple so as not to clash with my illustrated skin. I'd stood in front of many a shop window, considering investing in a few nicer things, but I don't really know how to put outfits together, and would definitely end up looking like I was trying too hard. I discard the shirt I'd worn all day and shrug on a thin strapped top under a gauzy gray sweater, and opt for a change of leggings. My flats are beginning to fray at the edges, but I doubt anyone really looks at my feet, or at least I hope they don't.

Before I depart, I decide to eat something. I'm usually a little teetery when I return from the bar, but I'd been much more than that after my last visit, and I'd prefer to avoid a repeat. I'm mulling over my choices when I notice that green glass bottle with the dark liquid inside, tucked away in a cupboard. It's probably time for another dose, so I measure out a minuscule amount and toss it back before carefully capping the bottle. I catch a glimpse of myself in the mirror as I lift my bag over my shoulder and pause, the bitter taste of the liquid still on my tongue. I sigh heavily at my reflection, and it stares disdainfully back at me, seeming to ask the questions spooling in my head.

What are you doing, it asks. *Why do you insist on enmeshing yourself in something you can't have? You're smarter than this. You know better. You know what will happen if — no, when — he finds out.* I scowl at my reflection and its judgmental stare, and close the door to the washroom so I can't see it anymore.

The club is crowded again, and I have to weave through a pack of people to get to the stairs. I don't see him when I reach the top, but as I slide into my chair I spy the top of his grayed head just beneath the counter. He's clanking through bottles on a low shelf. There are a few people waiting at the other end of the bar, and I hope they'll filter out so I can be alone with him. I rifle through my bag as I wait for him to notice me, my head already buzzing with anticipation. As I'm rummaging, I feel eyes on me, but it's not Rhys — it's two strangers at the other end. I dislike being gawked at, so I face them in hopes they'll look away. What I zero in on is their identical jackets — a skull embroidered on the front pocket, one of the eyes a glowing red. It looks familiar — I've seen it before. The man closest to me stands, and my pulse quickens when I get a better look at his face. There's a diagonal scar crossing the bridge of his nose. It was a cut last I saw it.

I freeze, and his grizzled pockmarked face twists into a sneer. "I've been looking for you, you fucking cunt."

My hand is still in my bag, and my fingers close around the knife at the bottom. Rhys is standing now — motionless, a bottle in his hand. I lock eyes with him for a millisecond as my mind races.

Run. I have to *run*.

Now.

I bolt, abandoning my bag and toppling my chair. I crash down the stairs and frantically push through the pulsing crowd, elbowing my way to the door and stumbling into the street. It's pouring rain, the heavy drops stinging my eyes. My flats become sodden and heavy, and it's not long before I lose both, gravel cutting into the soles of my feet. I don't know where to go, all I know is that I need to get away. I hear their heavy footfalls and shouting — I haven't lost them, they're still behind me. The rain is blinding and my lungs are on fire, and I curse myself briefly for taking up smoking again. My clothes are cold and cemented to my body, and my

34

stamina is starting to wane. Where do I go? Not home. I have to lose them. There — I know that alley ahead. It's a dead end, but I cut through it sometimes. There's a gap between the buildings I'm small enough to squeeze through, but they're not. I careen into the alley and skid to a stop, my heart dropping into my stomach. There's a dumpster blocking the gap. *Shit.*

I'm hoisting myself onto the dumpster when a blow to the shoulder knocks me to the ground. They're both rasping for breath, but they've caught up to me. Why did I run? Why didn't I stay in the bar?

"Stupid girl…" the scarred man wheezes. "…I got you now."

I dig my heels into the gravel to get to my feet as he lunges, but he catches me by the hair, forcing me back to the ground. I claw at his hands but he won't let go — all my flailing is doing is covering me with grit. The other man moves to grab my legs so I kick him squarely in the face, his nose erupting in a bloody faucet.

"*Fuck!*" he howls, clamping his nose.

I wrench away from the scarred man, leaving a clump of hair in his fist. My scalp burns hot, and my heart pounds in my ears as I back towards the wall of the building. They're blocking my way — I can't get around them, and I can't get over that dumpster quick enough. I fumble frantically for the knife I'd slipped into my pocket and hold it out in front of me. I cut him before. Maybe I can do it again.

The scarred man isn't threatened by it, and laughs. Bleeding man looks enraged, and a chill rolls through me as I realize there's no chance I'm getting away this time. Is this it for me? Is this really how it ends? Gravel crunches, and both men turn their heads.

"Fuck you doing here?" Scarred man spits on the ground. "Fuck off."

The figure emerging from the shadowed street doesn't pause — instead they continue to advance, and scarred man scowls.

"Are you deaf? *Get lost.*"

I shift my eyes from them to see who's appeared, and my heart sinks. Rhys. What is he doing here? It's obvious he followed, but why? I can't find my voice, so I shout in my head instead.

Run!

He doesn't — instead he speaks, calmly and cooly.

"That's enough. Let her go."

Scarred man laughs loudly and tilts his face into the rain.

"Ohhh, telling me what to do now, are we? Wrong move." He elbows bleeding man. "I'm gonna fuck his day up — grab her!"

Scarred man lunges at Rhys, but I can't watch them face off — bleeding man is closing in. I make wild swings with the knife, but I hit nothing but air. He reaches for my arm and I manage to make contact, slicing through his jacket. His face twists but it doesn't stop him, and he shoves me forcefully into the wall, the back of my head slamming against brick. I crumple to the ground, and he delivers a swift kick to my ribs with his heavy boot, folding me in half and leaving me gasping for breath. My vision is blurred, and the sky spins above. I can't move, and I can't call out. All I can do is lie curled and helpless on the cold gravel.

★ ★ ★ ★ ★ ★ EIGHT ★ ★ ★ ★ ★ ★

I'm groggy when I wake, and when my eyes focus I realize I'm indoors, wrapped tight in a blanket on an unfamiliar bed. I hear water dripping, and pick my head up to see a man with his back to me, draping a piece of clothing over a chair. Rhys.

Where am I? I survey my surroundings slowly, the fuzziness in my head receding further. The bed I'm in is under a skylight, and windows beyond the foot of it overlook the harbor. Clothing hangs from hooks on one wall, piles of papers and books are perched atop a high desk with what looks like a hundred small drawers, and a trifold screen sits in the corner with more clothing haphazardly tossed over the top. I pull the blanket closer and grimace as I shift. My body aches, and the bottoms of my feet sting. As I feel the soft fabric against my skin I realize my clothes are missing — I'm only in my underthings. A kettle starts to whistle, and footsteps echo softly as he pads across the room to turn off the burner. The whistling stops, and I hear liquid being poured.

He notices me sit up and approaches, steaming cup in hand. I attempt to stand, quickly clutching the blanket around my chest, but my legs buckle. He catches me before I fall, spilling only a little of the liquid from the cup. Instinctively I bury my face in his shirt, and I'm struck by his scent. He smells faintly earthy and dense, like the dragon's blood incense I keep in my apartment, and like something familiar I can't quite place. He guides me back to sitting and I have to force myself to look at him. I'm mortified — it's essentially just the sheet between us.

"It's all right," he says gently. "You're safe. This is my apartment."

"Where… where are my clothes?"

"Drying. They were covered in dirt so I had to soak them," he says, handing me the cup. "I'll get you something else to put on straight away."

I stare into the cup, a sweet smell rising along with the steam emanating from it.

"It's tea," he says, answering my next question before I ask it. "Mint and lemon balm. Should bring you around a bit more."

"How long have I been here?"

"Nearly a day." He pushes himself up from the bed. "I did worry you might've been worse off than I initially thought, given you slept for the whole of it, but that doesn't seem to be the case."

He opens the door to a wardrobe along the wall, and I watch as he pulls out two neatly folded items.

"These will have to do until your clothes dry." He hands me a worn t-shirt and soft sweats. "I'm sorry I have nothing that'll fit better. I would've —"

He quickly turns his head, averting his eyes as I stiffly pull the shirt over my shoulders and slide my legs into the pants. I pull the drawstring as tight as it will go and roll them up at the bottom — they're much too long. He clears his throat loudly after I'm decent, and sinks down on the edge of the bed. I feel awkward, so I shift my eyes to my feet. They're clean, and I realize I have no dirt on me anywhere, though I'd been covered in it.

"Did you really need to undress me?" I ask, and it comes out as a harsh whisper.

"I had no ill intentions. I assure you I made every effort to maintain your dignity — I only wanted to be certain you didn't have any broken bones or lacerations." He scratches behind his ear. "And I couldn't very well leave you sopping wet and filthy."

I clasp my hands together and swallow hard. I'm wholly embarrassed, and more than a little frightened. That man — is he still out there? What do I do now? I have to bite my lip to stop it from trembling.

"You've had an awful scare," he says gently. "Don't worry — I won't let anything happen to you." His grayed brows are raised softly, deepening the slight creases that cross his forehead, and my heart flutters. This is a situation I'd never prepared for, and I don't know what to say. I let my feet drop onto the floor and wince when I put pressure on them.

"I think the right move would be to bandage them," he says. "You're lucky you didn't need a stitch or two. Now that —" he nods to the purple hematoma spreading across my shoulder. "That may require more ice. I have a salve that should help — it cuts the healing time in half. How's your head feeling?"

I reach up and touch the sore spot where my head met the brick wall. "Tender, but no headache."

"Any nausea? Blurred vision?"

"No."

"Good. That's good."

He rifles through drawers at the desk, and returns with a handful of items. A roll of cloth, cotton swabs and a bottle of liquid, and a shiny tin. He sits on the floor in front of me, and wordlessly sets my feet on his lap. I can barely believe any of this is happening — he'd saved my life, and now he's... Tending my wounds? Why?

It's quiet save for the rains pounding against the windows, so I try to fill the silence with an explanation.

"That... Man. The one with the scar. He... Assaulted me the day I moved here. I haven't seen him since and I guess I sort of forgot..."

He doesn't comment, and I wonder what he's thinking. He moves on to massage the salve from the tin onto my bruised shoulder, and my face grows hot. His hands are warm and very soft, and goosebumps raise on my skin at his touch. Once he's through I begin to stand up, but he stops me.

"No, no — don't get up. You should keep off them for a bit. Ehh... Are you comfortable staying for a while? I don't know if it's wise for you to return home just yet, which is why I brought you here instead."

"Do you think he... Do you think they're still lurking about?"

"They didn't follow me, but I'd prefer to be on the safe side and give it a little more time."

I both want to stay and don't at the same time. I worry I'm infringing. What I'm also worrying about is how they found me — was it by accident? If he's been looking for me, does he know where I live? He doesn't know my name, but to my knowledge there's only one heavily tattooed woman with a storefront like mine in the immediate vicinity. Me.

"I should probably go — I really want to check on the studio." I get to my feet and they hurt, but not too bad. I can walk. "Make sure it's locked tight."

"I really don't want you out there wandering in the dark until I'm sure it's safe. You've told me where it is — I can go and check up on it for you. Survey the area."

"Really? You'd do that?" Why is he being so kind to me? We're friends, but that's the extent of it — at least on his end. Clearly he's the sort who would do this for anyone in need. Or would he?

"Of course," he smiles slightly. "Oh — that reminds me. I believe this belongs to you. I made sure to collect it after the... Incident."

He treads across the room and unloops something from a hook near the door. My bag — he must've gone back to the club when I was asleep. I'd completely forgotten about it.

"All right," he says, shoving his arms into a leather jacket. "Help yourself to anything you want, and *please* take it easy. I'll be back in a dash."

After he's gone, I sit in silence for a few minutes, watching the harbor lights grow brighter as the sky darkens. What an odd turn of events. I'm relieved he decided to bring me here instead of a hospital. The last thing I need is healers asking too many questions, or gods forbid running some tests. I'll just have to be more careful in the future.

I lie back against the pillows, and feel that fluttering sensation in my stomach when their scent hits my nose.

They smell like him. Immediately I begin thinking about how soft his hands were, and sit up quickly. I can't get caught up in these feelings — not now. There are far more important matters at hand. It's hard not to get lost in them given where I am, but maybe I can let that distract me instead.

Despite the concrete floor, the place is warm with an earthy feel to it, all wood and stone. Rows of herbs hang from a rafter in neatly tied bunches, and there's a table housing large shiny cylinders surrounded by various sized decanters in another corner. Shelves of books and glass vessels line the wall next to the tall desk, illuminated by a lamp with a green shade resting on its surface. What I want to do is poke around and see who he really is — what he likes, what his daily routines are — but even though he'd essentially welcomed me to do just that I wouldn't feel right. He's trusting me here, and I should respect his privacy. After all, I'm just a friend.

I run my hand over the pillow I'm clutching, catching his scent again. The linens are soft and slightly textured, like a cocoon of light gray clouds. What I should do is take his advice and attempt to rest, so I pull the blanket around me and curl myself into a ball.

****** NINE ******

I'm startled from sleep when the door opens, and I smell him before I even turn around. It's nothing like it was before — now he absolutely reeks of woodsmoke. He'd been gone a long time, and I'm about to rattle off a dim joke about him getting sidetracked at a stray bonfire, but his grim expression silences me. I watch him slowly hang his jacket on the hook next to the door, my heart in my throat.

Something's wrong.

"What is it?"

He doesn't answer. Instead, he sits down on the edge of the bed and stares at the floor. It's clear he's having trouble with what he's about to tell me, and it's scaring me. I'm too anxious to sit so I back away from him, and it prompts him to find his voice.

"Lynna, I... I'm so sorry." He swallows hard, and finally meets my eyes. "It's... *gone*. The studio..."

Gone?

No — it can't be. He must've scouted the wrong place. Buildings don't just disappear. He must be joking. This must just be a terrible prank, and I'm waiting for him to end it, but he doesn't. His expression is deadly serious, and that smoke smell came from somewhere. The combination dries up all my excuses.

"It's... Someone's burned it to the ground," he says quietly, clasping his hands together. "I could smell it before I even turned onto the street."

"Gone..." My voice is feathery. My ears are ringing, and it's becoming hard to breathe. "Everything's gone? The studio... My apartment..."

"I spoke to one of the firemen present and he assured me all was lost, though he wouldn't give me any further details. They couldn't contain the fire — it tore through your place and demolished part of the neighboring building before they got it out."

I feel like I've been hit with a cold wave.

Everything I've built here — gone. Burned to ash. Why? Was it them? Had I pissed them off by getting away again? It *had* to have been them. I know no one else with such a grudge — I barely have a friend in this place, let alone enemies. I feel like a rug's been yanked out from beneath me and I stagger, sinking to the floor and bowing my head in my lap. I cover my face with my hands as I struggle to take a breath, a long silent sob twisting my mouth. The tears fall hot and fast — I can't keep them in. I tried to make a home in this city, but it's been torn from my grasp. Slipped through my fingers. I have nothing left, and I'm all alone.

But I'm not. I feel cautious arms around me. He's sitting on the floor with me now, softly running his hand over my arm as he squeezes me against him. He's trying to comfort me, but it's only making things worse. My feelings for him are much too strong.

I pull away and rest my back on the floor, tears streaming into my ears. Panic begins to rise in the pit of my stomach. This is too much — the terrible loss coupled with the flood of longing — and I'm losing control of my emotions. I have to get out of here before I fall apart completely. I get to my feet and hobble over to the clothing draped over the chairs. My gray sweater and black leggings. They're still damp, but they smell of lavender and soap now, and I hear him get up as I'm changing.

"What are you doing?"

"Rhys, I… I'm sorry…I have to go…" My voice wavers as I fumble with the strap of my bag.

"I'll go with you. Just tell me where…"

I don't respond. Instead I blindly rush past him as I choke back a sob.

"Wait — Lynna, *wait*! Please —" he pleads, but I close the door behind me.

* * * * * * TEN * * * * * *

I cry quietly as I make my way down a greenish fluorescent lit corridor, my sore feet slapping the cold tile. I follow it until I come to a set of stairs, a metal door at the bottom. There's a humming behind it, and when I push it open I pause. I'm in the upstairs bar at the club, and it's in full swing. He lives in the building? I had no idea it had residential space.

I at least know where I am, but I don't know where to go, so I float down the stairs into the crowd, neon lights illuminating their bodies. It's loud, the pulsing beat drowning out the static in my temples. The bass moves through me as I stand in the middle of the room, utterly hopeless and helpless. Lost. I have no home, no studio, no money. I don't even have shoes. Gods, what am I going to *do*? Anguish rises in my throat as I stand motionless, the oblivious crowd surrounding me. I wish it would swallow me up. I wish I would disappear completely.

I feel a light hand on my shoulder, and when I whirl around he's there. Why did he come after me? Can't he see my threads are coming unraveled?

"Why are you following me?!"

My pulse soars when he gently places his hands on the sides of my arms, the music loud in my ears. "Let me help you. *Please*."

Tears are coursing down my cheeks, and I'm trembling. How desperately I want him to — to the point of nearly caving in on myself. My emotions are a tidal wave about to come crashing down and it's taking everything in me to stop it.

"Rhys… I *can't*."

"Why?" The neon lights are reflected in his dark eyes, and the softness in his expression sends my heart tumbling. "Have I done something wrong? Said something? I only meant to —"

I'm at my breaking point. "Because I *love* you!"

The wave crashes on the shore, and my heart feels like it might've stopped completely.

I've said it out loud and I can't take it back. He looks shocked, and I regret everything. I regret ever setting foot in this place. I regret letting myself slide into the daydream that kept me coming back.

I have to drop my eyes. I can't take this — I can't stand looking at him for one more moment knowing everything's in ruins. He steps towards me, and leans in so close the hair on his cheek grazes my face, sending a delicious shiver into my spine.

"Lynna," he says into my ear. "Lynna… I love you, too."

Every hair on my body stands on end as the room blurs. All I can hear is the echo of his words meshed into the pulsing song in the background. Is this real? Did he say what I think he did?

"Rhys… Did you —"

"Not here," he interrupts, taking my hand.

I don't know what to do besides follow him — back up the stairs, back through the corridor to the front door of the apartment. Once we're inside, I lose his hand and take shaky steps towards the windows. My thoughts are humming at a million miles an hour, and I can't get my bearings. This can't be right. He must've just said it to comfort me — he cares for me as a friend would. He can't possibly feel like I do. I take a shuddering breath, and force myself to look up at him.

"Did you… Did you say that because it's what you thought I wanted to hear?"

He shakes his head slowly, his brows knitting. "I wouldn't… I don't…" he starts, and sighs heavily before beginning again. "I'm not in the habit of saying things I don't mean, Lynna. I don't know what you thought, but this is no game to me. You're not just another random patron — another interlocutor with whom to pass the time. You've been… It's… *Fuck. None* of this is coming out properly. Don't you understand? I haven't felt *anything* like this before. I *love* you, I —"

I can't hold back any longer.

I cut him off mid sentence with my mouth, pressing my lips against his in a blind flurry of emotion. My heart soars when he pulls me against him, kissing me back with equal intensity. His thin lips are softer than I'd imagined, his body warm and his grasp strong. I want to lose myself in him. I no longer care what's at stake.

"You're sure?" I whisper between kisses. "You're sure it's me you want?"

"More than anything."

My feet ache from standing, so I step back until I feel the edge of the bed and pull him down with me. He's cautious and tender, his hand protecting my bruised shoulder as he presses me against the gray blanket. I'm frantic, clumsily attempting to unbutton his shirt, and in my frenzy I tear it, the last few buttons flying across the floor. I'm immediately embarrassed, but he doesn't seem to mind, and smiles softly as he shoulders out of it. Dark tattoos mottle his torso, and I want to trace every one with my fingertips, my lips. His skin smells faintly of woodsmoke mixed with dragon's blood, and I finally recognize the scent I couldn't name. A scent I'd savored over and over before. Petrichor. The smell in the air after the rains. All my rationality has left me, replaced by need and love. I love him — so much I think I might burst with it.

I let him remove my damp sweater, and he sweeps my hair to the side before planting soft deliberate kisses along my collarbone. He shivers when my fingers graze his stomach, fumbling with the buttons at his waist as he helps free me of my leggings. Static like tingles run the length of my spine as his mouth finds mine again, and I feel his heart thudding beneath his ribs when he embraces me. His touch is invigorating, and strangely familiar. It's almost like he knows me already, as if I'd been in his arms once before. My body takes over, desperately wanting to connect with his, and I'm amazed by my own boldness as I press him back against the headboard. My skin tingles as his hands slide up my thighs to my waist, and if there was ever any doubt as to whether or not we're on the same page, it's all but gone. He tightens his grip, and I inhale sharply as we find each other.

"Heavens…" he whispers. "Darling… my darling…"

I'm dreaming. I must be dreaming.

It feels real enough — his warm body beneath my hands, his breath on my neck, his fingers digging into my skin. I'm awash with a myriad of pleasant sensations I haven't felt in a long time, but among them is something new. Something electric, almost like the distinct hum of live wires. My questions start to pull me away — is this as meaningful as I think, or is this just a small life raft in the middle of a raging sea of devastation? A reprieve? A brief and passing thing? I don't know yet and I don't want to waste it by dissecting it before it's even over, so I let myself become lost again in his arms. I want to freeze time — I want to live in this forever — but I can only stretch it so far.

Slowly we melt onto the sheets, our hearts thudding in tandem. I press my cheek against his shoulder as our breathing evens, and feel him gently tracing the lines in my palm. Rain pounds against the windows in a comforting rhythm as we lie entwined beneath the storm clouds — chest to chest, my heart laid bare.

I feel I should be the first to speak, but nothing comes. Maybe we've said everything we needed to without words. I struggle to find my voice anyway, and am relieved when he locates his own.

"Penny for your thoughts?"

"Really? Do people actually say that?"

"Probably not," he laughs softly. "I wanted to say something profound, but that's all I could manage. A silly way to ask what you're thinking."

He rolls to the edge of the bed and reaches towards the floor, thin muscles stretching taut in his arm. I notice black winged birds covering the length of his back, the feathered tips on the sides of his neck belonging to one between his shoulders. He pulls a cigarette from the pocket of his ruined shirt and lights it, taking a long drag before offering it to me. I accept and lie back against the pillows, exhaling a curved plume.

"You haven't answered," he says. "Did I ruin the moment?"

I hand the cigarette back. I forgot he'd asked a question. "I keep feeling like this is a dream."

"A good dream? Partially, at least?"

"It is, I just... Didn't think this was something that would actually happen."

"I admit I didn't either," he says, depositing the ash into a small dish on the side table. "This is wildly out of character for me. It's not something that happens often — or at all, really. I never wanted to change that or anything else about my life before I met you. Gods, I'd think about you all day long. I'd count the minutes until your next arrival. I'd grown to look forward to that single day, and..."

He trails off as I push myself up and silently tread to the kitchen.

"I've ruined it now, haven't I?"

I don't answer. He hasn't, but the afterglow has cooled enough for me to second guess myself. I think about what he said and what had just happened as I fill a glass from the tap. Had I been incredibly stupid for giving in to this? Was I just looking for something to soothe the ache of everything I've lost? Is this the universe messing with me? This is exactly what I'd fantasized about minus the incident that brought me here, isn't it? Him reciprocating my feelings? I take a deep drink before abandoning the glass in the sink, and feel his eyes on me. I'm suddenly self-conscious in my nakedness, so I quickly move to cover myself as I walk back to the bed.

"Please don't," he says, stretching his arm out. "I think I've made it abundantly clear how I feel about you. Come now, let's get a little rest. We can talk more in the morning."

I'm not sure I'll be able to sleep, but taking time to process this is probably a good idea, so I let him tuck me tenderly against his chest. We lie quietly as we listen to the rain, his heartbeat steady beneath my palm. The heat from his body is comforting, and so is the way his fingertips drift on my shoulder in soft circles. My head is spinning with questions, but I feel safe and warm in his arms, so I swallow my doubt for the time being. I hope when I wake he won't have changed his mind. I hope I won't have either.

* * * * * * ELEVEN * * * * * *

The sky is still overcast, but the clouds have a certain glow to them, meaning it's morning. For a moment I forget where I am, and sit up quickly. He's not in the bed, but I hear clinking, and smell a delicious familiar smell. Footsteps, then a warm mug of coffee is being held in front of me.

"Good morning," he says, smiling down at me. I accept the cup and hold my face over the hot mist swirling from it. He treads back to the kitchen, and I hear a drawer open and shut. "Are you hungry? You must be. I'm limited in what I could make you, but —"

"Thank you, but I'm all right." I pull the sheet tighter around me. I don't feel much like eating. I've been transported back to when I found out my life was set ablaze. "I'm still reeling from yesterday. There was nothing left? Nothing at all?"

"I'm afraid not. I did wait around to search it myself, which is why I smelled so fragrant when I returned, but there was nothing salvageable."

I remain silent, and he shuts the drawer. "Well, what shall we do? Do you want to contact the authorities and have them investigate? Is there anyone you might wish to call? I prefer to live a bit more... off grid, so I don't have a phone here, but there's a landline in the bar you can use."

I stare into my cup. I don't want an investigation. It won't help anything, and I don't want to have to describe what happened to me or explain myself. It might only call attention to pieces of my life that don't add up, and it won't bring back what I've lost.

"I don't have anyone *to* call. I know what happened already — I know it was them. Maybe they'll at least leave me be now."

"The studio though," he says. "Surely you'll need to —"

"I was subletting," I interrupt. "The lease wasn't even

in my name, so I've got nothing coming to me from it."

I swallow hard, feeling the loss rush up. It wasn't mine, but everything in it was, and it's gone. I don't want to cry in front of him again, but I don't know how much longer I can hold it in. I wish I had a little time alone to think.

"I know it doesn't seem like it, but everything will be all right," he says gently. "Why don't you just take a moment — try and get your bearings? It's time I washed up a bit, but I'll be quick. There's more coffee on if you'd like."

I hear a door shut and I'm alone, almost like he's read my mind. I stare up at the clouds through the skylight as I let the tears course down my cheeks. The loss of my livelihood is the most devastating, but the rest were just things. I have my life, and right now I'm safe — that's what's most important. I've started over before, though never from the ground up, but I can find a way to do it. I can face whatever lies ahead. My tears begin to slow, and I feel better now that I've released them. I needed that more than I thought.

I search the floor, and when I can't find my sweater I select one of the shirts draped over the screen. My shoulder feels surprisingly better so I tentatively press the bruise, but the pressure doesn't make me wince. It seems he was right about that salve. I'm more comfortable about being curious now, so I inspect the shelves of jars and hanging plants. Vervain, echinacea, lemon verbena, yarrow... the list goes on and on. What does he do with them, and what are all these containers filled with? I find a bundle of dried Yerba Santa, the ochre leaves shiny and stiff, and pull a crisp piece from it. It makes me a little sad to think of the small amount I had in my own apartment, all burnt to bits now. As I'm staring at it I hear the washroom door open, and Rhys emerges shirtless, combing back his wet grayed hair with his fingers.

"Found something you like?"

"You know, I actually kept some of these things myself, but your collection is far more extensive. I used to go to this little shop near the harbor for them." I set the leaf on the desk. "Seems I'll have to pay it another visit in the future."

The corners of his mouth tilt up a little. "The one with the red door? Next to the bridge?"

"Yes — the apothecary. Makes sense you'd know it. Is that where all this came from? Some of the bottles look similar."

"More like where they go *to*. It's my shop."

"You're kidding," I half laugh, and stop when I realize he isn't. "For real? You never even mentioned it."

"You never asked," he chuckles. "And I didn't elaborate. I probably made it sound like my horticultural pursuits were merely a hobby, but they're much more than that. I was equally unaware you frequented the place — it's sort of amazing we've never crossed paths there before, though in truth I'm not often in it. The man who runs the shop is an old friend who wanted something to do. He's the face of it, and I'm the production end, essentially."

"I admit I'm a little shocked. Pleasantly shocked, but shocked nonetheless. That's quite a venture."

"It does well enough, but it's not my only venture. You… Ah… you might also be a little shocked to find out this place is mine too."

"This place? As in, the *building*?"

He scratches behind his ear. "Yes. It was… left to me, some time ago. I have a managerial staff run the club downstairs while I maintain my space up top. Bartending is the true hobby. I don't need to spend time there, but I enjoy it, so I like to take the weekend shift."

I sit down at one of the chairs near the table. I'm realizing I know him fairly well, but I also don't know him at all.

"I have to say. I'm impressed, but mostly I'm taken aback I didn't know any of it."

"It's not something I really advertise," he says. "And like I said — it never came up. I was too consumed with learning more about you — nosing about in your work and the like. Mostly in a desperate attempt to make good conversation, though I never really had to try. Talking with you has always felt… easy. Natural."

"I've always felt the same," I sigh. I'm realizing I'll have to open up about how I came to feel the way I do about him, since it seems that's where this is going. Though we'd been intimate only hours ago, I'm hesitant. My guard has come back up now that I've had a little time to process. "And those conversations were the ongoing highlight of these past few months for me. I suppose it was excruciatingly obvious I'd developed quite the crush on you, against my better judgment."

He looks slightly pained, and sinks down in the chair across from me. Shit — I've offended him. I didn't mean it like that. How do I explain why I tried to keep my distance without giving myself away? I can only tell him partial truth, and that'll have to be enough.

"Not because of who you are, but you know… I've been in a few relationships before. All of them ended, and every single one has hurt me, even if just a little. I'd sworn off the whole thing entirely. It was easier to be alone, though that comes with its own problems. Solitude breeds loneliness. It's a harsh cycle."

"I must agree with you on that. Even though I'd grown accustomed to being alone there's always that lingering desire to share your life with another, worried it'll mean nothing if no one else is there to see it. It never really bothered me, if I'm being truthful. I've had my fair share of propinquities, but nothing at all in years. It just wasn't worth it — I haven't had the faintest desire to follow through on any sort of interest in or from another in ages. Until now, that is. Now my world's been turned on its ear. I haven't felt anything like this before. Nothing's ever come close."

I have no idea what my expression is, but it prompts him to go on.

"Skeptical," he sighs. "But I don't blame you. The

intensity I'm projecting likely sounds downright... *unbelievable*, but I'm attempting to articulate my intentions and feelings with the utmost sincerity. None of what I've expressed is fake, and none of my words fabricated. I'm offering you complete honesty."

I do feel he's being honest. Truthful. I like to think myself a good judge of character, but I'm not sure I trust my intuition. It's betrayed me before. I've opened up and been sharply rebuked, shunned, and worst of all, threatened. I must register my apprehension on my face, and he shifts in the chair.

"I don't... bend my life, as I'll put it — for anyone. That sounds terribly arrogant, I know, but it's true." He leans forward, elbows on his knees. "Now I'd move the heavens and earth if you asked. Even if you didn't. It's wild — I feel like I've been run through with the quintessential cupid's arrow. When those men went after you, I didn't even think about the consequences. I didn't care — don't care. I'd do it night after night to keep you safe. I..."

I haven't responded at all — I haven't said a word. I want to, but I don't know what to say, and he scratches behind his ear.

"Gods. I'm completely overwhelming you. I just can't seem to shut up, can I?"

My heart is doing that thing where it wants to go live in my stomach, and something between bliss and nausea washes over me. His loquaciousness isn't the problem — I'm afraid of what this means. Afraid I've stepped into something I'm still not sure I belong in, even though I want it desperately.

"Rhys, if you want honesty, I'll give it to you. The future is... so full of question marks. I'm a little scared."

He looks relieved I've finally said something and stretches his hand out. I let him pull me into his lap, and he wraps me in his arms.

"Darling, the future is perpetually a question. It always will be. I don't want you to worry about what's going to happen."

"I think it's more complicated than that. Apart from what's going on here, there's the matter of my life up in flames. I don't know where I'm going to live — or work. I've become both homeless and unemployed in a flash. Not to mention stalked by a pack of unsavory men, of all things." I shift my weight to stand, but he doesn't let me go.

"I'll protect you from them — whatever it takes. That I promise," he says. "As for the rest, I've been thinking about it — possibly with more hopefulness than I should. You can… I'd love for you to stay with me."

Stay here? With him? He's just offered me the world. Do I take it? How can I let him do that?

"I suppose I have no choice at the moment. You must feel it's only right to offer me your help."

"You're not some obligation I must see through. Having you here is something I want — truthfully, I wanted it before any of this even happened. What I *don't* want is for you to feel unease, or that being with me is your only option. It can be temporary until we get you back on your feet if you'd prefer."

"I don't know if you're aware of what you're potentially getting yourself into — clearly trouble seems to follow me. It never did before, but my life has taken a sudden turn for the dramatic."

He laughs softly. "I believe I know exactly what I'm getting myself into. Haven't you been listening?"

Have I been listening? Here I am — in his home, in his arms — yet I'm having trouble accepting what he's telling me. He's staring into my eyes, and I can still recall the feeling of his lips on mine, butterflies dancing in my stomach at the thought.

"I… Think so."

"Well perhaps I haven't made myself clear. I'm trying to tell you… what I'm failing to get across is that I want us to be *together*. I'm offering myself to you — I want to be yours and I want you to be mine. You and all that comes with you — drama included. I'm becoming more nervous by the minute, since I'm not entirely sure what your answer will be."

He does look nervous, and I'm realizing this is much more than the brief and passing encounter I worried it might be. This is real. Something is beginning. He's just poured his heart out to me — risked opening himself to me — not knowing if I'd catch him when he falls. I'm out of reasons to disbelieve him, and though I have plenty making the case for why I should deny myself this, I don't want to. Damn the risks. I love him, and I don't want to see that worried expression on his face as a result of my hesitancy.

"Rhys I… I want to be with you more than anything. I'm completely mad about you, so if you really mean it, I'll…"

I'm watching his crooked smile take over his face, the small wrinkles at the corners of his eyes creasing deeply. He stands suddenly, nearly tumbling me out of his lap, but he doesn't let me fall.

"My darling, this is just… *wonderful!*" He swings me around, and I can't help but laugh. "I was beginning to think you were having second thoughts."

I hug him tight as I kiss him, and feel him smiling as he kisses me back. It's hard not to match it. I'm happier than I've ever been in my life, and the weight of the past twenty-four hours has lifted exponentially. I've dismissed my second thoughts along with my inner voice, telling me this is a disaster waiting to unfold. How could anything that feels this magical be a bad decision?

"I know you've just experienced a terrible and devastating ordeal," he says, setting me down next to the counter. "But I absolutely cannot hide my elation right now, so please forgive me." He opens the icebox, cold air swirling forth in little streams, and pulls out a bottle. "It might be a tad early in the day, but I'm advocating for a small celebration. Poor taste, or no?"

"Not at all. I think it's a great idea."

My bag is on the counter, so I dig for my cigarettes

only to find them crushed, and stare disdainfully at their remains.

"What've you got there?" he asks when I frown.

"A tragedy. What's left of my cigarettes."

"Not to worry." He nods to a cabinet. "Have a look."

I open the cabinet door as he removes the foil from the bottle top, and behind it are stacks of sweet smelling boxes filled with dried tobacco leaves. Cases of rolling papers are piled next to them.

"Did you dry these yourself?"

He pops the cork expertly. "I did."

"Gods, there are heaps! Where did you find all the plants?"

He smiles slyly. "I've got something I want to show you."

Champagne glass in hand, I follow him through a narrow door near the kitchen, and inside is a spiral staircase. The surrounding walls are dark with water stains, and the air becomes more humid as we circle up the metal steps. How curious — what has he got up here? The door at the top has a fogged over window, and the smell of wet earth emanates into the stairwell when he opens it. My jaw drops when I duck in behind him. It's a sprawling greenhouse, with multi paned windows and spaced vents cracked open ever so slightly. Three huge metal fans turn lazily behind rows and rows of raised beds with all matter of vegetation springing forth. This is an actual urban jungle — how had I not known it was up here? Through the glass is the harbor, brick on the side opposite, and I realize that's what shields it from the club entrance. How many more hidden gems *are* there in this city?

I hurriedly make my way down one of the aisles, caressing soft leaves, and running my fingers along the tops of wispy seedlings. I want to see everything all at once, but there's so much. I breathe in the aromatic peat filled air and exhale in a delighted sigh, and realize he's watching me.

"Do you like it?"

"*Like* it?" I laugh. "You must be joking. I could absolutely *live* in this!"

"You can — you do. I know it won't make up for what you lost, but with any luck it'll ease it just a little."

"I honestly feel… *lighter*… in here. This place is like magic." I sweep my palm across a large bed of the greenest moss I've ever seen; a sheet of forest floor laid out in front of me. I want to immerse myself in it, so I hop up onto the edge of the raised bed so I can touch more. As I'm carefully letting my fingers drift over the soft edges, I feel his hands at my waist, and turn to smile up at him.

I love the way he looks at me, his dark eyes crinkling at the corners, and I'm suddenly overcome with affection for him. I grasp his shirt in my fists and pull him in, his mouth cold and delicious, the taste of champagne still on his lips. We kiss slowly at first, then fervently as the big fans hum softly, rain thrumming loudly on the glass. He starts to lean me back onto the raised bed, but I stop him.

"Wait — the moss! I'll crush it!"

"No you won't," he laughs softly. "It's resilient."

I lie back as carefully as I can, and though it dampens my shirt, I love it. He lies beside me on the spongy terrain, and plants a line of kisses down the side of my neck. I'm amazed at how the smallest touch ignites a white hot fire in my core, tingling static taking over my body, and I feel like I might combust from the layered sensations. His warm soft skin, the delicate moss tickling me. The scent of peat, and that hint of petrichor. I pull away, and place my hand against his fuzzy cheek, needing to remind myself he's real — that *this* is real — it's not a dream. He smiles and presses into it like a cat, briefly turning to kiss my palm. I fit myself against him, and we stare up at the rain racing down the paned glass above. I could drink this in for an eternity, and I want to freeze this moment away in my memory.

✶ ✶ ✶ ✶ ✶ ✶ *TWELVE* ✶ ✶ ✶ ✶ ✶ ✶

We're back in the warm gray cloud that is his bed, and though I'm still encased in a giddy bubble of happiness, reality is beginning to creep in. What comes next? I can't solely depend on him — the thought of it makes me nervous, not to mention uncomfortable. I've always been independent — for good reason — and the uncertainty of how to move forward is starting to weigh on me. I don't want to ruin the atmosphere of the day, since I'm enjoying this leisurely interlude, but it's a conversation we need to have. I pick at a stray thread at the edge of the oversized shirt I'm wearing as I consider how to begin, and he sits up against the headboard.

"We'll have to do something about that," he says. "Though I like the sight of you wearing my clothes, I doubt you find them suitable."

"They don't exactly fit, but I suppose they'll do for now. It's not like I have the means to go out and get a whole new wardrobe, which brings me to a subject I have to address. I can't just… lounge around for the foreseeable future. I have to find some sort of work."

"You could lounge around indefinitely if that's what you wanted, but I'd imagine you'd like to get back to tattooing?"

I think about it for a moment, and realize I'm not sure I do. The studio catching fire had extinguished that part of me, and it would take a massive effort to rebuild. Gone is every piece of equipment, every reference book, every drawing, every client record — not to mention the building itself. Tattooing had been the cornerstone of my existence — my purpose — but it had evaporated overnight. Maybe this is the universe paving the way for something new. Maybe it hasn't forgotten me after all.

"No. I think that may be over for me."

"Are you certain?"

I nod. "Everything's gone, and I can't help but feel like

it's time for something different, though I'm not sure what."

"Well," he says, clasping his hands over his stomach. "I could definitely use some help here, if you're open to it."

"Here?"

"Yes — here," he smiles. "Home is where I work. Contrary to what you've seen over the past day, I don't usually spend my time lazing about. The greenhouse needs a great deal of upkeep, and I have long lists of tasks when it comes to the apothecary."

I consider what he's offered as I stare out at the harbor. I like the idea immediately. Imagining spending my days surrounded by that lush greenery appeals to me, and I'd never had the opportunity for anything like it. Why not? The majority of my drawings revolved around my love of botanicals, so it might be the the the perfect segue.

"If I'm being honest, the greenhouse is like a dream come true, and the apothecary is one of my favorite places. I'd love to be involved with them, though I have to warn you — I only know the basics when it comes to horticulture."

"I have no doubt you'll pick it up quickly. You absorbed a fair amount of information from those books with ease, and this would be less intense than that."

He's not wrong. I'd always been decent at retaining information when it pertains to something I'm interested in. I think I can handle it. I cross my legs under me, and rest the pillow I'd been lying on in my lap.

"Well, we should discuss terms then, shouldn't we? I'm just not sure how this is going to balance out, what with me living here in addition to working for you."

"Working *with* me," he says, smiling faintly. "And as for the rest, what's mine is yours — in every capacity."

"But you can't just take care of everything yourself, and I already owe you for —"

"Please — don't worry about any of it," he interrupts. "You're not beholden to me, you're part of this equation now."

I still feel a little uncomfortable, but I've also never lived with anyone before — especially not in a romantic sense. I'm not entirely sure how this is supposed to work, and what I don't want is to be an unnecessary burden to him. I tell myself I'll work as hard as I can, and hope it's enough until we can figure it out on paper. I'm at least glad I don't have expensive tastes.

"Are you sure you're all right with me being in your way every waking moment? You might get sick of me."

"I highly doubt it," he smiles, leaning on his elbow. "And I'll still request that you keep me company at the bar. I'd miss our nights if you didn't. I'd miss watching you dance, too."

I'd only joined the crowd a handful of times when I began frequenting — usually because of a song I couldn't resist — and it's clear he noticed more than I gave him credit for.

"You really *watched* me?" I playfully smack him with the pillow, and he laughs.

"That makes it sound a bit obsessive, but it really wasn't. You do realize that wall is made of glass, and somehow you always managed to pick the center of the room — *directly* in my line of view. I couldn't *not* watch, and I admit I was sad when you stopped."

"I stopped so I could spend all my time with *you*," I smirk. "That and it left me far too sweaty."

"I know. It was a little intoxicating."

I wrinkle my nose. "Oh… Gross."

"Not at all," he laughs, tracing the outline of a leaf on my knee. "It was earthy — sweet, almost — not pungent. I just have a very sensitive olfactory system."

"Well you're pretty redolent yourself." He raises an eyebrow, and I laugh. "I don't know how, but you smell… like the air after a storm. It's one of my favorite things. Petrichor."

He smiles. "A favorite of mine too. Here — my secret." I watch him stride towards the shelf overflowing with vessels. Glass clinks as he searches, the dark bird imprinted on his shoulder raising its wing with every movement of his arm, and he returns with a handful of tiny vials. I carefully uncap one, and lift it to my nose. I'm hit with the scent of fresh earth — so strong I can almost feel the soft particles between my fingers. The next is a crackling campfire, and the third hot pavement after rain.

"These are perfumes! Did you make them?"

He nods. "They were meant for the apothecary, but I never fine tuned them enough for my liking."

I'm continuously amazed by him. Every new facet he reveals is another fascinating and complex layer comprising who he is, and enchants me even more. One after another I waft the scents — a riverbed, freshly rained on grass, the night sky just after dusk. A sweet smelling hearth, warm soft sheets that have been slept in. I've never encountered anything like them, and they bring to mind a sort of latent feeling. Something deep and moving — the quiddity of a memory. I'm mesmerized by how he's managed to capture it in a tiny vessel.

"Rhys, these are incredibly evocative," I sigh blissfully as I lie back against the pillow, surrounded by tiny vials. "What lovely experience do you intend to bottle next?"

He leans in close, the hair on his face tickling my neck as he plants a kiss on my shoulder. "Maybe it'll be you. I'll just need to get you drunk and dancing to make a few notes."

I'm about to retort with a dry remark, but before I can even open my mouth, my stomach growls. Loudly.

"You can't pretend you're not hungry now," he laughs.

"I have to admit I'm sort of starving. You must be, too."

"Let me see what I can scrounge up — I don't usually keep much here."

"Actually, before that do you mind if I wash up? I won't be long." My hair feels a little greasy, and despite the fact that he professed to enjoy the smell of my sweat, I'd prefer it not become overpowering.

"Darling, take all the time you want. It'll give me a chance to run down to the corner shop. Here — I'll show you where everything is."

After he's gone, I step into the small white tub. I can barely stretch out in it, and I wonder how he manages since he's much taller — this washroom definitely wasn't constructed with him in mind. It's a narrow room, the walls the same stained cement as the stairwell leading to the greenhouse. There's no window, but the light from the pendulum fixture suspended from the ceiling is soft, not harsh. I lean my head against the rim, my eyes moving over the jars and bottles lining the shelf next to the tub. They have no labels, so I open them to inspect their contents, and am delighted to find a variety of scented salts among the soaps. There's lavender, eucalyptus, lemongrass, and one that smells strongly of vetiver. After deliberating, I decide to try the lavender, and it fills the washroom with a heavenly aroma as I sprinkle the crystals into the hot water. I sigh contentedly as I submerge myself, but my quest for complete relaxation is compromised. There's one thought eating away at me, and I've been staving it off all day. That green glass bottle had been lost along with everything else.

The water sloshes as I physically push the thought away. Nothing good can come of telling him, and maybe it won't matter. Maybe we can go on for a long time just like this. I haven't ever been granted anything like what I think we might have, and I'm not about to ruin it now. My secret will have to stay secret.

I stay in the bath until the water begins to grow cold, and when I emerge from the washroom he's at the kitchen counter, unloading a brown paper bag.

"What's all this?"

"I wasn't sure what you like, so I got a little of everything," he says. "And I have to be upfront — I'm an absolutely terrible cook, so it's probably best that I don't attempt anything myself."

"It seems we've got that in common." I pick up a container of cold noodles, slices of cucumber buried beneath them. "I wonder which of us is worse."

"I'm sure we'll find out in time," he laughs, placing the rest of the food in the icebox.

"Aren't you having any?"

"I keep an odd schedule," he says, shutting the door. "Maybe later. I do think I might open some wine, though. Would you care for any?"

I nod, my mouth full of cucumber. I'm so famished I have to consciously slow myself so I don't inhale the entirety of the container too quickly. We stay up late into the night, finishing the bottle of wine, and stretching the joy of the day as far as it will go. As I fit myself next to him in bed, I think about the conversation we'd had at the bar only weeks earlier. Had I been wrong about destiny? That perpetual feeling that I was missing something — was it him all along?

✶ ✶ ✶ ✶ ✶ ✶ THIRTEEN ✶ ✶ ✶ ✶ ✶ ✶

I sleep far longer than I mean to the next day and am shocked at the time when I wake. I'm usually up at the crack of dawn, but my schedule has been thrown way off. He's nowhere to be found, but I hear water running through the exposed pipes on the wall next to the greenhouse door and assume he's up there. He is — in the far corner, pruning herbs. I wonder how long it'll take to get used to the fact that in a few days' time I'd gone from loving him afar to living with him.

"Hello darling. Sleep well?"

My heart flutters. He's called me 'darling' more than once, and I think it's time I mention it. During all the hours we spent at the bar he never referred to me or anyone else with a term of endearment, casual or otherwise.

"Can I ask why you've chosen to call me that all of a sudden?"

He places the pruning shears on the edge of the raised bed and scratches behind his ear.

"Ah… Well," he says, a shy smile on his mouth. "Honestly it just felt… *right*. Like I've always called you my darling. I hope it doesn't bother you. It might be difficult to cease."

He looks a little embarrassed, but I don't want him to be. It does feel right, just like everything else between us. Like it's always been there. I sidle up next to him and slip my arm around his waist.

"Not at all — I love hearing it. I was just curious." I wonder what I might begin to call him as I observe his progress with the herbs. "Can I help with this?"

"Of course. Here — I'll show you."

The afternoon passes quickly as I try my hand at my new future. We trim leaves from long stems, harvest buds and flowers, and uproot whole plants. He shows me his process of cleaning them before either tying them into bundles to dry or spreading them thin on wide trays inside a whirring machine. After we're through, he walks me down the rows of the greenhouse, explaining each plant and its purpose, along with how to care for them. Several need to be closely watched, since they have to be harvested before they go to seed, while others must be collected in stages. A few require far less water than most, and care must be taken so they don't rot. There's pruning and feeding schedules, and replanting cycles to ensure a continuous supply. It's a lot to take in, and I begin to think I need to make notes.

"It's a little overwhelming, I know," he says, watching me mentally list what he's detailed.

"Maybe you can draft me an itemized sheet. I don't want to forget anything."

Later I find myself sitting at the table across from him, stacks of papers and books between us. Though we're working quietly, the room isn't silent. I'd discovered another interesting part of him — his extensive record collection. It's a media I hadn't ever delved into myself since it would've been too burdensome to transport, but I'm happy to have it at my disposal now, and ambient synth plays softly in the background. Given what I know of his tastes I think he's trying not to scare me off — he took forever when selecting it. I'm recopying the list he'd given me since his handwriting is nearly illegible, and he's paging through an open book, writing a series of equations on a piece of paper.

"I'm continuously impressed by your perfect penmanship," he says, glancing over at my neat lettering, a stark contrast to his loopy scribbles.

"I don't know how you decipher yours," I laugh. "I'm amazed I can read it at all. It's terrible."

He smiles slightly. "It was never my strong suit." He continues scratching out numbers and symbols, replacing them with new ones, and I wonder aloud what he's doing.

"Calculating a formula for a new elixir," he says without looking up.

"I have to ask — how do you even know how to do that? Or how to make all this?" I gesture to the rows of medicines and ointments on the shelves.

"An excessive amount of schooling. I probably put myself through far more education than was warranted, but I felt it necessary."

I'm intrigued. The last time I experienced formal training of any sort was during my apprenticeship.

"What did you study?"

"Anything and everything, but there were certain concentrations. Let's see… Alchemy, healing, mathematics, botany…" he muses, tapping his pencil on the table.

"Just a few classes?"

"More than a few. I completed those programs in their entirety, but there was much I never pursued fully. I'm certain I'm forgetting something."

"*All of them?!* Gods, and here I was only days ago assuming you were just the bartender with the lovely personality. Talk about misguided assumptions. You've spent most of your life on this, haven't you? It must've taken years and years."

"It did." He scratches behind his ear. "But I'm still that bartender you love."

"You must think I'm highly uneducated," I frown. "I never even considered schooling."

"Not at all, darling," he says, shutting the book. "I wouldn't ever call you uneducated. I told you once I didn't think you ignorant, and I meant it. I also know you've worked tirelessly to perfect your craft — I've witnessed some of it in action."

It's not my craft anymore, and I'm hit with a sudden wave of sadness. All the years I'd worked at it seem almost wasted because I'd given it up, though not entirely by choice.

"Well, I have something new to learn now. I'm sure I can perfect it too, in time."

He's noticed the change in my voice, and places his hand over mine.

"I'm sorry. Have I upset you?"

"No, it's just… This change is still fresh, is all. I'm still processing the fact that I'm not a tattooist anymore, and it makes me sad when I think about it."

"Completely understandable," he says gently. "And it would be odd if you weren't. I know it meant a lot to you."

I don't want to think about it anymore. There's nothing to be done about it — not really — so I pick up the list and push my chair back.

"It's about time for the evening watering, isn't it? Do you mind if I give it a go on my own?"

"Of course," he says. He pauses for a moment, chewing the edge of his lip. "You know, I have a bit of an errand to run. If you feel you're all right, I might pop out for a moment."

"Go on. I'm not going anywhere."

"I should hope not." He bends to kiss my cheek. "I'll be right back."

The sorrow I feel for my lost trade begins to drop away as I walk the rows of the greenhouse. Maybe I just need more time to adjust, and I'm hoping that pouring my focus into this will help. There's a misting system, which takes a fair amount of the legwork out, so I walk the perimeter of the room while I wait for it to finish, letting the wet green leaves tickle my arms. The air does wonders for me, and I feel worlds better after just a short amount of time. I descend the stairs to find the apartment empty, so I plop down on the bed to watch the lights on the harbor while I wait for him to return. After a long while I hear the door open, and he appears with another bag, but it's not from the grocer.

"What's this?"

"Well, you can't continue traipsing around in my old clothes," he says, setting it on the bed. "So I thought I'd take it upon myself to find you some new ones for the time being."

"Seriously? You actually went out shopping for me?"

"I thought it might cheer you up a bit. Is it an unwelcome gesture?"

"Not at all." I smile as I pick up a soft black t-shirt, size appropriate. Beneath it are more dark items — a sleeveless black tank made of silklike fabric, a loose gray knit sweater, and leggings that have a sheen like leather. "And you've certainly grasped my adoration for all things monochromatic. Where did you find all this? These are exactly the sort of things I'd choose myself."

"There's a shop a few blocks away that looked like it might have something you'd prefer, so I figured I'd give it a shot." He falls back against the pillows as I hold up the sweater. "Try them on, then choose something. We're going out tonight."

"You mean to the bar? Are you working?"

"No — somewhere different. I think you could use a little time away from here. It's safe, and it's not far."

We're going out — together. A first. The idea of it erases the last of my lingering sadness, and I can't keep the smile from my face. I pull on the leggings and sweater, pleased to find they fit as they should. The simple canvas lace up shoes he'd chosen are a little tight, but they'll likely loosen with wear.

"Well?" he asks, watching me admire my new outfit. "How did I do?"

"This is perfect. I have no idea how you knew it'd fit though."

"I didn't," he says, shrugging on a fresh shirt of his own. "It was an incredibly stressful guessing game, if I'm being completely transparent. You're smiling though, which I'll take as a good sign?"

New clothes were a gesture I didn't know I needed, and I'm touched by his thoughtfulness and attention to detail. My heart is terrifyingly full, so I throw my arms around him, and he laughs as he returns my embrace.

＊ ＊ ＊ ＊ ＊ ＊ FOURTEEN ＊ ＊ ＊ ＊ ＊ ＊

It's raining as usual, and we duck in and out of doorways as we traverse the sidewalks. I'm wondering where we could possibly be going when he pulls me by the elbow into a graffiti covered stairwell, then down a set of rusted diamond plate steps.

There's a familiar pulsing behind the metal door at the bottom, and a single red lightbulb burns above, its glow making our shadows long and sinister. Beyond the door is a smoky bar, and I comb back my damp hair with my fingers as I glance around. More red lights glow from corners, illuminating dark figures and a crowd swaying in front of a live band. The bartender is young, with slicked back hair and a thin mustache, and he smiles when we settle into the tall chairs surrounding the counter. Rhys says something to him I can't hear, and he disappears into a back room before returning with a dingy looking bottle. I sweep my eyes across the red lit cavern as he opens it, really taking it in this time. There are all sorts here, though most are dressed similarly — lots of spiked boots, leather, black eyeliner. I feel like I could belong here.

"I hope you don't mind — I ordered for you," he says, sliding the glass towards me. "This is likely some of the best wine on this coast. A little different than the cocktails you're used to, but I'm hoping you'll like it."

I pick it up to smell, and I'm met with a rich earthy scent. It tastes warm and velvety, and I like it very much. As I sip, I'm aware of a few patrons casting their eyes in our direction. Do I not blend in as well as I thought?

"Is it me, or are people staring at me like I have five heads?"

"It's probably the combination of me *and* you," he says. "I have a few acquaintances here, and none of them have ever seen me with a date. What I'm hoping is that they don't invite themselves over for conversation before I have the chance to introduce you to — ah! There they are."

We're approached by a tall smiling man, his teeth and his green eyes gleaming. He's not thin, like Rhys, but thick and muscular, his long dirty blond hair knotted on top of his head. He's in a leather jacket, and his t-shirt bears a band logo I'm unfamiliar with. On his arm is a beautiful woman, her eyes a deep gray. She's very petite, but is wearing the highest of platform boots that swallow her legs past the knee. Her shining black curls extend to almost waist length, where her silky blouse meets her short denim skirt. She looks a little taken aback by the sight of me, though she flashes a bright smile beneath her dark lipstick.

"Rhys! Where've you been all week?" The man exclaims as they embrace, clamping his meaty hand on Rhys' back. Clearly they're more than just acquaintances. He turns his gaze to me, and extends his big hand. It completely envelops mine as he grips it firmly. "Hi — I'm Julien. This is my better half, Cordelia. You must be —"

"Ah…" Rhys interrupts, placing his hand on my shoulder. "Julien, Delia — I'd like to properly introduce you to Lynna, my… Er… Girlfriend? Partner? Well, regardless of the term, we're *together*."

"No shit," Julien says slowly, smiling wider, but Delia raises an eyebrow.

I'm trying to get a better sense of these people he's introduced me to, and look Julien over again. His presence is formidable, and there's a hint of a dark scar stretching across his cheek, but his smile is incredibly disarming. I feel he'd be more likely to hug someone than hurt them, and I like him immediately. I'm intimidated by Delia though, and it only increases when she crosses her arms.

"You've got to be kidding." Her voice is low and sultry, not at all high pitched like I'd expected. "Well then. Does this mean no more evenings alone? Sadly draining one of those dusty bottles?"

Rhys half grimaces, and I'm wondering if her rudeness is purely jest or if there's bite behind it. She looks me up and down, but before I can think of anything to say she takes me by the wrist.

"Come along Lynna — accompany me to the ladies'."

Delia leads me into the black tiled bathroom and perches herself on the sink. Three giggling women exit as we enter, and it becomes very quiet after they've gone. She slides a cigarette from a silver case in her pocket and presses it between her lips. She's staring at me intensely, one of her perfectly arched brows raised above her heavily shadowed eyelid, and the longer she looks at me the more nervous I become. She's breathtakingly beautiful, her small round face registering a hint of smugness as she exhales a cloud of smoke from her smirking mouth. She taps the edge of her cigarette with one black clawed fingertip, the ash falling into the sink.

"Mmm — you and Rhys? Surprising. He's been alone so long I didn't think he had it in him. Comes off a little desperate, doesn't he?" She takes another drag from the cigarette. "Is that what you go looking for? The lonely old saps? Someone to pave your way for you?"

I'm not sure what to make of what she's said — has she just insulted us both? Before I can think of an appropriate response, she continues her rapid fire stream.

"Clearly you've gotten him into bed, given the way he looks at you." She leans closer, lowering her voice. "Good manipulation tactic, isn't it? And how is that going?"

I blush deeply. She's very rude, and unapologetically blunt. I need to say something. Quickly.

"I didn't... seek him out for anything like that. I didn't seek him out at all — we met at his bar. For months we'd been having long conversations that just... Turned into something more. Something... *Real*."

I don't know if I should mention the drama from only a few days previous to prove my point. Him saving my life. My livelihood up in flames. Briefly I see an image of the scarred man, wet with rain, and stifle a shudder.

"Oh, come on," she asks, her gray eyes steely. I have to

concentrate on keeping my composure. "He's out of your age range for anything real. Just how old are you, anyway?"

Is she serious? Furthermore, is she actually his friend?

"You're concerned with the age difference? It's a little judgmental, in my opinion, and he's not *that* much older. I'm not a teenager, I'm thirty-five."

I hope it sounds like a reasonable number. She opens her mouth, but I'm not quite finished.

"And this is more than real. I love him, and he's made it explicitly clear he feels the same. Your suggestion that I'd have ill intentions in pursuing him is abhorrent, and offensive to us both. You don't know me, and I'm wondering how well you know *him* — if at all. What kind of friend are you to talk about him like that? He's amazing to say the least, and he deserves more credit than you're giving him. Honestly… So do I."

She studies me carefully as she ashes her cigarette, and I will myself not to drop my eyes. I'm rarely assertive, but she's put me on the defense. I *do* love him, and I refuse be questioned on it. Her gray eyes grow suddenly warmer, and her smirk turns into something resembling a smile.

"There it is," she says. "That's what I was after. I might've given you the impression I think ill of Rhys, but that couldn't be further from the truth. He means a lot to Julien and me, and we can't let him get his heart broken, now can we?" She jumps down from the sink and adjusts her skirt. "I only wish he'd told us he was seeing someone — well, he likely told Julien and left me out, but I aim to get to the bottom of *that* later. It's obvious he's smitten with you, and it warms my heart to see a smile like that on his face." She links her elbow through mine. "I just had to be sure."

"You know," she adds she leads me to the door. "I have this feeling that we'll become great friends. I hope I'm right."

I'm taken aback by her abrupt change in demeanor,

considering how she'd just spoken to me minutes earlier. What the hell *was* that? A test?

When we return to the bar, Rhys and Julien are downing shots, and she groans.

"Already into the hard stuff, I see," she quips, and Julien shrugs. He swigs the last drops and sets the glass on the counter before taking her hand.

"Come on — we've barely seen any of the band!"

I watch them saunter off towards the back of the bar as I lean on my chair, still trying to process the interaction with Delia. Rhys takes the bottle and tops off my glass, and when it's full I take a gulp more than a sip.

"Sorry," he says. "I should've prepared you for that. I hope she didn't ask you anything inappropriate."

"Inappropriate is putting it lightly. Julien seems nice, but she threw me for a loop."

"She can be a bit abrasive," he chuckles. "She has good intentions though, and I'd trust her with my life."

"Have you known them long?"

"Very long. Julien and I have been nearly inseparable since we met, and bounced around the continent together some years back. Occasionally there are spans we've spent apart, but it's always like no time has passed when we reconvene. I consider him as best a friend as any. She's a close second."

"I'm afraid I don't have any friends of my own for you to meet. Are there more of yours I should ready myself for?"

"There's another you'll meet eventually. Dimitri's been traveling, but I'm certain he'll make an appearance when he returns." He finishes what's left in his glass, and empties the bottle into it. "Well? Shall we join them?"

I shift my eyes to the crowd. Julien's hair is visible, but Delia's too short for me to locate. Despite her change in attitude I'm still scared of her, but I don't want to make a bad impression by being standoffish. Maybe a little more liquid courage is in order. I take a hearty sip of the velvety wine, and two more for good measure before I nod.

"Let's go."

✶ ✶ ✶ ✶ ✶ ✶ FIFTEEN ✶ ✶ ✶ ✶ ✶ ✶

The excitement I'd felt for my new life is diminished when I wake with a pounding headache, cursing the amount of wine I'd consumed. I hear him up and about, and when I'm finally able to raise my head I see him standing next to the table, paging through a newspaper with coffee in his hand.

"Good morning darling," he smiles. He's far too cheerful, and I'm wondering why he's not in the same state as I am since he'd imbibed much more. "Oof — not feeling so hot, are we?"

I drop back onto the bed. "I've been better. Ugh, my head."

"I've got something for that." I hear his footsteps as he makes his way across the room, presumably to one of the shelves. There are a few clinking noises, then the bed shifts as he sits down. "Here — this should help."

I don't know what's in the cup he hands me, but it tastes awful. For a moment I regret drinking it, since it almost makes a sudden reappearance.

"Gods, what was that?" I ask, pressing the back of my hand to my mouth.

"It works better than it tastes. Give it a little while. In the meantime, just rest — I'll get you some coffee."

"How come you're so perky?" I ask as he hands me a steaming cup before climbing into bed next to me. "Did you take some of that… Whatever it was?"

"Nah — I have a high tolerance," he says, unfolding the newspaper in his lap.

I sit for a while, listening to the crinkling of the pages as he turns them, grateful the throbbing in my temples is beginning to recede. The foul tasting substance seems to be working. I think about the night at the bar, and further dissect what Delia had barraged me with in the washroom.

"I wasn't exactly expecting an interrogation like the

one last night. Does Delia always do that? Pull your dates aside and grill them?"

"No," he laughs. "There hasn't been anyone to do that *with*. I wasn't putting you on when I told you I preferred to remain… Unattached."

"She made it a point to comment on that." I pause to take a sip and it agrees with me, so I take another. "I was taken aback by some of the things she said. For a moment I couldn't tell if you were friends or foes. I think she meant to shock me. See how I'd react."

"I figured she was up to something, but it seems you've passed the test."

It appears I had. She'd been dramatically different after our conversation, and I'd felt more comfortable around her for the remainder of the evening. One thing sticks in my mind though — her insistence that I'm somehow too young — and it brings up a question I hadn't wanted to ask him since I have difficulty with my own answer.

"You know, she seemed to think there's this huge gap between us. It occurred to me that I don't know your actual age. I guess it's a bit odd not to, considering we're living together."

"Forty six," he says without missing a beat, not lifting his eyes from the paper. "What was your estimate?"

"It didn't matter to me, so I hadn't given it much thought, but I'm not sure that's the number I'd have landed on. I'm… Uhm… Thirty five, so I was at least right in that we're not *that* far apart."

"It's the hair," he sighs, tucking a few silvery strands behind his ear. "Makes me look ancient. I was cursed with the early onset of it — been completely gray since I was quite young."

"Well, I think it suits you. I like it."

"I'm glad to hear you do," he says, smiling slightly. "Since it seems it won't be reversing itself any time soon."

I smile back at him, but inside my stomach is turning uncomfortably. I can't tell if it's because of the lingering effects of too much wine, or because I'm realizing he's gone into this with complete transparency, and I'm still hiding things from him. Now's my chance — now's when I should tell him — but I'm afraid to lose him. I'm far too happy, and though I know I'm being selfish and dishonest by keeping my secret, I can't bring myself to undo everything. I push down the guilt, and concentrate on the peace of the moment instead. This quiet morning, this warm bed, and the one I love sitting next to me.

✦✦✦✦✦✦ SIXTEEN ✦✦✦✦✦✦

Days turn into weeks and I lose track of time, the hours passing fluidly from one to the next. My sleep schedule finally adjusts, and it turns out we're both early risers. We establish a gentle routine of long slow mornings drinking coffee and paging through the newspapers before tending to the daily tasks waiting in the greenhouse. I love this new path more than I ever thought I would. I spend the days covered in dirt — harvesting, pruning, propagating. I'd taken over the inventory lists after seeing the scribbled mess of his handwriting, and I think he's relieved he doesn't have to attempt to keep it legible anymore. I don't participate on the days he creates, but it quickly becomes my favorite activity to observe. Elixirs, ointments, powders, and tonics. Incense, tea blends, and scented salts. I never fathomed the depth of his capabilities when I fell in love with him, and watching him in his element only intensifies it. I wonder if I'll ever stop being amazed by him.

On the weekends I join him in the club for at least a little while, since I still enjoy sitting across the bar, though I no longer have drawings to complete. Instead I take one of his many books with me, so I can further my understanding of the plants and their uses, and he leans across the bar to read alongside me. We frequent the red lit bar, meeting up with Julien and Delia, who I've come to know as rare stones of great friendship. We laugh loudly, and drink and dance, now the obnoxious foursome in the corner. I love being part of something — finally — and like them both immensely. Julien flashing his toothy smile, and Delia tapping her nails on her silver case as she lights one after another. I hadn't spent any length of time alone with either of them, though she continues to insist I let her take me on a lunch date. I agree, but Julien insinuates her suggestion might not mean what I think.

"She's got ulterior motives," he says during a moment we're left alone in the booth. I'm not sure what he means, and it makes me nervous. I thought we'd been getting along spectacularly. Had I misread her?

"Don't panic," he laughs, cupping his beefy hand around his whiskey glass. "She's a bit of a clotheshorse, is all. What she wants is to get you out shopping."

"Well if that's all it is, I'm sure I can oblige her. She might be disappointed — I know very little about fashion."

"Oh, she'll take the lead. You'll find that out quickly." He grins as he takes a sip. "You seem to do well enough. That's pretty."

He nods to the pendant hanging around my neck, and I blush.

"I can't be credited for this. Rhys gave it to me. He's full of surprises."

"More of them than you even know," he says, lifting the glass to drain it.

I touch the cool stone as Rhys and Delia rejoin us, and smile as I recall how I'd acquired it.

***

"Hello darling," he says, shutting the front door behind him. He's just returned from an errand, and I'm busied washing the dishes I'd dirtied from my lunch. More cold noodles, but I'd made them myself, and had drastically undercooked them.

"What's that look you've got on?" I ask.

It's not a bad expression, but I don't recognize it. I dry my hands on a dish towel as he shrugs off his jacket. From his pocket he produces a wad of tissue paper, and begins unwrapping it.

"I've got something for you. I saw it while I was out, and it was too beautiful to pass up."

He lifts a long thin chain from the paper, and on the end is a chunk of metal with a teardrop shaped stone embedded in it. Rainbow streaks glint as it turns in the light — labradorite. I'd always been drawn to gemstones, and I'd had a small collection at one point, but that hobby had gone by the wayside when I began moving around. This particular one is my favorite, though I'd never told him that. He holds it out, and I watch it swing on the chain as I take it from his hand. He's right — it's absolutely beautiful — and I don't know what to say. I can't remember the last time I'd been given something like this, if ever.

His smile fades. "You don't like it?"

"No, no — it's lovely." I quickly dissolve my stunned look. "I'm just not used to this sort of thing, I guess."

"Well," he says, smile returning. "I admit I'm not used to seeing a piece of jewelry and immediately wanting to gift it to someone, but here we are."

He lifts it from my fingers, and softly sweeps my hair aside before clasping it around my neck. I don't know how to thank him, so instead of saying anything I grasp his shirt in my fist and pull him in to kiss him.

***

Everything is in essence, perfect. As perfect a life as I'd ever imagined, but thought well out of my reach. I feel at home with him, and I'd never felt truly at home anywhere. Though I'm encased in a bubble of domestic bliss, wistfulness for my past as a tattooist occasionally creeps in. I'd wander past the blank space between the buildings that once housed my studio, remembering everything I'd created within, remembering everyone whose lives I'd peeked into. I'd left it as is, but it hadn't left me. I'd catch myself wondering about some of the people I'd met, missing their stories and smiles, and I'd absentmindedly doodle in the margins of the pages meant for bookkeeping. I don't pay it much mind, but he does.

"You know," he says, tapping his pencil against the table. "We have surfaces other than that ledger, if you're interested in decorating them. I'd enjoy seeing more of your artwork, if you feel so inclined."

I'd been taking inventory while he fine tuned another elixir, and don't immediately register what he's said. An ornate border now frames the neatly penned words detailing the supplies we have in stock. I stare at it for a moment, then close the binder. He sets the pencil in the crease of his book.

"You miss it."

It's a statement, not a question, and I know he's referring to my craft as a whole. Drawing, tattooing. I do miss it — much more than I thought I might — but I don't want to get caught up in what once was. I have to put it away.

"Sometimes."

"Well," he smiles gently. "If it's something you still want, I'm certain we can find a way to make it a reality for you."

"No. I'm perfectly happy with what I'm doing now. Unless you think I'm not properly holding up my end of things."

His smile falters. "Of course you are. That's not at all why I brought it up. You could be doing nothing and I'd be completely fine with it. I only want to be certain you don't feel like you're missing something. I want to do all I can to ensure your happiness."

I grin at him, trying to reassure him I'm indeed content with what I have, and I am. Missing it is one thing, but it would be a dreadful undertaking to rebuild, and I don't feel right asking him to take that on. I tell myself I'll think of it less with more time, and that I just haven't fully adapted to this change, given it was the only thing I knew for so long. I'd begun the second act of my life, and I have to let go of the old one to embrace it.

* * * * * * SEVENTEEN * * * * * *

"Mmm — no," Delia muses as I hold up shirts for her to inspect. "Those won't do. The fabric's all wrong, and they'll fall apart in no time. I'm certain I can find a similar cut that's better quality."

She resumes shuffling through a pile of tank tops as I hang the offending shirts back on the rack, wondering what I'd gotten myself into when I accepted her invitation to go to lunch. I had no idea it was going to turn into several hours in a nearby boutique, having forgotten Julien's warning, and the one we're in is making me uncomfortable. Everything is far beyond my price range.

I'd demanded that Rhys separate the exact amount I'd earned by working — down to the very last cent, even though I know he's padding it disproportionately in my favor. I also insisted on giving him my half for what it costs to live in the apartment, but he's always one step ahead of me, telling me it's already covered. He'd given me free access to his funds — or *our* funds, as he refers to them — connected to the apothecary, but I don't even want to know how much is in the small safe near his desk let alone touch it. I worry it'll only make me feel worse about essentially sponging off him. He continues to assure me I could have whatever I wanted anyway, but I don't want to spend frivolously. He doesn't seem to care, but I do.

"This one's better," she says, holding up a light gray top with small buttons adorning the front. "We should get the black one, too. It doesn't hurt to have a staple item in several shades. It'll suit you — I can tell already."

I accept the garments from her outstretched hand, and she's right — they're much nicer than the stiff shirts I'd selected. The fabric is soft, and feels heavenly under my fingertips. I glance down at the tag, and my heart sinks. I'd never spent this much on an entire wardrobe, let alone two items.

"I'm not sure I —"

"Hush, doll," she says, tossing a sweater at me. "I invited you out, and I fully intend to spoil you. I know that shirt belongs to Rhys, and though I find it adorable you wear his clothes, you should really have more things of your own."

I look down at my oversize shirt, knotted tightly at my waist. He'd gotten me a few items himself, including the leathery tights I'm wearing now, but they're all I have since my own wardrobe was incinerated. I'd resumed wearing some of his clothes anyway, despite having commented on the fact that they don't fit. I feel more connected to him this way — his shirts smell like him, as if he's ingrained in the fibers themselves.

"Come along — shoes are next," she says. "Nothing I love more than a pair of new shoes."

She pulls pair after pair from their boxes, instructing me to try every one. I don't think I need anything more than the single pair I have already, but I oblige her anyway. I shake my head when she hands me a pair of lace up boots, the heels much too high for my liking.

"Not a fan?" she laughs. "Oh, please. Humor me."

"No, not a fan at all." I'm struggling with the laces, and have to pause to flex my hand.

There's a stiffness in my fingers — a sensation I haven't felt in a long time. I tell myself it must be from the long hours of pruning and continue lacing. I stand shakily, teetering when I step. Delia loves them and encourages me to walk the length of the aisle, so I do. I nearly fall and they pinch my toes, so I make my way back to the bench to begin the tedious task of untying them.

"I can't. Regardless of how they look, I hate how they feel. I don't know how you do it."

"Sometimes beauty is pain, doll," she laughs, admiring the platform heels on her own feet. "Fine. No heels. I won't force them on you if you hate them. Ooh — how about these?"

She's found a pair of black boots with rows of straps instead of laces, and they're flat — a far cry from the near stilettos I'd just had on.

"Try them. I'm willing to bet they're much more up your alley."

They are, and I love them immediately. They're comfortable, fitting perfectly around my calves, and the material is buttery soft. I glance at the box, and immediately remove them when I see the cost.

"Oh, come on," she groans. "Don't even look at that. Do you like them or not?"

"Delia, I absolutely cannot let you do this. They're far too expensive. Thank you, but I have to insist on declining."

She rolls her eyes. "If you insist. All right — I've done enough damage for one day. I'll have to get someone to pack this all up. Here —" She hands me a cigarette. "Go have a smoke. This could take a minute. I'll meet you outside."

I lean against the glass window while I wait, staying beneath the awning so I don't get the cigarette wet with rain. My elbows ache now as well as my hands, but I tell myself it's the weather — all the rain must finally be affecting my bones. Deep down I know that's not it, but I'm not ready to face facts — I prefer to lie to myself instead. Maybe I'll start to believe it.

Delia emerges from the shop with an armful of bags, so I stub out the cigarette to help her, laughing when she almost drops them all on the sidewalk.

"Delia!" I exclaim when she thrusts a box at me, a smirk on her lips. It's the expensive boots — she'd gotten them anyway. "I told you I can't accept these! We'll have to return them."

She shakes her head dismissively. "I'll be offended if you do. This is something I love, and I've greatly enjoyed our time today, so please — not another word. Now where are we going for lunch?"

***

"Hello darling," he calls as I struggle to swing the door open, my arms full of bags. "How was — heavens! I see you got the full Cordelia experience."

He laughs as he pads across the room to help me, taking the bags as well as the box.

"Did I ever. She's very demanding. She insisted on buying all this for me, even though I told her several times I didn't want her to."

"Demanding is a very gentle description." He notices me rubbing my shoulder, and his brows knit. "Are you all right? Did you carry these a long way?"

"I'm fine — I think the excursion just wore me out."

I sink down into a chair, and my stomach turns at the little white lie. It's spreading. It's gone from my hands to my elbows to my shoulders, and I worry it'll continue until it consumes me entirely.

"Just relax, then. I'll make some tea. I really must hear more about how the two of you got on."

I shake the stiffness from my arms as I watch him fill the kettle. I want to freeze us here — press pause. I don't want to tell him, but I'm realizing I may not have a choice if this continues. I don't even know how to begin such a conversation, and the fact that I'm considering telling him at all scares me on so many levels. I'm not ready yet, so as long as my hand isn't being forced I'll wait a little longer. Just a little longer.

⋆ ⋆ ⋆ ⋆ ⋆ ⋆ EIGHTEEN ⋆ ⋆ ⋆ ⋆ ⋆ ⋆

I don't find it in my heart to tell him, and it happens. The smooth line of my existence comes to a screeching halt. I wake one morning and can barely move — everything hurts, from the inside out. My joints are stiff, my heartbeat slow, and my skin is sallow. The worry in his eyes terrifies me, and I finally acknowledge what's happening instead of pushing it aside.

The mixture in that green glass bottle.

I hadn't taken any since the night of the incident with the scarred man, and the reality is that my body's finally catching up to its real age. I'd been living with the false hope that I could continue without it, not wanting to face the inevitable. I didn't want things to stop being so wonderful now that I finally have something good.

Two days pass before I decide I have to tell him. He'd been beside himself for the entirety, trying everything he could think of to cure me, and I can't let him continue. I can't listen to him speculate about viruses or bacterial infections for one more moment when I know the truth. I finally break when I see him bury his face in his hands, and hear him sniffle.

"Rhys… There's… Something I need to tell you." The words are heavy in my mouth. It's a sentence I'd been dreading.

He slowly raises his head, his eyes wet. The guilt for keeping him in the dark is almost as bad as the pain coursing through my body, and I struggle to swallow the lump in my throat.

"I'm not… I'm not nearly as young as I seem. I was taking… Medicine… And it had an effect on me that I think is wearing off."

His expression changes abruptly, a wave of realization washing over his face.

"Gods, of course… Of course that's it! It's accelerated withdrawal for certain — I should've recognized it. Tell me — what were you taking? I should be able to reverse the effects…"

He's on his feet, then he's over at the desk, ripping drawers open and hurriedly pulling bottles from the shelves. I'm stunned. Did he hear what I said? Does he not care that I'd kept it from him? My deep dark secret? The one that's controlled my life for so long?

"Lynna," he says over his shoulder, papers rustling as he sweeps them to the floor. "What were you taking? Please — tell me quickly."

"Elixirs three and nine," I mumble. Not a lie, but not the truth.

"Nonsense. Those won't completely…" He pauses, his hands flat on the desk. "There's something else. What is it?"

"Aeonia."

He doesn't respond — instead he turns around, a look of disbelief on his face. I don't know how to further explain it to him, since I know very little myself. I'd come by it through a vendor many years ago, and I recall that particular afternoon vividly.

***

"Have you got anything else besides what's here?" I ask as I scan the tins littering the table.

The man doesn't immediately answer. He's sitting in a folding chair behind the table, and I can't see any of his face besides his mouth beneath the hood of his coat. His pale lips spread into a half moon smile, and he pulls back his hood to reveal sharp features and almond shaped eyes of milky viridian green, his pupils small as pinheads. I'd never seen anyone with eyes like that.

"What is it you're after, dear? To stay awake for days? No no — to sleep, perhaps?"

"Uhm… Well…" I'm struggling to articulate what I'm looking for. His eyes are boring through me and it's unnerving. "I just need something to keep me in good health. My job — it's wearing on me."

I show him the shakiness of my hand as I curl it into a stiff fist. The repetitive motions of my occupation had already begun to take their toll, the arthritic decline making long hours of tattooing painful. Nothing I've tried thus far has helped, so I'd decided to seek out a less mainstream remedy.

"Ahh, I see," he says, reaching across the table to take my trembling hand. He unfolds my fist and presses his fingers into my palm. "Your wish is to reverse this, yes?"

"I don't think it can be reversed, I just want to... Slow it down. Ease the pain, if I can."

He's grasping my hand with both of his now, his eyes moving over my face as if he's lost in thought. It's making me uneasy so I pull it back, and he silently tents his fingers together. I'm wondering if I should've picked a different booth to inspect when he finally speaks.

"I've got just the thing."

He smiles eerily, and turns to a stack of cardboard boxes behind his chair. He unearths three green glass bottles, and delicately lines them up on the table.

"What is it?" I pick up one of the vessels to examine. Dark liquid sloshes around inside.

"Careful," he says. "It's very rare. This is no ordinary medicine. It's derived from blood belonging to a long extinct civilization."

I set the bottle down, rolling my eyes. Blood from a lost civilization? If he's trying to sell me on it by being hyperbolic he's failing.

"Choose to believe, choose to not," he shrugs. "Regardless, it cannot be mimicked, and it's the last of its kind."

"And why is this... Mysterious substance what I need?"

"It's called Aeonia, and it will do as you wish. Your hands will regain their dexterity, and you will be able to continue your work... Indefinitely. One hundred percent guaranteed."

"If it's so great, why haven't I heard of it before?"

"The desire for Aeonia has all but wiped it from existence," he says, leaning closer. "And you'd do well to keep it to yourself. This will change your life, my dear. I don't offer it to just anyone."

He grins again, never blinking, his green eyes still piercing me. I've struck out everywhere else, so I shrug and pull out my wallet.

***

Later I'd thought the vendor was crazy, and that I'd been conned into blowing a wad of cash on nothing, but as the pain diminished and the years crept on I realized he wasn't peddling snake oil. Nearly five decades had passed, though I still looked and felt like I was in my thirties. I'd been frozen in time, and though he hadn't warned me of the anti-aging effects, he *had* warned me not to stop dosing regularly.

"Under no circumstances do you skip doses," he'd stressed. "It is of *utmost* importance."

I had stopped. Abruptly. The last of it had burned up in the fire.

Rhys' head drops, and he sinks to the floor. "You've got to be mistaken. Aeonia… It doesn't exist anymore. Hasn't for a long time. You can't *possibly* have…"

He meets my gaze, and there's a wild look in his eyes. I don't have to explain anything — it's clear he knows *exactly* what Aeonia is, and what this means. Nothing he concocts will reverse this.

"*No!*" He's up again, and glass shatters. He's throwing vial after vial at the wall. "*Fucking no no no no NO!*"

He sweeps an entire shelf down with one swing and slams his fist onto the desk into the glass, blood trailing from his forearm when he raises it. Tears stream down his contorted face as he gingerly pulls a piece of glass from his palm, and he leans heavily against the desk, wiping his face with the back of his hand. I've never seen him like this, and my heart feels like it's caving in on itself.

"Rhys," I whimper, and he rushes over. "I'm so sorry. I'm —"

"No, my darling — don't. I just... I can't create what you need, but I refuse... I won't just stand by and let you..." He trails off as he cradles my face with his soft hand, and his expression suddenly changes. "Gods... I think I know what to do. It could work. It *has* to work..."

"What could?" It's becoming more and more difficult to talk, and I don't know how many more words I have left in me.

"I have an idea," he says, quickly kissing my forehead. "I love you. Rest if you can."

I watch him hurriedly shove his arms into his jacket, but before I can make my mouth move to respond, he's out the door.

✶✶✶✶✶✶ NINETEEN ✶✶✶✶✶✶

I'm in a dreamlike haze, unaware of the day or the time. I regain enough focus to recognize the sound of people talking, but I can only discern bits and pieces. I hear Rhys and a woman's voice, but I'm not sure if it's real or a hallucination.

"… Dangerous… We don't know what this could do to her…"

"… Can't lose her…"

"… Not giving her the choice… This is pure selfishness…"

"… No choice to be had…"

"… Could happen to her too…"

"… Die anyway… Hand me another vial…"

The sound of glass clinking, and a man's voice, whispering furiously.

"… Gravity of this… At what cost…"

"…Another vial — *quickly!*"

The voices recede, and I'm in the dark again. Suddenly I'm being shaken awake, and a soft floral scent fills my nose. It's Delia.

"Lynna?" She rattles my arm, so I slowly open my eyes. "We might be able to save you, but it could have dire consequences. You may not want this. I need you to choose —"

"There's no time," Rhys interrupts, gently pushing her aside. Something pierces my arm, but I can't look down to see what it is. I feel his hand behind my neck, and he carefully lifts my head.

I feel smooth glass as he touches a vial to my lips, and hear Delia inhale sharply. He leans my head back so I can swallow, as I can no longer unassisted.

"All of it… All of it, darling… *Please…*"

My body jolts, and the vial falls to the floor with a clank. My throat is on fire, and the searing heat spreads quickly — I feel like I'm burning from the inside. It's melting my organs, seeping out through my skin. Hellfire is nothing compared to this. I'm submerged in lava, engulfed in flames. I'm convulsing, dimly aware of Rhys forcefully holding me down, and someone's screaming.

It's me — *I'm* screaming, and I can't stop.

The pain is white hot, and I can't escape it. If I'm to die I wish it would take me, just so this will stop. Just make it *stop*. My thoughts are jumbled, my mind a tunnel I'm receding down backwards. My vision blurs, and soon there's only pain and blackness.

Things begin to appear to me in the dark. An explosion of swirling fire, the scarred man's face. Vast cities teeming with life. The cities disappear, replaced by dark landscapes of metallic ruins, the moon rising and setting above. Hundreds of bodies in an enormous pyre, smoke billowing into the sky. Fire and blood — so much blood — and it's so dark it's almost black. A feeling of being yanked through time itself, my body ripped to shreds, disassembled. An infant, slick with blood and vernix, its mouth open in a permanent wail. Twinkling lights like embers, a glimmering string stretching on in an endless line. The bizarre images plague me until it's again just dark, and the white hot pain recedes. Instead of hot it's now cold blackness, and I feel I might drown in it. I sink beneath it, deeper and deeper. I can barely string a thought together — I can't tell if I'm alive or dead, and I no longer care. Then nothing.

Endless… Black… Quiet…

Nothing.

✶ ✶ ✶ ✶ ✶ ✶ TWENTY ✶ ✶ ✶ ✶ ✶ ✶

Slits of light. Bright light. So bright I have to close my eyes, and I realize I have eyes to close. Am I still here? I'm aware of my body now, and I feel no more pain. I try to open my eyes again, but the light is blinding, and I instinctively raise my hand to shield them. I hear chairs scraping back, and quick footsteps.

"Hold her — hold her up." Delia's voice.

Someone pulls me to sitting, then props me up. My hand is clamped over my face, and I open my mouth to speak, but no words come out. All I can manage is a gravelly noise.

"Shh — don't try to talk. Keep your eyes closed." My hand is placed in my lap. "You'll have to be patient."

I sit motionless and concentrate on my breaths, feeling the air move in and out of my lungs. My mouth is dry, and I'm painfully thirsty. I feel a cup at my lips — water — so I drink deeply.

"No, no — slowly. Not so much at once. If you're not careful, you'll —" Delia stops mid sentence as I immediately regurgitate all of the water. "Yep. Just like that. Sit tight — I'll get a fresh shirt."

The wet shirt is pulled off me, and I shiver as a new one is gently fitted over my head. The brightness is fading, and I gingerly open my eyes to reveal blurry shapes.

"Delia?" I feel like I've never said words before, and clear my throat.

"Yes, doll. It's all right — you're out of the woods now." She grasps my hand, and I squeeze it back as hard as I can.

The scent of a strong bitter chemical is heavy in the air, and when my eyes focus I notice her beside me. Her hair is piled on her head in a messy bun, but her v neck sweater is unwrinkled. She smiles wanly, and shifts her eyes behind me. I turn my head sharply, expecting Rhys, but it's Julien.

"Welcome back," he says. "Thought we lost you there for a minute."

I clear my throat again and sink back onto the pillows, my thoughts racing. What happened? I thought I was dying, but now I'm here, and I feel so strange. Is this a dream? It doesn't seem like one. Why are they here — where's Rhys? I scan the room, but there's no trace of him. His shoes aren't by the door, and his jacket hook is empty.

"He'll be back shortly," Delia says, seeming to know I'm looking for him. "He went out to collect a few things we thought we might need to revive you, but you're up now, thankfully."

Before I can ask her anything, he bursts through the door as if summoned, a cardboard box beneath his arm.

"Delia, I was able to procure most of what's on the list, but not all. I may ask you to see if the hospital has —"

He notices me sitting up, and drops the box. In seconds he's across the room, nearly diving onto the bed.

"Gods… Darling… My darling…" he repeats as he inspects my body — looking into my eyes, gently turning my head, feeling the pulse in my wrist. My skin is back to its normal coloring — not sallow and sickly anymore. I'm tired, but there's life in my limbs, and more comes back into me when he hugs me so hard it takes my breath away. I'm not dreaming and I'm not dead. I feel his heart racing, and the softness in his touch — a far cry from that hot pain and cold darkness. I've never been more grateful to feel pleasant sensations.

"This is lovely and all, but she's through it," Delia says, and I see her cross her arms. "I think it's time to have a little chat, don't you?"

"For fucks' sake — give her a minute," Julien says. "She's —"

Delia shoots him a look filled with daggers, and he stops talking. A chat about what?

"What happened?" I ask Rhys. "I thought… I thought I was dead."

"You were very close, but clearly you're not. It worked. What we —"

"No small feat," Delia interrupts. "Rhys, we're out of runway here. It's time."

The room grows silent as he turns his head to look at her. He returns her stony stare with calm coolness, and she sighs.

"We'll give you a moment, then. Lynna — don't rush things. Take it slow."

After they're gone, he shifts back on the bed until he's sitting beside me. It's stopped raining for once, and bits of sun poke through the overcast skies, shards of light piercing the windows. No wonder I thought it too bright. He sighs heavily, and picks up a cigarette from the end table, rolling it between his fingers.

"How long were you taking... How old *are* you?"

This is the chat, then. It's revolving around what I was hiding. He hadn't so much as batted an eye when I'd told him, but will he react now? Will he be angry, like I expected? He has every right to be, so I prepare for the worst.

"Well... I started taking it when I was in my thirties, though I can't recall exactly when. I think about fifty years has passed between then and now."

I've said it, and it's slightly relieving to actually speak the words out loud. I'd tried telling a few people I thought were friends a long time ago, but they all told me I was crazy, and soon stopped interacting with me altogether. I made the mistake of telling a boyfriend I trusted once, and he's the one who scared me the most. He called me a liar, a monstrosity, a freak of nature. He confirmed my worst fear when he threatened to out me publicly, assuring I'd be cut apart to expose what made me this way, and I knew he was right. Later he wanted what I'd taken, and when I wouldn't give it to him he said he'd kill me for it. That's when I disappeared for the first time. I realized I couldn't ever share that information again, and never have until now. My nerves are returning. What will *he* do?

"Rhys… I'm sorry… I —"

"No," he says quietly. He's staring at the cigarette instead of smoking it, and continues rolling it between his fingers. "I have an apology of my own to make. I knew what I was doing and I… Didn't stop myself. I couldn't."

"What do you mean?" His reluctance to look at me is making me anxious.

"I haven't… I haven't exactly been honest with you either. I'm not the age I led on."

Is he serious? Is this an attempt to make me feel better?

"So… Not forty six, then?"

"Add your real age to forty six and it's more accurate."

My math skills aren't great, and the simple addition takes me a moment. If I'm in my eighties, that would put him at around… *a hundred and twenty*? I'm stunned, my mind racing. I thought for sure there was about to be a confrontation regarding my deceit, but things have taken a turn. I'm not sure how to feel — I'd failed to inform him of a vital piece of information in regard to my existence, so I can't blame him for not disclosing his, can I? How had he done it? Is this why he knew what Aeonia was when I mentioned it? Had he concocted something of his own to lengthen his life? Had we both been hiding a similar secret?

"You were taking something too, weren't you? Gods, this is unbelievable. I can't believe we both were."

"Not… Quite. I'm this way naturally."

It takes me a moment to fully register what he's said. Naturally? How is that possible? I'd never heard of anyone achieving what I had via the mixture, let alone come by it naturally. He finally meets my eyes and I realize he's as fearful as I was when I made my own divulgence. His secret is just as big as mine, but I both understand it and don't.

"Are you… What… *Are* you?" I choke out, and his face falls. I didn't mean to say it that way so I gently place my hand on his, and he responds by threading his fingers through mine.

"Well, I'm human — just like you — only a different sort of human. My kind have experienced... evolutionary changes, resulting in longevity that far surpasses the norm. It's... Difficult to explain. I don't have complete answers when it comes to *why* we've progressed in this way."

No wonder he'd always been so reluctant to talk about his past. I'd asked about it here and there, but he'd answered vaguely, though admittedly I did the same. Now I know it's because he couldn't reveal it, but is it also because he doesn't fully understand it himself? Questions, questions, and more questions — all alighting in my head like too many butterflies.

"So you don't know why you're... *Like* this?"

"I do, and I don't," he says, setting the cigarette back on the end table instead of smoking it. "A large part of the reason behind my excessive educational pursuits was unraveling our development — which I did, but only partially. Evolution is the most logical explanation, as biology and fact are undeniable when put to the test, but there are gaps in those evolutionary jumps. Gaps I can't fully rationalize. I've met others throughout the years, and the search for answers became more complicated, as there were conflicting beliefs. Some were like me, driven by fact and logic. Others, however, went in a more fantastical direction, convinced we're some alien race that had been dropped here centuries ago. I don't buy that angle. Never have. It's just a story made up by those who can't wrap their heads around something they don't understand, much like the population's belief in the gods. I prefer hard evidence, and the years I spent poring over our molecular structures has given me enough. It's not worth obsessing over anymore. At least not to me."

"But how did you find out? Your parents didn't tell you?"

"I was raised by my mother alone," he sighs. "We had sort of a... Tumultuous relationship. She kept it from me until I was nearly grown, when it started to become apparent I was different."

"Gods," I whisper, sinking back against the pillows.

"How is this real? How have I lived my whole life not knowing there are people like you?"

"Likely because we go to great lengths to hide it," he says. "It's problematic. I've mentioned my time spent traveling, and that's mainly the reason. When you stay in one place for too long it becomes noticeable when you haven't changed at all — people don't like that, and they start asking invasive questions. I've known others who've exposed themselves, and it didn't go well for them so I've avoided doing so all my life. It's so odd to me how existing as an unnatural being can be so dangerous, but that's how the world is. The slightest deviation from the norm seems to incite only anger or fear."

I know that all too well. Now that I think about it, I recall seeing a handful of news articles citing abnormal beings, but they always disappeared without a trace before I could find them again, and I ended up convincing myself I invented them to make myself feel less alone. That's what they must've been about — people like him. The way he lives — operating his businesses by proxy without a single document in his name, intensely scanning the newspaper each morning, paying cash for everything — it's all starting to make sense.

"That's why you keep such a low profile, then. I get it now."

He nods. "I chose to start the apothecary because I can stay behind the scenes, and though the club is decidedly riskier, it's yet to be an issue. Do you think anyone really notices the bartender? What he looks like? How long he's been there?"

"I mean, *I* noticed."

A ghost of a smile crosses his face. "Even so, the vast majority frequent those sorts of establishments for only a couple of years before abandoning it, and the cycle repeats, keeping my secret for me. The staff will catch on eventually, so despite my best efforts, it'll be a matter of time before I must leave here too."

"That sounds all too familiar." We've been living almost parallel lives, haven't we? Staying hidden, keeping people at arm's length. "It's why I jumped from place to place myself. I understood what I became less than you, though. I tried to go back and find the vendor to make him explain, but he was gone…"

I'd been reeling from what he'd told me and had momentarily forgotten he'd done something I can't fathom. He'd brought me back from what I thought was certain death.

"Wait — how did you reverse it? My withdrawal?"

"Our blood," he says. "It contains a specific compound, similar to one present in Aeonia. I couldn't replicate the components, but —"

"The vendor," I interrupt. "He said Aeonia came from some… Lost civilization, he called it. I thought he was making it up. Was he? Is that what —"

"An interesting theory, but one I have no evidence to support. There haven't been many who've encountered Aeonia, and though its origins are subject of debate, the effects are definitely known. I thought it might be possible to rectify what damage had been done by its absence by imbuing you with something close to it. We applied a formula — one designed to change a normal human into one like us. You've been infused with blood from my kind, and that coupled with a combination of specific substances altered you once again. When it comes to longevity, you should continue to age at a snail's pace. With any luck, it'll be centuries more."

I think about what the vendor had said, and what I've just learned. How much strange blood is in my body that doesn't belong to me?

"Where did the… Who's blood did —"

"Mine," he says.

I stare at my legs, imagining the intricate red web beneath my skin, blood coursing through it. He'd just told me I'd been placed right back where I was — frozen in time. Infused with his blood. Brought back to life by him, a part of him forever alive in me. I want to be relieved, but his expression carries a fair amount of concern.

"What we did for you — to my knowledge a procedure like this has only been successful once before. There are side effects both known and unknown, and I only hope you've managed to escape them all. Delia reminded me of the failure rate — reminded me what could go horribly wrong. She agreed to help me run the formula, but only after I begged her. It's complicated for her, and she ultimately believed you should've had a choice."

I'm speechless, and I need a moment to wrap my head around everything, even though I think it might take much more than a moment. I sling my legs over the side of the bed to stand, and immediately crumple to the ground. He rushes to help me up, but I push him away gently. I make my way to the kitchen counter on quivery fawn legs, and lean on it to steady myself as I stare through the windows at the sun on the water. A new day is born. A new *me* is born. I don't know how to feel about any of it.

"I'm sorry," he says, sinking onto the edge of the bed. "She was right — it was incredibly selfish to do what I did, but I would've rather had you alive. Even if it meant you'd resent me. I just… I couldn't let you go…"

How could I resent him for this? It's true, there's plenty I don't understand, but I don't care about that right now. He'd just saved me a second time and given me the opportunity to live a long life with him. Had I been able to make the choice on my own, I would've chosen it. I cross the room, steadier now, and fit myself onto his lap. He wraps his arms around me and holds me tight against him as he sniffles.

"Gods," he whispers. "When I thought I'd lose you I…I couldn't *bear* it. If you'd have died, I would have too."

I lean back so I can see his face. His dark eyes are bloodshot, and a tear spills over his cheek. The shadows beneath his eyes are deep from exhaustion, and his hair is wild and uncombed. I suddenly feel like I might drown in the depth of my affection for him. Tenderly I press my palm against his fuzzy cheek, and lean in to kiss him. The second our lips meet I feel a bolt of electricity surge through me and jerk back, a tingling sensation running the length of my spine. What *was* that?

"Did you feel that? Did you?"

He nods, taking my hands and pressing them to his chest. His heart races beneath his ribs, static in my fingertips.

"I feel it sometimes — when I'm with you," he says. "It's… Bizarre. Wonderful. Sort of an… Electric magic, if I'm to put a name to it. I'm not certain why —"

Before he can finish I kiss him again, and my body sizzles. I no longer care about anything but the fact that I'm alive — not what I am, not what he is, not what lies ahead. My senses are heightened, as if everything's been highlighted in bold — his soft touch, the scent of his skin, the taste of his mouth. We kiss more and more furiously until I'm tearing at his shirt and he's yanking mine over my head, our bodies pressing together like they want to exist in the same space. I'm fierce, untamed, and vibrating with new energy, and he's matching me step for step. I'm pulling his hair with both hands, his fingers are digging into my skin, and I feel his teeth grinding against my shoulder. It's feral — rapacious, even — and I've never felt more alive in the whole of my life. That faint electricity builds, intensifying with us and radiating from our center afterwards. I'd felt something before — a distant hum, a tingling on my skin — but this is something else entirely. I hope it'll always be like this now.

I lean my head on his shoulder as he wraps the sheet around us, and we hold onto each other as the clouds overtake the sky, changing the light in the room to familiar dismal gray. In this moment I'm exceedingly grateful for the potentially endless years stretched out before me, and to not have to hold what I had festering inside any longer. Though things had turned out far better than I imagined, I still have an amends to make.

"I should've told you," I murmur into his neck. "I'm sorry. I —"

"I'm sorry, too," he interrupts. "I find it almost laughable now, given we were harboring similar secrets. Delia felt you were trustworthy enough to know, and thought me wrong for keeping it from you. I had to agree with her, but I put it off anyway. I didn't have the first idea of how to explain it to you, or what you'd make of it if I did. I was desperate to keep you."

I'd felt the same. I knew what I was doing by essentially lying to him, but I'd been just as selfish, and unwilling to risk giving him up. We'd gotten lucky — incredibly lucky — but we can't go on like we had.

"It doesn't dismiss the fact that I lied to you — that we lied to each other. I don't want us to have any more secrets between us. I'll tell you everything from now on."

"Likewise," he says, gently caressing my cheek. "It's a promise."

There's a knock at the door, and another follows as we scramble to dress ourselves. He's still buttoning his shirt when he opens it and Delia side eyes him, but Julien laughs.

"Really? Already?"

Rhys ignores him and follows them to the kitchen, where they unload the brown paper bags in their arms. I observe them both with new eyes now that I know what I do, and wonder if this will change how we get along.

"Are you hungry?" Delia asks as she pulls a jar of olives from the bag, followed by a large block of cheese. "Even if you're not, you should try to eat. Your body will likely be adjusting to this for some time, and there's a fair chance you may not want to as often."

Rhys' odd habits are beginning to make more sense. He'd pick at things when it came to mealtimes, or tell me he'd eat later. Is that another part of what he is? What I am? What else should I expect? I watch her unwrap the cheese, and just the sight of it makes my stomach growl. I'm ravenous.

As she plates the food, she continues to cast her eyes between Rhys and I, and he sighs.

"All out in the open. She knows everything now, so you can give it a rest."

"Sorry," she says, though unapologetically. "I just didn't think it was fair — especially when it became obvious the two of you were headed towards a long-term type of thing. This latest development certainly threw a wrench into things, though. I never expected a twist quite like it."

I can't help but feel like she's upset with me, even though she hasn't been unpleasant. I can understand why, and begin to think I might owe her and Julien an apology too.

"Delia, I'm sorry. It wasn't fair of me to hide what I did either, and I can't thank you enough for —"

"I don't want to be thanked," she says, her gray eyes shifting to me. "I was against it from the start."

She *is* upset, and the air in the room becomes suddenly tense. Against it? Against saving my life?

"Did you... Would you rather I'd have... *Died*?"

"No." She pauses slicing cheese. "Not at all. If I'd wanted you to die, I'd have left Rhys at the door when he came to me. I wanted you to have a choice in it."

"I'm sort of bewildered by that take. You act like it's this terrible thing — like choosing it or death would be a difficult toss up. Of course I'd choose this over death. It's simple."

"It's absolutely *not* simple!" She slams the knife onto the counter, rattling an empty glass. "You have *no* idea how many things could've gone awry during the process, and you slipping away is the least of them, if I'm being truthful."

I'm speechless, and watch her slowly walk around the edge of the counter.

"And that's not all — that's barely scraping the

surface," she says. "You could've been left barely alive, suffering immeasurable pain. The only reason I opted to embark on this reckless endeavor was the fact that you'd *certainly* die without it, so I prayed the outcome would weigh in our favor."

"But I feel fine." My voice is small and timid, as I'm nearly in tears. "So I don't think arguing what *could've* happened has a point. It didn't, and I'll apparently be alive for some time now."

She takes a deep breath and lets it out slowly, her cheeks flushed. "You can't even *begin* to understand what sort of burden this longevity is at times." A shadow of despair crosses her face, and her brows knit. "You love him, don't you? Can you imagine your life now — without him? Without Rhys? Can you imagine being trapped here if he was gone?"

A cold wave washes over me, freezing me in place. Without him? What does she mean?

"Delia," Julien says quietly. "That's not fair. She doesn't know."

"Of course she doesn't," she says quickly, stalking towards the windows. "It's… That formula has me out of sorts. I hadn't seen the words in so many years, and the last time I looked at them he was still alive. He's the reason they exist at all."

He was still alive? Who's 'he'? I'm utterly perplexed, and suddenly shaken. I have no idea what I said to prompt her to put that idea in my head, but it's all I can think about now. I'm failing at holding my tears back, so I quietly tread to the washroom to let them fall in private. Rhys follows, catching the door and closing it behind him.

"What's happening?" I sniffle. "I don't understand. Why did she say that? Does she hate me all of a sudden?"

"No, and I know she didn't mean to hurt you, but I wish she would've chosen her words a bit differently. Her opinions are strong for a reason, and revisiting the formula undoubtedly brought up some painful memories for her." He steps forward and pulls me into his arms. "The formula we used to change you — it's hers. She'd begun developing it a long time ago for someone else."

Someone else? "Not… Julien?"

He shakes his head. "Someone she loved — deeply. Vincent. She intended to change him so they'd have more time together, but he was… He died. I don't think she's truly recovered from the loss, despite the years that have passed."

"The formula… Is that how he died?"

"No. She never implemented it, as she determined it too great a risk — hence her reluctance with you. She wasn't confident we'd succeed, and she didn't want you to suffer. If she's angry with anyone, it's me for essentially forcing her into it, but mostly I think she's just relieved and sad. I'm sure she'll come around."

My heart breaks for Delia. I had no idea something like that happened to her, and now have a better understanding of why she'd said what she did. Even still, I feel bad for making it seem like I'm taking what they'd done to me lightly.

I trail behind him sheepishly, unsure of what to say to her, but when we reemerge from the washroom she's calm. Before I can speak she's in front of me, her small hands in mine.

"I have to apologize," she says. "It's been an intense few days, and clearly they've taken their toll on me. Forget what I said — put it right out of your mind. What you need to concentrate on is the fact that you've survived a near impossible thing, and I couldn't be more thankful that you have."

Her tone has changed completely, and her gray eyes are soft. I'm exhausted and ready to cry all over again, and she laughs quietly when my lip trembles.

"Come on," she smiles, leading me to the table where Julien is already heaping a plate full. "Let's get you something to eat, then I think we should all have a rest."

✶ ✶ ✶ ✶ ✶ ✶ TWENTY-ONE ✶ ✶ ✶ ✶ ✶ ✶

Falling back into our steady routine is relatively easy, and there's comfort in normalcy in addition to relief at having no more secrets between us. I begin to think their concerns were misguided, as I'd clearly come through the transition physically unscathed, but there were other changes that occurred within me. Changes I didn't expect.

I feel… Lost, and unsettled. Moody and erratic. Happy one moment, and in tears the next. Anxiety I'd never felt before sets in, and I'd be going along normally then suddenly I'd be doubled over, panic ridden and gasping for breath. I start disassociating with no warning, finding myself staring into space with Rhys startling me back to reality. Usually I can't remember what's going through my head during these interludes, but sometimes it's the visions that spanned the dark time when I think I was momentarily dead. The moon sped up across the sky, the crying baby, so many bodies on fire. What did they mean? Did they mean anything at all?

On one such occasion, we're cleaning up the kitchen after a mutually failed attempt at cooking, the recipe gone awry. One moment I'm drying dishes, and the next I'm dazed, shattered glass around my feet.

"What… What happened?" My heart is racing, and I'm aware of his hand on my arm.

"It's all right," he says gently. "You lost time again. Just… Don't move. I'll get it."

I realize I'd dropped the glass I was holding, and instantly I'm irritated. I ignore his instruction and bend to scrape it up myself, and one of the pieces embeds itself in my hand. I suck in my breath as I jerk it back, a bright bloom of red spreading across my palm. I leave the mess on the floor and storm off towards the windows, my irritation turned to anger, and hear him quietly disposing of the vessel.

"Darling? Come on — let me see."

He inspects the cut, and I'm surprised to find it's only a tiny slice, as the heavy bleeding led me to believe it much worse. It certainly doesn't hurt enough to warrant this amount. It hurts when he pokes at it though, and I jerk my hand back. I don't want him to touch it — or me. I'm livid at nothing in particular, electricity buzzing around me as I turn my back to him, and he sighs.

"I know this has been a lot for you," he says quietly. "These... Pauses. They should hopefully lessen until they stop altogether. I know it feels like —"

I reel around to face him. "You know what it feels like? How? You were *born* like this — not made! How can you possibly know what it's like to be completely out of control of your own body like this? I feel totally disconnected from who I am — to the point that I don't even *know* who I am anymore! Is it you who's being snapped out of a trance multiple times a day? You who's seeing things — visions? Things you'd rather not see but can't get out of your head? No? Then don't pretend to identify when you have no *fucking* idea what this is like for me!"

I'd never shouted at him before, and hurt flashes in his eyes. It snaps me out of the fury that's enveloped me and I burst into tears.

"Oh gods, Rhys. I'm sorry."

He doesn't hesitate — he just takes me in his arms and holds me tight to him.

"You're right," he says. "I *don't* know what it's like for you — I can only imagine. I've been anticipating the possibility of moments like these, and prepared to face them head on, however uncomfortable they may be for me. I just want —"

"What, do you curse every woman you cross paths with?" I blurt out, and immediately I regret my words, their taste bitter.

Why am I behaving like this? I can't stand it, and I worry he'll tolerate it less and less if it doesn't let up. If it bothers him he doesn't show it — instead he shifts his eyes to my hand, blood trailing down my fingers.

"Would you let me handle that, please?"

"Oh… Shit. I'm sorry. I didn't mean it. I didn't mean any of it. I don't know what's come over me."

"Like I said — it's all right. It likely won't be the last time, but don't worry. You can't scare me away," he says. There's a small smile on his lips, and I'm comforted that he's forgiven my outburst.

I sit down at the table forlornly while he rifles through one of the desk drawers. I suck in my breath when he douses the cut in antiseptic, and he rubs a scant amount of ointment on it before circling a bandage around my palm.

"There. Good as new. Now how about some tea?"

He kisses my cheek in passing, our bad moment over. My hand is mended and my mood shifted, and I begin to feel curious as I watch him fill the kettle. How is it he knows so much about this?

"Rhys? Have you seen this before? Someone right after they've been changed?"

"No. Unfortunately I haven't. It's rare anyone's able to be changed at all, let alone by means of a formula like this one. Delia's seen it once. She was invited to witness a similar procedure, and she took what she learned from it to design a different version after she met Vincent."

"Why didn't she change him with it?"

He pulls two cups from the cupboard, and pauses after setting them on the counter.

"Two men were the subjects in question," he says, spooning dried herbs into the little mesh strainer. "The first died — a terrible death, as I'm told. The second survived, but he suffered a great deal, both during and after. When it changed his body, it altered his mind too, and he experienced a few… Mental effects. Among those effects were a series of visions in the form of night terrors, which I'm speculating are something akin to what you're dealing with. They did stop in time though, from what Delia said."

"So he was all right? That means I will be too, doesn't it?"

"I'm hopeful you'll continue to acclimate as you have been, and that what you're going through will cease after more time, but I'm afraid I can't be sure." He turns to face me. "The man — even though his effects lessened, they destroyed him. He took his own life."

My shock must be evident on my face, because he quickly strides over and crouches beside me, taking my hands.

"When I said there might be side effects, this is what I meant. They aren't limited to the physical, and though you've come through that part of it with ease, it was a bit naïve of me to believe you'd have no effects at all. This — what you're experiencing — it's completely my fault, and I feel terrible. I'm sorry."

He presses the top of my hand to my cheek, and I try to make sense of everything he's said. Should I be worried for myself? Though I'm having a hard time with it, I don't think what I'm going through would cause me to want to do myself harm. I can get through this — I just have to try a little harder.

"I'd never do something like that. I'll… I'll be fine. Really, I will. Just… Keep being patient with me. I promise I'll do my best not to take it out on you."

"Even if you do, I can handle it," he says, standing as the kettle begins to whistle. "It's worth having you here."

★★★★★★ TWENTY-TWO ★★★★★★

In time it seems luck is on my side, and the disjointed staring spells diminish along with my mood swings. I slowly feel more like myself, though not quite the same as before. I almost feel better now — rejuvenated — and my energy is at an all time high. It's not all positive, as the downside is that I'm constantly restless. I pace back and forth in the apartment, unable to keep still, and it proves distracting for him when he's attempting to concentrate on his work. I can tell he's bothered even though he doesn't mention it, so I take it upon myself to find a remedy. I begin going on long walks around the harbor like I used to, and when walking doesn't quell my vibrating limbs I begin running — something I'd never done electively. It helps, and soon becomes a daily ritual.

I'm jogging down the slippery streets when I see a familiar form, also out for a run, his blonde hair bouncing with each stride.

"Hi," I pant when I catch up, falling into step beside him.

"Lynna!" A smile of recognition spreads across Julien's sweaty face. "You never told me you were a runner!"

"I'm not. Well… I am now, I guess. I just started a few days ago — I was driving Rhys crazy by pacing about the house. I'm restless a lot now."

"Mmm. I know what you mean," he says. "It never really goes away, but you find ways to deal. I'm looping around to the other side — want to come with?"

"Sure."

As we jog along my head begins to fill with questions. I'd assumed he was like Rhys and Delia, but what he said is making me wonder if he's something more like me. How could he be, given Rhys said it was rare?

"Julien… Are you… Changed? Like me?"

We run nearly the length of a block in silence, and I begin to regret my inquisition. Maybe he doesn't want to talk about it? Maybe he didn't hear me? He must have, because he finally speaks.

"I am, though not the same way you were. It's a long story."

We run for a while longer, and I wonder if he means to elaborate or if he's going to leave it at that. I don't want to press him further, and even if he did continue I wouldn't be able to concentrate. My stamina is nowhere near his, and I drop behind. He notices me struggling, and chuckles as he slows to a stop.

"Let's walk a bit, hmm? How you feeling otherwise?"

"Besides not being able to breathe right now? All right, I guess."

He laughs. "Besides that, yes. I know you were having a bit of trouble for a while, but I'm glad you're getting out — it'll help to keep a routine. Going through something like that can make you feel sort of lonely, can't it?"

"I hadn't really thought about it, but yeah. Sort of."

"I haven't spoken of it in a long time, but maybe it'll help you feel a little less so if I do."

As we walk alongside the water he talks, recounting his years as a sickly child and his family's growing impatience with his health while I catch my breath. I listen attentively — we'd chatted many times before at the red bar, but it had always been light conversation.

"We were poor. As in, barely had a roof over our heads poor. I had a number of siblings, and it was hard not to notice how resentful they were of me and how much attention I needed. My parents said they were taking me to a family friend who offered to help — I'd met him before, but I didn't know he was a healer. What I also didn't know was that they meant to leave me there. Permanently. I never saw them again."

They'd abandoned him? For something he couldn't control? What kind of family would do that? I try to think of my own family, but the memories are too fuzzy to recall, so I focus on him instead.

"Julien… I'm so sorry."

"Doesn't matter," he says, his expression unchanged. "The thing that gets me sometimes is wondering if they knew what he was going to do. If they did, they're lucky they never came back. They're all dead now anyway."

We reach the edge of the harbor, and stop to peer over the wall at the dark water. It's a little foggy down here, and mist rolls gently across the waves.

"Whatever he did worked in the end," he says, but the small smile on his face is contemptuous, not at all the pleasant grin I'm used to. "But things turned out far different than I ever thought they would. I spent the first few months same as I always was, never getting any better, never leaving the house. Hooked up to this machine or that. Downing different pills, drinking all sorts of disgusting mixtures. Then he began bringing home others, a few at a time. Some were older than me, some younger, but I soon found out we all had something in common — we had nowhere else to go. For a while I thought he'd taken us in out of the kindness of his heart, but that soon changed. He kept us under lock and key — for our safety, he said — but we were less safe in there than probably anywhere else."

I stay close to his elbow as we turn back towards the city, mostly so I don't fall off the edge of the dock, but also because I don't want to miss a word. I'm both disheartened and fascinated by his story. He'd never opened up to me about anything before.

"As time went on it became more and more obvious what we were there for. We were his own personal lab rats — for years on end. Those of us who weren't sick already became so soon enough, and I was worse than ever. I can't even describe the pain I felt, or the horror when they started dying off one by one. Those kids had become my friends — I was all but ten or eleven when I met them, and by the time he was through I was nearly seventeen. They were all I had, but I lost them too. In the end, I was the only one who survived."

My stomach twists as I imagine what that must've felt like — to lose everyone you love. To watch them die.

"Gods. How did you manage to get away? Did you overpower him?"

"Wish I had," he laughs softly. "But I never got the payback I wanted. When I was finally strong enough I did have a few fantasies of beating him senseless — maybe even to death — but I didn't get the chance. Someone ratted him out — the house got raided one night, though I never found out if it was by the authorities or someone else. I slipped out the back and ran, and when I returned he was gone. Him and everything else — all his notes, his medicines, his records. Everything."

"How do you know... How did you figure out you'd been changed though?"

"He didn't keep it a secret. He'd go on and on — telling us we'd be 'transformed' from our lowly states into something divine. Saying he was doing the work of the gods. I thought he was full of shit, to be honest. Crazy. Insane. I'd read some of what he'd documented and thought it just the scribbles of a madman — a murderer — but over time it became more and more apparent that he'd definitely altered something drastic in me. I got stronger than I ever thought I would, and I stopped aging normally. Did you know I'm as old as Rhys?"

I'm trying to process all he's just said, but it's difficult. Almost as difficult as it'd been when Rhys explained what he is. I'm silent, and he nudges me with his elbow.

"Sorry — got carried away. What it boils down to is that we're sort of alike, you and I. Circumstances were different, sure, but we've got common ground, and you can talk to me about it if you ever want to."

It takes me a moment to respond. It's wild to me that he and Delia had been through so much and lead such normal seeming lives. "Thank you — and thank you for sharing that with me. My life feels like it's been an absolute cakewalk in comparison. You suffered for years when it was only days for me."

He shrugs. "It's all relative. You shouldn't try to compare them — both experiences were hard, but we've come through them all right." He adjusts his knot of hair, and jumps up and down a few times. "Well? You ready to give this another go?"

He takes off before I can answer, and I have to sprint to catch up. By the time we make it to the far end of the harbor I'm properly winded with a pain in my side, and have to bend over to ease it.

"Not bad," he says, unfazed by the exertion. "That was fun!"

"Was it?" I pant, and he laughs.

"Sure it was — we should do it again. I've tried to get Delia out, but she hates it."

"I imagine having to wear running shoes is the biggest barrier."

"Exactly," he grins.

"What are you doing now? Rhys is home — do you want to come up for a coffee?"

"Thanks — I'd like that."

I think about this new layer to our friendship as he follows me up the steps to the apartment. I feel closer to him now, and less alone knowing I'm not the only one who's come into this life differently. I smell the coffee brewing as soon as we're through the door, which means Rhys had been anticipating my return.

"Well, look what the cat dragged in," Rhys grins upon seeing Julien. "Pew! I can't tell which of you smells worse."

"Definitely me," Julien laughs. "Had quite the surprise today — didn't know this one shares my enthusiasm for exercise."

I sink down at the table and kick off my shoes. "I wouldn't label myself 'enthusiastic' just yet, but I'm willing to give it another go."

"I'd be out there with you two," Rhys says, tapping a cigarette on the table. "But it's definitely not my thing."

We sit and sip for a while, catching up. After my second cup I excuse myself to change out of my sweaty clothes, and when I emerge from the washroom Julien is gone.

"He wanted me to tell you goodbye," Rhys says. "I'm not surprised you bumped into each other — he's out there pretty much daily."

"It was nice to have company. We talked a bit, and he told me about some of his history. He's always in such good spirits for someone who's suffered a thing like that."

"I would've told you myself, but I didn't think it was my place to share it. I know what we did for you brought some feelings up for him as well, given what he endured. He didn't want you to experience the same sort of suffering."

"I sort of got that impression. Both of them have big hearts, don't they? I'm really grateful to know them."

"Speaking of Julien and Delia, I've been meaning to ask your opinion on something, and he just reminded me that time is of the essence. It's been weeks now, and from my perspective you seem to be doing much better. How would you feel about taking a little trip?"

"A trip? What sort?"

"Well, there's an exposition coming up — a medicinal vendor event, per se. I've been before and wouldn't mind returning, and Delia is expected to attend. She suggested we accompany her, and make a sort of holiday out of it — the four of us. It's a ways down the coast, but a bit of extra sun can't hurt now and then, can it?"

I consider it as I take our empty cups to the sink. I hadn't traveled for pleasure ever, really. Every time I'd taken a trip it was to get from one place to another, then settle until it was time to leave forever. It's exciting to imagine an actual adventure.

"I think I might love that — it sounds fascinating."

"Wonderful!" He smiles. "We can pick up a few things for the apothecary, and it might give me the opportunity to take you to a fancy place or two. Even get drunk and lie on a beach, if that sounds enticing."

"It does, actually." I circle my arms around his shoulders, and plant a kiss beneath his ear. "Is that all we'll be doing there?"

"I highly doubt it," he laughs, pulling me into his lap by my arm. "I can think of another activity you might enjoy."

I giggle as he kisses my neck. "Such as?"

"Don't worry. You're about to find out."

★ ★ ★ ★ ★ ★ TWENTY-THREE ★ ★ ★ ★ ★ ★

I'm once again bumping along on a train, but the situation is vastly different. It's not gray darkness outside my window — instead the scenery is rife with colorful foliage and sunny fields. I'm not packed like a sardine in an economy car this time either. I'm sitting beside Rhys in a more spacious private car, across from Delia who's casually filing her nails, and a snoozing Julien. I like having them with me, as I'd only traveled alone before, but it feels strange, and my excitement begins to turn to anxiety. Every jolt and bump of the car takes me further from where I now call home, and I almost wish we hadn't left.

After a long ride we arrive in a large coastal city, its glistening buildings jaggedly piercing the sky. White beaches and clear blue water splay out on the edges, dotted with green tropical-looking plants. We end up in a swanky hotel, and I follow Rhys into what's probably the nicest room I've ever been in — all dark blues and gold and shining white marble. A wall of windows looks out onto the city, and double doors open onto a terrace. I leave him inside to inspect it, leaning over the railing as the wind blows my hair into my face, and discover there's a door leading to Julien and Delia's adjoining room. It's bright, and the ground is too hot for my feet, so after shuffling uncomfortably for a few minutes I head back inside.

Rhys had dropped our bags beside a massive bed dressed in a shimmering moss green duvet. It reminds me of the moss bed in the greenhouse, and I smile as I recall when I first discovered it. I run my hand over the soft fabric; not a terrible substitute for the moss, though it leaves me even more homesick. It's beautiful here, but it's too bright and smells too new — nothing at all like our quiet dark apartment. My feelings are confusing at the moment. I'd traveled to so many unknown places on my own and had adapted — for years — but now I feel off, like I don't belong. Like we'll be different here.

"Not quite home, is it?" He asks, closing his arms around my waist. Somehow he always seems to know what I'm thinking.

"No, but it *is* nice. I'm just… not used to it."

"Perhaps you'll feel better after we settle in a bit. What do you say to a bath? Wash away the grime of public transportation?"

He unclasps his hands, and I follow him through another set of doors behind the bed, the washroom all glittering white marble. In the center of the room is an enormous sunken tub, filled to the brim with bubbles. They smell like fresh roses, and my homesickness begins to melt away.

"Did you do this while I was inspecting the terrace?"

"I did," he says, tossing his clothes aside after disrobing. He climbs in and sits back, water up to his chest. "Well come on. You'll like it. It's far roomier than the one at home."

He pats the edge, encouraging me to join him. His crooked smile is invitation enough, and I can't help but grin back as I pull off my clothes and slip into the bath across from him. The water feels divine, and I savor the sensation of the rose scented water on my skin. This isn't so bad at all — we're still the same, it's only the setting that's different. I can manage this strangeness as long as he's with me. I let myself relax more, and nudge him underwater with my feet.

"Tell me — what can I expect tomorrow?"

"If it's anything like it was previously, there'll be a copious number of vendors to visit. We'll likely be there all day."

"Well, what are you looking forward to seeing most?"

"Everything, really." He sits up abruptly, sloshing water out of the sides of the bath. "There'll be a rare book dealer, and I might be able to find a few spare parts for the distiller… Oh, and the seeds! Gods, the greenhouse could use a bit of updating. I could order what I want but not at this volume or variety. Last time there were absolute mountains of seeds to sort through, so I'm hoping that'll be the case again. We might even be able to find a few obscure herbs…"

He's lost in thought, smiling as he stares into space, but he notices me stifle a small laugh.

"What?"

"Oh nothing. Just never thought I'd hear someone rave about seeds like that."

"You devil," he laughs as he splashes me. "I thought you might be equally enthused."

"I never said I wasn't."

"Mmm," he smiles. "So you haven't feigned interest all this time just to mock me in this moment?"

"You give me too much credit," I laugh, floating through the water until I'm just in front of him, our lips nearly touching. "In all seriousness, I absolutely love that look you get about you when you're passionate about something, so please — do go on about the seeds."

✶✶✶✶✶✶ TWENTY-FOUR ✶✶✶✶✶✶

Once we're through in the bath, where he made no more mention of seeds, I pull on one of the hotel bathrobes and tread onto the terrace. The wind is cooler, and I feel my hair drying as it blows around. The sun is finally setting, and I admire the glints of color reflected on the windowpanes of the surrounding buildings. He was right about settling in — I feel much better than I did when we arrived.

"Well there you are."

I turn towards the voice and see Delia on the far edge of our shared terrace, also in a bathrobe. I pad over to sit in one of the lounge chairs next to her, and she eyes my matching robe.

"Seems we had similar itineraries. Those bathtubs are heavenly, aren't they?" She produces her silver case from the pocket of her robe, frowning at the single cigarette inside before pressing it between her lips. "I have to say — this heat disagrees with me, but it's starting to feel nice now that it's getting dark."

"You're right about the heat. I was never really one for hot weather."

"Are you excited about tomorrow?" She asks, tucking her feet beneath her. "There are some top botanists attending, as well as several horticulturalists."

"We were just talking about tomorrow actually. I think he's a little more excited than I am, but that's because I've never been to anything like this."

"You'll like it," she smiles, tapping the ash over the railing. "And I think we should skip the lectures and go straight to the vendors. I expect we'll both be adding several bags to our luggage for the return trip."

The door slides open, and a sleepy looking Julien emerges, rubbing his eyes. "What'd I miss?"

"Nothing dear, just talk of what we mean to acquire tomorrow."

"Oh yes, the plants," he groans. "You and your phytomania. All three of you."

He's not wrong. I'd discovered Delia shares some of that enthusiasm for horticulture, as it's closely intertwined with some of the remedies she employs as a healer. Though she works in a hospital she occasionally treats patients in her home, and often picked up boxes of medicinal supplies from our apartment that Rhys created for her. Our greenhouse supplements her work just as it does the apothecary, and she has her own list of things she wants to procure so we can grow them. The other set of doors slides open, and Rhys joins us.

"So what's the plan for the evening?" Rhys asks as he settles in next to Julien, and I assume he's addressing Delia.

"I took it upon myself to make some reservations," she says. "I can't wait for you to see the restaurant. It's fabulously upscale."

"How upscale is it?" I suddenly feel bad about my small selection of predictable garments. "I don't think I've brought anything appropriate."

Julien and Delia exchange a look, and she smiles slyly.

"Not to worry — I've got you covered." She nods to Julien and Rhys. "You two go get dressed. We'll just be a moment."

I follow her into their identical room where heaps upon heaps of clothes are strewn about. How all this fit in the small bags they brought is beyond me. She opens the closet door, and inside are several spectacular looking dresses — all in black, since that seems to be her usual. She pauses, and pulls two out.

"Try this." She hands me the hanger. "Then we'll see about taming that wild hair of yours. Air drying in this climate might be worse than it is at home."

I retreat to the washroom and close the door behind me, letting the robe drop before hanging the dress on the back of the door. I pull it off the hanger and slide it over my shoulders, relieved it isn't scratchy. My arm won't bend to reach the zipper, and after struggling with it I exit so she can assist me. I find her inspecting herself in the mirror, clad in a short bandage-style dress that hugs her figure.

"Perfect. I *knew* it would suit you," she smiles as she positions me in front of the mirror before zipping me up the back.

Two thin straps traverse my collarbones to meet the bodice of eyelash lace, a satiny black fabric overlaid with tulle below, hitting me right at the knees. It's astonishing how well it suits me; I'm never short of amazed by her eye for fashion. She sits me on the dressing bench and curls my hair into soft waves like hers. It had grown longer still, and now cascades down my back nearly to my waist. She rummages in one of her bags to retrieve a pair of peep toe spike heels, and I begin to question her judgment. Does she mean for me to wear those? Really?

"Oh I hope you didn't —"

She laughs as she slides them on her feet, and hands me a pair of flat sandals.

"Act like I don't know you. There — all finished. Shall we?"

We head back to my room, where presumably Julien and Rhys are waiting, as we've been much more than a moment. They're standing in the small kitchenette, and I'm stunned to see them both looking so polished. Julien is wearing dark pants topped with a shiny shirt patterned in silvery damask, paired with his everyday chunky combat boots. He looks very handsome — his long blonde hair slicked back in its usual knotted heap on top of his head, face freshly shaved. Rhys is in a black satiny button down, rolled to the elbows as always. His regular shirts are always neatly pressed, but not as nice as this one, and his gray pants are new and unfrayed, though his signature worn out boots are on his feet. He looks absolutely dashing, and my stomach flutters a little. He sets down his glass when we enter, his ever alluring crooked smile overtaking his face.

"Darling, you look… Incredible."

"You're welcome," Delia laughs as I blush, tossing her hair and smacking her now crimson lips. "Now let's hurry. We're late already."

We arrive at what appears to be another large hotel, the restaurant on an upper level. As we follow the hostess through the crowded restaurant nearly all eyes are on us — what a spectacle we must be, a troupe of eclectics dressed to the nines. Rhys continues to cast glances at me as I float along next to him, my arm laced through his elbow. I can't stop smiling. Delia had outdone herself with the surprise dress, and it's filling me with a newfound confidence I didn't know I possessed.

We're led into a large room housing a handful of widely spaced tables, and the hostess gestures to one. I'm overwhelmed with the atmosphere — the space is covered with shiny ceramic pots in geometric shapes overflowing with foliage of all kinds. Thousands of stringed bulbs form an intricate web above, their glowing lights dancing on every surface. It's magical, and I can hardly believe places like this exist outside of stories and magazines. Julien and Delia whisper to each other with their heads bent over a menu, but I sit in silence, taking it all in. I realize my wonder is being observed — Rhys hasn't taken his eyes off me since we sat down. There's a dreamy look about him I haven't ever seen before.

"Is there something on my face?" I joke. He laughs and takes my hands, kissing them one by one.

"Darling, you always look beautiful, but this… This is something else entirely. I doubt I'll be able to concentrate on anything else at all tonight."

I've never felt myself beautiful, but Delia had done me a solid, and I almost believe him.

"I'll have to start wearing this around the apartment then. I have to say — you clean up nicely too."

"You're welcome," Julien pipes up, pretending to polish his nails on his shirt. "He'd never have managed on his own."

"I'd argue that, but it's a fair statement," Rhys laughs.

"I can't believe you've done this for us," I smile, unable to contain my gratitude. "Thank you for this."

"Of course, doll," Delia says, winking from across the table. "I assure you it was great fun for me. Nothing I love more than an excuse to go shopping."

I barely touch the heap of delicacies Delia orders, but the champagne empties quickly. As we drink and talk and laugh I find myself assessing everything that had happened to lead me here — to this dream I'm in. I can scarcely remember the vast expanse of time before we were all together. The four of us here feels… Right. As if everything is exactly the way it should be. I feel his hand in mine beneath the linen shrouded tabletop, and realize my half circle is finally not feeling so incomplete.

* * * * * * TWENTY-FIVE * * * * * *

The exposition turns out to be much more than I even imagined, and they were right to be excited for it.

I'd thought traditional and herbal methods of healing to be more underground, but here it all is — in bold print, nonetheless. It's more prevalent than I'd ever realized, and the huge building is packed tight with booths crowded with all manner of alchemic goods. Thousands of bottles and vials cover tabletop after tabletop, there's an entire wall of musty smelling books stacked high, and rows and rows of flora with a misting system surrounding them like a skeletal structure. Crowds of people mill about like schools of fish, darting here and there to look at all manner of interesting wares.

I'm experiencing sensory overload, but Rhys and Delia seem right at home. Julien looks immediately bored, and wanders off to presumably find somewhere to entertain himself until we've finished. Delia and I head towards the horticultural section, while Rhys squeezes my hand and departs in the direction of the long tables crowded with metallic tanks and tubes, the machinery shining beneath the bright fluorescent lights.

An exotic looking woman with long silvery hair smiles as we browse the rows of labeled plant life, encouraging us to ask questions if needed. I begin to wish I'd composed a list of what to look for, since the selection is incredibly overwhelming. We spend what feels like hours inspecting everything carefully, reading descriptions and calculating growing times along with potential medicinal uses.

There are bright yellow flowers — for show, mostly — the preferred root decocted to treat respiratory issues, or ground up for an ointment to soothe skin infections. One plant's dark bristly leaves and stalks are particularly useful as both a diuretic and emollient, its bright blue flowers used only as a cuisine related flourish. Smooth stalks and small round buds contain hidden haemostatic properties, meant for healing wounds. Striated green stems topped with pink tinged flowers provide pain relief, its root most commonly used as a sedative. The list goes on and on, and I feel my brows knit in concentration as I make my assessments.

I'm a little proud of what I'm able to recall without a reference. I'd worked diligently to absorb as much information as I could while working alongside Rhys, and Delia seems impressed when I recite what I know to her. We decide it impossible to cart whole plants with us as there wouldn't be room for more than one or two on the journey back, so we choose a variety of roots and cuttings stored carefully in humid little boxes. After I've chosen what I think we'll benefit from most, I begin pulling packet after packet out of the rows of alphabetically labeled seeds. There are indeed mountains of them, and I'm hoping Rhys will be pleased as I load my arms with small squares.

After we pack our selections up, we say our farewells to the elflike vendor. What seemed like hours digging through greenery actually was, and it's very late in the day. We circle the huge space twice in search of our respective partners, and soon Delia's footsteps begin to stomp in annoyance. Finally she spots Rhys standing in a lounge area, leaning against a table and conversing with a seated Julien. Not only is Julien holding a drink with an umbrella in it, he's wearing sunglasses in addition, which makes him look very much like someone on holiday. Beside Rhys is a large box, and a bag packed full with books and rolled up papers. I'm a little disappointed when I realize he'd gone to the book vendor without me, but I'd taken over the botanical excursion entirely, so we're sort of even.

"We've been looking for you forever," Delia groans as she collapses in the chair beside Julien. She kicks off her platforms and flexes her feet with a grimace.

"Hello darling — how'd you do?" Rhys asks as I drop

my bags on the floor, and we both grin when I bend to pull out a fistful of packets. Seeds.

"I may have gone overboard. We'll be busy when we get back, that's for sure. I'm hoping I can get them all to take."

"Oh, you'll be busy all right," Delia says. "I've gone and doubled your workload."

"I see you found a number of things too." I nod towards the books.

"I got a little carried away myself," he says. "I hope it's all right I went to the book stand alone. I did find a few I think will interest you — I made sure to keep you in mind. If you like we can go back? Give you the chance to have a look yourself?"

The lingering disappointment I'd had about him exploring it without me has all but evaporated, so I shrug. "I'm sure whatever you found will do just fine. What's in there?"

"A new expeller," he says, nudging the edge of the box with his foot. "And extra parts for the distiller — plus a few updates."

Julien yawns loudly, and Delia sighs as she gets to her feet. "Let's get all this safely back. I'm exhausted, and ready to resume much more leisurely activities."

"Best thing I've heard all day," Julien grins, picking the small umbrella out of his glass before draining it.

˟ ˟ ˟ ˟ ˟ ˟ TWENTY-SIX ˟ ˟ ˟ ˟ ˟ ˟

A few hours later it's nighttime, and I'm lounging on the breezy terrace with my feet up on the railing. Delia had retreated to her room to nap, and though she assured me she'd get a second wind, I suspect I might not see her until morning. I have yet to become tired enough to sleep, and am watching the full moon rise between the tall buildings when Rhys' face appears over me. He'd disappeared on some secretive errand with Julien, and I hadn't noticed them return. Out of the corner of my eye I see Julien slip in through their terrace door, and catch a glimpse of Delia in the bed. She's definitely out for the night.

"What's with the mysterious look?" I ask, noticing his peculiar expression. "And where have you been?"

"Here and there," he smiles slyly. "Come on — we're going on a little excursion. Just you and me."

I'm trying to figure out what it is we're doing as I follow him through the hotel, and we end up on the sidewalk, waiting for a taxi. He's quiet the entire ride, mystifying me, but I'm unworried. His small smile leads me to believe I'll probably like whatever he has in store. He has an unfamiliar bag with him, but I know better than to ask more questions at this point. If he was going to let me in on where we're going he would have already.

The taxi weaves in and out of traffic, then finally out of the city altogether. We cruise up a road that looks to be going nowhere, the huge bright moon reflecting millions of tiny lights on the ocean beyond. Finally the driver stops and after exiting the car, Rhys motions to a sandy path leading up a steep hill. I can see the city shimmering in the distance, and I'm beginning to wonder how we'll get back as I watch the taxi's taillights shrink smaller and smaller.

"Did you bring me out here to murder me?" I joke, and he laughs. "Seriously — what are we doing all the way out here?"

"I think it's best if you see for yourself."

He takes my hand as we trudge to the top, and find a grassy knoll extending to the beach on the other side. It's dotted with thousands of long leafy stems sticking up from the ground, their yellow flowers waving synchronically in the moonlight. It's ginger — *Zhingiber Officinale*. We'd run dry of it long ago, and it had been almost impossible to import, as the once common plant had become increasingly scarce over the past few decades. There wasn't even a single one to be found at the exposition. Even twenty of these rhizomes would last us quite a while, and have several medicinal uses as well as being the star of a favorite cocktail.

"Gods, there are so many! How on earth did you find these? I had no idea they were native to this place."

"They aren't — someone had to have started them long ago for them to have taken over like this. I got a tip from one of the vendors, and Julien and I came up here earlier to investigate."

He slides the bag from his shoulder, and now it makes sense why he has it. We begin the work of pulling them from the ground, decapitating the rhizomes of their foliage before packing them neatly into the bag. Once it's full, our stores restored, we tread down to the beach and walk along the ocean. We take our shoes off to feel the water, its warmth surprising in the cool night air.

"Are we walking the whole way back?" I'm enjoying the trek, but it might become tedious after a while since the city's such a ways off.

"Not yet."

We round a group of trees and I notice dark shapes nestled on the edge of the sand where the grass drops off. As we approach I start to make out the shapes a bit more — it's a beach umbrella stuck crookedly into the sand, a large square blanket piled with pillows beneath.

"I'm not sure if you recall me mentioning lying on a beach as one of the elements included in this escapade, but I thought you might enjoy it with a bit less sun and a bit more privacy," he says. "Cliché romantic beach stroll, check."

"Is foraging on that checklist, too?"

"Mmm — quite right," he says, miming checking off a piece of paper.

I can't believe he's gone out of his way to to do this, and smile as I survey the cozy scene. I sigh as I flop back onto the blanket, the pillows cool and comfortable. This is so much better than during the day. I'd be endlessly trying to avoid the scorching sun — not to mention the crowds — and suffering through the heat.

"I'm assuming this is what you brought Julien up here for? To help stage this?"

"Of course," he says, twisting the top from a bottle he's pulled from the sand next to the umbrella. "Do you really think he'd agree to accompany me solely to investigate a rumor about some wild plant?"

"Well I'm pleased he went for it — this is really nice. I can't remember the last time I was on a beach," I muse, staring out across the endless expanse of sapphire water. "And I certainly never thought to try it in the nighttime."

We pass the bottle back and forth until it's empty, recounting the events of the day. He details descriptions of some of the books he picked up, and we both laugh when I tell him about Delia schooling the vendor on her own wares.

"You should have heard her. Arguing with the woman over a few mislabeled herbs."

"What was the dispute?"

"It wasn't that important, nor was it about anything we need more of. She had fennel marked as anise, but it seems a common mistake. They're both so similar. I think Delia just wanted to argue about something."

"You *have* picked up a few things, haven't you?" he jokes, smirking.

"I like to think I learned a good bit more than the difference between a few herbs. You should've seen the look on Delia's face when I pronounced 'trimeniaceae'."

He bursts out laughing, and I realize I've mangled the word yet again. Generally I'm fairly strong when it comes to vocabulary, but I still trip over my feet when it comes to the multi syllable proper names. I feel my face redden, but I laugh along with him.

"That's probably why she made the face," he snickers.

"I'll get it right one of these days," I groan, and he pulls me into his arms. "It and all the others I've been butchering."

"You don't need to become a master of linguistics," he says, planting a kiss beneath my ear. "In fact, I find your horrendous mispronunciations to be quite adorable."

"Well, I can at least *spell* what I can't properly articulate — and legibly, mind you."

He laughs again. "Fair enough."

As we watch the moon move across the sky, the water begins to call to me, and I decide I can't contain my desire to submerge myself in it.

"Where are you off to?" He asks when I get to my feet.

I pull my shirt over my head, dropping it in the sand before shimmying out of my leggings. I take a few steps before glancing back, and smile as I continue my path to the dark ocean.

"Fancy a swim?"

The sand turns to gritty pebbles between my toes, the pull of the waves luring me out to waist deep. The water is wonderfully warm, and the sea foam swirls around me in cloudy spirals as the gentle breeze lifts my hair from my shoulders. I hear splashing, but before I can turn around he tackles me into the surf. We both come up laughing, wiping the salt from our faces. I splash him and dive away, turning over to float on my back, my body illuminated in the moonlight. He swims out next to me, and we linger in the glittering blue water under the moon, watching stars twinkle in the dark sky above. It's magical — the steady hush of the waves lapping the shore and the weightlessness of my body, a small speck in the vastness of the sea. I turn my head to see him smirk before sinking into the water, and feel his hands pulling me down with him. We resurface in an embrace, and he kisses me the moment we break through the water, the taste of salt on his lips. I never imagined I'd experience anything like this. Submerged in the sea with the one I love, both of us baptized by the ocean.

* * * * * * TWENTY-SEVEN* * * * * * *

We sleep through most of the next day, as we didn't return to the hotel until near dawn. The taxi driver who ferried us back didn't even raise an eyebrow, as if he regularly picked up soaking wet passengers at all hours. I awake to Delia tapping our glass door, and Rhys sleepily crosses the room to let her in. The sun is already setting behind her, and I'm shocked by how late it is.

"Have you both gone mad?" She's talking before he even opens the door. "The afterparty starts in an hour!"

"I admit it slipped my mind completely," he says sheepishly, and she whirls out of the room only to be back in seconds, garment bag in hand. She tosses it on the bed, and turns towards the door.

"*One hour!*" She calls over her shoulder. "I have a meeting with the advisor and I *won't* be late!"

"Oh dear," he laughs. "Now I've done it. I can't believe I forgot."

"Afterparty?" I unzip the bag she tossed at me. Inside is a floor length gown of black silk, a single strap holding up the cowl neckline. Its simplicity is elegant, which leads me to believe the party it's meant for might not be one I'm cut out for. "I wish I would've been prepared for such a... Formal event."

"It's not my thing either," he says. "But if we don't go, Delia will have our heads by the looks of it."

We arrive only a few minutes later than Delia intended, and I'm stunned by the transformation that's taken place in a single day. The multitude of cubes stacked with goods have vanished, replaced with dozens of circular high top tables draped in black fabric. Hundreds of globe lights of all sizes hang from the ceiling, appearing as if they're suspended in midair. The walls are layered thick with tall potted palm, bird of paradise, and cavendish banana, the sterile white space transformed into a warm glowing jungle.

I'm uncomfortable the moment we cross the threshold, a stark contrast to the floating lightness I'd felt in the restaurant. It's far too crowded, and I feel suffocated. It's near impossible to walk through the room without bumping into people, and I have to dodge my shoulders as I step. I stay close to Rhys' elbow as we follow Delia, who's decked out in another lavish ensemble — a short dress of black lace overlaid on white, accented with fingerless gloves. Rhys is walking stiffly, and I sense he's reacting similarly to me, his face expressionless. He's dressed the same as he was two nights previous, save for exchanging his black shirt for a fresh one. Julien has swapped his silver damask for thin pinstripes resembling spiderwebs, and even though Delia had scolded him he's wearing his sunglasses. She didn't find it amusing, but I think it's hilarious.

She leads us to an empty lounge, where Julien immediately parks himself in one of several tufted leather couches. Glowing orb lights the size of beach balls litter the space, reflecting on glass windows boasting an impressive view of the city.

"Well, it's obvious none of you are interested in rubbing elbows this evening," Delia says. "Just stay until I've finished my conversation with the advisor. It might not go as planned, and I'll need support afterwards in the form of company and a beverage or three."

One the way over I'd asked about her meeting, and she'd explained that the board of healers she's involved with meets annually to discuss their individual practices. One of the higher ups decided a few of their new methods crossed regulation boundaries, and was moving to instate a ban on any he personally declared unconventional. It sparked her desire to meet with him one on one.

"Utter bullshit," she hissed, her heels clicking angrily down the sidewalk. "There's always risk involved in saving lives, and nothing they've been doing has shown an increase. It's politics is what it is, and I intend to give him a piece of my mind. Gods I hate this administrative nonsense. One of these days it'll be enough to make me hang up my hat for good."

After she departs, presumably to give that particular advisor an earful, I sink down onto the couch beside Julien. Rhys makes his way to the bar within view without a word, and I know without him saying that he'll return with some sort of refreshment. I watch him lean against a chair as he chats with the bartender, and both laugh intermittently. He looks much more relaxed now, being off the hook from making dull conversation with any of the partygoers. As I observe him from a distance I feel that familiar flutter in the pit of my stomach, and smile a little. I can scarcely believe he belongs to me, and think of all the nights I spent pining for him. That time feels far away from now, and so does the first night I ever set eyes on him.

***

I'm nervous upon entering the dark club, and hover just inside the door. I must pause a little too long, because one of the doormen leans over and speaks to me.

"If you're looking for the bar it's to the left, and there's another up those stairs," he says, pointing to a staircase on my right. The closest bar is packed full, so step by step I climb to the second level in hopes it'll be much less busy.

It is, and I immediately spot the bartender, a slim man in a white button down. He's conversing with a couple sitting on the end, so instead of getting his attention for service I decide to wait until he notices me. Quietly I slide into a chair, scanning the rows of bottles for something familiar. When I don't find anything, I busy myself by pawing through my bag in search of nothing in particular, hoping I haven't made a mistake by coming here.

"Hello. What can I get for you?"

"Oh… Uhm…" He startled me, and I hadn't yet

prepared my request. Now I've apparently forgotten how to string together a full sentence. He isn't annoyed, or if he is he doesn't show it.

"Take all the time you need — no pressure."

He glances up at me as he washes a glass in the sink under the counter, and I'm oddly struck by him. I'm noticing all the little details — his silvery hair, his tattooed skin, the sinewy muscles moving in his forearms. There's a small smile on his thin lips, and it's further distracting me.

"I haven't... Been here before. I don't recognize any of the bottles, so maybe that's why I'm having some trouble deciding. Usually I'd go with a standard champagne cocktail, but I'm really not sure. Sorry, I know that's terribly vague."

"I've distilled many of these myself, so they're sort of off brand," he says, gesturing to the rows of hand labeled spirits. Distilled himself? How interesting. "If you're feeling adventurous, perhaps you'd allow me to take a wild guess? If you decide it's not to your liking we can try something else."

His kindness is enough to make me drop my guard a little, and I start to relax.

"Sure. I mean, yes please. Thank you." I'm relieved he's made a suggestion so I don't have to. I locate the pack of cigarettes I'd just bought, and before I can ask if it's allowed he sets a glass ashtray in front of me. I sigh quietly, happy to have something to occupy myself with while I wait. I'd like to have my drink in hand before diving into my book.

I turn to the club below, pulsing electronic music filtering through the glass. Neon lights are being projected onto the dark walls in geometric shapes, the crowd a single wave lapping back and forth. The vibe is much different up here, with the first floor being much more high energy. It's calmer, with just the right volume of music that it's quiet enough to hold a conversation. My client was right — this is much more my speed.

"There we are," I hear from behind me, and when I turn he's there with a fancy looking glass, lavender liquid inside and a sprig of something resting on the rim. I think it's thyme. He leans back against the shelves, watching me. "Have a go and let me know if you like it."

My face reddens, and the realization makes me blush even more. Why am I so nervous all of a sudden? Maybe it's because I'm hyper aware of the fact that he's barely taken his eyes off me. I sample the cocktail, and to my surprise it might be one of the best I've ever tasted. Tart and spicy with a pleasant burn.

"This is wonderful." I sip again. "What is it?"

"Sort of my own invention. The recipe is a bit of a secret. If I told you —"

"What, you'd have to kill me?" I finish his bad joke, and he laughs. I like the way his brows soften and his eyes wrinkle at the edges when he does. My nerves are subsiding, and I'm beginning to feel almost comfortable. "Seriously — it's lovely. Thank you."

"Of course. I'm pleased you like it," he says, and I can tell he genuinely is. He leans on the counter with his elbow, his crooked smile sending a flurry of butterflies into my stomach. "Welcome to our little club — I believe you'll fit in nicely. My name is Rhys."

I return his smile. "I'm Lynna."

***

While we're waiting for him to return, Julien and I muse about Delia's meeting, and laugh at the idea of her pointing a gloved finger in an old man's sour face. It seems unbelievable that she won't get her way, as she's forcefully persuasive when she wants to be. I certainly wouldn't challenge her. Suddenly I see a fast moving figure crossing the room. A beautiful brunette, her hair streaming behind her as she runs, one hand clutching the hem of her emerald green satin dress. I watch in amusement — surely she's going to trip in those heels, but she doesn't. Instead she makes a beeline for Rhys, and my smirk turns to a frown when she throws her arms around him. When she touches his face I sit up straight, my teeth clenched.

"Oh you've *got* to be kidding me," Julien groans. He's seen her too. Does he know her? Rhys looks uncomfortable and removes her hand from his cheek, but she leans in and says something into his ear.

"Who's that?" I can't hide the iciness in my tone. Julien sits forward, actively observing.

"That's Morgan. She's a bit... Something."

"So she's... An old friend?" She's standing awfully close to him, and he doesn't seem to like it. If she is one, she's not giving him the space a friend would.

"I guess she falls into that category. She and Rhys sort of dated, if you can even call it that. I was never a fan, and Delia can't stand her."

My stomach somersaults. I'd been under the assumption he hadn't dated at all for some time, let alone been involved with someone like her. I watch her grasp his sleeve as she smiles, a twinge of jealousy uncoiling within me. I can keep my thoughts to myself, but I apparently can't keep them from registering on my face, and Julien notices.

"You've got nothing to worry about — it was ages ago," he says, nudging me. "Come on. Let's go and save the poor fellow."

He gets to his feet, so I follow. I attempt to compose myself but she's still touching him, and it's filling me with unexpected rage.

"Morgan. Been a long time," Julien says, and her face lights up.

"Jules! It's so wonderful to see you!" She exclaims as she embraces him. He stands stiffly, not reciprocating, but she doesn't seem to notice. "And who is your *lovely* date? Hi — I'm Morgan."

Here I am standing face to face with her, all the while attempting to swallow my residual irritation. She's incredibly beautiful — willowy, with flawless skin, full red lips, and shining perfect teeth. Her teal eyes are bright and accented with wisps of black liner, her eyelids softly shadowed. I wish I hadn't brushed Delia off when she asked to put a little more makeup on me.

"*My* date, actually," Rhys says, slipping his arm around me. "Morgan, this is Lynna."

Her smile disappears for only a second before it's back on her face, and I conjure one up to greet her.

"It's wonderful to meet you. Are you enjoying the expo?"

She doesn't respond, and there's an awkward pause as she looks me up and down. An image of them together flashes in my mind — I see her carefully manicured hands caressing him, and it turns my stomach. I feel him grip my side tighter and try to suppress my imagination. Julien silently collects the glasses from the bar and nods towards the lounge, clearly ready to end this interaction.

"Right," Rhys says as he starts to steer me away. "Nice seeing you, Morgan."

"Oh, there's so much to catch up on! Let me grab a drink — I'll be right over," she says, motioning to the bartender.

"Can't take a hint," I hear Julien say as we make our way across the room. I hear her heeled steps clicking behind us, and wonder what I'm in for. I don't think she likes me very much, and I don't think I like her either. Maybe I should give her the benefit of the doubt?

Rhys and I sit together on one of the couches, with Julien across from us. I watch in near amazement as she slides a chair close to Rhys and sits down next to him, her elbow on his armrest. I decide I definitely don't like her.

"So what's it been? Fifteen years? Are you still holed up in that dismal city up north?" She asks, resting her chin on her fist. "I hated it there. Too much rain."

"I think we like the rain," I speak up, but she ignores me. Fifteen years? She looks young, so she must be one of them.

"Are you still running that apothecary? And that incredible greenhouse? I've been absolutely swamped at work — we've been doing some really interesting diversity studies to increase plant resilience. What are your thoughts on the significance of chimeric holdfasts as genetic reservoirs?"

Though I don't understand what she's going on about, Rhys seems to. He answers politely, his flat remarks an obvious sign he's trying to stifle the conversation, but she doesn't seem to care. I observe her cooly as she drones on, leaning forward and batting her long eyelashes. Why is she putting on such a performance? I'm growing tired of it, so I might have to try and steer this in a different direction. I clear my throat and lean forward to address Julien.

"I wonder how Delia's doing. Do you think she's making headway with the advisor?"

"Cordelia is here?" Morgan asks before he has a chance to weigh in. "How wonderful! It's so nice that you two are still together." She turns back to Rhys. "Remember when we used to go out — as couples? That one restaurant we visited in the middle of the city? Dreadful service. A fun memory, though. We should do it again."

My skin crawls as she runs her finger down his arm. He immediately pulls it away, but my chest tightens. I want to snap that finger in half, and it's becoming more and more difficult to hold my tongue. I need a moment to collect myself, so I stand and adjust my dress before excusing myself to the washroom. Once I find it, I stand over the sink and stare at my reflection. The night has taken a turn, and I hadn't expected to find myself engaged in a contest to vie for his attention. As I gaze into the mirror I can't help but compare myself to her — my lips not nearly as full, my teeth far from perfect. I have wispy wrinkles near my eyes where she has none, and though I'd thought I looked nice in this gown, my body isn't the sculpted silhouette her tight dress implies. Not only is she gorgeous, she's apparently far more intellectual than I. How am I supposed to compete with someone like her?

I sigh heavily. Am I really in a competition, or am I just jealous because I wish I looked more like her? Because I wish I understood what she was talking about when it came to plant genetics? He'd given no indication he welcomed her presence, mostly he looked uncomfortable. I must be getting in my head too much. There's a reason they're not together anymore, isn't there? He's with me now, so what I should do is not let her get to me.

When I return I have to stop from rolling my eyes when I notice she's moved seats. She's taken my place right next to him, though I find it interesting he's standing instead of sitting beside her as she continues to talk to him.

"Hello darling," he says when I reach him. He pulls me close and kisses me much longer than he normally would for a public greeting, and I realize he's doing it on purpose. It's his way of subtly reinforcing his attachment to me, and I hope she takes the hint. Out of the corner of my eye I see her watching us, expressionless. Her eyes shift to one of the waitstaff passing close by, and she catches them by the sleeve to speak to them, but I can't hear what she says. I can tell Rhys is ready to leave and so am I, but we're waiting on Delia, and I get the feeling Morgan would follow even if we relocated. She makes no effort to move from her spot in the middle of the couch to let us sit together, and I'm becoming annoyed with this all too polite dance we're doing. I don't want to be rude, and clearly he doesn't either, but this is getting a little ridiculous.

"Here," Julien says, patting the seat cushion before moving to a chair. "Trade you."

A hint of irritation flashes across her face as we sit across from her, but she quickly smiles and shifts to the edge of the couch as she adjusts her dress.

"So, Lynna," she says. "It's Lynna, right? What is it you do?"

She's eyeing my tattoos, and her eyes are all but drilling into my neck. I'm no stranger to being stared at, and I refuse to shrink under her eye, so I brush my hair over my shoulder, inviting her to judge me further.

"I was a tattooist for a long time, and now I'm Rhys' partner for the apothecary."

"A tattooist? Rhys I hope you're not planning on any more," she says. "I'm of the opinion that too many can render one a bit... Unsightly. You may end up having regrets when it comes to your choices — in every aspect."

By 'regrets' I know she means me. She'd just blatantly insulted me, and I have to bite the inside of my cheek to keep from saying something snarky. Rhys threads his fingers through mine, and chuckles lightly.

"That's a bit of an inconsequential opinion. I stand by my choices — all of them. I have no regrets."

"What is it *you* do Morgan?" I ask. Maybe if I shift the spotlight back to her she won't have room to say any more disparaging things.

"I'm a botanist," she says, her lips curving into a bow. "Oh, but you must already be familiar with botany if you're working alongside him. Tell me — what's your preferred grafting method to avoid incompatibility in regards to intrafamily species?"

I'm not sure how to answer. He'd given me a brief explanation of grafting at one point, so I'm not unfamiliar with the term, but I'm not versed enough to attempt it myself, let alone recall the ins and outs. She seems pleased by my silence, and as I struggle with what to say Rhys speaks up.

"I don't believe that's a relevant question. It's not required in much of what we do."

She inches forward, and rests her elbow on her crossed knee. Her dress strap has slipped down over her shoulder, revealing more of her cleavage than I care to see, but she doesn't adjust it. Instead she fixes her gaze on him and smiles sweetly.

"I have to wonder — isn't it a headache having to explain everything all the time? Wouldn't you rather be paired with someone who can offer you a challenge? Someone who's fluent in everything you know well?"

My face is growing hot with dim rage, and he squeezes my hand tighter. Before either of us can provide a rebuttal the waiter reappears, and bends to show her a bottle he's brought. She smiles, and it feels like an eternity of uncomfortable silence before he finally uncorks it and sets it in the middle of the table.

"I thought we might want to toast our reunion," she says, her voice sultry as she nods towards the sweating bottle. "Look — it's one of your favorites."

Briefly I imagine myself upending the table, glass flying everywhere and that expensive bottle exploding into a bubbling mess. It's what I'd like to do most, but I don't like imagining the shocked look on Rhys' face even though I'd delight in hers. I can't cause a scene — it would only give her more ammunition against me, and she has enough already. I have to regain control of this situation more subtly, but I'm not sure how. She reaches for the bottle, and a petty thought enters my mind, so I snatch it from the table before she can grasp it.

"This is so kind of you," I smile. "Please — allow me."

I fill the glasses slowly, and when I get to hers I tip the bottle a little too much. Bubbling liquid spurts out, sloshing onto her emerald dress. She gasps and jumps to her feet as she holds the wet hem away from her, and when Julien snickers I press my hand to my mouth so I won't laugh. I'm trying to look apologetic, but I'm not sorry at all.

"Just look — it's ruined!" She groans, scowling at the fabric.

"You might try a little cold water," Julien chuckles, and she shoots him a dirty look.

"I suppose so. Will you help me Lynna? I could use a hand."

Is she really asking for my help? I don't want to go

with her, but if I decline it has the potential to make things more uncomfortable. I deliberate for a moment before following her to the washroom. Maybe talking with her in private will be a good opportunity for me to set a few things straight.

Once inside, she pulls a few towels from the dispenser and dabs at the stain. I gather a few myself, but when I hand them to her she stares at me instead of taking them.

"You know you're on borrowed time, don't you?" She asks.

Borrowed time? "What are you talking about?"

She stops dabbing her dress, and wipes her hands off. "Come on, Lynna. You couldn't even answer a basic question about horticulture. Do you really think you'll be able to hold his attention long term?" She leans towards me, and I step back without thinking. "Admit it — you already know you're not good enough for him. He'll see it sooner or later, and move on to someone who can *really* pique his interest."

Did she really just say that? I dig my nails into my palms and try not to drop my eyes as she smirks. I have to say something, so I swallow the lump growing in my throat.

"And what, you think that someone is you?"

"I *know* it is," she says. "He wasn't ready to commit before, but he is now, and I'm more than happy to step back in. You should give up before you get hurt."

Tears are welling in my eyes, and I will them not to fall. She's a predator, and I don't want to show her I'm the weaker one.

"You're making an awful lot of assumptions, and you're wrong."

"Am I?" She laughs. "I suppose we'll see."

Her shoes click as she stalks past me to the door, and when she's gone I let the tears course down my cheeks. I'd meant to come in here to stand my ground, but I hadn't done a good job of it. I'd barely gotten a word in.

She's right. You know she's right.

It's a small quiet voice coming from somewhere inside me, confirming what I don't want to believe. Is it right? Is *she* right? What if I'm *not* good enough for him? I shake my head as I dab at my eyes with the towels. I can't let her mow me over like this, can I? She doesn't know him like I do — she can't. I have to get back out there, so I straighten my shoulders and push the door open.

She's nearly to the lounge, so I quicken my steps to catch up. Julien and Rhys are standing next to the window, and she walks right up and pulls him aside. Her hands are on his shoulders, and he shakes his head at whatever she's saying. I'm only a few strides away when she stands on her tiptoes and plants her lips on his. I suck in my breath and stop dead in my tracks, but it doesn't last more than a second, and I exhale audibly when he pushes her away.

"What the hell are you doing?!" He hisses. "You're being wildly inappropriate."

I feel a gentle hand on my shoulder — it's Julien, a scowl on his usually pleasant face. Morgan's face grows soft, and she steps towards him.

"Rhys, be honest with yourself... We both want this. I know you miss me." She places her hand back on his shoulder, but he closes his fingers around her wrist and jerks it away, his expression stormy.

"Enough! What I miss is your absence. You need to leave, and if you won't, *I will*."

He releases her and she takes a step back, pressing her manicured hand to her chest. She glances at Julien and I before smoothing her dress and tossing her hair over her shoulder.

"Fine," she says. "I'll go, but just remember — *you* did this. We could've had something again, and you've thrown it away for *that*. Goodnight."

She bumps into my shoulder as she passes, and I wish I would've been able to think of something clever to say, but I'm relieved she's finally out of sight.

"Gods, I'm so sorry," he sighs. "I never thought she'd have the audacity to —"

"Can we go? Please?" I interrupt. I suddenly want to be anywhere but here.

"Go on," Julien says, patting my shoulder. "I'll wait for Delia. She'll understand."

I'm quiet on the short walk back to the hotel, still reeling from the scene with Morgan. I have to consciously force the image of her kissing him out of my mind, and I'm angry at myself for letting her get away with it. Once we're in the room I kick off my shoes and fidget with the zipper on my dress. It's stuck, so I wearily sink down onto the edge of the shiny green duvet, flustered. He sits down next to me, sighing heavily.

"You haven't said a word," he says. "Are you all right?"

"I just… I never expected anything like that. Now all I'm doing is questioning everything."

"What are you questioning?" He asks, shifting so he's kneeling in front of me, taking my hands. "Don't think for one second that I'd fall for any of that nonsense. I owe you an apology. I should've told her to get lost much sooner. I never should've let you sit through that."

"I'm not angry with you for being polite, and it was clear you weren't interested in her, but it made me wonder a bit. When we were in the washroom she basically told me I'll never measure up, and that you'd come around eventually and seek out someone like her instead. I'm embarrassed to admit she got to me a little. Maybe more than a little."

"Darling," he says, his brows softening. "What she said couldn't be further from the truth."

"It was hard having it thrown in my face like that. Especially considering how attractive she is — and smart."

"And about as deep as a birdbath," he says, and I smile faintly. "The very brief time I wasted in her presence was nothing like this — nothing at all. We went out a few times and that was that. She's childish and manipulative, and once I understood that I wanted nothing more to do with her. I never felt so much as a shred of affection for her, whereas I *love* you."

I love him too, so I press my palm against his fuzzy cheek, and he nuzzles against it before turning to kiss my palm. She's taken up enough of our evening, so I decide not to dwell on it any further. I'll purge both her and the doubt she's planted in me.

"Do you think you'd be willing to help me out of this thing?" I ask as I fumble with the zipper. "I can't seem to get it."

He laughs quietly. "I've wanted to help you out of it all night."

Later I'm lying next to him with his arm draped over me, and though he's asleep I'm unable to drift off. I carefully untangle myself from him and slip quietly from the bed, bending to pick up his shirt before sliding the glass door open. I button it closed as I curl into one of the chairs on the terrace, hoping the sound of traffic will lull me. After a few minutes I hear a door open, and quiet footsteps.

"Can't sleep?" Delia seats herself next to me, knotting the bathrobe tie at her waist.

"No. I'm sorry we didn't wait for you. How was your meeting?"

"Squashed the whole thing," she smiles, offering me a cigarette. "That buffoon never knew what hit him. Gods, what a night you had — Julien told me all about it. The *gall* of that woman."

"I know," I sigh, pressing the cigarette between my lips.

"She's always been bad news," she says, the cloud she's exhaled drifting away into the sky. "I *am* a little sad I didn't get to watch you douse her in champagne, though. Nice touch — Julien thought that was hilarious."

"What I wanted to do was throttle her, but that was all I could manage."

"I think you certainly took the high road. She should be ashamed for having come onto Rhys like that, but I'm not sure if she's capable of feeling anything like embarrassment given how she behaves."

"I just hope I never have to see her again."

"I doubt you will. I should've known she might turn up here, considering it's where he met her in the first place, but it didn't even cross my mind. I thought we'd gotten rid of her ages ago."

"Has anything like this ever happened to you? With Julien?"

"I've gotten a little pushy with a few girls who've thrown themselves at him," she admits. "But I trust him, and try not to let my jealous streak get the better of me. That's not to say you weren't completely within your rights to feel the way you did tonight. I'd have knocked her out cold had she kissed Julien like that."

"Well if I ever see her again I hope I can muster up the courage to do just that," I laugh. "But I trust him too. I can't blame him for what happened — he certainly didn't invite it."

"I don't think there's any reason for you not to trust him," she says. "In all the years I've known him, I've never seen him like this. She can't hold a candle to what you clearly mean to him."

"I know, and he said something to that effect earlier, which did make me feel better. It's just… It's been a long time, but I've been replaced before. Cast aside for someone better. That feeling that it'll happen again never truly leaves you, I guess. I don't think he'd do that to me, but I think I let her get in my head a little."

"Don't," she says, patting my hand. "She's not worth wasting your time on, and she's certainly not better in any way." She uncurls herself from the chair. "Come on — let's go to bed. We'll be home tomorrow, and can put all this far behind us."

148

★★★★★★ TWENTY-EIGHT ★★★★★★

Our life settles back into a familiar routine when we return home, and I love the ease of it. We propagate the cuttings, and plant endless rows of seeds, joyously checking their progress daily. When we're not actively working we venture out into the city, frequenting markets and little shops. I don't eat much anymore, but I still love admiring the rows of colorful produce in the vegetable stands, and smelling street food simmering in stainless trays. We sit in restaurants I frequented when I first moved here — he enjoyed when I told him how I used to make up stories about what the other patrons lives might be like, so we continue it. We spend days in bed together, cuddling and reading side by side, or watching the rains trail down the glass. I like the mundaneness of our life together — the regularity — but what keeps me from settling back into it completely is the new twinge of nervousness in my stomach. It's often accompanied by that small quiet voice, and I begin hearing it more and more frequently.

This will end. Everything will end. It's a matter of time.

I push it away when it arrives, attributing it to lingering fear that what Morgan had said was accurate. He's as confident and reassuring as ever, but the spiraling thoughts shake me to my core. I'd never had this much anxiety in my life, and I'm unable to break free of the low level panic that continuously loops in my head, accompanied by an increasing number of intrusive thoughts. What if he changes his mind? What if a day comes when he decides he can't do this anymore? How will I go on? I shiver when I picture myself lying in the cold rain until it drowns me, and my body jerks when I imagine stepping over the edge of the harbor bridge. I don't want to see any of these things, but I do. I start holing myself away in the washroom, letting the running water drown out my tears. I'm driving myself crazy and I can't keep living like this, the fear and anxiety always lurking below the surface, waiting to sabotage me. Waiting to consume me entirely.

I finally vent some of my worries to Delia on a night out with just us two, hoping they'll go away if I let a few loose. I'm curious as to how she and Julien kept up a relationship that stretched over many years without growing bored of each other.

"You worry too much. I sincerely doubt that man will ever grow bored of you," she says. "But to answer your question, yes. Occasionally Julien and I can't stand the sight of each other. That's why we do things like this." She sips her martini, and I stare at the glass, confused. "You and me, I mean — not the martini," she laughs. "You need some time apart — other hobbies and whatnot. What's that old adage? Something about absence and the heart? I can't recall. Don't you think they enjoy their time on their own too? I'm willing to bet they haven't thought of us for one second since we've been out."

Julien and Rhys had resumed a longstanding tradition of theirs — a weekly card game, which turned into us essentially swapping partners. Those nights I'd spend with Delia, and we'd go out dancing or shopping — mostly whatever she felt like. She and Julien have it different than us, though. We work from home together, whereas they keep fairly opposite schedules. She spends a few days a week in a hospital, and he works some nights in multiple establishments as a bouncer, as he preferred to get paid to enjoy the bands. Julien was often prone to insomnia, referring to it as his own brand of restlessness — and he slept odd hours or not at all, while Delia preferred a steady sleep regimen. It worked for them, the time apart, but Rhys and I hadn't ever gone more than a few hours without each other. Is that really what it might come down to? I can't imagine separating myself from him to that degree as a maintenance strategy.

"Maybe I'm overanalyzing things," I sigh, swirling my cocktail.

"You are. Let yourself enjoy the day to day, and don't give it another thought."

It's easier said than done, but I take her words to heart and try to focus on the now. Right now time apart is the last thing on our minds — we can't get enough of each other. Nothing feels stagnant or boring yet, so why am I convinced it'll become so? Why am I waiting for this imaginary other shoe to drop? I decide I have to mention it to him, so I do one night as we're lying in bed, sweat from the shared activity from moments before still dewy on our bodies.

"Darling, I must admit I've had a few of the same fears," he says, leaning back to rest his head on my thigh. "That you'd tire of this routine — or of me. It might become tedious for you after a while."

"I have an incredibly hard time imagining myself growing tired of you."

"Well, we're very much on the same page when it comes to that. I must say — I like to believe I know how you feel about me, but that's still a lovely thing to hear."

"I'll tell you every day then." I smooth the hair above his ear, and when he smiles up at me I wonder why I ever questioned him in the first place. He won't abandon me — I know he won't.

"If you do begin to feel like you want something more — that you are, in fact, growing tired of all this — all you have to do is say the word. I'll take you anywhere in the world you want to go, and I'll happily support any activity you choose to pursue, whether you decide you'd like to take up your old career, or even start a new one — anything. Whatever tickles your fancy," he says, reaching up and actually tickling me.

I squirm as I giggle. "That's very sweet of you. I'm not sure this is about my occupation, though." I pause as I think about it. Maybe I'm not worried about him at all, but if I'm not, what am I so worried about then? "Maybe it's baseless anxiety of what's to come. I've never had anything this good, and I might still not be used to it. I feel like I'm constantly waiting for something bad to happen."

"Well, our beginning came on the heels of something tumultuous, so I can understand your cause for a touch of anxiety now that things are more tranquil. You mustn't let it consume you — things are bound to go awry in one way or another, but if there are troubles that pop up we'll deal with them accordingly when they do. There's no sense getting worked up about something that hasn't even happened yet. What we should be focusing on is enjoying the present."

I shrug. Delia had basically said the same thing. "I know. I feel ridiculous even saying it out loud. How could anyone be anxious about anything when they have this perfectly beautiful life stretched out in front of them?"

"You're not ridiculous," he says, his face softening. "My intention wasn't to downplay your feelings. Anxiety is very real, and doesn't seem to bother with the logistics of any particular situation. In my experience, it's often more prevalent in calmer times such as these. Your mind searches for something that could go wrong, and you feel validated when it comes to pass, thus perpetuating the cycle."

I shift against the headboard. "That's exactly it. The feeling that something terrible is waiting just out of sight is awful, and it's worse not knowing what it is. The idea that I might be struggling with this fear I can't name forever is almost… Unbearable."

I say it without thinking, and as soon as the words leave my mouth I feel like I've finally put my finger on it. Superficial concerns about our dynamic aren't what's eating me, and neither is how he feels about me. It's not a question of him tiring of me — it's me tiring of myself. I'm worried about the daily battle with my mind, and how long it might stretch on. Hearing that small quiet voice assuring me of what will go wrong, and those intrusive thoughts interrupting my bliss. His expression changes to concern, and he sits up.

"What are you saying?"

"I don't know," I sniff, suddenly tearful. "I've never experienced something like this. I have these… Dark thoughts sometimes, and there's this constant underlying fear about nothing and everything. I can't help but long for its end. I don't want to long for it, but I do."

He doesn't speak. Instead he pulls me against him and holds me for a long time, smoothing my hair with his fingers. I feel his heart beating rapidly, and it makes me nervous.

"I understand," he says quietly. "This is the sort of thing I was worried you might face."

Is that it? It makes sense — I'd never encountered anything like it before, or at least not to this degree. Should I have recognized it?

"What do I do?" I mumble into his chest.

"I think we've caught it early enough, but I want you to tell me every time you feel this way. I refuse to let it destroy you. I'll do everything I can to keep that from happening."

I hadn't fully understood the gravity of what I'd been burdened with until now, and it feels heavy. Had I lost the ability to properly manage what's going on in my head? The concern in his voice tells me we're on the same page about this, too. This has to be what consumed that man, eventually driving him to suicide. I don't want to end up like him, and vow to myself that I won't. I'll have to manage the fear that comes in the form of that small quiet voice, and those vivid intrusive thoughts. The blessing I received by being changed is a long life filled with love, but it had come with a caveat — a curse deep within my head.

I survived the transition, but can I continue?

★★★★★★ TWENTY-NINE ★★★★★★

"Almost there!" Julien calls.

My legs are burning, and my heart feels like it might burst from my chest. I'm slowly closing the distance to where he's standing atop the hill, my feet sliding on the muddy trail. Once I reach him I bend over and rest my hands on my knees to catch my breath.

"...Fuck..." I mutter between gasps. He laughs and jogs in place.

"All right. Back down now!" He's not at all fazed by the fact that we've just done four miles uphill, and I watch him begin his descent. I take a few big breaths and shake my shoulders out, then follow him down the trail, letting my body weight do the work. He's already way ahead of me, but I know if I drop behind too far he'll circle back.

I've been running with Julien for a handful of months now, and he'd gotten me to complete distances I never thought I'd be able to. I think it's fun for him — coaching me, pushing me. I also think he knows about my internal struggle. We never speak of it, but I have the feeling Rhys must've mentioned it to him, because since that conversation Julien had shown up regularly to get me outside. He said it did wonders for his mental state, and went on a long rant about endorphins and the benefits of a steady routine. I complain frequently, but as much as I don't want to admit it, I'm enjoying it. The sweating, the sensation of my now strong legs propelling me forward, the feeling of accomplishment when I hit a new milestone — all of it is more exhilarating than it is tedious, and it's helped me more than I thought it would. The anxiety had begun to fade into the background, and I don't hear the voice anymore.

After we reach the city, we walk along the harbor to cool down. It's busy today, and crowded. The fish market is in full swing, and it smells something dreadful, but we don't mind it enough to stay away. As we're rounding a corner I hear loud voices and laughter coming from a group of burly men. My heart skips a beat when I notice their matching jackets — skull patches on their backs, each with one glowing red eye. I suck in my breath and jerk Julien behind the nearest market stall when I see a familiar face among them. The scarred man.

"What are you doing?" Julien laughs, frowning when I shush him. I cautiously peer around the side of the stall. He's still with the group, and he hadn't seen me. Glass smashes, and I notice the empty bottles surrounding them.

"Lynna, what —"

"It's him. The one with the scar."

I don't need to say anything more. Rhys had told both him and Delia what had happened the night in the alley, and I'd filled in my version of it during one of our jogs. He knew exactly who they were, as I expected, but what he'd told me next sent a chill through me. What I hadn't known was that the gang's presence was always accompanied by an uptick of grim news articles — brutal murders, bodies discovered in the harbor, and disappearances. If the woman who assured me I had nothing to worry about would've told me that from the beginning, I might've been a little less carefree in regard to my surroundings. I shudder as I think of my own bloated corpse being dragged from the water, my certain fate had Rhys not intervened.

"Shit," he mutters, joining me in peeking at them. "Come on. No sense in hanging around here."

We backtrack through the market, and take a side street to the apartment. My heart is racing just as much as it had been only a little while ago when I was running. I hadn't seen any trace of them since that night, and Julien had comforted me by explaining their transient nature, so I stupidly thought I might never have to again. They're obviously back, so it's clear I was wrong. What do I do now? I know without any doubt it was them that burned down my studio — will they find me again? Will I have to look over my shoulder every waking moment?

"Hello darling," Rhys calls when he hears the door open. "You've been gone a while. Did Julien take you on a tour of the entire continent?"

His back is to us, metal clanking on the kitchen table as he reassembles the temperamental distiller. A valve had failed earlier in the morning, and there are pieces of it spread out all over. The entire apartment smells of ethanol. When I don't respond he turns around, and his smile disappears when he sees our faces.

"Julien? What is it?"

Julien removes his muddy shoes before crossing the floor, and I listen to him speak quietly to Rhys as I undo my laces. Rhys responds in a low tone, and I'm annoyed by them keeping their voices down. I want to know what they're saying, since this situation directly involves me.

"Are you about finished with your secret conversation?" I ask, crossing my arms.

"Sorry," Rhys says, setting the tool he'd been holding on the table. "Darling, would you mind putting the coffee on while I clear the table?"

"I'll do it," Julien offers. "Go ahead and change. You're all muddy."

When I emerge from the washroom they're both at the table, and a fresh cup is waiting for me. Neither of them look nervous or afraid, so I have to believe that whatever strategy they've come up with is a solid one.

"First, are you all right?" Rhys asks when I sit. "Seeing him must've put you on edge."

"It certainly did. I'm just glad I was paying attention to where I was walking or we might've run smack into them. What happens now? We're both at risk here — he knows your face, too."

"I'm aware," he says, tapping a cigarette on the table before fitting it between his teeth. "But I don't believe we have anyone to worry about besides him and the other fellow present that night. Did you see the latter in the crowd?"

I can't really remember what the other man looked like, besides the fact that he was big. Mostly what I recall is the blood trailing from his nose after I kicked him in the face.

"I don't know."

"It doesn't matter," Julien says. "You should avoid them all equally."

"I'm not the only one who should be avoiding them." I shift my eyes to Rhys, and he smiles gently.

"They know I work at the club, which could present an issue should they turn up there," Rhys says. "But I addressed that with security long ago, and I'll reiterate it again. I can limit my errands otherwise."

"I'd suggest you lay low, so we might want to put our runs on hold," Julien says, and I try unsuccessfully not to frown. "For a little while, at least. They never stay long, but I think it's a good idea to err on the side of caution. I'll find out what I can through work, and once we know more we can go from there."

Rhys reaches across the table and takes my hand, squeezing it. "It'll be all right. We won't let anything happen to you."

"Doesn't hurt to be proactive, though," Julien says. "You still got that knife?"

It takes me a second to realize what knife he's referring to. My old switchblade — Rhys had collected it for me after the night in the alley. I haven't touched it since.

"Yeah. It's somewhere."

"Wouldn't be a bad idea to keep it on you — just in case. You know how to use it?"

"I guess so," I shrug. "Clearly it's gotten me out of one situation already."

"Well let's make sure. Go and see if you can find it."

* * * * * * THIRTY * * * * * *

I do as they ask and keep to the apartment for nearly a week, and without the steady exercise I pace more and more frequently. Rhys had said he'd limit his errands but he doesn't, and I can't help but worry about him being alone with the gang lurking about. I know he's far more capable than I am when it comes to defending himself — at least, he must be if he got me away from them before — so I have to believe he could do it again.

I spend most of my time doing my usual tasks, replenishing items meant to be sold in the apothecary. I'd learned how to mix the salts and made a few tea blends of my own. I know which elixirs are ready to be bottled and how to label them, and how to extract the compounds hiding inside certain plants. Some require pressing, while others need to be boiled or steeped in alcohol. I enjoy the work immensely, but sometimes when I walk around the greenhouse my mind wanders, and I find myself daydreaming about embedding some of the beautiful foliage in skin. The longer I spend away from the art of tattooing the more I miss it, and I don't think I realized how big a part of me it was. I'm afraid to bring my longing to his attention. I don't want him to think I'm dissatisfied with what I'm doing with my life now because I'm truly not, but I feel guilty for wanting more. I try to remind myself to be grateful for what I have, and not get too greedy, but I'm not sure how long I'll be able to keep my yearning to myself.

"Do you want to help me cart this down to the apothecary?" He asks. He'd just finished carefully packing a series of fragile jars into two boxes.

"More than happy to." I'm eager to stretch my legs even though it's a short walk. "Load me up."

It's raining heavily, and I worry the boxes might collapse, but we manage to get them there safely. He rests the box on his knee as he fumbles in his pocket for the door key, and after a brief bout of swearing he locates it. Once inside, I busy myself with allocating the inventory we'd brought while he places it on the shelves. It's quiet, the only sounds being the clinking of the jars as he arranges them and the tapping of rain on the glass. I'm startled by a sudden flash of lightning, followed by booming thunder.

"Heavens," he says, tilting his head to peer through the front window. "It's getting worse out there. Let's hurry this up — the longer we're here the more interesting our trek back will be."

The rain as well as the wind picks up on the walk home, and by the time we reach our building we're both a little sodden. It seems we're in for quite a show, the rapid flashes of lightning illuminating the apartment like a strobe light might. Bits of hail clink off the windows and gather in the corners, and I quickly shut one I'd left cracked open, the floor beneath it wet. I haven't seen a storm this furious in a long time. He helps me mop up the water, and pauses suddenly.

"The greenhouse. I think some of the vents are still open." He drops the towel and races towards the door. "The wind will shatter them to bits if it keeps up like this."

I follow him up, and just in time. The wind howls much louder up here, and a few seed trays had blown from their tables. We hurry to the cranks controlling the roof vents, spinning them shut as streaks of lightning split the sky. We almost have them all closed when a strong gust of wind takes hold of the last vent, forcing it in the opposite direction and snapping the metal hinges like dry twigs. The vent slams back against the roof and shatters the entire section, glass flashing in the light as it crashes down. Instinctively I duck to the ground, but I'm not close enough for any of the glass to have hit me. There's a jagged hole in the roof where one of the slanted panes was, rain coming down hard through it. What a mess. I can only imagine what a nightmare it'll be to replace. I quickly get to my feet to ask what we should do about it for the time being, but he's nowhere in sight. I scan the aisles, and hear glass tinkling. When I find him he's on the floor, leaning up against one of the wooden table legs, his hand firmly clamped on his shoulder next to his neck. There's a large patch of blood seeping through the front of his shirt, and the sight of it freezes me in place.

He winces as he pulls his hand away, and the bloodstain immediately doubles in size. He reapplies pressure and rests his head against the table.

"Darling… Can you help me up?"

I'm so stunned it takes me a second to get my legs to move. After I've gotten him to his feet, we slowly make our way towards the stairs. The blood on his shirt is soaking into mine, the coppery smell of it thick in the air. I hope it's not as bad as it looks from the outside. We finally reach the apartment, and he sinks heavily into a chair near the table, still holding the wound closed. He's not saying much and he's very pale, which tells me it's painful. I'm starting to panic.

I'm frantically digging through drawers to find something to put pressure on it in place of his hand, and find a clean dish towel. Now what? I can't take him to a hospital — do I get Delia instead? Is she even at home?

"Rhys, what do I do?"

"You'll have to close it up," he says. "I'd tend to it myself, but I'm quite dizzy. Do you think you can do that? I can tell you how."

I take a deep breath and nod, willing my heart to stop pounding so hard.

"Third drawer from the top left, you'll find a square green jar containing a white powder."

I yank the drawer open, nearly spilling the contents. *Steady now, Lynna*. I find the jar and open it, the powder inside, and when I show him he nods.

"Now," he says. "When I remove my hand I need you to pour all the powder onto the wound. The moment you've done that, apply pressure and *don't stop*. Are you ready?"

160

I am, so I move the jar into place and wait. He removes his hand and a red stream trickles from the gash. It's worse than I thought — much worse. Without hesitating I dump the jar's contents into the wound and press the towel over it. Hard. He hisses, teeth clenched, and slams his fist on the table. When I shift my eyes to his face I notice how white his lips are, and the dazed look in his eyes. I've seen this before during a tattoo — he's about to pass out. Quickly I straddle him so he doesn't fall, and he slumps limply against me as I hold him up with my body. My breaths are coming in little bursts, adrenaline exploding into my limbs, but I pour all my concentration into the task at hand. I can't lessen the pressure.

After a few excruciatingly long moments his head stirs against my shoulder, and I feel his free arm wrap around me. Color is starting to come back into his face, though he still looks an unnatural shade of pale.

"Well done," he whispers. "Just give it a few more minutes to be sure it's stopped, then I'm afraid you have a bit of sewing ahead of you."

We wait a bit more, and when I pick the towel up the bleeding had indeed stopped, the powder turning the blood into jelly-like clots. The glass had split his skin neatly, and sliced right through muscle. How am I supposed to navigate this? I don't know what I'm doing at all, but I have to trust that he does.

I insist on moving him to the bed so I don't have to worry about him falling out of the chair. I listen from the desk as he calls out what I'll need — a curved needle, thread so delicate it's almost invisible, a strip of white bandage, and a brown vial of disinfectant. I cut the shirt off so he doesn't have to move his arm, and he instructs me how to carefully clean the wound. Through gritted teeth he tells me how deep to plunge the needle and how to knot the sutures, one by one. When I'm finished he lets his head drop back onto the pillows, exhaling heavily. I soak a fresh cloth in warm water to remove the rest of the blood, and clean his arm, his chest, and between his fingers. He watches me silently, a faint smile tugging at the corners of his mouth, and I'm relieved he looks so much better already. When I finish cleaning his hand he curls his fingers around mine.

"Thank you, my darling," he whispers. He looks tired, and his eyelids start to droop.

"Is it all right for you to rest now?" I ask, and he nods, so I kiss him on the cheek before taking the bloodstained cloth to the sink to rinse it out.

As the red water trickles down the drain I have to stop and place my hands on the edge of the sink to steady myself. What if I hadn't been here? What if it had been worse? What if he'd lost too much blood? The what ifs keep coming, filling my head until it hurts, and I slip into a downward spiral of intrusive thoughts, picturing myself finding his body on the floor of the greenhouse.

Can you imagine being trapped here if he was gone?

Delia's words ring in my ears, and I cover my hand with my mouth to stifle a sob. I hope this is the first and last time I have to experience something like this.

✶ ✶ ✶ ✶ ✶ ✶ THIRTY-ONE ✶ ✶ ✶ ✶ ✶ ✶

In the morning, I wake up in the same clothes from the night before. There's blood on me, but it's dried to a dark maroon, and the remnants of where he'd been lying are on the sheets. Where is he? Did he fall off the bed? I hurriedly rub the sleep from my eyes and hear water running. Is he in the washroom? The door is open and there he is, standing in front of the mirror. He's got a small pair of scissors in his hand, and he's carefully snipping the sutures I'd made less than twelve hours earlier.

"Good morning, darling," he says casually, as if this were a regular event in our household.

I'm confused, and become even more so when I see his shoulder. The wound is closed completely, a thin scab where the gaping hole had been. There's no way it should be at this stage yet — I'm not even a healer and I know that. I stand on my tiptoes to gawk at it further.

"How…"

He pulls out the last little string, and sets the scissors on the edge of the sink. Why does he suddenly look guilty?

"I think it's time we had a talk," he says. "I have something I should share with you."

I sink down into a chair at the table, my eyes sweeping over the residual gore strewn about from the night before. Bloody bandages, drops of blood on the concrete, his cut apart shirt — all of it points to a wound that's now barely more than a scratch. What exactly is he about to tell me? He sits down, wincing slightly as he threads his arms through a fresh shirt. After he buttons it from the bottom up, he picks up a cigarette from the middle of the table.

"I don't understand how it's closed up already." I can hear the disbelief in my own voice, and I'm staring at him in the same manner — he looks completely normal now. "Was there something in that powder? I thought it was a clotting agent alone."

"It was," he says. "But this — what's happened to the wound — it's... Part of who I am. My kind have the ability to heal at an extremely accelerated rate."

He begins to explain his theories on the rapid cellular turnover, but I'm barely listening. How had I not noticed that change in myself? I try to think back to any instance where it would be apparent, but there aren't any. The only time I'd been injured besides a stubbed toe or bumped elbow had been when I'd broken the glass, but though it bled quite a bit it was a minuscule cut, and had healed normally from what I can remember. Had it been faster? I'm no longer sure. Why didn't he say something then? Why didn't he tell me from the start?

"I don't understand why you never mentioned this."

"I didn't intend to leave you in the dark forever," he says. "I just thought it a trifle unnecessary to point out just yet."

"*Unnecessary?!* It seems rather crucial! You didn't think I'd want to know that about myself?"

He sighs, and reaches across the table to place his hand on mine.

"That's the thing. Though it's been proven possible to instill similar longevity in ones not like us — rare, but possible — the healing is another matter. No one's ever taken on this capability."

"No one? So... Not that man?"

"No."

"And not Julien?"

He sighs again. "No."

"And not me. That's why you didn't tell me. Because it doesn't matter."

He nods slowly. I pull my hand back and gnaw on my thumbnail as I stare at the splats of dried blood surrounding the chair. I'm full of conflicting emotions — irritation that I hadn't known, disappointment that my body can't do what his can, and wonder that his can do that at all. What else can he do that he hadn't shared?

"That gash you had — it was awful, and it's almost

nothing now. What happens if you're hurt worse? Can you recover from that with ease, too? Are you —"

"I'm not immortal, if that's what you're getting at," he chuckles. I don't smile. None of this is amusing to me. "I can be hurt — clearly — and I can die, same as anyone else. Had we not stopped the bleeding it wouldn't have done me in, but I'd be worse off than I am currently had I not been seen to directly."

"What does it take then? To die?"

"Well," he says, finally lighting the cigarette he'd been toying with. "That's a bit difficult to answer. It depends on a number of factors — timing and severity being the most critical. I know Delia's seen a handful of us recover from injuries she'd thought fatal beyond a shadow of a doubt during her time as a healer."

"Is there anything else? Any other odd thing I should know that you haven't divulged? Am I going to one day discover you can move objects with your mind or… Or… See the future?"

"No, darling. I assure you I'm incapable of either of those things," he says. "And there's nothing more."

I'm a little miffed, so I spend most of the rest of the morning in silence, pondering everything he'd told me as I change the linens and gather our bloodied clothing. I'd made it clear I didn't want to talk more, so he'd gone upstairs to assess the damage, and when I finally cool down I find him sweeping up the glass. There's water everywhere, and though the storm had moved on it would continue to be a flooded nightmare when the rains resume.

"I think I know someone who can replace the vent and the pane," he says as he empties the particles into the bin. "I should leave shortly to see if I can arrange it. I don't think it'd be wise to leave this as is for long."

I think about the fact that they'd been adamant I keep to the apartment as much as possible, yet he continues to venture out as if nothing's amiss. Is that why he hadn't been that worried about being a target himself — because of what he knew? I lean against one of the raised beds as he sweeps.

"Does this… Ability to heal quickly mean you're in less danger? Those men out there —"

"Yes and no," he says. "It's definitely not something to be cavalier about. I'm cautious when I leave here, and I don't linger anywhere longer than I have to. Though I've taken a beating from them before and recovered, I'd rather not experience one again."

They'd gotten to him before? Was it that night? He seems to know that's the question I'm about to ask, and answers it before I can.

"They thrashed me solidly before I got you away," he says sheepishly. "Nearly fractured my jaw. Had a broken nose, but I've had my nose broken before. I think they might've done me a favor in that respect. It's a little less out of joint now."

I hadn't thought he'd been hurt at all, but he had — he'd just healed before I woke up. He'd suffered that and I hadn't ever known. He smiles faintly when I press my hand against his cheek, softly tracing the bent line of his nose with my thumb.

"I'm sorry," he says, placing his hand over mine. "I promised no more secrets, and I think that counts as one."

I'm not irritated anymore. If anything, I understand his reasoning. Now that I know, all I wish is that I had that capability too, but nothing would be able to give it to me. My awareness doesn't matter much, all in all, since it changes nothing. I kiss him softly, and take the broom from his hand.

"I'm just glad you're all right. Go on — I'll finish up."

After he's gone, I do what I can to tidy the greenhouse before cleaning myself up. I'm sponging water from my hair when there's a knock at the door. It's Julien, looking pleased.

"Where's Rhys? I've got some news — good news."

"Can you share it with me instead? He's out seeing about having some glass replaced."

"Glass?" He laughs, pausing with one arm still in his jacket. "What's he broken this time?"

"I'll show you."

I tell him what happened as we circle up the steps — the storm, the shattered pane, the wound. He shakes his head as we stare up at the roof.

"You've had a fun night, haven't you?"

"And how. You can imagine my surprise when I found him this morning. It was almost like nothing ever happened."

"It's an odd thing to witness. You really stitched him up yourself?"

"I had to. He walked me through it."

"Well don't let Delia find out," he laughs. "She's apt to put you to work."

We circle back down the stairs, and I pour us each a cup before settling at the table.

"So what's the news? I've about had my fill of surprises for the day, so I hope it's something tame."

"They're gone," he says, undoing his knot of hair and scratching at his scalp. "The skulls. Asked around at that dive I work at sometimes — one of the bartenders is chummy with a few of them. He was under the impression I was asking because I was looking to partake in something unsavory, so I went with it, and he said I'd just missed my opportunity. They'll be gone for months now — at least."

"What kind of... Unsavory something did he think you were after?"

"Drugs, Lynna," he grins. "He thought I was looking to buy."

"Oh."

"Regardless, it means you're off the hook for now. You can get back to normal — breathe a little easier."

The word prompts me to take a deep breath, and let it out slowly as I think about what he's said. Gone or not, I still worry we're not forgotten. If the scarred man were to spot either of us who knows what would happen? What will solve this for good? Time? Will he eventually grow old and die — taking his grudge with him? I know I can't get caught up in these questions, but they leave a tendril of residual dread coiled deep within me. I don't think I've seen the last of him.

☆☆☆☆☆☆ THIRTY-TWO ☆☆☆☆☆☆

"Ugh," Delia groans, pulling garment after garment off the rack. "No… No… No… *Heavens*, no."

I pick up the clothes she's tossed behind her, folding them neatly before placing them in piles. She's every bit the clotheshorse Julien described, and she'd enlisted my help in a bout of manic closet cleaning. I like spending time at her and Julien's top floor condo. Her tastes are lavish — far different than the simple earthiness of Rhys' and my home.

Her walk in closet is a midnight blue, somewhere between indigo and deepest violet, the built in wardrobes containing an incredible variety of styles all in shades of black. I'd only seen her in more casual clothing, although nothing about Delia can really be considered casual. Skirts, printed tights, glittery tanks and shiny blouses are all things she'd wear out, but for work she dressed professional, in tailored fitted slacks and silky button up shirts. Sometimes I'd catch her at home in an oversized sweater or tunic, but they were never wrinkled, and most certainly never had holes in them like mine tend to accumulate.

Julien's section is more modest — a few dressy pieces here and there, but mostly consisting of band t-shirts and workout clothing. He only has a few pairs of shoes, and they sit in a single line beneath shelves of Delia's platforms and pumps. All are painstakingly organized by shade like the clothing, the closet itself separated from the rest of their home by patterned velvet curtains the same midnight color.

The apartment itself is walled in rich black woodwork, with carefully molded wainscoting and silver sconces illuminating the equally dark ceilings. On the walls are several ornately framed paintings, antique oils of shapely women draped in fabric — hair free flowing, breasts exposed. Their kitchen is all chrome and black marble, their countertops clean and empty. The dining area consists of a small glass table and chairs in the corner, but most of the room is taken up by a long stainless sideboard, littered with books and medical supplies for Delia's home practice. Tall shelves packed with vials and bottles cover an entire wall, her collection much neater than Rhys'. In the living room are two baroque style sofas with matching chairs surrounding a circular glass coffee table. A dozen half melted candles sit atop it, wax having melted into hardened pools in a silver tray. Their gigantic black bed sits facing the floor to ceiling windows in the bedroom, the four bedpost bases carved in a complicated floral design tapering nearly to the ceiling, the headboard the same delicate motif as the adjoining posts. The sheets are an exquisite black silk, and the duvet a black and white damask trimmed with tassels. Beyond the bedroom is the closet where I now sit, watching her decide which items from her extensive collection stay, or are disposed of. I pick up a soft shirt with a ruffled collar and hold it against me. It's much too small.

"I wish I could squeeze myself into some of these," I muse as I fold it.

"It *is* a shame. It'd be fun to be the same size — share clothes — though you should really count your blessings you don't need stilts to reach things on high shelves," she laughs, nodding at the tufted stool she's balancing on. She fills her arms with more garments, and carefully steps down from her perch to survey what she'd accomplished. "There. I think that's the last of it. I feel much better having cleaned all this out. Although..." she pauses, considering. "Now all I see are empty spaces just dying to be filled with something pretty. Why don't we do a little shopping after we pack this up? We need to find you something fancy to wear anyway."

Fancy? The last time I wore anything like that was when we traveled. I smile as I recall the eyelash lace, the floating tulle, and the way he looked at me when I was wearing it.

"For what? We're not going anywhere that I'd need anything new for."

She sighs disdainfully at the tears in my leggings, the leaves tattooed on my knees peeking through the ripped fabric. "No, those won't do. Not for this weekend."

I stare blankly at her, and she laughs and sits down next to me. "The weekend? As in tomorrow? Any special date come to mind? Possibly your and Rhys' anniversary?"

Anniversary? I quickly run the months through my head. Gods, she's right. Time has a tendency to get away from me, the days and weeks melting into each other, but we'd made a full circle. It's been a year since we've become officially involved. A year since he carried me home in the rain, since he told me he loved me. I can't believe I've forgotten, and start to panic internally. If she's remembered, he certainly has.

"Shit. He's going to know I forgot."

"Perhaps not," she says. "Why don't we swing by a few shops while we're out? Maybe something will catch your eye?"

I let her take the reins, and follow her through the wet streets as we visit shop after shop. Nothing jumps out at me, and I begin to feel defeated. We have everything we need, and I don't want to give him some afterthought of a gift. I'd almost rather give him nothing than something trivial.

"Hmm... Maybe try thinking outside the box," she suggests as she leafs through a pile of high end fabric. We'd ended up in a clothing store after all. "It's possible what he'll like most isn't tangible."

I sigh heavily as I sink down onto the white bench of the too upscale store. I'm letting him down with my absentmindedness — I know I am. She chuckles when she sees my forlorn look, and drops the shirts she'd been admiring.

"Oh, just relax. You're not on trial to profess your love, here. It'll be fine."

"What do you and Julien usually do?" I ask as she seats

171

herself next to me. "I'm so far out of practice. I could use a little inspiration."

"The usual. Flowers, a little wine," she says, looking thoughtful. "I always buy a new outfit and we go out somewhere fancy. It's a bit of a tradition."

"I don't think we have any traditions yet." Nothing she's said has resonated with me. It's far too late for me to set up any sort of reservation, and I don't think a bottle of wine is going to cut it. "I feel awful. If he's got something up his sleeve it's sure to be very thoughtful, and here I am scrambling at the last minute."

"I *am* going to push for a new outfit, so don't even try to resist me, but I'm sure we can think of something otherwise," she says, her arched brows knitting. "Let's see — Rhys is the sentimental type, clearly, so perhaps you'd consider writing him something? Detailing a favorite memory?"

Could I do that? Would it be enough? I don't hate the idea, but I have no clue where to begin. He remembers things down to the last detail — what if my recollection is different? Or what if I choose one that doesn't mean as much to him as it does me?

"Has Julien done that for you? I didn't imagine him to be the poetic type."

Her smile fades a little, a sudden faraway look in her gray eyes.

"No. Julien is a bit of a softy, but he's not generally one to be grammatically inclined. I did receive a gift like that once, a long time ago. I honestly hadn't thought about it in ages until now…"

She grows quiet, and leans back against the wall. She seems mildly upset, and I'm not sure what I said to cause it.

"Did I say something wrong?"

She shakes her head slowly. "No, doll — you haven't. It's funny how things pop up when you least expect, isn't it?"

I'm confused, and she sighs. "Vincent. I know Rhys

told you a little about him. Our first year, I forgot all about it, too. The date, the anniversary. He was so excited to give me something he'd poured his heart into — a long letter detailing all the special moments we shared, and it was absolutely everything I needed. I cried because I hadn't reciprocated, but he laughed and told me he didn't care. All he wanted was me, and I was ruining it by being distraught. Thinking I'd let him down. I always regretted my forgetfulness, because I felt I didn't get the chance to properly show him what he meant to me before he was gone. I guess that's why I'm so over the top all the time. Because of one lost moment."

She pauses to sniffle, delicately patting under her eyes with the edge of her sleeve. "Sorry. I usually have great control over my emotions. It still gets to me — even after all this time."

"I don't think she's ever recovered from the loss."

Rhys' words, only partially answering my questions. I knew he died, but I never found out how. I want to invite her to tell me if she wants to, so I take her hand. The second I fold my fingers around hers she grasps them tightly, and I take that as my cue.

"Delia… What happened to him?"

She's quiet for a long moment, still squeezing my hand. Just as I'm starting to regret asking about him, she speaks.

"He was a healer too. He was brilliant and kind, and didn't care about working in a proper facility, so he went out on his own. He'd go to the most dangerous parts of the city to help anyone who needed it. The poor, the homeless, the rougher around the edges the better, since they usually didn't have the means to receive the care they needed. I admired him for it, until he got involved with a group of men. I knew they were trouble from the moment he described them — the worst kind of trouble — but he waved me off. Said they deserved help just as much as the rest of us. They always had injured among them — definitely because of the sort of activities they pursued, and… Damn it. He just wouldn't leave them be."

She clears her throat and straightens her top, blinking her tears away.

"He roped himself into caring for one of their leaders. From what he told me, he was old, and too far gone — he couldn't do much more than palliative care. He tried to explain it to them, but when the man passed… They *murdered* him." Her voice grows quiet, almost a whisper. "They left his head in an alleyway for the authorities to find. As a warning to anyone else who might cross them."

A tear had fallen onto her pant leg, and she wipes at the wet spot. She's trying to hide her pain from me, but it's palpable. It's radiating into my core. She wipes her eyes again and clears her throat.

"Vincent was like you — before. That formula was intended for him. He didn't care what I was, and I wanted to keep him as long as I could, but… It was just too risky. I decided I'd be content with whatever time we had, but it wasn't much. They took him from me. Took him and tortured him and there was nothing I could do. I don't even think they understood what they'd done. They'd ended the life of the one person who cared most about them."

My heart is racing. An intrusive thought pushes through, and I see Rhys' head left bloody in the cold wet street. Hot bile is in the back of my throat, choking me. I'm going to vomit. I drop her hand and rush out of the shop, doubling over in the entryway near the street. I never thought what happened to him would be anything like that. I'd thought an accident, or old age — never cold-blooded murder. What sort of horrible people would do that to someone who was trying to help them?

Gentle hands pull my hair away from my face, and I realize she's standing behind me. I've finished, but I don't want to face her — I'm too ashamed at how I'd reacted. She waits a few moments, then gently turns me around and hugs me to her tightly. We hold onto each other for a long time, not saying a word. How she could go on all these years with that image in her mind is beyond me, and I have renewed admiration for her strength. I don't know that I could've continued on had it been me in her place.

"I'm sorry," she says into my shoulder. "I'm sorry to have put that on you — that wasn't my intention for today."

"Delia, I —"

"No," she says, stepping back. "I should've saved that gruesome tale for another time. Now I've gone and made the whole afternoon about me, which isn't any help to you. What I meant was to explain that you don't need to worry about forgetting — Rhys won't care. He'll love you all the same, and I think that's something you already know deep down. I'm the one who made you worry you're not doing enough by dragging you all over in search of the perfect gift." She glances down at what little I'd deposited on the sidewalk. "Are you all right?"

I nod quickly. "I'm fine. Really I am. I know that must've been hard — thank you for telling me."

"You know," She smiles softly. "I told you when we met that I had a feeling we'd be great friends. I didn't realize how right I was."

We're interrupted by a salesperson cracking the door, peeking her head out to scowl at us. Delia grabs my arm and laughs as she pulls me down the street.

"Right. Come on — we need a drink, and it looks like we'll *definitely* need a new shop to go to. We're probably banned for life after that scene."

I find nothing for Rhys during the remainder of our outing. The heavy bag I'm carting home is filled with clothing I probably won't wear, but I felt I had to get everything she suggested as penance for revisiting that painful memory. I think about what she said as I make my way through the street — her tradition with Julien, and the gift from Vincent that stuck in her mind. Would Rhys prefer something tangible or intangible? A remembrance instead of a thing? A tradition of our own? What would it be?

As I'm walking, I pass a store with an open door, booming bass spilling into the street to attract attention. It's a tourist shop, and I pause to let my fingers drift across a sidewalk display of snow globes and bumper stickers bearing the city's skyline. The music is too loud for me to want to go inside, but the tempo triggers a memory, and I suddenly have an idea. He's always seemed to be emotionally driven by music, and I know he has a lot of attachment to most of his records, as they marked memorable parts of his life. The night he caught up to me in the club all I could hear was the song that was playing, vibrating through me and embedding itself into that moment. Every time I hear it I think about the look in his eyes when I'd confessed my feelings, and the shiver that rolled down my spine when he returned them. I know he'll remember it, and I'm almost certain hearing it will prompt the same response in him as it does me. Maybe it's too simple — too cheesy — but I don't care. It's what I want to give him. I have to find it.

The first store I try is closed, and I'm out of breath by the time I reach the next. I pray silently as I flip through the records — this is the media I need. We have nothing save for a stereo and a record player — I don't mind that he's set in his ways because I love them too, but it limits my options.

"Help you miss?"

It's the store attendant, a thin man in a denim vest with a handlebar mustache. He's watched me race around unsuccessfully for more than a few minutes, trying to balance the bag on my arm as I search. I tell him what I'm looking for, and he thumbs through the records in the exact spot I'd been searching.

"If it's not here, we probably don't have it," he says, and my heart sinks. I must look as disappointed as I feel, because he pauses, his mustache shifting as he regards me. "I'll check in the back anyway. Wait just a minute."

I stand next to the front counter for what feels like an eternity. Rhys is out with Julien, and I want to get home before he does — regardless of whether or not this pans out. I almost gasp aloud when the man returns, a large flat square in his hand.

"Must be your lucky day," he chuckles. "Someone special ordered this, but never picked it up. We only hold it for thirty days before it's fair game, so it's yours if you want it."

I thank him profusely as I pay him, and smile to myself as I make my way home with it tucked beneath my arm. All I have to do now is figure out how to present it. Do I do it tonight? Wait for tomorrow? My smile fades a little. Will it be enough?

I sigh with relief when I open the apartment door — his shoes and jacket are missing, which means he's not home yet. I drop the bag of new clothes by the wardrobe, and peel the plastic from the cover. Might as well try it out. Just as I'm lifting the cover of the turntable the door swings open — it's Rhys, a look of surprise on his face.

"Hello darling," he says, hastily shrugging off his jacket. "Didn't think you'd be back yet." He balls up his jacket and strides across the room, opening the door of the wardrobe and shoving it in. Odd — he always hangs it up. Just as I'm about to ask what he's doing he notices the crinkled plastic on the floor. "What have you got there?"

I was distracted by his strange behavior, and momentarily forgot what I was in the middle of. I wish I'd hidden the record, or at least disposed of the plastic. I don't know what to do besides let him in on it, since I've been caught red handed. Instead of answering, I slide the record into place, and carefully drop the needle. The second I hear the song goosebumps raise on my skin, and he pauses in the middle of the room.

We stare at each other, frozen.

I'm transported back to that night — back to the middle of the club, barefoot and trembling, my heart pounding. I can almost see the staccato flashing of the neon lights casting their pink glow on his skin, and his crooked smile starts to spread across his face. It's clear he remembers, and I know without him even saying a word that this means something to him. I'm now confident I've chosen my gift correctly. He's in front of me in a few steps, gently grasping the sides of my arms just like he did then. His hands are warm, and he's so close I can smell him, the scent of petrichor drifting into my nose. He leans forward, and I know he means to kiss me, but I stop him before his lips touch mine.

"A year ago we began our life together," I whisper, and his brows soften. "But I loved you long before that night. Every time I think of this song it puts me right back in that moment. The moment you changed everything."

He's silent, and softly caresses my cheek. He hasn't said a word — did I choose right after all? I'm starting to second guess myself.

"I didn't know what to give you for our anniversary, and this is all I —"

"Darling," he says quietly. "You've given me something wonderful. A memory, and a monumental one at that." He takes my hand and holds it to his chest, his heart racing beneath my palm. "And it was *you* who changed everything. My heart caught fire the moment you said you loved me."

I open my mouth to say it again, but he presses his lips to mine. I don't need to say it this time for him to know, and I don't need him to convince me he feels the same. We don't need any more words at all.

★★★★★★ THIRTY-THREE ★★★★★★

It's nearly afternoon and I'm still lying in bed, rain casting ever changing patterns on the linens. I'm still tired as we'd stayed up far too late, having revisited another memory from that first night. He hands me a coffee before climbing back in next to me, and I rub the rest of the sleep from my eyes. I smile as I realize we're repeating the pattern we'd formed a year ago. Will this become a tradition? If it does, I'll happily look forward to it.

"It seems your visit with Delia yesterday was most productive," he says, nodding towards the bag abandoned near the wardrobe as he shifts back against the headboard.

"Oh, those aren't hand me downs. We went to a couple shops after the purge and she insisted I try a few new looks. I didn't have the heart to say 'no' after what she told me."

I take a long sip and watch his amused expression shift to a quizzical one. My stomach turns as I remember the details, so I set the cup on the end table.

"In short, I learned what happened to Vincent."

He sits forward.

"From the look on your face, she told you all of it. A terrible thing. Are you all right? You've paled a bit."

"I just… I could feel how painful it was and still is for her. It hurts my heart to even think about." I pause, and shake my head slowly. "Then I had another one of those dark thoughts. I couldn't help but imagine if it was *you* it had happened to, and I became so upset I had to run out of the store. It was incredibly embarrassing — I got sick all over the sidewalk. I don't think I'll ever show my face there again."

"Heavens," he whispers. His expression is so severe I give a small laugh to try and lighten the mood, but he isn't persuaded. He puts his arms around me, pressing me against his chest. "I know it's not something you can control outright, but please try not to think things like that. I don't want you worried that something so horrid will befall me."

I'm thinking of it even now. It's almost like I'd absorbed Delia's sorrow, and the remnants are still lingering in my body. I sniffle as I slide my arms around his waist.

"I'm sorry. I'm just… Too sensitive, I guess. I —"

"I don't think you're too sensitive. In fact, I love that part of you," he says, and I feel the soothing vibrations of his voice through my cheek. "But empathy can be precarious to manage."

I know what he means. I'd been guilty of letting it get to me, both now and in my life before him. It worked to my benefit sometimes when it came to tattooing, that sensitivity to the experiences and emotions of others. Every line I inscribed I felt an echo of in my own body, and did my best to be gentle and understanding, easing the pain however I could. Apart from the physical pain, I often encountered a different sort, as my clients would bring the very essence of themselves along with them, evident in their moods and life stories. Sometimes it wasn't painful at all, and I'd feel excited right along with them as they shared a joyous moment, their exuberance buoying me long after they'd gone. Other times I'd feel their grief, and wipe my tears on my sleeve as they shed their own. The hurt always lingered longer than the pleasant feelings, and it was difficult to separate myself from. I'd find myself imprinted with their pain, wearing it as my own for days on end. Living their lives. What I can't do now is live Delia's.

✶ ✶ ✶ ✶ ✶ ✶ THIRTY-FOUR ✶ ✶ ✶ ✶ ✶ ✶

I manage to pull myself out of that momentary despair, and let myself relax for the majority of the afternoon until I'm met with something unexpected. Though the anniversary had begun on a more languorous note, I find myself racing around to be ready on time. He'd made plans with Julien and Delia I was previously unaware of, and from what he tells me, the meeting time Delia suggested is not at all a suggestion. I'm starting to realize her nudging me into post closet cleaning shopping was probably pre planned, though I'm not yet sure why.

He insists on taking care of the evening watering while I bathe, and when I emerge from the washroom he's nowhere to be seen, so I assume he's still finishing up. I figure I should wear one of the outfits she'd pressed me on, so I empty the bag of clothes onto the bed. I'm still unsure about one of the new articles — a dress. Apart from the more formal occasions in the expo city, I don't wear dresses, preferring leggings and a sweater, or t-shirt on the daily. This one isn't quite as fancy as the ones she'd chosen for me before — it's a gauzy tank dress in purple tinged gray. It's shorter than I'd like, the hem hitting me right above the knees, so I'm certainly going to wear something under it. I pull on the pair of ripped leathery leggings, laughing to myself as I recall her disapproval, and shove my feet into the black boots she'd bought me on our first outing.

After I've dressed I gaze at my reflection in the windows facing the harbor. I remember all the times I'd frowned at it in the scratched mirror in my old apartment. I like how I look now — the dress fits me well, and though I wouldn't have chosen it myself, Delia's gift for styling has shown through once again. I comb out my hair and brush a little mascara over my lashes, and sit on the bed to wait. When he still hasn't appeared after a few minutes I decide I should hurry him along. If we dally much longer we'll be on the verge of running behind. I climb the circular staircase, and smile as I do every time I'm greeted with that lovely humid air, but something's different.

Immediately I notice the main lights are off, replaced by the twinkling glow of thousands of tiny string lights cast across the glass rooftop. They're beautiful — like stars against the black night — and the door shuts slowly behind me as I gaze up at them. Had they been here all along and I hadn't noticed? Surely I would have — he must've done it while I was in the bath, though I'd only been about an hour. The leaves are wet, which means he's completed his task, but I see no sign of him. The greenhouse is constantly undergoing change as juvenile seedlings morph into adult plants, and the whole place is currently overflowing with foliage, obscuring my view of the aisles. I don't have to go far — I find him in the center, leaning against the moss bed and staring out into the night. He's more dressed up than he was when I left him — in that same dark button down from the restaurant night in the expo city — and my heart flutters when he turns around.

"Hello darling."

"What's all this?" I look up at the lights sparkling against the glass. "They're so beautiful — I never want them to come down."

"Oh, just a little magic," he smiles slyly, offering me his hand. When I take it he pulls me against him, and dips me rather dramatically. I can't do anything but stare up at him, surprised, and he laughs.

"Too much?"

"Absurdly over the top." He rights me, clasping my hand in his and slipping his arm around my waist. He turns us slowly, and it's my turn to laugh. "This is a close second to absurdity. What's gotten into you?"

"I dial it back quite a bit, I'll have you know," he says, grinning as he gently twirls me. "I can be *much* worse."

I groan and smile back at him. He'd made it apparent since the first week we were together that he adored dancing with me — slow dancing in particular. I never got comfortable with it, and would roll my eyes and laugh every time. He's right — he's *much* worse right now — but as sickeningly romantic as it is, I have to admit he's won me over.

"Did you orchestrate this for your amusement alone?"

He smiles softly. "Not entirely."

He stops, and I gasp when he lifts me onto the edge of the moss bed. He's picked me up here and there, but it's always surprising. The moss is dampening my dress, but I don't really care — I want to know what he's up to.

"I had a whole speech prepared," he says. "I thought that might've been a bit much though. I try to show you every day what you are to me — what this past year has meant. How elated I am to spend the rest of my life with you."

He reaches into his pocket, and my heart begins to race. What is he doing? It can't be what I think — I know I've made it very clear how I feel in that regard. Has he forgotten that conversation? It happened a long time ago, but I remember it clear as day.

***

"Well would you look at that," he says, squeezing my hand. We're walking through the misty streets en route to the harbor markets, and across the way is a crowd of people. They're surrounding a couple — the woman in a white dress, and the man in an outlandish looking top hat. "A beautiful occasion, don't you think?"

I wrinkle my nose at the woman's dress. Even though it seems most people pine to wear one for most of their young lives, I've never been of that mind. It's pretty, but not for me. The ceremony itself is a similar story.

"It always seemed unnecessary to me. All that — for what?"

"What do you mean?"

I shrug. "The customs — the whole idea of matrimony itself — it's sort of irrelevant. Do you know how many stories I have from clients who had that sort of union unravel? *Hundreds*."

"Some of the customs *are* a bit silly," he laughs. "But I like the aspect of devotional and literal exchanges for commitment's sake."

"There can be commitment without, though. Just because two people tie themselves together with a few words and bits of jewelry doesn't mean they won't abandon each other. It's a nugatory societal obligation, and what it does is it changes people — for the worse, more often than not."

"Mmm," he says. "I suppose you have a point, though it's a bit of a cynical one."

"Maybe, but it's how I feel. Have I offended you?"

"No," he says.

The look on his face is telling me otherwise, and my heart sinks. Is that something he wants? To be married? I love him — desperately — but I don't know that it's something I can agree on. It changes everything from what I've seen, and I don't want anything about us to change. Ever. He's grown quiet, and I scramble to think of something to say.

"Rhys, I want to spend my life with you, but things are going so well already, aren't they? Why risk ruining it?"

He smiles, draping his arm over my shoulder. "Well then, spend our lives together we shall."

"Promise?"

"Ooh — that's *awfully* close to a vow, my darling," he laughs, kissing me on the cheek. "But of course. It's a promise."

***

He'd never brought it up again, and I thought I'd been successful at not so subtly conveying my bottom line. When it comes down to being officially wed, my answer was and still is a very firm 'never'. Surely he remembers. Surely he knows me by now.

I suck in my breath when he removes his closed fist

from his pocket. He takes my hand, and I'm suddenly terrified to look at him.

"Lynna," he says quietly. "I never thought I'd find anything like this — anyone like you. I've lived a long time, and I want nothing more in the world than to be with you for the rest of it."

I swallow hard when he uncurls my fingers to place a small item in the palm of my hand, warm from his pocket. I shift my eyes to it — a shining oval of the darkest green with scarlet streaked through it, set in simple white gold. It's not a diamond, but it's still a ring. What do I say? He seems to notice my obvious apprehension, and I watch him chew the edge of his lip as my mind reels. Is he about to ask the question? Will he leave me if I decline? Would he really make me choose? An expression I don't recognize flashes across his face, but it's gone before I can register what it means. He clears his throat quietly.

"It's a bloodstone," he says. "All it's meant to be is a tangible reminder of how much it means that you're here — that you've chosen me, and our life together. To remind you that my heart and my blood are yours. I'd give them both to you a thousand times over."

I exhale audibly. He's not proposing — it's just a gift. An extraordinarily meaningful one, and I'm glad for what it represents and also what it doesn't.

"Gods," I sigh. "For a moment I thought you were —"

"Not quite," he laughs softly, plucking the ring from my palm. "May I?"

I hold out my hand to let him slip it onto my finger, new happiness causing it to tremble now rather than fear. He knows me after all, and I wish I'd never questioned him. I'm overcome, so I grasp his shirt in my fist and press my lips against his. I feel him smiling, and I am too.

"I'll never doubt you again. Thank you — this is beautiful. I love it, and I love you."

"Happy anniversary, darling," he laughs, kissing me again. "Here's to a hundred million more. Now let's go — we're already late."

✱ ✱ ✱ ✱ ✱ ✱ THIRTY-FIVE ✱ ✱ ✱ ✱ ✱ ✱

The night is surprisingly warm, and the rains have stopped their heavy downpour, enshrouding the city in a fine mist. The diaphanous glow of the streetlights through the fog only adds to the magic of the evening, and it's moments like these that remind me why I love the city so much. Most people tend to gravitate towards the unclouded brilliance of fair weather. I, however, have grown to feel most at home in ethereal grayness. It feels mysterious and enchanting — every rainy noir scene speckled with shimmering lights evokes a haunting sentiment, as if the universe is waiting to whisper its secrets to me. I sort of want to wander around in it for a while, but we have somewhere to be.

When we reach the intersection that connects to our usual watering hole, the red bar, he leads me in the opposite direction.

"Aren't we meeting Delia and Julien?"

"We are," he says, sidestepping a puddle. "But we're going to a new bar that just opened. She mentioned she's got a surprise in store, which I admit I'm most curious about."

A surprise? I'm curious now, too. "Whatever it is, I hope it's nothing too grand."

"Well, it's Cordelia," he laughs. "Would you expect anything less?"

We arrive at a tall building, and it's deserted and completely devoid of furnishings, save for a simple sign instructing those who enter to take the elevator to the very top. When the elevator door opens, we both pause.

The entire room is completely enclosed in glass. Cement columns ascend to meet the transparent roof, and the space is dimly lit, giving it the appearance that the whole floor is floating in the air amidst the fog. Metal tables litter the room, candles in mercury glass vessels on each. Several of the windows are actually doors, leading onto a balcony that appears to circle the entire building. Electro Pop music pulses from speakers strategically embedded in the columns. I smile as Rhys grasps my hand, pleased Delia's picked this place. I love the atmosphere.

I see no sign of her or Julien, and just as I'm about to suggest we sit at the bar to wait, a man in a tie greets us and directs us to follow him. We wind through the furniture in the direction of the balcony, which is covered in an almost invisible glass awning. In the corner is a large U-shaped sectional on which sit Julien and Delia, as well as several others I don't recognize. The low concrete table nestled into the sectional has a round cutout in the center, and as I get closer I realize it contains a fire, small orange flames licking at the sides. Lined on the edge is a row of foil topped bottles and stemmed glasses. What keeps pulling my attention is the view — the corner directly overlooks the misty harbor, a chasm of light glowing far below the colossal structures jutting out of the fog.

"*There* you are," Delia stands, and as she moves to intercept us I take note of the newcomers. Julien is engaged in conversation with a man in a wild patterned green shirt, his mass of orange hair twisted on top of his head much like Julien's. Next to him is a woman with short blonde hair in a black lace babydoll dress, peering over at us from behind a pair of gold rimmed glasses. The third is standing to greet us — a dark haired man with bright blue eyes, in a navy suit with a long dark coat over it. He grins widely, and Rhys stops in his tracks.

"Dimitri! You're back!"

He passes right by Delia to the man, who immediately gives him a solid hug. I remember him mentioning that name — this is the traveling friend. Who are the others?

"Well, hello to you, too," Delia half laughs as she watches their exchange. "What do you think, doll? The place sounded too good to be true, so I had to see for myself."

"The view is absolutely mesmerizing. Uhm… Who are —"

"Oh, right," she shakes her head. "It was sort of unexpected how this came together — I found out our friend Sergio was in town, and Dimitri only just returned last night. They both wanted to meet you, so I invited them to join us. Is it too much?"

I would've preferred a quiet evening with just us four, but maybe this is better. I haven't met anyone besides Julien and Delia who are well acquainted with Rhys.

"No, not at all."

"Good." She looks relieved. "Come sit — I've ordered heaps of champagne. I want to introduce you to Sergio first and… Kiera, I think her name is? I can't believe he's up and married — I never knew him to be the type."

Sergio is pleasant and amiable, though very loud — he almost shouts when he talks. His white teeth flash beneath his red mustache as he greets me, and I smile shyly. He's extremely charismatic. He refers to the blonde woman as his wife, and she smiles warmly when I shake her hand, though she says nothing. I'm overwhelmed, and don't say much myself. There's a lot going on — Sergio and Julien talking over each other, Delia interrupting them both. Rhys and Dimitri are standing off to the side, engaged in their own jovial exchange. I sit primly on the chaise, and Sergio turns his attention to me.

"Bit much for you, eh?" He laughs. "I'd blame Delia — she knows what happens when I'm invited to a get together. All hell breaks loose!"

His eyes are kind, and his easy smile relaxes me enough to find my voice. "How long are you in town for?"

"Day or two at most," he says. "We're just passing through — came up to look at a potential property, but it was a bust. Not worth sinking any time into."

"Are you a realtor?"

"Depends on the day," he chuckles. "I have many hats

— *most* of them legitimate — but that's all very hush hush, you know? Mostly I'm accredited as an investor — hotels, restaurants, you name it."

I'm not sure if he's actually answered my question, but he's entertaining enough to speak to. "That's very interesting. How do you know everyone?"

"Used to own a bar they liked — back east. *Pre* Delia." He elbows Julien. "You and Rhys used to pop in on the regular to get soused — remember? I ended up joining in on far too many occasions. Ha! It was a time, for sure. Mostly it was Rhys and I trying to keep him from brawling with anyone who gave him the side eye."

"Oh come on," Julien laughs, his nose in his drink. "That's not accurate. I don't recall instigating a damn thing. What do you think, Rhys?"

"I'm siding with Sergio on this one," Rhys says, sitting down next to me. "Darling, might I pull you away? I'd like you to meet Dimitri."

Dimitri shrugs off his coat, and I inspect him more closely as he drapes it over the seat cushion. His eyes are a striking shade of blue, and he has an intense look about him even though he's smiling warmly. His dark hair is combed neatly behind his ears, and his face is freshly shaven, the shadow from the fire accenting the chiseled line of his jaw. He leans forward, and when I take his hand he surprises me by kissing the top. It's a formality I wasn't expecting.

"A pleasure," he says. "How enchanting to meet the one who finally caught Rhys' attention. I would have dared say his only love was books, but I am delighted to see he has found such a charming match."

I'm bemused by his greeting, and Rhys is a bit red in the face.

"Tell me," Dimitri says. "How did you meet?"

Rhys clears his throat. "In a bar. Trite, I know, but there was much more to it than that."

As they're talking I focus on Dimitri. His voice is low and deep, his enunciations drawn out. As he speaks I notice the skin on his neck just above the front of his unbuttoned collar — it looks textured, as if it's deeply scarred. Is it just the shadow from the fire? I'm not sure, and I don't want him to think I'm staring. I decide to take a break from all the conversation to let them carry on their own, and walk to the edge of the balcony. I rest my elbow on the high concrete wall so I feel more grounded as I peer over the edge. The fog hasn't subsided, the buildings still veiled in mist. As I'm looking out over the city, the awareness of exactly how high up we are dawns on me, and an intrusive thought makes its way to the foreground.

Jump.

It's that small quiet voice again. I gasp and step back from the wall just as Delia appears at my side.

"You all right, doll?" She asks, clamping a cigarette between her teeth. She offers me one, and I take it, still reeling from the image of my body plummeting to the concrete below.

"Yeah — just a bit dizzying looking down."

"I might advise against it, then," she laughs. Her smile turns to a frown as she fails to light the cigarette on the first match, but after a brief struggle with the second, she succeeds. She exhales a cloud into the night, and leans on the wall. "I must say — the reunion seems to have taken the night off course. That may have been an error on my part."

"Everyone seems like they're enjoying themselves, don't they?"

"Yes, but the whole *purpose* of this gathering was to sort of… *Celebrate*… The two of you. You know, since it's a special date and all."

I shrug and tap my cigarette so the ash goes over the wall. Her eyes suddenly go wide, and she grabs my wrist, pulling it towards her to inspect the ring.

"Lynna! What on earth… Were you not going to tell me?!"

"Oh — I honestly forgot. It's beautiful, right? He gave it to me just before we left."

I catch his eye when I nod to him, and he stands when he notices me showing her the new adornment.

"I can't believe you didn't announce this first thing!" she says, tilting my hand so the stone reflects the light. "No matter — it gives me the chance to congratulate you one on one."

"Congratulate me?" Is that what she thinks this is? "Delia, it's not *that* sort of ring, it's —"

"Just an anniversary gift," Rhys interrupts. "So? What do you think? Have I done well?"

Delia's brows lift. She smiles, but it seems oddly forced. "Of course you have — it's absolutely beautiful. I'll direct my congratulations at *you*, then — for being capable of choosing a nice piece of jewelry."

"Thank you," he laughs softly. "Now — Dimitri has been very inquisitive in regard to your past as a tattooist, my darling. I'm not about to pretend I know the first thing about it, save for being on the receiving end. Are you up for being interrogated?"

I nod, and he steers me back towards the sectional. I seat myself near Dimitri, and I'm suddenly distracted by the idea of discussing my past. It had been on my mind more frequently lately, and I'd begun to worry I'd abandoned it prematurely. I love spending my time tending to the plants and the apothecary, but my desire for it is still there.

"Tell me," Dimitri says, shifting closer. "What inspired you to pick up such an interesting career? Were you always an artist?"

I search my mind. Sometimes it's hard to remember things from way back, probably because I've lived so long.

"I think I always was. I filled notebooks with sketches, and ruined hardbacks by doodling in the margins. I was taught tattooing by an old man — I remember being completely infatuated with the permanence of his illustrations. It was like nothing else would fulfill me. I had to learn what he knew."

"Fascinating," he says, staring at me intensely as he rests his chin on his fist. Inquisitive barely scrapes the surface — he's much more interested than I imagined. "What was it like? His teaching?"

I explain in depth the rigorous apprenticeship period — more than a year's worth of training before I even touched skin with a needle. The old man was a curmudgeon to say the least, and Dimitri nods sympathetically as I admit to shedding tears on the daily — his way of toughening me up to face the world was by way of belittling me at every turn. It worked though. In the end, the constant criticism improved me for the better. As soft as I am now, I never would have made it very far had he not broken me down to show me the cruel nature of reality, and what it took to really commit to something.

"Dedication is an admirable trait to instill," he nods. "Where is he now? Your mentor?"

I hadn't thought about him this much in a long time, and sadness tugs at my heart when I picture his weathered face. As gruff as he was, he had a soft spot for me, and treated me like his own daughter on occasion. I cared for him, and I wanted to make him proud, but he never got to see it. He died shortly after I left, and I felt partially responsible, as if I were the sole thing that kept him going. My guilt for abandoning it resurfaces. What would he say if he could see me now? Would he be proud of me for what I accomplished, having been in the trade longer than he had? Would he berate me for letting it go so easily?

"Long gone, just like everything else," I sigh. "Honestly… It's strange to talk about it as a past venture even now. I thought I'd be doing it until I reached the grave, but life had other things in store."

"Rhys has told me what happened to you — I am very sorry," Dimitri says, a solemn expression shadowing his face. "I, too, have watched my life go to pieces, and I can empathize with your particular loss."

He smiles quickly and laces his fingers together.

"Have you considered reclaiming it — your trade? It is

clear that it still means a great deal to you. It seems a shame you should abandon it if it is not truly in your heart to do so."

I smooth the hem of the dress over my legs, considering his question. It does still mean a lot to me. I miss every facet of it, but the interpersonal aspect might be top of the list. The fulfillment that comes from watching a person's face light up when what I've drawn is exactly what they want. Feeling their radiance as they admire their new tattoo in the mirror. So much of my joy is derived from empowering others in their own skin, and without it I feel less than.

"If I can figure out a way to make it happen… I think I'd really like to. It's part of who I am."

I quickly glance at Rhys to gauge his reaction, and notice the corners of his mouth pulled into a small smile. He threads his fingers through mine, and I realize he's not shocked by my admission at all. He knew, didn't he? He always knew I'd want it back. I recall all the times he'd delicately offered to help me start over, and hadn't pressed me further when I expressed my disinterest. He's not upset by me wanting more — quite the opposite. He was waiting for me to be ready on my own instead of pushing me.

"Marvelous," Dimitri smiles. "I look forward to seeing your work — especially now that I have the time available. I am sure Rhys will provide you with the support you need for this endeavor?"

"Of course," Rhys says, squeezing my hand.

"On that note," Dimitri says, reaching forward to pick up his glass. "A toast, if I may — to friends reunited, to *new* friends, and to Rhys and Lynna. May you find only happiness in each other."

I'm simultaneously moved and embarrassed by his display. I dislike being the center of attention. I try to smile as my face reddens, reminding myself to be grateful. I'm lucky to have friends at all, let alone friends like these — all of them wishing for our happiness.

Finally the spotlight is off me, and I watch them interact for the next hour or so. Rhys and Delia laughing at something Dimitri's said, Julien and Sergio chiming in. Delia and Rhys smoking too many cigarettes, Julien spilling a full bottle of champagne on the table. Kiera doesn't say much other than thank you when her glass is refilled, and just as I'm wondering if I should approach her to try to include her more she yawns, and Sergio echoes it. He rises and begins collecting their coats, and Julien scoffs.

"Leaving already? Come on — it's early!"

"Afraid so, lad," Sergio laughs, and Kiera smiles shyly. "We've got an early day tomorrow. Always something cooking, am I right? Well then, let's not let years go by with our only correspondence being by post!"

"I am afraid I must follow suit," Dimitri says as he gets to his feet. "But I will see you again very soon — likely I will be far more present than you wish."

"You'd better," Delia says pointedly. "We have a lot to catch up on. You've been gone over a year!"

"Indeed," he smiles. "Goodnight my friends."

After they're gone I feel a little worn out myself, and we retire for the evening after I'm unable to stifle my own yawns. Hilariously enough, once we're home and in bed I'm more awake than I'd been at the fancy bar. I can't help but wonder what it will be like having Dimitri around more. I love the closeness the four of us share, and both hearing them speak about him and seeing them with him leads me to believe I'll grow to like him just as much. I like him already for instigating a discussion that allowed me to broach something I'd been nervous about.

"Did you really mean it?" I ask as Rhys fits himself beneath the sheets. "About letting me pursue tattooing again?"

"I'd never describe it like that," he says. "I'm not about to 'let' you do anything — I'm here to support you, not control you."

"I appreciate that. I guess I'm just a little surprised you'd be willing to embark on this with me."

"Are you really in that much disbelief?" He laughs, leaning on his elbow. "It was unfair how you were tossed out of it, and I always knew it was in the back of your mind. I told you I'd help you take up whatever you wished if it would make you happy, so why wouldn't I be on board?"

I sigh. "It's… It might be a dreadful undertaking, though. I'd be starting from scratch, and I've never had to before — not to this extent. I can't even begin to figure out what to do first — not only do I have nothing, I don't have a place to even do it if I did. Before I'd just fit myself in to gaps in other people's studios, and I got really lucky the last time with the one I took over, but there's nothing like that here. I don't want you to have to take that on."

"Darling, I'm happy to take it on. I'd give you the *world* if you wanted it," he says, lifting his arm to invite me to come closer. "And if it'll put a smile on your face, I just might throw in the heavens."

He sighs contentedly when I snuggle against him, but I feel sudden unease. I didn't want to put this on him — I hadn't from the beginning, which is partially why I avoided thinking about it. I can't regain what I'd lost on my own, and guilt begins to rise up when I think about all he'll need to do to help me. Should I even entertain the idea at all? I'd already been a great weight for him to carry, and I don't want to add more. I want to resume what I love — almost desperately — but all I'm having are second thoughts.

✱ ✱ ✱ ✱ ✱ ✱ THIRTY-SIX ✱ ✱ ✱ ✱ ✱ ✱

The rains are heavier than ever lately, and I'm regretting my decision to accompany Julien on a new path. The trail that traverses the slopes to the west of the city feels like quicksand, sucking my feet in with every step. It doesn't help that the rain has washed a good bit of the hillside away, resulting in a landslide here and there, which means we have to avoid the occasional drop-off in addition to the mud. It's a difficult slog, and we're both soaked to the bone.

"*Shit*," I mutter. My foot is stuck, and there's a sucking sensation as I free it.

"You good?" He calls back.

"Yeah. Mud almost took my shoe clean off."

He slows until he's next to me, and I'm grateful for his patience as I begin moving slowly.

"What'd you think of meeting everyone the other night?" He asks. I realize he's trying to distract me. It's obvious I'm struggling, and sometimes talking about anything other than what I'm doing will allow me to move through it more easily. It helps; recalling the details of the night nearly a week ago efficiently takes my mind off how tired I am.

"It was… Unexpected, but I enjoyed it. Dimitri seems nice — very formal. Was he around a lot before he left?"

"Here and there," he says. "He does that often — disappears for a while then circles back. He's much closer with Delia and Rhys than he is with me. He and I don't have all that much in common. He's very… How do I put it… *Scholarly*, and that's not exactly something I'm into."

I got that impression from him, and it worries me to think about. Will he not like me once he finds out I haven't been formally educated? He seemed interested enough when I talked about my former occupation, but what if I end up not pursuing it? Would he think less of me? Would it create a domino effect, causing *all* of them to think less of me? I flash back to Morgan's words and smirking face. Would it truly only be a matter of time before they realize I don't fit in?

"You all right?" Julien asks, breaking me out of my inward spiral. "Do you want to slow a bit?"

"No, no — I'm fine." I try to shake the disparaging thoughts away, and focus on something else. "Your friend Sergio seemed interesting. And Kiera didn't say much at all, did she?"

"No — I got the sense that that wasn't really her scene," he says, wiping the rain from his eyes. "But it's definitely his, so I'm curious what the attraction is there. He was never one to want to settle down, so I think we were all surprised."

I nearly trip over my lace and he stops with me so I can pull it tighter.

"From the sound of things, you were all much wilder at one point. I can hardly imagine Rhys being anything other than the way he is now."

"Oh, he's the same as he's always been," he says as we continue along. "The only thing different between then and now was that he tasked himself with keeping me out of trouble, which I'm sure he's relieved not to have to do these days. Poor fellow ended up with more than one shiner after I'd roped him into a fight."

"That's surprising — you've always seemed pretty level to me. I can hardly imagine you picking fights just for the hell of it."

"Used to have some anger issues — I know how to channel it better now. Delia keeps me in line too, for the most part. Let's turn around," he instructs, so we about face.

"You know," I puff. "No one's ever told me. How did you and Rhys meet?"

"That's a tale if there ever was one," he laughs. "There was a point in time where I was making a living as a fighter — boxing, mostly. It was all pretty straightforward, but the organization of some of those fights started getting sketchy toward the end of that career. My last fight was dirty — guy had a blade in his fist, and it caught me upside the face." He points to the scar on the lower part of his cheek — he's answered two of my questions in one, as I could never bring myself to inquire about it. "Would you believe who was in the bar next door? I showed up covered in blood with a gaping wound and everyone scattered — except him. He knew exactly what to do, and took me to where he lived to sew me up. Didn't even want anything in return. We became friends that very day."

"Case of the right place and right time, it seems."

"And then some. We got along so effortlessly from the word 'go'. Sort of changed my life, meeting him. I ended up leaving with him when he moved towns, and we've spent a fair amount of our lives together. A rare one, he is, as I'm sure you already know. I've never had a friend quite like him. Even the handful of times we were apart for a few months or so we always picked right back up where we left off, like no time had passed at all."

"Funny," I laugh. "He said the exact same thing about —"

I'm suddenly falling, the hillside crumbling beneath my feet. I scramble to grab hold of something, but it's all slippery mud, and I drop with the earth and rocks until I crash at the bottom of the hill. A splintering pain shoots through my leg as mud covers my body in heavy waves. I hear Julien yelling my name but I can't get my breath to respond. Am I going to suffocate? I struggle against the dirt as the landslide subsides, and see a blurry form skidding down the hill. Everything's muffled, and it's hard to focus.

"Lynna! Can you hear me?"

"Julien…"

"You're okay, you'll be okay — I've got you." He grunts as he pulls me from underneath the soil, and I see red as pain shoots through my leg. He gingerly sets me on the slope.

"Tell me what hurts."

"This whole… Side…" I'm breathless, the edges of my vision blurring. "But my leg… Hurts bad…"

"I should never have taken you up here with the rains like this. *Fuck*. Rhys is going to skin me alive."

He picks me up carefully, my arm slung around his neck, and we slowly ascend the hillside back to the path. I'm glad he's strong — there's no way I'd be able to walk by myself. It's going to be a long road back as it is — every step he takes sends lightning streaks of agony through me, and we're still a good two miles out.

＊＊＊＊＊＊ *THIRTY-SEVEN* ＊＊＊＊＊＊

I shift cautiously, trying to move as little as possible. I'm in bed propped up by pillows, having just woken up from a nap. The medicine Rhys had given me made me incredibly drowsy. I scrunch up my face in preparation to wiggle my toes, breathing a sigh of relief when the excruciating pain doesn't return. I gingerly rotate my arm, but it feels normal — luckily it had only been badly bruised and not broken. I readjust the pillow to sit up more, as the aching in my ribs has also subsided. I sit for a moment, enjoying the fact that no part of me is currently throbbing, and realize how quiet it is. I notice Rhys hunched over the table with his head resting on his arms, asleep. It's no wonder he's out cold. When Julien and I returned we made quite a scene — him cradling me in his arms, both of us dripping mud all over. Rhys had gotten to his feet so quickly he almost upended the table.

***

"What the *fuck* happened?! Bed — lay her on the bed!"

"Landslide," Julien says. "It's her leg, mostly. She fell pretty far and I think she landed on it."

Julien carefully sets me on the bed, and I hear a drawer slam before Rhys is at my side, cutting the length of my pants with a pair of scissors. I feel his gentle hands on my shin, and groan with pain when he palpates it. I don't want to squirm, but it's impossible not to when he presses down.

"It's broken," he says. "Feels like a simple tibial fracture — it'll need to be immobilized. Where else hurts?"

"My arm… And my ribs." I'm nearly gasping. The throbbing in my leg has me out of breath.

He inspects the rest of my body, though nothing is in as bad a shape as my shin. It's hard to concentrate, but as I watch him cross the room to the desk I notice his tightly clenched jaw. His voice had been calm, but his face says something different. Is he angry with me? With Julien? With *both* of us? He returns and begins clearing the mud from my leg, and I have to grit my teeth each time he touches me.

"I don't have a proper splint on hand, so this will have to do for now," he says. "Darling, I'm sorry. This is going to hurt, but it'll be over quickly. Julien, can you keep her in place?"

Julien sits down behind me, wrapping me securely in his big arms. I find out why this is necessary almost immediately — I want to stay still while Rhys tightly wraps my shin, but another wave of red pain floods my body, nauseating me and making me writhe against Julien's grasp. Rhys instructs me to drink a powder he's mixed into a glass of water, and I nearly gag at its bitterness, but manage to swallow the majority of the medicine. My whole body throbs as I sink back against the headboard, exhausted. I can hear them from across the room, Rhys' voice an angry whisper.

"What the devil were you doing all the way up there with the weather like this?! You *know* those hillsides are unstable! She's lucky all she sustained is a broken bone — it could've been far worse!"

"I know that — I'm sorry. I never —"

"She'll be off it for *weeks*," Rhys interrupts. It's clearly Julien he's angry with. "And that's *if* I can get it to set correctly. Oh, and she can forget about *walking* let alone running for the foreseeable future!"

"Like I said — I'm sorry. It was an accident."

It's quiet for a moment, then I hear footsteps and the door open and close, meaning Julien's gone. I wanted to thank him for pulling me out of the landslide and carrying me that long way, but it'll have to wait. Rhys begins helping me out of my mud caked clothes, and I try to speak — try to tell him it wasn't Julien's fault — but he shushes me gently. He doesn't even need to. The grogginess is taking hold, and I feel myself slipping into medicine induced sleep.

***

"Darling, you're awake!"

He's heard me stir, and sits down carefully so as not to jolt my leg. I peer disdainfully at the muddied linens on the floor.

"The least of your worries," he half laughs. "It'll wash out. How are you feeling? If you're still in a lot of pain I can give you more of that medicine. Gods, you gave me a good scare — I can't stand to see you hurt like that."

I realize I haven't felt any pain at all since I'd woken up. Am I still feeling the after effects from the medicine he'd given me earlier? I can't be — I'd rarely taken anything for pain throughout the course of my life, and when I did I could definitely tell when it was present.

"Rhys, it… Doesn't really hurt anymore. In fact, it doesn't hurt at all."

He eyes me skeptically. After a moment he pulls back the blanket and inspects my shin, watching my face as he presses here and there. I shake my head — it doesn't even make me wince, let alone writhe or scream. Strange. He pauses, then unwraps the splint and inspects the now faint bruise on my shin, barely visible at all through the tattoos.

"You're sure?" He asks. "I'd say it was the medicine, but that's had to have worn off by now. This should hurt just as much as it did a few hours ago."

"There's nothing." I flex my foot with ease. "Nothing more than a dull ache. All I feel is pressure from your hand."

He presses harder — then harder still, his brows knitting. "Gods. The bone… It… There's no fluctuation. It appears to be completely knitted. This can't be so…"

He lifts the hem of my shirt to examine my bruised ribs. The purple marks are gone, and they feel fine to me.

"Nothing here, either?" He asks, gently palpating my ribcage. It tickles more than anything, and I giggle.

"No," I laugh. "Stop that."

He returns to my leg, mumbling to himself as he manipulates it. Finally he sits back, chin in hand, his eyes wide.

"You've *healed* them… A broken bone… In almost no time at all…"

He's gone from sullen exhaustion to beaming excitement, but I'm not sure I'm fully grasping the situation. How is my leg healed already? He'd said that couldn't happen.

"It worked…" he says, standing and pacing next to the bed. "I can't fucking believe it. It *worked*. When we changed you… You not only survived, you absorbed the full capacity to heal. It's unheard of!"

"But… I thought you said it was impossible?"

"It is — it *was*," he says, pausing to bite the corner of his lip. "I don't… I'm not certain of the exact reason. I made a few slight alterations to the formula, but I never expected…" He shakes his head. "It doesn't matter how. What matters is that the evidence is clear — it happened."

I should probably be more excited to know I can heal like they can, but when my bone had broken it had hurt just as much as it would've even if I couldn't. I should be counting this apparent gift as a blessing, but it doesn't seem like I'll be spared any suffering because of it.

"Well Julien should be happy when he finds out. He was really concerned. I think he feels like it's his fault — or at least, you made him believe that."

He stops his pacing, and scratches behind his ear.

"I did — I should apologize. I still wish he hadn't taken you up there with the weather like this, but if you'd been on your own you might still be buried under that hillside." He sits down on the edge of the bed, shaking his head as he continues staring at my leg. "I dare say you might be up and about as early as tomorrow. I still can't wrap my head around it."

"Tomorrow? If it's fine why can't I get up now?"

"I'd really prefer you don't walk on it immediately — just to be on the safe side."

What I'd prefer is to ignore his instruction. There's dirt in my scalp and behind my ears, and what I want most is to wash it out.

"I really don't want to stay in this bed like this. I feel very… Gritty."

"I'll draw you a bath then. Stay here." He smiles, and disappears into the washroom. I sling my legs over the edge of the bed once he's out of sight — so far so good. I'm almost on my feet when he returns, but he slips his forearm behind my knees and picks me up instead of helping me walk.

"Not yet, my darling — please. Just stay off it a bit longer. I've got you."

★ ★ ★ ★ ★ ★ THIRTY-EIGHT ★ ★ ★ ★ ★ ★

The umbrella has a bent spoke, and water dribbles on us as we wind our way through the weekend markets by the harbor. It had barely been a day since my leg was broken, but the only evidence remaining is a slight limp, and I'm hopeful that'll be gone soon as well. I'd been a terrible patient, walking about frequently despite his protests — so much so that at one point he jokingly threatened to tie me to the bed. I'd begrudgingly relented and remained supine overnight, and come morning he'd been satisfied with the ease of my mobility, enough to agree to let me accompany him to the apothecary.

The little bell tinkles as the red door swings open, and the man with the glasses smiles up at us from his chair. I'd come to know him as Zep, a sweet small mouse of a man with a long braided beard that smelled of licorice and pipe tobacco. As Rhys unpacks the bag he's brought, I meander down the aisles, much like I used to before.

The shop smells heavenly, every corner a different sensory experience. There's sweet mint and lemongrass amongst the tea blends, containers of dried eucalyptus and chamomile on the shelf below. Colorful canisters of turmeric next to jars of loose soft lavender, crisp paper packets of medicinal powders, tiny vials of extracted oils. I let my fingers graze a row of consecutively numbered elixirs, feeling a small sense of accomplishment — many of these I'd put together myself. Funny how things turned out — I used to daydream about living in a place like this, smelling the lovely fragrances day in and day out. Now I have a hand in the entire process.

I hear Rhys and Zep chatting, Zep's raggedy chuckle drifting into the aisles along with a hint of pipe tobacco. When I round the last corner Rhys is folding up the empty bag, and Zep has disappeared — probably into the storeroom to put away the new stock.

"Ready to go?" I ask.

"One last thing," he smiles. "Follow me."

I trail behind him to a narrow door on the west wall — a closet, I always assumed — and he pauses in front of it. He produces a key from his pocket, elevating my curiosity. What's inside, and why is it locked? When he swings it open it's not a closet at all — it leads to the sister building adjoined to the apothecary. The layout is a mirror image, though it's empty save for a few cardboard boxes stacked in the corner, and there are no shelves closing it in. Dust swirls in the air, and it smells of must and pine and motor grease. The front windows are covered in crookedly taped brown paper, and the floor is layered with bits of sawdust and several sizes of footprints from whoever had been here last. I make a face as I brush away a cobweb. The ceiling is covered with them, their dusty loops hanging like forgotten chandeliers.

"What is this place? Been empty a while, hasn't it?"

"A couple years," he says. "It used to be a hardware shop, run by a rather grouchy old man and his two sons. After he died, the sons seemed to lose interest and closed it. They've decided to pull up their roots, and offered me first choice on the sale before they make it public."

I swipe my finger on a dusty shelf. "Are you considering buying it then?"

"I already have," he grins, leaning against the papered window. "And I thought I'd let you decide what to do with it."

"Me? Why would I decide? Expanding the apothecary is sort of *your* call, but I think it's a nice space for it."

"It could be an extension of the storefront, surely, but I was thinking it could be… Yours."

Mine? Why would it be mine? I glance around the room, and it dawns on me what he means. Tattooing. It would be perfect for a studio. I'm immediately excited, but it quickly turns to apprehension. I assumed when he said he'd support me that he meant it more in the ways of encouragement — not that he'd buy me a place to work. How can I accept this?

"Have I misread you?" He asks, his smile fading. "If this isn't up to par, we can find somewhere else, or —"

"No, it's ideal, I just… I thought I might rent something, so I'm not really prepared for this. It'll take me a long time to repay you, and —"

"Repay me?" He interrupts, shaking his head. "Absolutely not. I want you to have this if it'll make you happy."

He bought this place just for me, didn't he? I know I should feel grateful — and I do — but I also feel guilt. Guilt for having to lean on him after the loss of my last studio, and guilt for not being able to subsidize this on my own. He'd already given me so much and I'd barely reciprocated. What if it fails — what then? Will he resent me? Will it become clear I wasn't worth the effort? I can't let him do this.

"It's such an enormous gesture, Rhys. I don't even know that it'll be successful."

His grayed brows raise softly, and he treads around a pile of sawdust to take my hands.

"My intention wasn't to pressure you whatsoever — that's the last thing I want." He's searching my face, and I hate that I've caused the concerned look on his. He chews the edge of his lip for a moment before squeezing my hands. "I was… I purchased it a while ago because it's a solid investment, and I had the idea only recently that you might like to make something here. Please — I don't want you to worry. Should you have a change of heart, I'll simply expand the business."

I'm relieved — he didn't buy it just for me. My apprehension begins to ease when I realize what he's offering might be a way I can put more into our partnership. If it goes to plan, I'll be able to contribute far more evenly, and repay him for everything he's done for me whether he wants me to or not.

"You don't have to decide this very minute," he says. "I thought I'd show it to you and —"

I don't need more time to decide, and I want to see that

smile on his face again. I grasp the lapels of his jacket and kiss him forcefully.

"Darling," he laughs, hugging me close. "I do love that so many of your answers contain no words at all."

I'm still reeling from the morning's surprise after we arrive home, but it's not long before I'm met with another, in the form of both Julien and Delia at our door.

"How is she? I would've come sooner but I was working an overnight," she says, brusquely pushing past Rhys. She does look like she's come straight from the hospital — she's still wearing her name badge, and it throws me every time I see it since it doesn't read her name. She stops dead in her tracks when she sees me take a few steps. "You're… Walking? *Already?*"

She looks me over, both her and Julien sharing a look of disbelief. I'm not sure which one of them is more shocked. She looks to Rhys, confused.

"She healed it," he says, nodding.

"You're sure?" She frowns. "You're absolutely sure? It wasn't just a sprain or a… A bruise?"

He smiles. "I couldn't believe it, either."

I watch her face change from skepticism to the same beaming excitement Rhys had exhibited when he realized what had happened. None of it seems as illogical to me as it does them, though — maybe because I'm starting to accept bizarre circumstances as normal.

"Is it really that unheard of? I mean, wouldn't it make sense given what you've changed in me?"

"Lynna," she says. "I don't know how to make you understand. It's rare to survive the transition in any regard, so to take on this capability in addition makes this a unique situation all around. It's… *Incredible*."

"Pretty wild," Julien says, moving around Delia to fold me into his big arms. "But all I care about is that you're all right."

"Thank you — for bringing me home. I might be taking a short break from running for a bit, if you'll excuse the pun."

"Take all the time you need," he laughs softly.

Delia asks to inspect my leg herself, so I sit on the bed and let her prod at it. I hear Julien and Rhys whispering quietly in the kitchen, then laughter. I know Rhys felt bad for blaming Julien for my misfortune, and I didn't think Julien would hold it against him, but it's nice to hear them behave like they usually do.

Both Delia and Julien advocate for a celebration once she's satisfied with the state of my bone, and as Rhys opens a bottle the conversation shifts when he makes a new announcement. The idea for a studio next to the apothecary. Immediately Delia's eyes light up — she's much more excited about it than I thought she'd be.

"Have you thought about aesthetics yet? Wall colors? A theme? What sort of atmosphere are you trying to create?"

"I've no idea," I half laugh. "This only just happened, and there's far more to consider before diving into the interiors."

She raises an eyebrow as she lights a cigarette. "Interiors are crucial. You can't work out of a dusty old box, you've got to make it *inviting*."

"Well, I know that, but what I'm concerned about is the actual act of tattooing now that I've had some time to think about it. I'm more than a little rusty. I've taken breaks before, but never this long, and I can't help but wonder if I'll have forgotten everything."

"Not to worry, doll," she says, smoke curling from her lips. "I'm sure it'll feel like you never left it. You just have to get back into a groove."

I hope she's right, since it's been gnawing at me ever since the decision had been made. Will my body remember what to do like it had before? Is my muscle memory still there, in hibernation? What will I do if it isn't?

✶ ✶ ✶ ✶ ✶ ✶ THIRTY-NINE ✶ ✶ ✶ ✶ ✶ ✶

Julien answers the door when I arrive. He's in his track pants but he isn't sweaty yet, which means he's about to head out on a run. I'm wistful — I'd like to go with him, but I'm not quite ready even though my gait has returned to normal.

"Hi!" He grins. "I'm about to pop out for a bit, but Delia's in the other room with Dimitri. Coffee's on if you want."

Delia's curled in a chair, and Dimitri's on the couch, looking very smart in a crisp shirt and matching blazer. He looks more like he's about to give a lecture at a university instead of relaxing casually on a weekday morning.

"Hello doll," she says. "Wonderful timing — Dimitri's only just arrived himself. Come sit."

Dimitri stands to greet me, and once again takes my hand to kiss the top.

"Lovely to see you again, Lynna. Where is your counterpart?"

"At home. He was in the middle of something and I was bumbling around making too much noise so he suggested I might have a walk. I figured I'd come see what Julien was doing — I never expected to find you both here."

"I do get a day off once in a while," Delia laughs. "And sometimes I like to use that time to lounge around and do nothing. How are you feeling? You're not limping at all, which I'm happy to see."

"Good as new. It's still a lot to comprehend — one moment we're in such a bad way and the next it's like nothing happened. I don't know if I'll ever get used to it."

Dimitri looks confused, and leans forward to pick up his coffee.

"What do you mean by this? I am afraid I do not follow."

"She's recently recovered from a broken bone," Delia answers for me. "The speed at which she healed it took us all by surprise."

"Have you never received an injury before?" He chuckles. "It is difficult for me to believe you have gone your entire life without."

"No — I have, but I haven't experienced recovery quite like this."

"She's not used to any of it," Delia says. "The transition was one thing, but —"

"Transition?" He interrupts, his dark brows raising. "Do you mean to say she has undergone this recently? How?"

He sets his cup down, his blue eyes fixed on me. It's uncomfortable — I feel like I'm under an inspection of sorts, and I kind of hate being spoken about as if I'm not even in the room.

"More recently," she says. "Though it's been the better part of a year. I never thought I'd have cause to use that formula, but it proved worth the time we spent on it after all."

Dimitri looks more perplexed than ever. "What? You… Completed what we started? You made it very clear that your intention was to abandon it — for good."

"It wasn't planned, it was very much an emergency. The formula was still unfinished — just as we'd left it — and Rhys and I had to scramble to put the remaining pieces together in a rush. Trust me — I was just as hesitant about it as I'd been long ago."

He sits silently, rubbing his stubbly chin with his thumb and forefinger as he processes what she's said. I wasn't aware they'd partnered on it — I assumed it was hers alone because of what I knew of her intentions for it.

"The injury you sustained," he says. "How long until you healed?"

"Completely? Hours, though I did have a limp for a little while. Rhys thought it might be a psychosomatic response since it didn't hurt at all, and after he explained it it sort of went away."

He scoffs. "A broken leg. You managed to heal a broken leg in a matter of hours?"

"Believe it or not, she did," Delia says, and his face changes at the seriousness of her tone. Did he think we were joking before?

"Impossible. It has never been done. To assume that capability would make her one of a kind."

"She's always been one of a kind," Delia says, winking playfully at me. "But it's certain now."

Dimitri exhales audibly through his nose. "I suppose congratulations are in order, Cordelia. You have achieved what I was not granted the opportunity for. Not only have you completed the project — essentially my life's work, at one point — you have also managed to improve it. What are your plans for it now?"

"I don't plan to do *anything* with it," she says, pulling a cigarette from her case on the table. "It was a one time thing, and we got lucky — *incredibly* lucky. The risk of performing a procedure like that... Well, you're aware of how unpredictable it can be, so I don't need to reiterate. What matters is that she survived an impossible thing, and I'll accept the one small victory for what it is and leave it at that."

"Others have survived — she is not alone," he says. "She is simply the only one to assume this particular capability."

"*One* other," she frowns. "Only one survived using this method — that I've witnessed — and I'm sure you remember how *that* turned out in the end. Alternative cases are still few and far between, and have even *lower* statistics of survival than direct blood transference." She pauses, shaking her head. "Those other methods are lengthy, not to mention brutal."

I realize she's talking about Julien. Brutal was definitely a word that came to mind when he described his experience to me. Dimitri sits forward.

"This formula is... Clearly unique. It would be a shame to not test this further."

"We've already done the legwork on this. It's not something to use haphazardly. I don't see the point to it."

He folds his arms over his chest. "Abandoning it a second time would be absurd. A complete waste of so much dedication and research."

"I can't even guarantee the formula alone is responsible for the success," she says, and he looks at her questioningly. "I have a theory. She was taking Aeonia for years beforehand, and if you recall, the other survivor had been using it prior to his experience. What we don't have is any research on the effects of the formula and Aeonia used in tandem because there is none, but it feels like too much of a coincidence not to come into play."

All of this is news to me. Did the Aeonia have something to do with it? Both of them are frowning, and I'm bracing myself for them to continue their exchange. I can't tell if they're having a friendly discussion or if the conversation is taking a turn.

"You were using Aeonia?" He asks. "How does one like you come to be in the possession of a rarity like that?"

I shrug. "I didn't know what it was. The man who sold it to me said it would help me with pain I was having so I could continue to work."

"Interesting," he says, tenting his fingers beneath his chin. "And why did you agree to submit to this… Experiment? Did they explain the importance of it to you?"

"Dimitri, she had no idea," Delia says. "She didn't learn what had been done until well after the fact."

"Nonsense," he says, his brows furrowing. "I know Rhys — he would never implement such a formula on an unaware individual. He made that known in the past."

"This wasn't one of those situations. Lynna was near death — he only suggested we try it in an attempt to save her. I was against it at first — I thought she should make the decision herself, since I'm of the same mind as he when it comes to that, but he was desperate. I'm glad he pushed me to do it anyway. In the end it was the right call to make."

"So it was his idea," he says. "He was the one to finish it?"

"It took both of us to navigate the remaining calculations, but he did the bulk of the work. Why does it matter?"

He stares at me for a long moment, and just as I'm starting to wonder what it is he's thinking his cloudy expression vanishes. "I suppose it does not. What matters is that it has succeeded," he smiles. "Well, Lynna, it seems you were destined for something marvelous when you met him. It is an extraordinary thing that has happened to you."

"I'm just glad it's over," I sigh, and he laughs softly.

"I am sure it was far from pleasant. You must tell me of your experience sometime, but for now let us talk of something else."

I sit with them for a good while longer, drinking coffee after coffee. As morning turns to afternoon, I find I have less and less to contribute to the visit. They talk of Delia's work at the hospital, and discuss various remedies Dimitri had come across in his travels. From what I can gather he's spent time as a healer as well, though he often refers to his years spent in a research library. They cease talking to me at all after becoming engrossed in a discussion that's way over my head, so I decide to leave them to it and return home.

"That was a rather long walk," Rhys says when I close the door, pausing to kick off my shoes. "I didn't mean to chase you out for the whole day."

"I got caught up. I went to see Julien, but Dimitri and Delia were there, and we ended up talking for a while. They got into some long winded thing I couldn't follow so I figured it was time I came back."

"Yes," he laughs. "They tend to do that. It can be difficult to get a word in once they get going."

"He seemed taken aback when he found out I'd been

changed." I sit down at the table, and he moves his papers out of my way. "I had no idea he was part of it — the formula."

"Indeed he was," he says, tapping a cigarette on the table before pressing it between his lips. "He was the one to encourage Delia to pursue it in the first place. He knew her before I did — he was friends with Vincent, and I think that's what spurred the interest in teaming up to put so much into the formula."

He knew him? I had no idea about that either. What else don't I know? "Well, it's no wonder they're close, having shared a loss like that."

He nods. "A terrible thing."

"How did *you* meet Dimitri? Through Delia?"

"Dimitri was actually the one to introduce me to Delia. I'd met him on my own — we spent some time in academics together. It was because of our common ground that we ended up forming a partnership. We had a little practice for a short while, years and years back."

I'm intrigued. "Really? What sort of practice?"

"Well, we were both interested in developing medicine, and it worked as a combined effort since he was more interested in the patient side and I preferred to lean heavy on research and creation. That isn't to say he's not gifted in that area — he had many of his own projects he was pursuing in addition to fronting the business. I always thought he should focus on that. His bedside manner leaves something to be desired at times."

"Why is it you stopped working together? Did you have to move after so many years?"

"Not exactly," he says, his face falling a little. "We had a few... Differences in opinion, and it began to cause turmoil. He's very driven when it comes to his work, but he'd often skip steps and seemed to occasionally disregard the well being of the patient. There was an incident at one point with a patient who nearly died as a result of his neglect, and he was rather unapologetic when I confronted him. I spent a fair amount of time smoothing things over when patients returned with complications he hadn't bothered warning them about, and decided I didn't want to go on working with him. It was destroying our friendship."

I'm a little surprised. Given Dimitri's demeanor and what I know of his background, I can't picture him behaving carelessly, especially not to the extent that it would cause Rhys to back out of a partnership.

"Clearly you've salvaged that relationship. You speak so highly of each other, and from what I've seen you get along well now."

"I owe him a great deal," he sighs. "I caused him a lot of unpleasantness, and though I've worked hard to make it up to him I'm not sure I ever will."

Unpleasantness? "What do you mean?"

"There's… Something you should know. Something I should confess," he says. His expression is drawn, and it confuses me further. Is this yet another secret? What is he hiding now?

"Our practice," he says. "It was on the first floor of a little house. The second floor was where our lab space was, and the third where we lived. The night I told him I wanted to end the partnership we got into a nasty argument. I definitely said a few harsh things, and so did he. He stormed off and I went to bed, figuring we'd finish hashing it out after we both had time to cool down. I awoke in the middle of the night to the room filling with smoke and ran down to the lab only to find it engulfed in flames."

He pauses to stub out the cigarette, then immediately picks up another. He stares down at it before continuing.

"I couldn't get it under control. We were in grave danger of the whole place going up given some of the substances we kept. The door was jammed, so I had no choice other than run back upstairs to use the fire escape. The third floor entrance had locked behind me, and when I got it open I found him trying to pry apart one of the windowsills. It was an old building, and they were

216

painted shut — in hindsight that was something we probably should've fixed but thought nothing of it until then. We couldn't get it open, and all he said to me was that he knew I'd done it on purpose. I tried to explain that I would never do such a thing, but I didn't get many words out. We could barely breathe, so he shoved me through the window."

"Wait, he… *Pushed* you? From a third story *window*?!"

"He saved my life," he says, finally lighting the cigarette. "He meant to follow, but before he could the place went up. If we'd have waited a moment longer we both might not have survived. He did, so perhaps we would've, but who knows."

"I too have watched my life go to pieces. I can empathize with your particular loss."

When Dimitri said that to me I never imagined he meant in the exact same fashion. I sink into the back of the chair in disbelief. "I don't understand how either of you survived it. Gods — his skin. He was burned, wasn't he?"

"He was — quite badly," he says. "He barely managed to get out at all, and though I had a number of broken bones it seemed nothing in comparison to what he suffered because of me."

"But you didn't set the fire — how could it have been your fault?"

He bites his lip. "That's the thing. It *was* my fault. I can be absentminded at times, and was much more so then — occasionally he'd give me an earful for leaving a burner on in the lab. I was *sure* I'd been careful, but I wasn't thinking clearly that night — I went to bed angry. After we recovered I begged him to believe me, that I'd never sabotage him like that. He reminded me of my forgetfulness, and that it had to have been a forgotten open flame that caused it. He was right — I know it was me, and I ruined everything for him. He not only lost his practice and years of documented research, he was also disfigured and nearly killed."

I realize I'd pressed my hand to my mouth as I was listening and try to dissolve the shocked look on my face when I see how guilty he clearly feels. To me it was simply an accident — a terrible one, but an accident nonetheless — but to him it's something different. Dimitri had forgiven him, but it's apparent he hasn't forgiven himself. Quietly I round the table to circle my arms around him, and he sighs heavily.

"How Dimitri's managed to forgive me I'll never know, but I won't ever stop trying to atone for it," he says, resting his head on his fist. "You must be incredibly disappointed in me."

I'm not sure what to say. He'd just shared something difficult — something that had greatly impacted his life — and I feel closer to him than ever before. He'd been vulnerable, freely admitting his error, and had reminded me that we're the same. Capable of mistakes. I'd made too many of my own in my life, and I'm not at all disappointed in him, though I don't know how to properly convey it without making light of what appears to be a heavy memory.

"It was an accident," I whisper softly. He leans against me when I squeeze him tighter. "I can't tell you how to feel about it, all I can do is point out that he *has* forgiven you, and you should consider forgiving yourself."

"Mmm," he says. "Easier said than done."

✶✶✶✶✶✶ FORTY ✶✶✶✶✶✶

Something shifted the day he told me what happened between him and Dimitri. Their dynamic is different to me now that I know what I do, but it's not obvious in how they interact. Dimitri appears frequently, just as promised, but he's always pleasant and courteous. Nothing in his mannerisms tells me he's resentful, and he never once dredges up the past. He and Rhys seem to genuinely enjoy each other's company, and I like seeing the two of them laughing as they share wine over the kitchen counter, or talking quietly as they huddle over one of the books at the desk. I still find myself worrying I don't have anything vital to add to the conversations, but Dimitri is never dismissive, so instead of dwelling on it I throw myself into my own project. The studio.

There's a lot to do. The space hadn't been cared for in years, and though I have hours of cleaning ahead of me I don't dread it. I'd always enjoyed readying a space, envisioning how I might organize it as I went, and this one's a clean slate. On one afternoon I'm just starting to remove the cobwebs from the ceiling when there's a gentle knock on the window. I can't see who it is since the brown paper is taped up, but there's a mass of dark hair peeking through a gap.

"Hello Lynna," Dimitri says when I swing the door open. "Rhys mentioned you were here, so I thought I might look in on your venture. Have I arrived at an inopportune moment?"

"Not at all. Beware the sawdust — I'm doing some cleaning. It's not much yet."

He surveys the empty room and nods. "It is a marvelous space. All it requires is a bit more... Atmosphere."

"Delia made a big deal about that," I laugh. "She's demanded to be included in the decorating, but I have a lot to do before then."

"Of course she has," he smiles, placing his hands on his hips as he inspects a dusty shelf. "She has always had a good eye. I have allowed her to add her touch to a few of my residences in the past."

"Did you invite it, or did she bulldoze you into it?" I joke, and he laughs.

"Perhaps a little of both." He removes his long coat, revealing a neatly pressed shirt beneath a dark vest, a silvery chain hanging from one of his pockets. "Now then, would you care for some assistance? I am happy to lend a hand."

His outfit looks expensive, and I wince when he sets his coat on the floor. I haven't even been here an hour and I'm covered in sawdust, so there's no way he's escaping this unscathed. "Dimitri I appreciate it but you don't have to. You'll absolutely ruin your clothes."

"Nonsense," he says, already rolling up his sleeves. "Clothing can be laundered."

I can't help but notice his forearms as he folds his shirtsleeves. They're marred by red patterns, and I quickly avert my eyes. I don't know how he feels about the scarring, and I don't want to be rude by staring. I wonder briefly how it must have felt to experience those terrible burns, and can only imagine how Rhys feels every time he sees them.

I try to give Dimitri some of the lighter cleaning, but he's determined to work right alongside me, and plunges into the task with vigor. Together we begin clearing the place of cobwebs, laughing when they stick to our hair. Hearing him laugh puts me more at ease. I'd been nervous since he showed up — just like I'd been the first time I'd gone out with Delia, and that time I'd intercepted Julien on a jog. So far he's surpassing my expectations, and I hope I'm living up to his.

"You've been traveling a while haven't you?" I ask. "Been anywhere interesting?"

"I have visited plenty of places," he says, dutifully running the dust cloth down the corner of the wall. "I travel to work, as I find it easier than settling in one place — I am sure you understand the reason." He brushes his hands off before moving to the next corner. "However, most of my time is spent indoors. I do not often seize the opportunity for sightseeing."

"Right. I'm sure it keeps you busy." I feel awkward. Why had I asked him such a generic question? I have to do better. "So… Rhys said he met you during your schooling. Was that for you to become a healer?"

"I am a great many things besides a healer. Rhys and I share similar credentials, which is how we came to befriend one another. Aside from my practice, I enjoy expanding my knowledge however I am able. Unfortunately, there are too many things to be learned and not enough time."

I'm once again feeling guilty about my own lack of education. Does he think less of me for it? Should I just be honest? "You know… Discovering the extent of what the two of you have amassed academically makes me feel like I've wasted my life. I have nothing to show for it, and even less to add when it comes to your discussions."

"You have much to add," he smiles. "I found your trade particularly interesting, and it is something I am unfamiliar with. Diversity is important — can you imagine how boring the world would be if we were all the same?"

I shrug. "I guess you have a point."

"That being said, it appears you and I share a similar curiosity for education after all. Rhys tells me you have come a long way with horticulture in a short time. It is a difficult subject, and takes much dedication. I am impressed."

"Oh, don't be." I know he's probably just being nice saying that, but I hope it's genuine. I'm starting to realize how much I *want* to impress him. "All it means is that I can keep a few plants alive and memorized a few of their proper names. Just don't ask me to pronounce them, lest I change your view. I've embarrassed myself in front of Delia more than once by doing that."

He laughs, and stoops to start cleaning a low shelf. "I am certain Cordelia finds you charming. How has she been faring? I have been absent for far too long. I do not like leaving her alone with her troubles."

Troubles? In my eyes Delia had only ever been a force to be reckoned with. The only time I'd even remotely seen her emotions get the better of her was the day she told me about Vincent. I suddenly remember what Rhys had told me about their shared ties with him, and realize that must be what he means.

"She seems fine enough. I know it was hard for her to... Well... I know what they did for me brought up some feelings for her. About Vincent."

"Mmm," he says, nodding. I can't place his expression. Maybe it's difficult for him to talk about.

"Dimitri, I'm sorry. I heard you were close with him."

"He was like a brother to me. It is a loss I feel in my bones to this day." He stands slowly, brushing sawdust from his pants. "But what is to be done? One cannot continue to live in the past. I have encouraged her to move on from it, just as I have."

I'm marveling at his apparent ability to move on from all things devastating rather than dwell on them. As he straightens his sleeves my eyes shift to the scars on his arms, and he notices before I can avert my gaze. My cheeks flush with embarrassment and I scramble for an apology.

"I really don't mean to stare — I'm deeply sorry. Rhys told me about... Your practice. I didn't know when we met that you had your livelihood burn up like mine had…"

He stares at me, his blue eyes unflinching. Did I say the wrong thing?

"Another thing we have in common," he says, placing his hand on my shoulder. "Though it is most unfortunate."

He's standing very close, and I can smell his aftershave. It's woodsy, like an evergreen thicket, with a tinge of something else. Amber, maybe? He's a little shorter than Rhys, but I still have to look up at him, and he's broader, more muscular. I can tell just by the sensation of his wide hand on my shoulder that his grasp is strong, but it's gentle now. I know he means to comfort me with this gesture, but the second he touched me my body stiffened on instinct, and I can't seem to relax.

"It is devastating," he says. "To work tirelessly at something and have it snatched from your grasp. To long for it when it is gone, and have it remain just out of reach. I believe you may know the feeling I speak of."

I do know the feeling, but his words have spurred a question I'm afraid to ask. I'm suddenly scared. What if his answer isn't the one I'm hoping for?

"You don't... Resent him... For what happened, do you?"

He smiles faintly. "Our bond is stronger than you might think. Even at my angriest — when I believed he had done it intentionally — I still saved his life. I know he was and still is incapable of such a drastic measure."

Relief edges out my unease. Why was I so concerned he might secretly hate Rhys all of a sudden? Am I just projecting my own anxiety onto the situation after hearing Rhys' side of it? I must be, since it's clear they're on good terms. It's still that Dimitri had forgiven him, and all that remains is his occasional struggle with his guilt. He pats me on the shoulder, so I return his smile.

"My experience was different from yours though. Those men who destroyed what little I had — they did it with malice. It was no accident."

"True," he says. "But I have taken what I can from my experience, and you must take from yours. It can only make you stronger — more patient, more willing to do whatever it takes to recover what you have rightfully earned. I am finding my way back, albeit slowly, and I am confident you will as well."

I sigh as I lean against the now clean shelves. "*One* of us is confident. It's been so long. I'm worried I won't be able to do what was once the only thing I knew. The only thing that mattered."

"You doubt yourself?" He flashes a sideways smile. "From what Rhys has told me of your drawings you are indeed talented. Do not be discouraged by what has been lost. You still retain the most important part of this — in here." He points to his temple. "No one can take that from you. You must simply remember what to do with it."

His words are more than encouraging. He's reminding me that though I'd lost everything I haven't lost what I know. It'll be hard to replace some of the tangible things, but he's right — I have a good start, and in my heart I know it's still there. He's definitely a new inspiration for me. If he can rebuild his practice I can most certainly rebuild mine.

We finish the shelves and move on to the grimy baseboards. He's incredibly considerate — I know I could lift the heavy bucket of soapy water, but he won't let me carry it, and moves it slowly around the room as we continue.

"Do you mind if I ask of your experience?" He asks, dropping a fresh bucket of water beside me. "What it was like for you after your transition? It is a rarity to observe, and I am curious."

"It was… Strange more than anything. They were so worried I wouldn't come through it at all and what might happen after, but I guess I have a hard time grasping why because I don't really understand it." I rinse my cloth, wringing it out in the bucket. "Physically I felt fine, and it completely restored me. My body was all but falling apart before, but I was like new again. Mentally it left me… A tad unstable. It was rough for a while, but I think I'm mostly better."

"Cordelia and I," he says. "We witnessed a procedure similar to yours many years ago. The survivor had a host of issues afterward — instability of the mind being one of them. He did not take to it as you have." He shifts to his knees as we continue scrubbing. "Would you mind elaborating? How did you feel?"

I don't like describing that time. It conjures up everything all over again, but I feel like I can trust him. I don't think he'll judge me, or call me crazy, so I tell him everything. The visions, the dissociating, the violent mood swings. He listens intently, nodding grimly when I confess the fear I'd felt after learning what happened to the man he'd seen changed. I don't want to talk about him anymore, so I shift back to the awe I felt from finding out what Rhys had done to save me. He moves to empty the bucket of dirty water, the baseboards clean.

"It is fascinating," he says, shaking his head slowly as he pours it into the utility sink. "Truly a thing to behold, this. And to think — the entire process was finalized and executed in part by an individual who had never seen it before."

"Obviously you understand what went into it more than I do, but it's still miraculous. He's brilliant, isn't he?"

"Brilliant is an understatement. He wastes his talents on those simple remedies he peddles."

I have to agree with him, but I'd never say that to Rhys. I know he loves what he does.

"What was he like — when you met? When I picture that time all I can see is the two of you at a desk with your heads bent over books. Him talking too much, you shushing him so you can work."

"An accurate description," he grins. "He is very much the same now as then — soft hearted, talkative. Less adventurous, given his choice in occupation. Appearance wise, he has more tattoos now, in addition to being much more gray."

I can't help but smile. "I love all those things about him. It's nice to hear he's been like that all along."

"It seems he has become different in one way," he says. "He was only dedicated to his work before, whereas now he has shifted that dedication to another. How surprised I was to return and find him with you. He never showed interest in anyone until now — I believe you may be the most important part of his life. Why, I am caused to think he would do anything for you."

I'm blushing again. "He's said that once or twice."

"Well now," he says, nodding as he surveys the room, the space having been cleansed in half the time with his assistance. "I believe you are ready for the next step. I look forward to seeing it come to life."

"I really appreciate your help. Thank you for that."

"My pleasure," he smiles as he does up the buttons at his wrists. "I enjoyed it. Immensely."

He doesn't let me put away the cleaning supplies on my own, and insists on walking me home after. I like him much more than I thought I would. Despite his formal ways, he's kind and considerate, and I'm grateful he's put in the effort to get to know me. I hope I get a chance to return the favor.

★★★★★★ FORTY-ONE ★★★★★★

I knew Delia was opinionated about clothing, but she proved much worse when it came to decorating. I wanted her to be present since I like having her input, but her tastes aren't mine. I declined her vision of a baroque style parlor as delicately as I could, shaking my head at yards of velvet fabric and ornate wallpaper. This is the first studio that will really be mine from the ground up, and I want it to look the part. My spaces before all bore the mark of whomever owned it — even the one that burned. I want this to reflect the elements I love about the home I share with Rhys, all our things earthy, comfortable, and unfussy. She frowned at the two gray chairs I'd picked up with the intention of using them for a small waiting area, lamenting the leather ones she'd wanted to buy.

***

"I'm really not sure about these," she says, running her index finger over a hole in the upholstery. "They look a bit worn in."

I'd disclosed that I'd salvaged them from a business undergoing a remodel, but I didn't tell her I'd found them in a dumpster. The chairs most definitely reflect me — they're a little rough around the edges, but they'll do their job just fine.

"It's just a tear — I can patch it."

"The quality of your stitching isn't the issue here," she laughs, abandoning the chair to hold the door for Rhys. He's carrying in the last of the potted plants we'd brought down from the greenhouse. Mostly ferns with new growth, the spiraling fiddleheads uncurling into soft tendrils. "It's the fact that you have to stitch them at all. Are you *sure* you wouldn't rather have those gorgeous armchairs I —"

"Quite sure," I laugh, and she rolls her eyes.

***

Despite her derogatory comments about my choice in furniture, she seemed to like the studio's appeal well enough. The walls and shelves are a matte black, mirroring the apothecary, complemented by the chairs and planters, all in varying shades of gray. It's fairly dark, but the lighting is good, and the green plants surrounding the windows add plenty of vibrancy. I think I've done well — both Rhys and Delia offered to purchase anything I might want beyond the necessities, but I had a strict budget in mind. That and I didn't feel comfortable amassing expensive new things when I knew I could find perfectly fine used ones for almost nothing. Besides the chairs, I'd scoured the local resale shops and found a beautiful set of framed botanical prints, and stacks of worn hardbacks for reference material — both for a steal. Dimitri offered me one of the folding medical tables he'd used in his travels, and I'd been delighted to find an old cabinet that would be perfect for a workbench in the back room. With a slight amount of refurbishing, it looks like new again.

Everything had come together easily, apart from one very important thing. The suppliers I'd used before are still in business and I'm able to get most of what I need, but only most. I still have no machines, and I'm out of places to find them. I'd thought that since the equipment to run them was available they would be too, but I hit roadblock after roadblock. The times had changed without me, and I hadn't paid much attention to it as I'd never needed anything more than what I had already. The machines I'd lost in the fire had been given to me by my mentor at the start of my career, and I'd simply replaced the parts that had worn out over time instead of the entire apparatus. I don't want any of the newer models available — I want what I know, and I'm only becoming more frustrated.

"No luck?" Rhys asks, shaking the rain from his jacket before hanging it up.

I'm sitting in the same spot at the table I'd been in when he stepped out, but I'd been more determined then. Now I'm forlornly resting my head on my arm, a scratched out list of potential avenues in front of me. I'd gone down to the bar to use the phone as a last ditch attempt to track down anyone I used to know from past studios who might be able to help, but no one could. Those I did reach didn't even remember my name. That's what happens when you don't let anyone get to know you — they forget you ever existed.

"No," I sigh, pushing the list across the table. He sits down across from me, mirroring my pose.

"Do they really not make what you're after any longer?"

"The problem isn't that they're obsolete, it's just that they're not the standard anymore. Everything evolves whether or not you decide to participate, but I don't know that I want to start over with something I'm unfamiliar with. I happen to be very particular about what I like."

"Something I understand very well," he says, smiling gently. "Although reluctance to change with the times can often make one's life more difficult, it's a matter of preference. As long as the end result is what you're after, it doesn't really matter how you get there."

"Exactly, but it's leaving me at an impasse currently. I don't know what to do. I can't even find the parts to put one together from scratch."

He watches me huff and sigh, chewing the edge of his lip like he does when he's rolling an idea around in his head.

"Darling," he says, sitting up to pull his cigarettes from his pocket. "What would you need to be able to construct it?"

"Why? Do you have some sort of solution?"

"Possibly," he smiles. "I'd be happy to utilize any connections I have to find what you're after, but I'm completely in the dark when it comes to the components."

I pause for a moment, then drag the list back across the table and flip it over. Illustrating what I'm looking for is probably the best way to communicate what's in my head.

"It's complicated," I explain as I begin to sketch. "It's the frames that are the true obstacle — the measurements have to be precise."

He moves his chair closer as he watches, and for a while the only sounds in the apartment are the scratching of pencil on paper and rain tapping the skylight. When I've finished I push it towards him. On the paper are diagrams for two machines from two different views to show how the steel would need to be angled, and a long list of parts — all with specific lengths and gauges. Iron cylinders, a long coil of copper wire, a thin sheet of tempered steel, washers, screws. I don't list the tools needed to put it all together — I know he has them already. I watch his eyes move over the page, the corners of his mouth tilted in a small smile. I tap the pencil on one end.

"Does that make sense? Am I making an impossible request?"

"This should suffice," he laughs softly, running his finger along the edge of my sketch. When he looks up I notice a certain twinkle in his eyes. The same one that appeared every night he'd watch me draw at the bar, and I have to laugh. It's a look I now know well.

"I never thought you'd be this enchanted by a hastily sketched diagram."

His crooked smile grows wider, and my heart flutters a little. "I'm mesmerized by everything that pours from your fingertips," he says. "I've been fascinated from the start. I admit it's… Incredibly stimulating to watch."

"Why? It's just pictures — far from any of your carefully calculated equations."

"Because," he says, placing his hand over mine. "Those 'pictures' are a reflection of *you* — how you view the world. You know how to make an image come to life through shape and color, whereas I see things differently. My view is mostly analytical — all numbers and overcomplicated wording."

I shrug. "It's a skill anyone can learn. Some are more naturally inclined as I am, but it can be taught."

"I'm aware of that," he says. "But I imagine when it comes to visual interpretation each individual's perspective is different from the next, and I quite prefer yours. I remember watching you pinpoint the very essence of your subject matter, turning them into more than just lines on a page — into something one can almost... *feel*. I'd recognize your work anywhere, and I'll always think it beautiful and interesting." He taps the diagram. "Even a list of mechanical pieces."

I rest my chin on my fist as I consider what he's said. His explanation has me blushing — I hadn't realized he thought that of my artwork, and I hadn't ever really dissected it before. To me it's always been more than just translating something line for line, but my interpretation does appear to be centered on touch, since I can't help but imagine how things will feel against my skin. Wispy fern tips and lush petals that tickle, thick serrated leaves and thorns that catch. Delicate striations and fragile stems requiring gentleness. It's more than just flowers, and for a moment I think about the feverish night I sketched him, tracing the line of his jaw and wondering what it would be like to feel in reality. I no longer need to use my imagination — I know what he feels like, and it's better than anything my brain could conjure up.

There's a tingling sensation in my fingertips, static coursing between his hand and mine, and I have the sudden need to experience it again. The look in his eyes has changed, and it's telling me we're on the same page.

Without a word he pulls me into his lap, letting his lips brush mine before kissing me. It's not ever difficult to identify the details of his particular touch and why I love them. The softness of his thin lips, the spiky hairs on his cheek against my palm, the sensation of his scratchy neck as he moves to plant small kisses on the side of mine. The strength in his arms when he picks me up to carry me to our bed, the scent of petrichor on his skin. The radiant heat from his hands as they move over my body — pulling me closer, grasping me tighter. That electric hum between us is the one thing I can't pinpoint, but I love its presence nonetheless.

"Is this the sort of distraction I'm to expect when I start sketching on the daily?" I joke as I pull the sheet up around me. "If so, I might not get much work done."

He chuckles, turning to rest on his elbow. "Mmm — I believe I'm only half responsible here, but I'll try not to initiate *too* many distractions in the future. I might find it incredibly difficult, so I can't make any promises."

"I'm only joking. I'd never demand such a promise." I roll to face him, running my fingers over the soft skin of his stomach. He shivers in response and pulls me so close our lips are nearly touching.

"Do that again, my darling, and I'll make you any promise you like."

✶✶✶✶✶✶ FORTY-TWO ✶✶✶✶✶✶

It's pouring rain, and we're both a half hour late and nearly soaked by the time we burst through the door of the red bar. It's one of our regular nights out, but it'll no longer be just the four of us. Dimitri is supposed to join in, but when we approach the booth he's nowhere to be seen. I feel a little less bad for running behind even though it wasn't my fault. Rhys had lost track of the time.

"Sorry we're late. It's *really* coming down out there," Rhys says as he helps me out of my dripping jacket before removing his own. Julien shakes his head, a half smirk on his face.

"You do know they make this apparatus… Oh, what's it called?" He laughs, jokingly scratching his head. "Ah — that's it! An umbrella! Have you heard of this miraculous invention? They're incredibly useful."

Rhys laughs, and Delia rolls her eyes. "They're only useful if you actually *have* one, and we don't either because you lost the last five I bought!"

"But *we* didn't use a rain delay as an excuse for being late," Julien grins. "Do you think Dimitri's going to have a better one? Where is he anyway? He's usually fairly punctual — and better prepared."

Just as the words leave his mouth the heavy door swings inward and Dimitri ducks in, looking every bit as sodden as we do. I'm watching Julien gear up for another sarcastic comment, but Dimitri speaks before he can let one fly.

"Apologies for my tardiness," he says, slicking back his damp hair. "I did not mean to keep you waiting. Perhaps I could make up for it by purchasing the first bottle?"

"Now *that's* how you apologize for being late," Julien laughs, raising an eyebrow at Rhys. "Thanks — we'll get this one. You go on and settle in. Rhys?"

They head to the bar while Dimitri removes his dark coat, and I know it's mostly so they can down a few shots before returning with our drinks. Dimitri smooths his pant legs and sits at the end, adjusting the cuffs of his crisp white shirt beneath his suit jacket. The sleeves ride up when he crosses his arms, revealing the scars marring his skin. Briefly an image of him trapped in a fiery blaze flashes through my mind, and I have to blink to dislodge it. He scratches at his freshly shaven cheek, and the gold watch adorning his wrist glints in the dim light.

"May I?" He asks, gesturing towards Delia's silver cigarette case. She smirks and slides it towards him.

"Funny," she says as he clamps one between his teeth. "It used to be *me* bumming them from *you* all the time."

He smiles and shifts his eyes to me. "Do not listen to her. I usually abstain, but our Cordelia here is… How shall I say… A bad influence."

"Hardly," Delia laughs. "You got me started in the first place! I didn't smoke at all before we became friends."

I find that hard to believe, and it's my turn to laugh as Julien and Rhys return.

The wine is poured and the night ensues, and I like having Dimitri among us. He laughs at Rhys' bad jokes, and chuckles along with Delia as they recall anecdotes from their shared history. He makes it a point to include me in the conversation, and I appreciate him all the more for it. He definitely paid attention to my comment about feeling inept.

"Cordelia tells me your studio is nearly complete," he says, reaching over to top off my glass. "She mentioned that you did not heed her decorating advice. You are *quite* the rebel."

"Oh, come on," Delia groans. "Make me sound like a bully, why don't you. I think she did a marvelous job of it anyway — save for those awful chairs."

"Hey," I laugh. "I like those chairs!"

"I have to admit I like them, too," Rhys adds, slipping his arm around me.

"Yes, you're lucky you don't butt heads about that sort of thing," she smiles, elbowing Julien, and he scoffs.

"Be real — I don't put up a fuss. Whatever makes you happy makes me happy," he says.

"It seems you are all quite lucky in that regard," Dimitri says, watching Delia lean against Julien. "And my hope is that I will be as well. I have a bit of news to share, and it pertains to the reason I was delayed tonight."

There's a pause as we wait for him to continue, and Delia raises an eyebrow.

"Are you about to reveal a new love interest?"

He smiles, crossing his arms. "An old romance, in fact. I am happy to announce my reconciliation with Sierra."

Delia balks, but Julien laughs. "Are you kidding? The two of you fought like cats and dogs from the time —"

"Dimitri, that's wonderful!" Delia interrupts. "I'm sure if you've reconsidered it must mean she's become less pugnacious. Will she be joining us any time soon or does she still despise me?"

"We have come to an understanding," Dimitri says. "She has assured me she intends to pursue only peaceful interactions."

"Well, I'm glad to hear that. She always behaved as if I was some sort of threat to her, and I don't want that to be a continuing issue."

"Indeed," he says, helping himself to another cigarette.

"That's quite an announcement," Rhys says, plucking his own cigarette from his pocket. "Congratulations."

Dimitri nods. "While we are on the subject of announcements, there is something else I have been considering since my return. Rhys, I feel it is a waste for us to continue our separate endeavors. As things stand, it appears I have much to learn from you."

"Nonsense," Rhys laughs. "You were and still are the smarter out of the pair of us. I'm certain of it."

"On the contrary. You have done what I was unable to in regards to the formula — with limited resources at that."

Rhys shrugs. "It's not like I took it up as a hobby, it was pure necessity."

"What matters is that you have done it," Dimitri says,

leaning forward. "And it causes me to wonder what more we might accomplish."

"You've seen what I do now — you'd be terribly bored with the nature of my work. It's nothing like what we were into before."

"But you have clearly not lost your touch," Dimitri says after exhaling a cloud. "Not only have you successfully changed Lynna, you have altered the formula so she assumed the healing capability. It is a magnificent accomplishment — one I wish to share in — and I would like to further our explorations."

Rhys' brows knit. "It was mostly by chance — I had no idea she'd take that on. I can't say I care to delve back into the realm of experimentation, and I don't intend to implement that particular formula ever again."

"It would be a shame not to," Dimitri says. "But for now I will simply implore you to consider. I will be in need of a new venture now that I have decided to discontinue my travels."

"You're giving up your practice?" Delia asks.

"It is time for a change," Dimitri says, a smile creeping across his face. "It has been wonderful to return to the steady company of friends — old and new. What I want most in life now is to settle down with Sierra and resume a partnership with a very dear friend."

Rhys' jaw twitches as he slowly stubs out his cigarette. "Well Dimitri," he finally says. "You've given me a lot to think about."

Rhys is unusually quiet on the walk home, and his silence continues as we prepare for bed. We lie next to each other without a word, and though I think I already know the answer to my question, I decide to ask it anyway.

"What's wrong?"

He jumps when I speak. He must've been completely absorbed in thought. "Sorry," he says, sitting back against the headboard. "I'm just thinking of what Dimitri asked. It's… Stressful."

It's exactly the answer I expected. "Really? Would working with him again be that terrible?"

"It wasn't easy the first time, and I don't want to risk our friendship all over. We don't anymore, but all I can think about is how often we argued back then."

I'm trying to imagine them arguing — trying to imagine him arguing with anyone — but it's difficult to picture.

"I mean, surely you can negotiate a way to have reasonable discussions, can't you? You seem to be doing just fine with it now."

"We have, but all that could change quickly," he says. "Dimitri can be a little... Moody, and historically it's been exacerbated if things don't go his way. Once he makes up his mind he's difficult to sway, and even more difficult to reason with. He always wanted to push the envelope when it came to our projects. He wasn't satisfied with mundane things like healing lacerations or coaxing immune responses, which is about the extent of my work currently. Granted, it does get a little tedious at times, but I don't feel comfortable going above and beyond with what limited resources I have here, and I really don't want to change anything to accommodate those pursuits."

"What do you mean by 'above and beyond'?"

"Dimitri was always most interested in the human mind above all, and was hell bent on focusing all our attention there. Among our endeavors were a series of formulas intended to recall lost memories, and erase some completely. They had marginal success at best, but he found them promising. He took it further, and became engrossed in theories regarding memories, mannerisms, physical attributes — even consciousness as a whole. He was even convinced he could find a way to... Pull it out of someone. What he dreamed up was well beyond the scope of the possible, but where I had to draw the line was when he began putting patients at risk by actually attempting it — without their knowledge. It didn't work

— not even close. One nearly died, hence the explosive argument at the end of our previous partnership, if you'll excuse my poor choice of wording."

I wasn't aware of their pursuits until now, and Dimitri's comment about Rhys wasting his talent on simple remedies makes more sense. Controlling memories? How? It's wild to me that they're both capable of things I can't comprehend, and makes me think of something he said early on. I'd asked him why — why he was so drawn to alchemy, to biology, to the inner workings of so many things I'll never understand — and his response intrigued me.

"Well," he'd said. "The universe can't be controlled, and neither can the laws of alchemy, but if you're precise enough, you can find elegant ways to make those laws bend to your will. It's always fascinated me, as it's the closest thing to actual magic."

Magic indeed. He'd bent the rules to near breaking for me, and the result had rendered me more unbelievable than I was before. Had I not experienced it firsthand I would've said it wasn't real — or possible. To me, what he can do is definitely magic, but it's obvious that taking it to that degree again is not something he's after.

"And then there's that formula," he sighs, folding his arms across his stomach. "It's my greatest concern, in all honesty. It was such an ordeal for him to discontinue it at Delia's behest, and now that we've gone and completed it he's intrigued by the potential to see it for himself. It's just… Well… None of this is ideal."

"Can't you just tell him working together isn't an option?"

He closes his eyes and sinks down into the pillows. "Darling, I can't deny him this. I owe him far too much."

I already knew the answer to that question, too. He's stressed because he's already made up his mind to do whatever Dimitri requests because of their past, regardless of what he wants. It seems like an easy solution, saying 'no', but I understand why it's not. I only hope it'll be different for them this time.

✶✶✶✶✶✶ FORTY-THREE ✶✶✶✶✶✶

The mists are heavy, blanketing the city in a hazy white glow, and Julien and I are attempting to navigate them as we jog through the wet streets. It's surreal how foggy it is — I can barely make out his shape less than ten feet in front of me, and we constantly have to stop and reroute when an obstacle appears out of nowhere.

"I think we might have to settle for walking," he says after nearly running face first into a streetlamp. "Lessens the chance of smacking into things."

"Probably a good idea. The last thing I want is to surprise Rhys by returning home with a broken nose."

"Yeah, let's not push our luck," he laughs. "Or his buttons."

It's stifled our activity, but I love the ghostly appearance of the city, the dim outlines of the rectangular buildings disappearing into the white void of sky. As we walk we encounter a couple trying to locate their car in a parking lot, and I overhear their frustration at the task. It makes me think about how Rhys and I would approach the same situation, and leads me to wonder about the dynamic between Dimitri and his apparent love interest. He's such a proper and polite person — what'll she be like? Does she actually hate Delia?

"So Julien — you've met Sierra. Fill me in."

"Heh," he grins. "She's a bit of a handful from what I can recall. It's been maybe fifteen years or so since he brought her around. I'm surprised he's trying again — it was short lived, likely because she took such an issue with Delia. I've heard them fight about it. We'd be in the other room and they'd start whispering, but it was impossible not to overhear. I guess she felt he spent too much time with Delia and accused him of comparing them, and he thought she was being inappropriate and overly jealous. It was apparently too much for him and that was that."

"I can't say that sounds like fun."

"She was nice overall — very chatty. We had a couple smooth outings with her along, and I'm hoping that's what's in store for us now that she's back in the picture."

"I hope she and I can get on. I got lucky with Delia. I never thought we'd be as close as we are."

"Honestly, neither did I," he says. "And I don't mean that to offend, it's just that she's not one to make friends easy."

"I like her abrasiveness," I shrug, and he laughs. "I think we balance each other out."

"I think so too," he says, dodging a low hanging sign. "All right — that's enough of this. Let's head back."

* * * * * * *FORTY-FOUR* * * * * * *

I'm sitting on the cement floor of the greenhouse, frowning up at the ceiling. The roof had been mended well enough but a few places still leak on occasion, and no matter where I move I continue to be interrupted by dripping water. Another droplet splats loudly on the page of my sketchbook, smearing the line I've just drawn. I tear out the page and crumple it up before tossing it into the growing pile of similarly crushed papers at my feet. This is only adding to my frustration.

I've been spending more time in the greenhouse lately, filling pages upon pages with sketchy illustrations with the hope of getting back into that groove Delia mentioned. There's no shortage of vegetation, but we don't have much in the way of ornamental flowers, and the repetitive leaves are starting to become just that. Repetitive. I know I can get different references from books, but I'm hankering to approach this more organically, and the lack of viable subject matter is only making me more irritated. This shouldn't be this difficult. I know I've had trouble with this before, but how did I approach it? I think I'd just gone for a walk, or investigated someone's nearby garden, but there are none in the immediate vicinity I can think of. I'm not sure what's even in season presently. The greenhouse is on a cycle all its own.

I tap the eraser against the page as I think, and when the answer comes it's so obvious I feel like an idiot. The markets. Anything I could ever want to sample onto a page is there. Fresh flowers, fruits, vegetables, and even the fish with the rainbow shine of their evenly patterned scales. It's the inspiration I need, and just in time. The stalls will be closed tomorrow, so I'd better get a move on. I clank down the spiral steps into the apartment, and find Rhys where I left him — bent over the desk with several open books in front of him.

"Hello darling," he says, sliding a piece of paper between the pages of one before closing it. "What's that look you've got on?"

"I had an idea. I'm heading down to the market and then I think over to the studio. Do you want to come along?"

"Mmm — I've got a few things to finish up here and then I'll join you. How's that?" He tilts his face towards me, so I kiss him and shove my sketchbook in my bag.

The market doesn't disappoint, and I wander row after row observing the bounty laid out within the stalls. I want to draw all of it — find a corner to sit and immortalize this afternoon — but there'll be time for that another day. For now I need to focus on what might best become a tattoo.

I collect oranges and lemons with their stems and leaves still attached, gleeful to find a small blossom on one. I debate whether or not to delve into the piles of fresh vegetables, but I pass them and move on to the floral stands. Best not overdo it. I choose thorny white roses, unfurling coral lilies, feathery pink astilbe, black centered anemones, and the lushest blood hued peonies I've ever seen. On my way to the studio I pause in front of a fish stall. I have no idea what I'm going to do with it after, but the scales are good practice, and it's too pretty to resist. When I finally reach my destination I have to knock on the apothecary door for Zep to let me in. My arms are so loaded with my market treasures I can't get my key out for the studio.

"All those flowers — just for me?" He chuckles, tapping the edge of his pipe against the counter.

"I have far too many so I'll certainly leave you with some once I'm through," I smile. As I'm walking towards the connecting door, a box of colorful bottles waiting to be stocked catches my eye. I like the way the light glints from their surfaces. I have to include them.

"Do you mind if I borrow these?" I call over my shoulder. "I'll return them intact. I promise."

"You don't need to ask, dearie, this is your place too," he says, polishing his glasses on his shirt. "Take anything you want. Here — let me get that door for you."

I deposit everything on the floor, and return next door for an armful of different sized bottles, their little tags twirling as I carry them across the room. I carefully curate small still life arrangements, pairing citrus and buds, spreading out leaves and blooms. The scent of the fish in its brown paper hits me before I even unwrap it. It's not a spoiled smell but it's too visceral for my liking, so I tread back into the apothecary for a handful of incense to mask it.

Several hours later the floor of the studio is covered with pages of new drawings, and I feel satisfied with what I've created. Plenty of what I've drawn is suitable for tattoo designs, and the rest is mostly studies — leaves, petals, and a variety of scale patterns. Rhys hasn't appeared yet, and I'm accustomed to him running late but more time had elapsed than I thought. Maybe I should just head back anyway.

As I'm packing up my hoard Zep appears in the doorway, asking after my intentions for the fish. I'm grateful he wants to take it off my hands — that solves my dilemma of what to do with it. Even if I could do it any sort of justice by cooking it neither Rhys or I would eat it, and I didn't want it to go to waste. Zep laughs when I hand him one of the bundles of flowers. I know he was teasing me before, but the smile on his face tells me he's pleased I've left him some, and I'm glad I followed through.

The apartment is unnaturally quiet when I return. I set down my bag and look around, but there's no sign of him, and his shoes are gone. Maybe I'd missed him if he'd come to meet me? It's highly unlikely — the path to the apothecary is fairly direct, and it'd be unlike him to take a secondary route. I begin kicking my shoes off and pause when I see a piece of paper on the counter where I'd be guaranteed not to miss it. It's Rhys' scrawling handwriting, his words forming an apology along with a request to meet him at Julien and Delia's. I sigh as I pull my jacket back over my shoulders, and pick up the bouquet of flowers I'd brought home. I think Delia will like them.

"Hi!" Julien says when he opens the door. "Woah! What are these for?"

"Could you hold them for a moment?" I ask as I thrust them towards him. "I was using them for a project and thought Delia might enjoy them."

"Will she ever," he muses, tilting the bouquet to inspect them. "Awfully nice of you."

As I'm removing my jacket I hear bits of conversation from the other room — Delia's voice, and someone I don't recognize.

"Dimitri and Sierra are here," he says, and I raise an eyebrow.

"And? No fistfights?"

"Smooth sailing thus far," he grins. "But let's see what happens once they get a little wine in them."

I see Dimitri first, and I'm unsurprised to see him sharply dressed. He's in a studious looking sweater, dark knitted cables twisting down the front with the white collar of his shirt peeking over the neckline. Seated beside him on their sofa is a small woman with wavy black hair, and when she turns her head I notice she bears a striking resemblance to Delia. Her blue-gray eyes are wider, and lend an intensity to her expression that Delia doesn't possess, along with the lines creased beside her mouth. She's beautiful and very polished, her carefully manicured nails shining as she clasps them in her lap over her indigo shift dress. Delia's curled up in the chair next to the sofa, gesturing as she talks, her cigarette smoke wafting in loops. Rhys is leaning against the windows, and his mouth creeps into a smile when he sees me.

"Hello darling. I'm sorry, I did intend to come and meet you," he says as I sidle up next to him. "Things went a bit astray, as you can see. How was the market?"

"Productive, which is exactly what I wanted. Delia, I brought you some leftovers."

"Doll, you shouldn't have!" She exclaims when I present her with the bouquet. "These are gorgeous! Thank you — this has made my whole day. Julien? Could you bring a vase, please?"

"Yes dear!" He calls from the kitchen, and she smiles as she buries her nose in one of the roses.

I realize both Dimitri and Sierra are watching me, and I have yet to greet either of them. Quickly I offer my hand, and he rises to take it.

"Hello, Dimitri. So good to see you. I take it this is —"

"Lovely to see you again as well, Lynna, " he smiles. "Please — allow me to introduce you to Sierra."

Before I can address her she's on her feet, grasping my hand forcefully. "It's so nice to make your acquaintance Lynna! I've heard so much about you!"

Her vibrant smile doesn't do much to soften her features, but she's very animated, so I try to match her excitement by offering my best smile. As I'm seating myself on the sofa opposite I notice the bottle of wine already on the table, a ribbon circling the top. They must've brought it as a gift — Dimitri's manners are always so on point, and I wonder if mine will ever come close. I gifted flowers though, didn't I? Maybe I'm already well on my way.

"We were just reminiscing about some of the old days," Delia says, inspecting each bloom before arranging them in the vase. "I was recounting the particular evening Dimitri introduced me to Rhys. Lynna, did he ever tell you about it?"

"No, but I'm sort of dying to hear it now." I am. I love hearing about their histories.

"One of the more awkward moments of my life, as I recall," Rhys says as he sits down next to me. Dimitri picks up the wine to open it, and slowly unravels the ribbon.

"Awkward indeed," he says. "They both assumed I was

intending to set them up, when in reality I was merely looking to merge my small collection of friends."

"Despite the fact that it wasn't his intention it was very clear that neither one of us was remotely interested," Delia says, putting the last rose into place. "No offense, Rhys. You know how I cherish our friendship."

"No offense taken. You're not my type either," he says, and she laughs. "But honestly — I felt bad for Dimitri. It was obvious the poor fellow was trying to cheer you by taking you out and there we were, scowling at each other and not speaking."

Dimitri rolls his eyes. "Once the ice was broken you both spoke far too much. It is true — I am not suited for the task of matchmaking, but I do believe I was spot on in my assumption that you would indeed find common ground. These many years in between have proven me correct."

"I think we've all benefitted from each other's company," Delia says as she accepts a glass of wine from him. "Though I chose a slightly different path than the two of you. I didn't start out with the intention of abandoning alchemy, I simply wished to focus on my skills as a healer."

"It shows," Dimitri smiles. "You are truly gifted in the art."

I notice Sierra frown, but she resumes smiling when she sees me watching. She obviously still has a bit of distaste when it comes to Delia. I wonder how long it'll stay under wraps.

"All right, that's enough," Delia laughs. "You mustn't flatter me — it might go to my head."

"It is not flattery if it is truth," Dimitri says, and Sierra links her arm through his as she quietly clears her throat. Now is probably as good a time as any to change the subject, so I decide to divert the attention to someone who clearly wants it.

"Sierra, how did you and Dimitri meet?" I ask, and she perks up instantly.

"Oh goodness," she says. "It was probably about fifteen or so years ago — when I was *much* younger, I'm afraid — in a library of all places. I used to work there, and he somehow always chose my counter when selecting his books."

"Clearly you caught my eye," he says, and she blushes. "Though if I recall correctly you did not approve of my reading."

"I find all this stuff about... Alchemy, and anatomy... To be a tad dull, don't you?" She asks. She's staring right at me and I think she wants me to back her up but I'm not sure that I can.

"I mean, it's true that I'm unfamiliar with the bulk of it, but I wouldn't exactly describe it as 'dull'."

"Well *I* for one could stand to hear less about it," she says, threading her manicured fingers through Dimitri's. "I quite prefer the *romance* genre myself."

With that, she pulls his face towards her, planting a long slow kiss on his lips. I'm waiting for him to respond to her but he doesn't — he just sits there like a mannequin — and the one sidedness makes the kiss awkward rather than endearing. Maybe he's just not one for displays of affection? I glance around to see if anyone else is as uncomfortable as I am after witnessing it, and the look on Rhys' face tells me he feels similar.

"Dimitri?" Sierra asks as he not so covertly wipes bits of her lipstick from his mouth. "All your friends are here now — isn't it time?"

"Patience, my dear. There is much to discuss, and the evening has only begun."

"But I can't *wait* any longer!"she exclaims. She moves to the edge of the couch and looks at each of us to make sure we're listening. "Everyone — Dimitri and I are getting *married!*"

"You're what?" I hear Julien utter, but no one else says a word. My instinct is to say something congratulatory but I don't want to be the first to do so. To my relief, Delia finally speaks up.

"It seems congratulations are in order. That's… Fast, isn't it?"

"I know it's terribly fast, but it was just meant to be," Sierra gushes, grasping Dimitri's hand. "And I know why we broke up before, but all that's changed now." She leans forward and lowers her voice to a near whisper. "I know what he is. I know what you all are."

She's normal? Like I was before? I had no idea, and I wish someone would've prepared me for that. If he's told her his — our — secret it must be serious, but it seems strange given they'd only just rekindled their relationship. When he said he intended to settle down he obviously meant it, and he wasted no time.

Delia is staring daggers at Dimitri. "So you've told her. That's a big step Dimitri."

"Oh, but tell her *why*," Sierra says, nudging him. "Tell her why it's going to be just fine that I know."

Dimitri hasn't moved since she made the announcement and his face is expressionless. I can't tell if he's overjoyed or irritated. Finally, he nods.

"I suppose it is the time for it after all," he says, straightening his sweater. "Now that Rhys and I have decided to partner once again I feel it is the perfect opportunity to move forward with this new beginning as well."

"Dimitri," Rhys half laughs. "We haven't even discussed the ins and outs of it yet. I have a few things I need to broach first."

"But we *will* be working together," Dimitri says firmly. The smile that crosses his face isn't pleasant like usual, and it's making me uneasy. I'm suddenly aware this is a demand. There's no choice in it for Rhys.

"I'm sure —" Rhys clears his throat. "I'm sure we can work something out. I just thought we'd have the chance to privately discuss —"

"There is no need for further discussion," Dimitri says finitely, reaching for one of Delia's cigarettes. "I will not allow the tedious work I have done to go to waste. All that time and effort had purpose, and I am seizing this chance to implement it so that I may keep her with me."

Before I can fully process what he's just said Sierra grasps his hand and squeals with excitement.

"I'm going to be *one* of you! Lynna, I'm going to be like you are — he's going to change me!"

Instantly all the air seems to go out of the room, and I realize I've been holding my breath. The tension is palpable, shock on both Delia and Rhys' faces. I'm stunned myself — not only had he announced a whirlwind engagement, he'd basically strong armed Rhys into a decision without even hearing him out, and to make things even worse he not only told Sierra what we are, he also told her she'd be changed. I don't want to be in the middle of this conversation, and I'm starting to wish I'd ignored Rhys' note and stayed home.

"Dimitri," Rhys says, clasping his hands together. "You know that's not an option. When we altered Lynna we nearly lost her."

"But you did not," Dimitri says, tapping his cigarette against the ashtray as he picks up his wine glass. "She has come through it with ease, and is perfectly well. I have forgiven you for using my work for your own purposes, but now is the time for me to gain from it. This formula is different — this formula will be one to alter the future, and you are going to help me see it through."

I sink into the couch, my body acting of its own accord and trying to make itself smaller since all I want to do is disappear. I'd never seen Dimitri like this, and I don't like his sudden change in attitude. I watch him pick up his wineglass and take a casual sip.

"Don't be impetuous, Dimitri," Delia snips. "You know the gravity of the potential outcomes. The only reason we attempted it with Lynna is because we were out of options and very much out of time. That is not at all the case here."

"Regardless, it has been done and it can be repeated."

"No," Rhys says. "There were other factors at play in

that situation — ones that aren't present here — and we theorize it was a very specific chain of events that might've led to the successful outcome. Even with those factors the potential for drastic complications is extraordinarily high — the procedure is simply untenable. You recall why development was ceased in the first place, don't you? I *know* you understand it could end badly."

"Nonsense," Dimitri says, setting the glass down with a clink. "She has suffered no drastic complications, and what I *understand* is this formula." He scowls as he sits forward, pointing his index finger into his chest. "*I* was the one to assist Cordelia in the creation to begin with. You have simply taken what I have made and called it your own because you ran a few numbers, made some slight tweaks. It belongs to *me*, so do not explain it like I am some layperson. By rights I should have completed it myself. I should never have let you stop me, Cordelia."

Delia balks. "I had a perfectly valid reason to —"

"What… What sort of… Complications?" Sierra interrupts, looking between Rhys and Dimitri. Her excitement has evaporated, replaced by consternation. "You said… You said it would go off without a hitch. You were certain."

"Of course it will," Dimitri says, looking sharply at Rhys. "I see no reason for your continued attempts to convince me otherwise. How can you justify denying me this when it is what you have for yourself?"

"Stop it — just *stop*!" Delia shouts, exasperated. "We have gone *over* this! There's undeniable evidence supporting our theory that the successful transition is *solely* the product of prolonged prior use of Aeonia. It's the only known shared factor between the two survivors. Even if we were to attempt it again we couldn't prepare Sierra in the same way — that particular substance hasn't been in circulation for close to a century! There's no suitable replacement, which is what began the merry go round of Lynna's transition in the first place!" She shifts to the edge of her chair, one clawed fingertip pointed at Dimitri. "You've seen others who didn't make it — many more than I have, even — and those who did for a brief period of time. Do you want to risk having her end up severely mutilated if she does pull through? What sort of life would that be for her — and you? The likely outcome is that there won't be a chance for that at all and it'll kill her outright!"

Rhys and Delia had drilled the dangers of what they'd done into me, but I'm only now really understanding how incredible it is that I'd lived at all. I'd heard Delia mention Aeonia to Dimitri before, and he was clearly familiar with it — why hadn't he listened to her? Why is he going against what's plain as day even to me? Sierra's face has gone pale, and she inches away from Dimitri.

"I could be... *Mutilated*?!" Her voice is a harsh whisper. "Or *die*? That is not at *all* what you described!"

She sniffles and stands up, smoothing down her dress before walking to the windows with her arms crossed. Dimitri looks furious, and shoots Rhys and Delia an icy glare before picking up his glass and stalking into the kitchen. I watch them go after him, and Julien and I exchange a look as they pass him — it's clear he doesn't want to be here either. He'd been leaning against the doorway to their dining room, and he sighs heavily as he turns to follow them to the kitchen. I hear intense whispering and decide I'd rather remain here and let them sort it out. The sniffling is growing louder behind me. Sierra's full on sobbing now, so I push myself up.

"It's just... It's just that..." She stammers. "When he... When he came back to me after all these years I couldn't believe it. He hadn't aged a *day*. He told me what he was and why he left me before, but he said it would be different. He promised he could change me too — just like you. He... He promised if I did it we could truly be together, then we could get married like I'd wanted, and I was... I was *so happy*. Oh, it's so horribly *unfair*!"

She covers her face with her palms as I stand

awkwardly next to her. I don't know what to say or do. I feel terrible for her — she'd come into this visit excited to share her news, and now she's faced with the realization that what Dimitri told her would happen definitely won't. I gently place my hand on her elbow in an attempt to comfort her, but she jerks it away. Her blue gray eyes flash angrily, so I take a step back.

"Don't," she hisses. "Just *don't.* It's her behind this — I'm sure of it. She's always had it out for me... Trying... Trying to steal him away when she already has a man just because she doesn't like me. You're in on it too — you're *all* in on this ruse. Making up wild stories and the like — is it fun to torture me? Did you do it just for a laugh?"

"Of... Of course not," I stammer. "This is far from a joke, Sierra. What they described to you is very real and very serious."

She stares at me for a moment, her bottom lip quivering.

"Well... if it *is* real he obviously didn't know the details before. Why didn't any of you tell him? Why did you let him believe it could be done? Dangling your life in front of him as if he could have... As if we could have something like it? Gods, the cruelty of it all is too much to bear!"

I'm shocked. She's angry and not thinking straight. It's the only explanation for the conclusions she's jumped to. I wish I hadn't gotten roped into this.

"Sierra... This isn't at all what you think. Dimitri knew the risks already — he had to have known given how involved he used to be with it."

She's nearly hysterical, hugging herself tight as her shoulders shake, tears streaming down her face and dampening the front of her dress.

"I wanted this so bad," she sobs. "I'm... I'm only getting older... And he *never* will..."

Despite how she'd lashed out at me, I feel for her. Her pain feels desperate and hopeless, and I know it's what I'd feel if I was faced with her situation. If things had turned out differently for me. I imagine Rhys presenting me with impossible solutions to our mismatched lifespans, the clock ever ticking. Had my last bottle of Aeonia not disappeared in the fire I might've kept taking it, but even with it I would've had a looming expiration date. As things are now I'm not completely sure of any of our progressions — he'd told me it was likely to be centuries more, but nothing was set in stone. Sierra should only be about halfway through her life as she is, but it still seems like no time at all in comparison. I'd be upset too — just as she is — and maybe I'd want to blame whoever I could.

"It's… Not fair," she hiccups, her tears streaming in torrents. "Why… Why do you get to have this and I don't?"

She's hurt and confused, so I need to be as gentle as possible. "I didn't ask for this. I didn't have a choice in it, and I would never parade something you couldn't have in front of you intentionally." Tentatively I step closer. "You *do* have something though. You have each other, and that's more than many are able to find. You can still get married and have the happiness you want — I'm sure of it. I'd rather have a brief time with Rhys than none at all if I had to choose."

She meets my gaze, her icy eyes rimmed red.

"Choose, then," she scoffs. "Trade with me. It's so easy for you to spit this nonsense at me from where you're standing. You've got nothing to lose while I stand to lose everything, and now you're just… Trying to make it all better? *Don't bother*. You've ruined my life. *Ruined* it!"

She turns her back, and I'm left in a state of bewilderment. They must be meant for each other — neither one seems to be able to hear what's being told to them. I'm angry she's accused me — accused all of us — and I'm on the verge of tears myself even though I don't want to be. I can't make heads or tails of what she actually believes, but it's certainly not the truth — that Dimitri had lied to her and not us. Why can't she see that? Is she so blindly devoted to him that she'd believe anything except what's right in front of her? I leave her to sulk and stalk back to the sofa. I'd tried to console her once — no, *twice* — and she'd rebuffed me, so I'm not about to try for a third. The angry whispers from the kitchen have grown louder. I can't make out what they're saying but I'm not about to insert myself into another unpleasant conversation, so I lean against the cushion and think about what sort of earful I might give Dimitri after this. Just because he'd been in a horrible accident doesn't give him the right to treat Rhys — treat us — like that, and he needs to clear the air with Sierra. She's right — none of this is fair to her, but what's also not fair is her blaming us for it.

My thoughts are interrupted by the sound of glass shattering and a few muffled thuds. When I round the corner into the dining room I see the broken wineglass first, red liquid trailing from it. Julien's elbow is hooked around Dimitri's neck, and both their faces are red. Is he restraining him? Why? Delia is pressed against the wall with her hand over her mouth, and Rhys is leaning on the dining room table, his palm covering his eye. I'm incredibly confused, and my next thought leaves my mouth of its own accord.

"What the fuck is going on?"

No one answers. Dimitri wrestles away from Julien, adjusting the neck of his shirt before grabbing his coat. He storms into the living room and is back in seconds with Sierra. He stops in front of me, and Rhys quickly stands between us, putting his arm out to keep me behind him. Dimitri shifts his eyes to me, his intense stare making me shrink. I can feel fury pouring off him in waves, and I'm suddenly afraid of him.

"*I* did it," Dimitri spits, moving so close to Rhys that they're nearly chest to chest. "I did the work that gave you all you have now. She is only alive because of *me*, and it disgusts me that you would even *dream* of refusing me after all I have done for you. After all you have done *to me*. Have I not suffered enough?"

"Dimitri, that's not fair," Rhys says. "What you're asking —"

"And you," Dimitri interrupts, turning to Delia. "I gave you everything I could. Accommodated your every need, and still you deny me this. You have always felt me unworthy of reciprocation, and it has been made clearer today just how much so."

He grasps a still sobbing Sierra by the wrist and pulls her towards the door.

"Come along. I thought them friends, yet they will not assist me in my pursuit — my desire to only live as they do. I am nothing to them, and now they are nothing to me."

He shoulders past Julien with Sierra trailing behind, and slams the door so hard it shakes the cabinets. His residual anger is hanging in the air and it's almost suffocating. It's dead quiet, but his words are still ringing in my ears, and the explosiveness of his outburst is lingering in my body. I sniffle as I attempt to hold back my tears, and Rhys turns around and folds me into his arms. I'm at a loss — why had Dimitri reacted like this? Why had he turned on everyone? When I pull away I notice a tear in Rhys' shirt collar, then my eyes land on his swollen cheek.

"Gods, did he *hit* you? Whatever for?"

Julien rummages around in their freezer as we sink into the chairs surrounding the glass table, and I wait for an explanation while Julien wraps ice in a towel.

"Because I told him 'no'," Rhys says, pressing the ice against his cheek. "I refuse to assume responsibility for her life, and if I'd agreed I would be. He's not accustomed to hearing a 'no' from me, and became further enraged when he demanded the completed formula and I declined." He pulls the ice away and gingerly touches his cheek. "Thus the act of aggression. He obviously feels we've failed him, and in a way I suppose we have, but there's good reason for that refusal. It's not that I don't want him to have a long happy life with Sierra — what I won't do is end it prematurely for them. I don't understand why he would've gone ahead and told her it was a definite."

"She's irrelevant," Delia says. "He only sees one aspect — that we're keeping the formula from him and denying him both the credit and the benefit."

"But he knows we didn't finish it to somehow spite him."

"I'm not sure he does," she says, striking a match to light the cigarette pressed between her lips. "He's completely delusional — you heard him. He's under the impression we've gone behind his back in order to claim this as our own. I can't fathom why he believes that — it's as if he's dismissed all logic. Not to mention whatever he's filled her head with."

I think I have to speak up. "She's just as delusional. I tried to console her and she snapped at me. One moment she was convinced you were making it all up to play games with her, and the next she implied you lied and led him on about what the procedure entailed."

Julien scoffs. "Seriously?"

I nod, and Delia frowns. "She tried to blame me too. She said Rhys and I dangled what we have in front of them and then yanked it away on purpose. She seemed to think you're somehow behind all this, Delia. She made it very clear she believes you planned this whole thing to steal Dimitri from her."

"That's *insane*," she says, exhaling an angry cloud. "I've never been anything but gracious to her, and I've only supported his decision to pursue her despite my opinions."

"You know what?" Julien half laughs. "Fuck this. He knows what's at risk and he didn't even blink at the idea of putting her through it. I have to wonder if he actually cares about her at all."

Dimitri has to care about her though, doesn't he? Why else would he want to change her so badly? I think about what she said for a moment, and I start to wonder too.

"She did tell me he said he'd marry her if she'd go through with it. That's odd, isn't it? I mean, I thought that engagement sort of came out of nowhere, but I chalked it up to not knowing their history well enough."

"Odd indeed," Julien says. "If he truly cared for her he'd never bribe her with a promise like that. Nevertheless, it's appalling that either one of them would behave like this. All you were doing was trying to remind him that it'd most likely kill her and he wouldn't listen, and though it was plain he'd misled her she chose to blame everyone but him instead."

"Something must've gotten misconstrued," Rhys sighs. "Maybe I should've… Phrased things differently…"

"We both know how he gets," Delia relents. "Everything's personal. He might just need some time to cool down before he can see this in the right light."

Julien sighs heavily, and flings open a cabinet door to pull a glass tumbler from inside. He fills it to the brim with amber hued whiskey and takes a deep drink.

"I know how you feel about Dimitri," he says to Rhys and Delia. "You have ties with him that I don't, and I know you think I don't understand him, but what he did today… That doesn't sit well with me. Honestly, after that little display I think you should stay away from him for a while and really consider what his friendship means to you."

He takes his glass into the living room and sits heavily on the sofa, leaning his blonde head back and closing his eyes. I'm conflicted. I want to give Dimitri and Sierra the benefit of the doubt. Maybe they'd been so disappointed at the realization that what they dreamed up wouldn't come true that they'd lashed out. I can only hope that they realize how they've treated the people who care about them and try to mend things. Julien has a point though, and what happened isn't sitting well with me either. I hate how Dimitri had spoken to them and how he looked at me before he left, not to mention the assault. Regardless of how it might impact their relationship, I'm proud of Rhys for actually having the guts to say no to him. I can only imagine what it would do to him if Dimitri wore him down enough to perform the procedure and have her not survive it.

* * * * * * *FORTY-FIVE* * * * * * *

Everything's different after the episode with Dimitri and Sierra. Rhys is in a visible slump — he'd been angry after we'd left but it quickly changed to guilt, and I know he'd let what Dimitri said start to eat away at him. I thought it might blow over like Delia said, but days passed without so much as a word from them. He finally decided to make the first move and had gone to Dimitri's apartment to speak to him, but I opted to stay out of it. I figured it would be better for them to talk one on one, and I'm hopeful when he returns.

"Well?" I ask as he shoulders out of his jacket. "How did it go?"

He's not smiling, which tells me all I need to know. My hopefulness dissipates further as I watch him sigh heavily.

"He wasn't there."

"Did you leave him a message or something?"

"No," he says, sinking into a chair. "He wasn't there as in he doesn't live there anymore."

"Do you think he decided to travel again after all? Maybe he thought it best?"

"Perhaps, but the odd thing is that he appears to not have lived there for some time. The neighbor I ran into said it's been years. I haven't been to his place in quite a long while, but he never once mentioned having moved. He always kept that apartment as a home base — even when he traveled." He pulls a cigarette from his shirt pocket and taps it anxiously on the table. "I can only deduce that he's at Sierra's, but he's been in town for weeks now and only just revealed his reconciliation," he says, tapping it once more before clamping it between his teeth. "But the apartment…"

"What about it?"

"I don't know why he wouldn't have told me he'd vacated. I've been sending him money for it. For decades."

I sit down across from him. "What? Why are *you* covering that?"

"He's always had issues with his funds," he sighs. "I did all right after our place was destroyed, but he never seemed to recover. I felt it only proper to help him when he asked since it was my doing that put him in that position, so I jumped at the chance to provide him with whatever I could."

He's been paying Dimitri's rent — for decades? Dimitri seems capable enough of providing for himself. It's strange to me, but I can understand why he's done this. If I were in Rhys' shoes and had the means to help someone I'd hurt I'd probably do the same.

"I suppose it doesn't matter what he did with it," he says. "But if he's insistent on cutting me out he's on his own. If he wishes to salvage this he'll have to come to us."

More days go by with no contact, and it becomes apparent Dimitri meant what he said. We're nothing to him now. I'd been leaning towards Julien's stance in that if he wanted to behave like that we didn't need him around, but it's clear Rhys feels differently. Imagining what it must be like to have one of my oldest friends violently erupt and cut me from their life causes me to soften, and I begin to wonder if I'd done something to warrant their reactions. Rhys doesn't talk about it, but his actions and expressions tell me it's always on his mind. I'm torn between wanting to both console him and give him space to come to terms with the situation on his own, but he remains the same, and I feel like I'm somehow failing him.

We hadn't seen Julien or Delia since, either. Usually we'd meet up with one or both on the regular, but nearly two weeks passes with no visits. I'm fairly sure Delia feels similar to how Rhys does even though she'd initially been upset with Dimitri, and wonder if she's having the same difficulty letting him go. I feel stuck. What I want most is to fix everything — paste the pieces back into place so things can go back to the way they were — but I'm not sure how. I finally decide to stop hovering around him and busy myself in the studio, but I'm faced with a completely different standstill there. I still don't have the tools I need to complete any actual work. Everything in my life seems to be stuck in a strange holding pattern, and I have no idea how to snap out of it.

I'm watering the potted plants in the studio when there's a knock on the window. It's Delia, peering in at me. The door creaks as I swing it open, the tiny bell jingling.

"Well," she says, eyeing the piles of drawings on the table. "You've been busy. Any closer to opening?"

I shake my head no. I notice her gaze disdainfully at one of the gray chairs before reluctantly sitting in it, but she doesn't comment.

"I have to apologize for being so distant," she says, tapping her nails on her silver case. "I tend to throw myself into work when I'm stressed, so I've been pulling a few extra shifts at the hospital."

"Have you heard anything from them?"

She shakes her head. "I wanted to go over but Julien insisted I don't. He feels an apology is necessary before any reconciliation can be made. I was on the fence about it for a while, but I think he may be right. I'm still a little hurt by what was said and I don't think I should apologize when I'm confident I did nothing wrong." She snaps her case open. "Mind if I smoke in here?"

"Go ahead — it's not like I have customers," I shrug. "Rhys did go to see him but he wasn't there. He said it was strange — Dimitri apparently hasn't been living there for years, so he must've moved straight in with Sierra when he came back."

"Really?" She pauses before pressing the cigarette between her lips. "He never mentioned that to me. I don't understand why he wouldn't have. Maybe he thought I'd judge him?" She lights the cigarette and shakes her head again as she exhales. "No matter. I wish I had an answer for a lot of the things he's done lately, but I'm afraid I don't. Enough about Dimitri — how are you holding up? How is Rhys?"

Her question gives me pause — I don't know if I should explain how depressed he truly is, but I'm helpless where I stand. Maybe if I confide in her she'll know what to do, so I sink down into the chair next to her and hug my legs to my chest.

I tell her that I'd catch him listlessly paging through books, or just staring out the windows. That he'd fallen behind on the apothecary tasks, and had been sleeping more than ever lately. That he hadn't been cold to me, but he wasn't his regular warm self, and that I long to hear him laugh again. The biggest tell was that he'd started sitting in complete silence, when before we'd barely go more than a few minutes in between some sort of music in the background. It's so unlike him it's worrisome. Delia nods knowingly, and taps her ash in an abandoned cup on the floor.

"He always was a sensitive one," she says. "He cares a great deal for Dimitri, and I don't think he knows how to write someone off — even if it's necessary for his own well being. The things Dimitri said — I know they got to him because they got to me too. He likely feels he's betrayed their friendship, and though I think he's put his time in when it comes to restitution, I'm sure he's wondering if there's something more he could've done."

"He's always going to feel this way isn't he? That no matter what he still owes Dimitri his life because of what happened?"

She sighs. "I think so. It's this unspoken thing between them, and Rhys has always bent over backwards for Dimitri without question because of it. Honestly, I understand it. I feel I owe him something too."

Really? What could Delia possibly owe him for? "Why?"

"Vincent introduced me to Dimitri," she says. "They'd

261

only just met, but they got along well from the start, and Vincent thought we might begin including him since he was a bit of a loner. Gods… He was there for me day in and day out after Vincent died." She sighs, pausing to stub out the cigarette. "He saw me at my worst, but he never judged me — it's because of him I was able to start living again. He introduced me to Rhys, and through him I met Julien. If he hadn't pulled me out of my misery I don't know if I'd be here right now."

I'm a little stunned. I didn't know any of that.

"It's only part of why this has been difficult." She leans her head against her fist and sighs. "Dimitri's the only other alive who still carries any memories of Vincent at all. If I don't have him in my life, it's like I lose a piece of Vincent all over again."

"Gods, Cordelia," I whisper. The situation is far more complicated than I even realized. Both their ties to Dimitri are delicately intertwined with things he'd done for them and memories he shares with them, and it appears neither are able to justify cutting him out so easily. I'm not sure I could either if I were them.

"I know. It's a lot," she says, brushing her dark curls over her shoulder. "But I'm fine, and this will work itself out — I'm sure of it. What we need to do now is get Rhys back on track. See if you can't convince him to go out with us tonight. It'll be good for him to see Julien — he and Rhys have a way about them, and if anyone can reassure Rhys that he did everything he could, it'll be him."

Rhys isn't home when I return, but the note he's left suggests he'll be back shortly. Where did he go? He didn't mention any errands to me when I left. I'd done some cleaning at the studio, so I decide to take a long hot bath with the expectation that it'll both make me more presentable and give me a little clarity. He's sitting at the table when I emerge, and his small smile makes me hopeful.

"Hello darling," he says. "How was your afternoon?"

"Delia came to visit me." I pause to pull my shirt over my head. "She asked how you are, and I was honest."

He sighs. "No sense in lying to her. It's true I've been a total recluse, not to mention a complete sad sack. I'm getting past it, but it's just been more difficult than I thought. I'm sorry you've had to put up with me this way."

He stretches out his arm, inviting me to sit with him, so I accept. "You don't need to apologize. It's a hard situation, so of course you'd be a bit of a mess over it. I've honestly felt like I've been failing you in some regard — like I've abandoned you to your thoughts. I just wanted to make everything better but I couldn't figure out how."

He brushes a damp strand of my hair from my cheek. "You haven't failed me at all. You've been patient and understanding, and you just *being* here makes things better. I've spent enough time dwelling on this. I'm ready to be done with it." He kisses me softly, and I'm instantly soothed. Somehow we've switched and he's the one who's lifted my spirits.

"Where were you this afternoon?" I ask, and he smiles.

"Picking something up," he says. He reaches behind me and slides a small box across the table. "It's for you. Go on — open it."

"Really? Did you finally get me that pony I've always wanted?" I joke, and he laughs. I love hearing it. It's the first time he's laughed in days.

I pry back the corner and am met with something covered with brown paper, and he nudges me to further investigate. Slowly I lift the paper and immediately jump to my feet. Inside the box are two machine frames, cut and welded as per my instructions, the swirling patterns of steel shining in the light.

I'm astonished, and my mouth drops open.

"How did you…"

"I got lucky — Zep knows a welder." He says. "Are they up to par? If not I'm sure I can commission others.

The rest is underneath." I lift another layer of paper, and there in the bottom is everything else on my list. It's essentially a bag of mechanical confetti. I'm speechless. I don't even know how to begin to thank him for this. He's watching expectantly and I realize I haven't given my approval, so I throw myself into his arms so energetically I force his chair on two legs. He laughs as he returns my embrace.

"That should be the last piece, right? You're all set now?"

I nod. "I mean, I'll need customers, but essentially yes."

My heart flutters as he smiles his crooked smile. "Well you've got one right here whenever you're ready. Now, I think this warrants a little celebration don't you?"

I'm on board with celebrating for several reasons, but the machines are actually in second place. He seems so much better, and it leads me to believe the fallout with Dimitri might be behind us. If Dimitri wishes to remain absent, then so be it. We can get along fine without him.

✶ ✶ ✶ ✶ ✶ ✶ FORTY-SIX ✶ ✶ ✶ ✶ ✶ ✶

I'm sitting at the table, tinkering with the machine parts as quietly as possible. It had been a late night and Rhys is still asleep. I hadn't had to do any convincing to get him to go out, and spending a little time with Julien and Delia had done to bring us up even further. He and Julien had gotten far too drunk, but I like when they do — it only ever makes them silly and full of too much love, laughing and hugging each other repeatedly. Despite his excess consumption, I know Rhys will be as perky as ever when he wakes, as the alcohol never seems to affect any of us in the ways of a hangover. I'd asked him about this interesting detail shortly after I'd been changed, and was pleased to find my theory on the right track.

***

"Why is it I never wake up in the state I used to?" I ask, surveying the empty bottles on the kitchen counter. We'd had Julien and Delia over the night previous, and had mowed through a gluttonous amount of wine. "Even a fraction of that would've rendered me immobile for a day or two before — especially since I barely eat anything — but I feel great right now. Is it because we... Process things differently?"

"Exactly that, darling," he says, eyeing the carafe as it slowly fills with coffee. "Our metabolisms have their own patterns when it comes to nourishment and processing, and it's why we can imbibe a fair amount without experiencing the effects a normal person might. We're able to rely heavily on alcohol to sustain our needs more than food, though we do require it occasionally. There are plenty of other ways to maintain ourselves, but this has always been the easiest, I've found."

***

I'd been relieved to know I wasn't doing myself a disservice by drinking too much and not eating. Delia had been right when she warned me that I might not want to as often, and I'd lost my appetite shortly after I'd been altered. He'd told me that it's something that seemed to occur during adolescence for most of them, but I'd been catapulted into it so it took days not years. There are only a handful of things I can stomach even when I do feel the urge. Everything else tastes weird now, which only furthers my lack of appetite.

I finally get the machines together, but I'm too impatient to wait until he's up to see how they'll run. I jot a quick note and quietly close the door behind me to head down to the studio. The city is in its usual foggy morning state, the moisture in the air so thick that my hair and jacket are damp almost immediately. Coils of white mist rise from the harbor, giving it the appearance of an enormous steaming bowl of soup.

When I go to slide my key into the lock the door swings inward — it's already open. The hair stands up on the back of my neck and I glance around, but the streets are empty save for a few vendors peeling back their stalls near the market. I gently nudge the door so the bell doesn't sound but I see no one, and nothing looks out of place. I cautiously check every corner but the studio is empty, and I survey the apothecary anyway even though the shared door is locked. I think I've inadvertently spooked myself. I must've forgotten to lock up after I talked with Delia, and I've really got to be more careful. I'm lucky no one made off with anything.

I sit down next to the workbench and clip in the first machine. Right away the familiar buzzing begins, and I'm proud I still know how to put them together. Even though I know he'd be pleased if he were here, I can still hear my mentor in my head, telling me my coil wrapping left much to be desired. I smile as I remember him, and clip in the second. Nothing. Not a sound. I wiggle the wire, but still nothing happens, and my mentor's voice pops up again.

You frustrate too easily. Come on, child — troubleshoot. Start with the points of contact.

It's not the wire, since the other machine ran perfectly. Maybe the spring? No, it's not that, either. Did I put a washer where one doesn't belong? I remove the screw and the washer, then replace just the screw. Immediately it works. Take that, old man.

I hear a door shut in the apothecary and my stomach drops. Had someone been hiding in there and I'd missed them? My pulse elevates as the shared door opens, and I exhale audibly as I lean against the workbench. It's just Rhys.

"Are you all right, darling?" He laughs. "You look like you've just seen a ghost."

"You scared me! When I came in the studio door was unlocked. I'm pretty sure it was my fault, but I think I'm still on edge."

He pauses, the smile dropping from his mouth. "Nothing out of place, is it?"

"Thankfully, no."

He strides to the door and inspects it, opening it and closing it again before locking it. "I'm sure it was just a little absentmindedness, but should you find the door open again I'd much prefer you not investigate if you're on your own."

"Fair enough."

"Well? Everything satisfactory?" He asks, nodding towards the machines. I show him as my answer, and he smiles when he hears the noise. "Wonderful. Ready to test them out?"

"What, right *now*?"

"Now's as good a time as any, isn't it?"

"You haven't even told me what you want!"

"I can't say I have anything particular in mind…" he says. He scans the room, and his eyes land on the piles of sketches. "But I can think on my feet. May I?"

"Be my guest."

He sets the pages on his lap and shuffles them slowly,

carefully considering each design. Finally he lands on an image — a single rose, complete with the flower's signature triad leaflet. I should've known. Roses are one of his favorites.

"A classic choice," I laugh as I begin cutting it out to make a stencil. "You can never go wrong with a rose. Well, where's it going?"

He chews the edge of his lip as he thinks it over. "Hmm… I'd like to see it, so I suppose that limits my options." He pulls his shirt over his head, and after surveying the landscape of his torso he points to a gap of open skin beneath his clavicle. "Perhaps here?"

I finish the transfer and hold it up to his chest. A perfect fit. He agrees, so I gently clean his skin before pressing the stencil against it. As I pull it away I notice a familiar look in his eye, the corners of his mouth raised. His expression betrays him every time, and it's how I know when he wants to kiss me, and when he wants it to go much further than just a kiss. I'm amused — and interested — but now is not the time.

"Oh no — don't even think of it," I laugh, playfully smacking his arm. "I'm trying to concentrate here."

"I doubt there's anything you can do to *stop* me from thinking of it, darling," he laughs. "But I promise I'll keep the distractions to a minimum. I won't do anything inappropriate."

He sits casually on the table as I finish preparing, but I'm suddenly a ball of nerves. I'd been away from the familiarity of this routine for an extensive period of time, and I'm about to retest my skills by permanently inscribing him of all people. No pressure.

I exhale as quietly as I can before I start. My heart is thudding beneath my ribs, and I feel like it's echoing throughout the room, in tune with the buzzing of my new machine. He scrunches up his face as I pull the first line, then the second. My hands move as if on autopilot, and I start to relax. Thank gods. My body's remembered.

"I know I've asked you *where* you got these, but I don't

think I've ever asked *why*." I nod to the dark birds spanning his torso. All of me has remembered — I'm talking without thinking in an effort to distract him from the long lines. "It's obvious why you chose the foliage and alchemic symbols, but why the birds?"

"I thought they might increase my street credibility," he says seriously. It's a ridiculously terrible joke, and I have to pause to laugh. He's pleased by the outcome, and once I've resumed he continues. "In actuality, I had an interest in ornithology at one point. It was never something I wanted to make a career of, but birds are really fascinating creatures, so I decided to make them part of me, so to speak. It was hard to narrow down, so I went with the classifications that interested me most. Corvidae, Ardeidae, Strigiforme…"

"Can you dumb it down for me?" I laugh softly. "I know what those words mean about as much as I did the botanicals when I first got into them."

"They're families of birds, darling," he smiles. "When it comes to my particular illustrations, I'm referring to the crows, the heron, and this owl over here. I wouldn't mind adding more one day."

I'm delighted to learn something new about him, but I already sort of knew he'd chosen them because they mean something to him. He's gone about it in the way he does everything else — with intent. Nothing enacted on a whim, everything on purpose.

It takes me a little more time to complete than it had in the past, but I know my fluidity will improve with repetition. I'm just a little rusty. I'm happy once I'm finished — for two reasons. One, my machine had worked just how I'd wanted after only a few minor adjustments, and second because it felt good to know I've still got it. I can do this, and the future doesn't feel as shaky as it did before.

"Mmm," he says, turning in the mirror as he inspects it. "I'm afraid you have a new problem to face."

I suck in my breath. Does he not like it? I thought I'd

done a good job, but now I'm worried all over again. I've always despised this part of the process — waiting to see if who I've marked permanently will either love it or hate it.

"What do you mean? Is something wrong with it?"

"Not at all," he chuckles. "It's perfect — I like it so much it's ignited the desire for another. The problem is that you'll definitely have your work cut out for you now. I might demand to occupy most of your time."

I'm relieved, and I have to laugh. "Don't *do* that. I'm happy to indulge you, but you *cannot* toy with me after. At least not until I'm back in the swing of things."

"Fair enough," he smiles. "I apologize. How can I make it up to you?"

I return his smile. I have a pretty good idea of how, and it's the proper time for it now that the tattoo is out of the way. I tilt my face up to invite him to kiss me, and he does. Softly, with intent.

＊＊＊＊＊＊ *FORTY-SEVEN* ＊＊＊＊＊＊

The time has finally arrived, and I start out slowly, flipping the closed sign on the door to read open only a few days a week. Tattooing Rhys was one thing, but the thought of reacquainting myself with complete strangers brought a whole other cascade of uncertainty. It goes well despite my nerves, and soon enough I have a slow but steady trickle of business. I've been busier in the past, but it's enough to pay for my expenses, and even save a little if I'm stringent. I'd tried to give most of what I make to Rhys to offset his part in my workspace, but he wouldn't accept it, so I told myself I'd put it away for anything we might need in the future. I'm happy to finally feel like I'm pulling my weight.

I'm pleased to find a few of my old clients making their way through the door, equally as surprised to see me as I am them. The only unfortunate part is that they come with questions about where I'd disappeared to for so long. I answer as reservedly as I can, and it's another thing I have to reacquaint myself with. The game of truth and lies — how to not give myself away. I'd become too used to speaking openly within our close circle, and I have to consciously choose my words carefully.

"I *cannot* believe this!" The woman exclaims, the bell on the door jingling furiously when she shuts it. "I was worried when I saw the state of your old place, and then you were just… *Gone*! What happened?"

It's Claire, the woman I'd covered up the name for, and she greets me with an unexpected hug. I have a prepared answer — the same one I'd been telling the others.

"Electrical fire. It took a while to get back on my feet."

"Gods, how *terrible*!" She says. "Well, I'm glad to see that you're in one piece — *and* back in business. I was starting to think I might have to travel for something new. There aren't really any other places around here."

"And I'm glad to be at your service," I smile. "What can I do for you?"

She wants more flowers, which I'm not at all unhappy about, and chooses an amethyst hued iris, the long leaves trailing up the side of her leg. As I work we chat casually — as if I'd only just seen her the other day instead of well over a year previous — and she asks me a question I should've expected from her.

"Well? What happened with that man you were talking to?"

"Really? You remember that?"

"Of course I do! I have a good memory," she laughs. "And I'm way too invested in everyone else's life, or so my boyfriend tells me."

I can't help but smile, and she leans forward excitedly.

"Ooh, it's something good, isn't it? Did he make a move?"

Clearly her boyfriend is right, but I don't mind it at all. I no longer have to lie to myself when it comes to how I feel about Rhys, and it's something I don't have to lie to anyone else about either.

"He did. Well, we sort of *both* did. It worked out better than I could've imagined, honestly."

"Lynna, that's *incredible*!" Her leg jolts with her enthusiasm, and I pause. "Sorry — I'll stay still, I'm just excited for you! You look much happier than you did when we first met."

"I am. Quite a bit more."

"So? What's he like? Tell me about him."

"Well, he's —" I start, but the apothecary door interrupts me. It's Rhys, appearing as if we'd conjured him up just by talking about him. "Right here, actually. See for yourself."

"Don't mind me," he says apologetically, shifting the box in his arms as he closes the door. "Just bringing in more ointments. Carry on."

We'd moved some of the apothecary inventory into the studio. The back room has ample space for storage overflow, and I want to use a few of the items here anyway. I watch her gaze follow him as he disappears into the back, and after he's gone she leans closer.

"Wow," she whispers. "He's a bit... *Distinguished*, isn't he?"

"If you mean 'old' by that, he's really not," I whisper back, trying to simultaneously not laugh and keep my voice down. It's a lie, but it's a necessary one.

"No, no — he's very handsome, just not what I was picturing. I *love* that hair. I think he's —"

She stops whispering when he reappears, and a smile spreads across her face.

"Sorry to interrupt," he says. "Which did you like better? I want to be sure I don't hide it away where you won't be able to locate it easily."

"The green salve." I nod to the squat round container in his left hand. "The consistency is more what I need. The other one is fine, it's just a bit more globby than I'd like."

"'Globby' is it?" He chuckles. "Well I'll certainly make note of that for when it comes time to produce more."

"Hi," Claire says, and I suddenly remember I hadn't bothered to actually introduce them.

"Oh, sorry. Claire, this is —"

"Rhys," he says, taking her extended hand. "A pleasure. Hopefully Lynna isn't torturing you too much."

"Not at all — I enjoy it. I missed her when she up and disappeared. You can't imagine how thrilled I was when I walked in today."

"Glad to hear it," he says. "Darling, I'll put these up and wait for you next door. I don't mean to be in the way."

"Oh please," Claire laughs. "I don't mind at all."

She clearly wants to find out more about him right from the source, and I'm happy to let her. I also enjoy having him here and it seems he wants to be, so I glance up. "You're not. Stay if you like."

He does, and Claire peppers him with questions about the apothecary while I continue. I like talking to her, but it's sort of nice to be able to fully concentrate on what I'm doing while she's distracted otherwise. They continue while I move on to shading, and when I'm almost finished she discloses something I'd never told him — the fact that I'd talked about him to a client, however vaguely.

"I have to say — I'm *so* happy the two of you figured it out. I'll be honest — I wondered about it for *days* after I last saw you, Lynna."

I feel my face start to redden, and he laughs. "Wondered about what?"

"I mean, you should've seen her," she says. "Agonizing over whether or not to tell you she had feelings for you. She never said so directly, but I knew." I press my lips together, and she finally notices my red face. "Oh no, did I say too much? Sorry, I tend to do that sometimes."

"No," I laugh sheepishly. "It's just a little embarrassing to recall. The fact that everyone around me — Rhys included — seemed to know I loved him when I was trying so hard to keep it to myself."

"Well, I *didn't* know at the time," he says, smiling softly. "But I certainly hoped."

Claire is pleased with his response and smiles triumphantly as I give her tattoo a last wipe. I'm a little pleased by it too — it's a tiny window into the past, when everything was still in flux. I like knowing we were on the same page even then, aware or not.

"I love this," she says, turning her leg. "It fits so well."

"Nicely done, darling," he says. "I'll let you finish up while I put the rest of that inventory away. Claire, it was lovely chatting with you. I do hope you'll be back again."

"Count on it. It was nice meeting you too, Rhys — just do me a favor and don't let her up and vanish from here."

After he's gone, I rub a small amount of the salve I like over the iris, and dig in my drawer for a bandage.

"He's wonderful," she whispers. "Very charming."

"I have to agree with you there," I whisper back, circling the bandage around her leg.

"He's obviously crazy about you — I could see it in his eyes. Will we be hearing wedding bells any time soon?"

I'm thrown by her question, and pause before resuming

taping the bandage. I don't know how to answer — truth or lie? How do I concisely explain that I don't hold much stock in such an archaic notion without offending someone who clearly approves of it? I decide to go with truth.

"We're very happy just as we are. No bells necessary. It's not even something I'm considering."

"Mmm — we'll see about that," she smirks. "I recall you once saying you were fine all by yourself, and now look at you. I don't buy it. It's in the cards for sure. When it *does* happen, I'll happily remind you 'I told you so'."

She seems certain I'll change my mind, but I'm not so sure. Even if we cut all the parts we found silly, there's still one main reason I'm opting to shy away from it. It might change us, and I don't want anything to change about how we are. Why risk ruining something that's already so perfect? We were lucky enough to end up here after being exposed to each other, and what I don't want is to throw a wrench into things. If I could tell her all that maybe she'd understand, but I can't, so I shrug instead.

"I suppose we'll see."

We share a long goodbye, and after she's gone I find myself hoping she meant it when she said she'd be back again soon. I enjoy her company, and her nosiness always prompted me to think about things more carefully. I'm finishing wiping down my table when I feel his arms around my waist, so I lean back against him.

"She was very nice," he says. "Very talkative too. Possibly more than I am, which is difficult to achieve."

"A trait I seem to gravitate towards, since I like both her and you."

"Well according to her, you definitely more than 'like' me," he says, releasing me so I can continue cleaning up.

"If I recall correctly, I'm pretty sure she said I have *feelings* for you, but no one specified what those feelings are," I joke, and he smiles faintly.

"Fair enough."

I finish the surfaces and put my bottles of ink away

while he leans against the shelves, watching me. It's only when I begin fitting my arms into my jacket that I realize he's been silent a while, which usually means something's on his mind.

"What are you thinking?" I ask.

"Darling," he says, uncrossing his arms. "Are you happy? Truly?"

Why is he asking me that? Maybe my joke hadn't landed the way I intended.

"That comment about my feelings was just me kidding with you. Of course I'm happy. Are you?"

"More than I've ever been. I just like to know you are, too."

He's usually not put off by my jokes, and I realize he must've heard us whispering about a hypothetical wedding when he was in the back. There's a small shred of worry in the pit of my stomach. Would my stance on this eventually cause an issue between us? He'd once made it apparent he might welcome such a thing, but I'd done the opposite. No — he'd never given me cause to think he wished we were something else, and I don't think he'd ever pressure me into something I'm unsure of. If he feels differently I have to believe he'd tell me, and should that day ever come I hope we'll be able to work it out. Right now it seems like all he's asking of me is a little reassurance, and that I can give him honestly.

"Rhys, I'm happier than I've ever been in my life. Truly."

The smile that appears on his face washes away my bubbling concern, and I let him fold me into his arms. Nothing's changed, and it's a reassurance I didn't know I needed, too.

"Good," he says. "That's all I want."

★★★★★★ FORTY-EIGHT ★★★★★★

A few more weeks go by, and I'd forged a new routine of waking early to tend to the greenhouse and share part of my morning with him before heading into the studio. Occasionally he'd accompany me, but more often than not he'd stay behind and meet me later in the day. Sometimes I wouldn't see him until I returned home, or later still if he was working at the club. Tonight is one of those nights, and I'm happy to be cleaning up from my last client of the day so I can visit him at the bar just like I used to. I recall Delia once telling me we needed more time apart to truly appreciate each other, and I'm starting to realize there might be something to that. I never got tired of being around him all the time, but I like having something to do that's just mine, and it's sort of invigorating for us to be able to fill each other in on what we did during those hours spent away. I'm always excited to see him, but maybe more so now if that's even possible.

The bell on the door jingles while I'm cleaning my hands in the washroom, signaling a customer. It's already late, and though I could probably squeeze something small in I really don't want to. I'm preparing myself to ask them if they wouldn't mind coming back another time as I round the corner, but when I see who's standing in my lobby I drop my towel.

"Hello Lynna," Dimitri says. I watch his eyes move over the books and prints lining the walls. "It appears your studio is doing well after all. How wonderful."

I regain my composure and toss the towel into the waste bin. He startled me — what is he doing here? He's been missing for weeks on end. He doesn't look angry or upset and I feel a glimmer of hope — has he patched things up with Rhys? He must have if he's here. I'm not expecting any sort of apology myself, but if he wants to mend things I'll gladly accept. He's opened by saying something pleasant, so maybe I should return the gesture.

"It is, and I have to thank you for being right. You said not to lose sight of the fact that I still had it in me, and I did."

He smiles. "It appears I have made a correct choice then, since you are clearly the only one who listens when I speak. Is he here?"

Correct choice? About what? And why is he asking if Rhys is here if he's seen him? Shouldn't he already know?

"Rhys? No — he's working tonight. Didn't you... Did you not talk to him?"

"And why would I have spoken to him?" He asks, running his fingers along the table that once belonged to him. "I doubt he wold be receptive to what I have to say, since I have not changed my stance on any of it."

My stomach drops, the hope gone. He hadn't made up with Rhys — he hadn't seen him at all — and he doesn't intend to reconcile anything. He's staring at me with those intense blue eyes, and I'm starting to feel just as small as I did the last time I saw him. I'm pretty sure Zep had gone home for the night, and I'm acutely aware of the fact that he and I are alone. I once felt a sort of kinship with him, both of us having lost everything, but now I only feel fear. I don't trust him anymore.

"I really think you should try and talk to him. I know he wants things to be good between you again."

"I am afraid the time for that has passed. I have come to talk to you instead."

"Why?" I'm trying to remain calm, but it's difficult. I'm glad there's at least a table between us.

"Because I thought you might be one to listen to reason. I have shown my loyalty to both Rhys and Cordelia many times over, but they have cast theirs aside. Now," he says, casually adjusting his wristwatch. "I have done something for *you* as well. You stand here before me — alive, and as one of us — as a result of something I carefully developed. Where does *your* loyalty lie?"

My *loyalty*? What is he talking about? "Dimitri... I don't understand. What is it you want from me?"

"You are aware, I am sure, that Rhys and Cordelia declined my request. They have not dissuaded me, but I am in need of the information they keep. They have a combined series of notes — a journal, if you will — containing the entirety of the completed formula. I require it to proceed. What I am asking is for you to honor this request."

Gods. He wants me to go around them and get him the formula. Does he think he's entitled to ask this of me... Because I'm *alive*? I don't follow his logic, but I couldn't acquiesce even if I wanted to, and I definitely don't.

"Why do you you think I could do that? It's not in my possession."

"It is, though," he says. "You cohabitate with Rhys. You have access."

"Access or not, it's not mine to give. If you want it, you should really —"

He slams his fist on the table, making me jump. My pulse rages as he walks around it, closing in on me, and I take a step back but there's nowhere to go. I'm literally up against the wall. He doesn't stop until he's so close I can see the individual specks of stubble on his chin.

"You will retrieve it," he says, puffs of air hitting my cheek with each syllable. "And you will bring it here where I will collect it. I am not an unreasonable man, but this gatekeeping has gone far enough."

I want to say yes. I want to say whatever it takes for this to stop, but I can't.

"No," I whisper.

He grasps my arm, squeezing it painfully. I can't twist from it — he's too strong, he's got me pinned. He bends closer so he's staring right into my eyes.

"You will bring it here for me to collect," he repeats. "Your loyalty is at stake, and both it *and* your life are closely intertwined. I know Rhys would hate to see anything happen to you over something so small as a book."

"What's going on here?"

Zep's voice from the shared door. He hadn't left after all. I shift my eyes to him — the most unthreatening and sweet man if I'd ever met one — and silently beg him not to get involved. Dimitri smiles coldly and releases my arm. He saunters across the room as I catch my breath, pausing when he reaches the door.

"I will be seeing you very soon, Lynna. Do enjoy your evening."

The bell jingles as the door closes, and I sink down to the floor. Zep rushes over, kneeling beside me.

"Are you all right, dearie? What happened?" He asks, the comforting scents of pipe tobacco and licorice surrounding him. He's like a small grandfather I want to cling to — to feel him pat my arm and tell me everything will be just fine. Everything is definitely *not* fine, and I suddenly want to be anywhere but here.

"Nothing… I just… I want to go home."

"Come now," he says, helping me to my feet. "I'll accompany you."

He insists on walking me the whole way up to the apartment door, and I hug him tight before he leaves. I'm grateful he'd been there just when I needed him, but I don't tell him what Dimitri said. I'm not sure I want to tell anyone. He seems surprised — I'd never hugged him before — but he pats my shoulder gently, and for a moment I feel just a tiny bit better.

The dread returns once the door closes. I don't know what to do. I can't keep it from Rhys, and I'm not about to give Dimitri anything. He'll be back, and though he'd given me a veiled threat, it's a threat nonetheless. I feel helpless. I feel like this is somehow *my* fault, like my presence has complicated everything. Had I not been changed their relationships with Dimitri would've remained the same, wouldn't they? I shake my head, physically attempting to dislodge the thought.

I pace back and forth in the kitchen while I deliberate my approach. I'm supposed to meet him, but I don't want to bring it up while he's working. There's a fair chance he'll know something's amiss even if I pretend. Do I wait until he arrives home? If I don't show up he'll worry, so it appears I'm going with the first option.

I was hoping the bar would be at least momentarily deserted, but there's a couple sitting at the end. This was a bad idea. I don't know if I can hold it together, and I don't want to make a scene. I should've just waited, but it's too late to turn around now. He's already spotted me.

"Hello darling," he says, just like he always does when he greets me. I never tire of it, and under normal circumstances I'd say something pleasant in return, but all I can muster is a wan smile. I can do better than this. Maybe if I proceed as usual I can put it aside for now, and he won't know.

"I'd love a drink, please."

His grayed brows are knitted and the smile is gone from his mouth. I'm a terrible actor — he knows something's off.

"I think you should probably tell me what's wrong first," he says.

"I was trying to wait." I glance at the couple. "This isn't the place for it."

"Well, I'll *make* it the place for it," he says. "I won't be able to simmer in suspense wondering why you're so clearly distraught. Just a moment."

I don't know what he says to them, but they both nod and head towards the stairs. He follows, and once they're down them he clips the chain across the entrance, signaling the bar closed.

"All right," he says, sliding into the seat next to me. "Put me out of my misery. What is it?"

There's a familiar lump in my throat, and my eyes are already burning with unwanted tears. What will happen now that Dimitri's crossed a line? Why did he have to do that? If he'd only been open to talking through it maybe none of this would've happened.

"Dimitri came to the studio."

"He did?" He's surprised. I'm not sure what he was expecting me to say, but it wasn't that. "You talked to him then?"

He looks almost hopeful, and I feel worse knowing I'm about to dash whatever's there.

"I told him… I told him he should try and have a conversation with you, but he declined. Rhys, he wants me to steal your notes. The formula. I think he wants to try and change Sierra on his own."

I watch the optimism drain from his face, and he sets his elbow on the bar, resting his head in his hand.

"For fuck's sake," he says, exasperated. "Why on earth did he think coming to you would make any bit of difference? And to ask that of you? Absurd. Completely absurd. I assume you didn't agree to it?"

"*Of course* I said no." My chin trembles, and I bite my lip to stop it. He picks his head up, his brows soft.

"I'm sorry." He reaches for my hand, and it feels cold in his warm one. "I never wanted you in the middle of this, and I'm not questioning you. I just want to understand what's going on."

"He said I'd… He said I'd *have* to honor his request." I'm failing at not letting my voice waver, and his concern is growing. "He went on and on about… Loyalty, and…"

"And what?" He asks softly.

I don't want to say it. Once I do it'll shift everything, just like it had when Dimitri uttered the words to me. He's clutching my hand tightly, waiting.

"Lynna — what did he say?"

I swallow hard. "He said my loyalty is at stake. That it's… Intertwined with my life. He said… He said you'd hate to see something happen to me over a book."

His expression changes in an instant. Gone is the concern, replaced by a deep scowl, and his grip on my hand lessens. He stares at the floor for a long moment, his eyes darting back and forth. He's visibly angry — more than I've ever seen.

"Dimitri threatened you? He actually *threatened* you?!"

I don't think he needs me to confirm, but before I can, he's on his feet. He paces erratically, and it doesn't seem like he knows what to do with his hands. "I can't *believe* this. I've felt… *So guilty*. I'd gone *over* and *over* it… Wondering what more I could've done…How I could've helped him without *risking her life*…" The volume of his voice is growing, and he's almost shouting. "He made me start to believe I'd betrayed him, and now *THIS*?!"

He suddenly stops pacing, and his angry scowl dissipates. His face is soft, and so is his hand on my cheek.

"He didn't hurt you, did he? *Did he*?"

I shake my head no, and it's truth. Dimitri had shown me a different side of him tonight — one I'd never expected — but though he'd scared me quite a bit he didn't hurt me. I think scaring me is what he intended to do, and he had.

"Gods," he says, pulling me against him. "I should've known he wouldn't give up on something he wants so easily, but I never thought he'd resort to anything like this."

I press my face into his shirt, hoping it'll absorb my tears. "What happens now?"

"I don't know yet. I've got to speak to Delia."

★★★★★★ FORTY-NINE ★★★★★★

They're both home when we arrive, and I feel terrible for interrupting what's obviously a quiet night in for them. They're pleased to see us at first, but their expressions change quickly when Rhys explains what I'd told him. Delia's eyes widen and Julien looks angry, muscles in his jaw flexing as he listens. The conversation becomes a blur as I get lost in my thoughts, replaying Dimitri's words in my head as I watch them react. I hate how this is affecting them. Julien notices my trembling hands and instructs me to sit down.

"It'll be all right," he says. "Let's get you some tea. I know we have it somewhere."

We sit in silence for a while, the only sound being the rain tapping on the windows. Finally the kettle whistles, and Delia gets up to tend to it.

"Careful doll," she says, gingerly handing me the cup. "It's very hot."

I sip anyway. It burns my lip immediately, so I set it on their coffee table to cool.

"Darling," Rhys sighs. "I'm afraid you might have to stay home until we sort this out."

Stay home? While I agree that this is an alarming situation, I'm not sure that's the right move.

"I don't like the idea of Zep having to deal with him when he comes looking for me, and it's not like he couldn't just show up at our home — he knows where we live, after all. Me not being there might not do anything but provide an unoccupied storefront for him to take out his wrath on. What I *really* don't want is for this studio to meet the same fate as my last one."

He sighs. "A fair point."

It's quiet again. I'm trying to think of something — anything — to suggest. This is more complicated than I thought.

"What if... Couldn't you give him something made up?

An imitation?" I ask. "I mean… Something that might give similar effects but wouldn't do her in?"

"No," he says. "Dimitri isn't stupid. Reckless, yes, but despite his poor judgment he's a brilliant alchemist. He'd most certainly catch on given his familiarity with the information already. It would only escalate things."

"Sorry — I wasn't thinking."

"It's all right," Delia says, leaning forward to pat my arm. "None of us are having any good ideas at the moment."

Julien shifts against the sofa, crossing his big arms over his chest.

"This might be my opinion alone," he says. "But have any of you thought of just giving him the damn formula? He's clearly hell bent on mowing down anyone in his path to get what he's after, and Sierra apparently wants to blindly follow him into it. You've already explained what could happen to no avail, so you're not really saving her from anything. I'm inclined to think we should leave them to take their lives into their own hands."

Rhys stands and walks slowly towards the windows, and Delia snaps open her cigarette case. Both seem to be contemplating what Julien said, and so am I. Part of me wishes I would've just told Dimitri yes. Maybe then we could've avoided all this.

"You may be right," Rhys says. "He's got us — well, he's got *me*. He knows I won't jeopardize Lynna."

I'm suddenly aware that I hadn't thought I was in any real danger. His words had done enough on their own. Were they not just an intimidation tactic? Did Dimitri actually mean what he said?

"Do you really think he'd… Do something to me?"

"I can't know for sure, which is why I'd prefer a little caution," he says. "I didn't ever think he'd threaten you to begin with, so I must relinquish any doubt I have about him following through in favor of believing he will."

I'm scared for real now. Maybe I should stop making suggestions of my own and listen to theirs.

"What should I do?"

"Well, I don't want you in the studio alone, and I won't be swayed on that. We'll both have to make a few schedule adjustments, but I think we can work it out."

"Don't worry about that — I'll mind the studio with her for now," Julien offers. "I have more time on my hands than you do anyway."

"Thank you, Julien. I appreciate it. I'll be there every minute I have available, too."

I watch as he and Delia exchange a look. It seems they've arrived at a decision, and she sighs heavily.

"I can't believe it's come to this. Throwing away decades' long friendships over what? Pride? A few pieces of paper?"

"He's given you no choice," Julien says. "If he were a true friend he'd never ask this, and he'd definitely never say he might hurt someone to get it."

"I know," she says, reaching her hand over to grasp his.

"I'd like to avoid you having to deal with him altogether," Rhys says to me. "I want to give it to him myself if he's to have it, though it may be tricky since we don't know exactly when he'll be back, nor do we know where he is presently. I'm sure one of us is bound to intercept him sooner or later."

"Do you think he'll show up if he knows you're there with me?" I ask Julien.

"He will," Rhys answers, turning to look out at the rain. "If he's gone this far, he'll most certainly make good on his word."

* * * * * * FIFTY * * * * * *

Julien begins appearing at our door in the mornings as promised, and walks me the short distance to the studio. It's been a week now with no sign of Dimitri, though I still jump every time the bell on the door jingles. Julien spends long hours parked in one of the gray chairs, waiting. It's comforting to have him there, but I worry he's terribly bored. He never complains though — he just sits and watches the door. Rhys arrives to relieve him as soon as his own work is finished but he stays anyway, and the two of them chatter away while they wait for me.

Two weeks and still no Dimitri. I can tell Julien's beginning to grow impatient since he occasionally abandons the chair to wander over and watch me work. He hovers over me, hands clasped behind his back, observing quietly as I fill in blank spaces of skin with flower after flower. Long silvery stalks of lavender, lush hellebore blooms, bright pink peonies, and striated dianthus. After a day or so of quiet, he starts asking questions.

"Can't you do it all with just one?" He asks, pointing to the needles in their neat little packages.

"I could, but it would take an awfully long time, and you wouldn't necessarily get the same result. It's better if you have different sizes for the line weights."

He laughs softly. "I don't know what that means."

"Look — see this line?" I point to my client's shoulder where the stencil I'd placed is drying. "See how it's much thicker than the others? Bolder? Varying line sizes — line weights — give the image more depth."

"Makes sense," he says. "But what about this one? I've only seen you use it for color. Is that what it's for? It looks like it'd make an awfully thick line."

I hadn't realized he was watching that closely. "It's for shading in general. It's shaped like that so I can fill in larger areas at a time. Essentially a series of awfully thick lines."

"All about efficiency then, is it?" He smiles, and I have to smile back at him.

"Something like that."

He starts following me around all day every day, watching me set up my tray and break it down after each client, asking a question here and there. Our dynamic has changed. Instead of my bodyguard Julien has become something like an assistant, offering his help with anything I need retrieved during my process, and greeting customers if I'm busy when they walk in. He seems to like it well enough, and I'm at least happy he doesn't seem bored.

Soon enough I have a slow day with no customers, which isn't uncommon from time to time. He'd sat in the chair for most of it while I drew at the table, the room quiet save for my crackly radio and the scratch of pencil on paper. I'm referencing from a book of moths, and though I'd love to go out and collect a few real ones, now is not the time for any extracurricular excursions. Julien has been silently hovering over my shoulder for the past half hour, and I suddenly have a curious idea. In lieu of standing around watching, I'm wondering if he'd be open to participating a little. I'm aware of his eyes on me as I walk to the bookshelves, and I search until I find a thin book of simple floral vectors. I set it on the table, then tear out a blank sheet of paper from the sketchbook. He stares at me blankly when I hand him a fresh pencil.

"What do you want me to do with this?"

"What do you think?" I laugh. "Go on, then. Do you think you can copy them?"

He shrugs. "I guess I can try."

I observe him out of the corner of my eye — drawing, erasing, drawing, more erasing. Soon his page is filled with shaky doodles, all smudged from the eraser. I tear out another page and silently slide it in front of him, and this time he's steadier, the eraser marks blurring the page a little less. The third begins to resemble the illustrations even more.

"Julien, have you ever drawn anything before?"

"No, not really," he says. "I mean, I like art — always have. I just never really had an opportunity to give it a shot. Met a lot of musicians as a bar bouncer, but no artists. At least, no one who's asked me to sit and draw with them."

"Did you enjoy it just now?"

"Yeah, actually. It doesn't seem like I'm any good, but I did like it."

I pick up the pages, studying the progress he's made from the first page to the last. "You've definitely got the concept down. No one's good right away — well, *most* people aren't. There are always prodigies, but they're the minority. Everything takes practice."

"I wouldn't mind practicing more, but I have to admit — I don't much like flowers. No offense," he laughs, shutting the book of vectors.

"None taken." I pick up the vectors along with the book of moths and slide both back on the shelf. "It's late enough — how about we close and take a little walk to the bookshop? See if we can't find you something you like better?"

His face lights up. "Really? All right — sure!"

We stay too long at the bookstore, but though Julien's already late for his bar shift he drops me off at my door anyway. Rhys calls to me when he hears it swing open.

"Hello darling. How was the day? Uneventful, I hope?"

It had been nearly a month with no sign of Dimitri, and I'd started to forget why Julien was there in the first place. We'd both loosened up — I don't jump at the sound of the door anymore, and he's all but stopped sitting by it. I have to remember not to get too cavalier. Dimitri's arrival is still looming.

"Uneventful, yes, though it was… Unusual." I sit down at the table across from him. He's carefully applying labels to a few dozen blue glass bottles. Despite my additional workload, I'd still been keeping up with as much of the apothecary tasks as possible, and

I'd penned each one of those labels this morning.

"Unusual? How so?"

"Would you believe I actually had Julien drawing today? He's been really inquisitive lately. We actually just came from the bookshop — he doesn't like the flowers so I thought I'd find him something else to copy. He left with an armful."

"Really?" He pauses, thumb pressed against a label. "I had no idea he had it in him."

"Neither did I. He said it always interested him but he never got the chance to try it."

"Seems you've got yourself a student," he says, flashing me his crooked smile. "Do you intend to teach him anything other than drawing?"

Teach him? I guess I sort of had been doing a little of that, however briefly, but the thought of actively teaching hadn't ever occurred to me. I'd never had a student before, but I also hadn't ever wanted one. I didn't think I'd be any good at it.

"I don't know. If he's this interested, I think I owe it to him to see where it could go. I thought he was just bored, but you should've seen him today. It was like he... Unlocked something inside himself, almost. I'm not sure I'm cut out to be any sort of instructor, though. I barely know what I'm doing myself, even though I've been at it forever."

"Darling," he chuckles, setting down the bottle. "*No one* knows what they're doing. That's the big secret. We're all led to believe that the masters of trades and keepers of high accolades are infallible in their knowledge and performance, but once we finally achieve the same level of mastery we find out they're just like everyone else — all of us doing our best. Trying not to... Fuck it all up, if I'm putting it plainly."

I've felt like that my whole life, and there's not a day that goes by without me wondering if I'm going to do exactly that. Fuck it all up.

"Well I sort of hate that, but I'm relieved it's not just

me. Do you know how amazing it is to me sometimes? That people willingly let me transform their bodies? I mean, who deemed me worthy of that? I'm a stranger — these people don't know me from a post in the ground, yet they trust me. I think it's that blind trust that drives me the most. All I want is to live up to what they believe I'm capable of and not disappoint them. Make sure they're happy when they leave."

"And that's why you're successful," he says, covering my hand with his. "Because you *care* about it — *and* them — truly. Your whole heart is in the endeavor, and it might extend past that, even. Tell me — how did you feel today? Did it make you happy to watch him take that first step?"

I think about the excitement on his face when I presented the idea of finding him custom reference, and those not so shaky doodles on his last page. I did like it. Maybe more than I initially thought.

"Honestly, yes. It was… Fun. Especially picking out those books. I just wanted to feed him more — nurture his inspiration."

"Thought so," he smiles. "Your instinct was to nurture, which an important element in any sort of teaching, and it came to you naturally. Despite this doubt you have about yourself, I think you'd make a wonderful instructor." He picks up a new bottle, and lines up the label. "I hope it continues. I think this new development could be very good for the both of you."

⋆⋆⋆⋆⋆⋆ FIFTY-ONE ⋆⋆⋆⋆⋆⋆

It's a quiet morning, and I relish these early hours spent in the greenhouse, my feet bare on the warm wet concrete. Today I'm thinning seedlings, and I'm glad Rhys isn't awake yet. I hate trimming them — I know it's necessary, but I feel like a sort of executioner. Deciding which ones to cut and which to let thrive. He maintains that trimming is the better method, but I'd rather separate their tender roots and carefully place them back in the soil. If he were up he'd have already cut them himself.

A section of lavender has matured, so once I've finished with the seedlings I move on to harvest their long stems. I don't mind trimming these — the plant endures, and produces even more. As I'm clipping the last few strands Rhys' arms creep around my waist, and I smile when I feel his lips on my neck.

"Well good morning to you, too," I giggle. "I started to think you might sleep the day away."

"Not likely," he laughs. "Come on, it's not even that late. I know you were up early to save that calendula from me."

He's seen the seedling trays. "Maybe. You know I don't like how you thin them."

"I'm aware," he says, turning me around to face him. "It's a matter of risk, however unfortunate, but I'll gladly let you do it your way."

I know he's right. When you pull them out you risk damaging the whole lot, and there've been times I've killed more than I saved. I still feel the need to try, extra work or not, and I like that he indulges me anyway. I have a soft spot for the seedlings, and he has a soft spot for me. He's smiling gently, and I love the way he looks when he first wakes up. The shadows under his eyes are deeper, but his dark eyes are always bright, and his silvery hair is a little unkempt. I enjoy the sleepy scent of his skin, the faint trace of petrichor always on it, but today he also smells of resins — frankincense and dragon's blood. He was making incense yesterday, and must've put on the same shirt. His hands move to the small of my back when he leans down to kiss me, and though the greenhouse is warm and humid, goosebumps still raise on my skin. I have more work to finish before Julien arrives, but the way he's pressing me against the edge of the table leads me to believe I might not complete it. There's a tingle of static in my limbs, and I decide it can wait. I'd rather live in this moment, his warm body against mine, the scent of fresh earth hanging in the air. The tasks become an afterthought as I throw my arms around his neck, and let the few strands of lavender I'd been holding fall to the floor.

Miraculously, I'm right on time despite the delay. I'm pulling Rhys' sweater over my head when Julien arrives, and I only have a few more things to pack up before we head in. He's got a stack of books under his arm and seems a little impatient, so I hurriedly lace up my shoes. I'm glad he's eager to get started, and I'm curious to see his progress. He's practiced his sketching daily with me, and Delia said he'd even been doing it at home.

***

"I've never seen him so focused," she says, pursing her lips as she fiddles with the bottle opener. "Good gods. Would you mind?" She hands me the wine bottle, and with two twists the cork is free of its prison. I never figured out why she has such a hard time with opening wine. At first I thought her nails might be impeding her dexterity, but she does just about everything else without issue. "Thank you, doll. I'd be completely out of luck if I washed up on a deserted island."

"It seems you'd be *in* luck," I laugh. "Washing up on a deserted island with cases of wine seems pretty fortunate."

She pours the wine as loud laughter erupts from the

other room. Rhys and Julien are playing cards, and it's their turn to host, so we've sequestered ourselves to the kitchen. She sits down at the glass table as I continue leafing through Julien's artwork. He's gravitated towards fauna rather than the flora that is my standard, choosing to copy images of bears, wolves, and big jungle cats. His drawings are improving little by little, and I'm pleased to see very few eraser marks on the paper. I forbade him from erasing at all for now — I want his sketches to become looser and less rigid. He needs to get used to refining an image after forming the basic shapes, and to stop trying to make them perfect the first time.

"He sits here for hours on end," she says, lighting a cigarette. "He comes home from the studio, goes to work at the bar for a couple hours and then gets right back to it. That television hasn't even been turned on in *days*. That's a long stretch."

Of the four of us, Julien is the only one who spent any amount of time flipping through channels. Delia would give in once in a while, and would fill me in on some film they watched together, but it's not my thing. I've always preferred reading, and so does Rhys. We don't even own a TV.

"I don't know what you did to ignite such a spark in him, but I definitely approve," she says, tapping the edge of the cigarette on the ashtray.

"I didn't press him on it. I honestly never would've suspected he'd take to it like he has."

I hear Rhys groan, accompanied by Julien's booming laugh. Sounds like he's won the round.

"You know, he's always had a good eye for art," she muses, spinning her glass on the table. "We used to go to museums and the like, and I think he enjoyed it far more than I did. *He* picked all these paintings." She gestures to the framed oil on the dining room wall. It's beautiful, the delicate brushstrokes making the woman's flowing garment look like real silk. "I framed them, of course, but I can't take credit for the subject matter."

I didn't know that. She's the decorator, so I assumed it was all her. Maybe his inclination was there all along and no one noticed.

"For us it's always been about me and my work. I love that he has something to call his own," she says. "It's nice to see him inspired for once instead of bored."

***

Julien looks bored now, though. He's standing by the door waiting for me to say goodbye to Rhys, and it's clear I'm taking too long. I don't want to leave him today. The static from the morning is still lingering between us, drawing me to him, making me want to fit myself against him like a puzzle piece. Part of me wants to toss the whole day and do just that, but I have responsibilities. I kiss him one more time, and Julien clears his throat loudly.

"Go on," Rhys chuckles. "I'll be down shortly. One more moment and he's apt to leave without you."

"I just might," Julien laughs. "Come on — hurry up."

Finally we're out the door, and I shift my thoughts to the day ahead. I need to come up with some sort of structure. The flow of business is steady but unpredictable, and I'd like to have designated time to spend working with Julien instead of leaving it to chance.

"I've been doing the shapes like you said," Julien says as we round the corner to the harbor road. Every object has a base shape — triangle, square, circle — and I've had him start breaking everyday things down as an exercise. "It was fun until I tried it on Delia last night. She was *not* pleased."

I have to laugh as I imagine her reaction to her circle head and oblong limbs. "Maybe stick to inanimate objects for now. We'll try people later on."

There's a food truck near the harbor bridge, and the smell of coffee hits me just as we're reaching the studio. I notice him stare longingly at it, and decide I'll run over and get us some once we've settled in. It's raining and his books are getting wet. I hurriedly pull out my key, but when I go to put it in the lock the door swings inward. It's already open. My body tenses — I *know* I locked it yesterday. He watched me do it, and the look he gives me suggests he remembers that clearly.

"Stay here," he instructs, handing me his books. The door creaks as he cautiously swings it the rest of the way open. I watch him quickly survey the room, then disappear into the back. I shift the books in my arms as I wait. From what I can see it looks like everything's in place. Maybe there's something wrong with the lock?

A hand clamps over my mouth and I drop everything. I'm dragged away from the doorway, tripping over my own feet as I stumble. I scream, but the only sound I can get out is muffled. I'm being marched forward, and no matter how much I writhe I can't break free — I'm continuously pushed on through the winding desolate alleyways. I finally get a glimpse of a long black coat, but I already know it's Dimitri.

Finally he stops, slamming me against a wall of cinder block, his hand still over my mouth. I'm struggling to speak — to tell him he didn't need to do this — but he doesn't let me.

"Did you think you might somehow evade me?" He hisses. "That I would simply slink off empty handed when I saw that brute following you around? Know this — Julien does not scare me."

His hand is covering my nose and mouth and I'm having a hard time breathing. It's making me panic and I claw at it, my fingers digging into his skin. He doesn't seem to care — he looks annoyed if anything.

"Make no mistake," he says evenly. "If you scream, I will break your neck."

He releases me, and I gasp for air. He watches scornfully as I double over, my hands on my knees. I don't understand why he's done this. What was the point of getting me alone in an alley, surrounded by dumpsters and reeking trash? Why won't he just stop and listen? Does he enjoy being this dramatic? Making big speeches about loyalty? I'm starting to think his scare tactics are just for show, and they're not scaring me anymore. They're making me angry. I step forward and look him square in the eye.

"If you're so unafraid of Julien why didn't you just come into the studio? Is it because you knew he'd call you out on your bull —"

The heel of his palm connects with my face, and instantly my ears ring. The metallic taste of blood is in my mouth. He's split my lip.

"Do not taunt me — I warn you." He's moving towards me, backing me up against the wall again. I'm still stunned from the blow, and fresh fear is pricking the back of my neck. This isn't an act at all. He's crossed another line and actually hurt me. His eyes narrow, and I start shrinking. "Now where is it?"

"Rhys… Rhys has it."

"That was *not* the arrangement. You were supposed to bring it to *me*."

I spit blood on the ground. I'd like to spit it in his face. "He wants to give it to you himself."

"You *lie*," he snarls, his blue eyes flashing. "This is simply another scheme to derail me. I am *finished* with this — he has only ever wanted to keep me from succeeding, and I will *not* allow this game to continue."

Has he lost his mind? Who is this person standing in front of me? Where did that kind and thoughtful man go? He's nothing like he was when I met him. He's cold and mean, and he thinks everyone's turned on him when it's the exact opposite. I wipe my mouth, and my lip throbs. It's still bleeding.

"Dimitri, he *cares* about you — the only thing he wanted to keep you from was doing something you might regret. Can't you see that?"

"You know *nothing* of regret," he hisses. "What I regret is believing I could trust him."

His shirt collar has come unbuttoned, the edge of the scarring on his chest visible. He hadn't gotten past what happened, had he? He must think Rhys is just out to ruin everything for him all over again. He's clearly held on to that resentment, and it's clouding his rationality. He should know better — Rhys does a lot of things with intent, but hurting people on purpose isn't one of them.

"Dimitri... It was an accident. He didn't mean for it to happen, and he's been desperately trying to make things right ever since. He definitely wasn't trying to hurt you again by doing this. Please — you have to understand that."

He chuckles, and it takes me by surprise. Is he really *laughing* right now? He is — he's shaking his head and staring at the ground. Laughing.

"An accident, indeed," he says. He slicks his wet hair back, flinging the water from his hand with a flick of his wrist. "I thought he showed promise. I thought he wanted to build something together — something *magnificent*. Do you know what he did instead? He took every opportunity to stand in my way, lecturing me as if I were beneath him. All because he was afraid. Weak. I was so close to discovery but he shut me down, and I lost *years* of research as a result. I will *never* forgive him for that, and I *refuse* to let him ride my coattails now. Using my hard work for his own benefit only when it suits him." He steps towards me, and I suck in my breath when he points his finger at my face. "My loyalty to him died the moment he turned my patients against me, and he should have died *right along with it*!"

I'm stunned. This is much deeper than I thought. He doesn't just resent Rhys, he *hates* him, and it's apparent he's hated him for a long time. My clothes are soaked at this point, but I'm not sure if I'm trembling from cold or fear. I have a question I need to ask, and I'm terrified of the answer.

"Why... Why did you save him if you hate him so much? Why..."

His mouth creeps into a hideous smile, and it sends a shiver through me. He steps closer, and I press myself against the cinder block. I wish it would swallow me up.

"Oh, Lynna," he says, shaking his head. "How disappointing. You are as easily fooled as the rest."

My heart is pounding in my ears. He's so close I can smell him — his evergreen aftershave, cigarettes on his breath. I'm shaking fiercely, and I recoil when he brushes his thumb against my lip.

"He was supposed to die in that fire," he says casually, rubbing my blood between his fingers. "But then he went and interrupted my escape. The fall did not kill him either, though I meant it to."

I feel sick, and my knees buckle. He closes his hand around my arm and holds me up against the wall. I don't want to hear any more. I want him to stop. I turn my face away but he wrenches it back, squeezing my jaw as he forces me to look up at him.

"He begged my forgiveness when he saw my burns," he says, his icy eyes boring into mine. "*Begged*, like a dog. I reveled in his groveling. He did anything I asked, because after all, I had risked my life for him — I had *suffered* for him. He is only alive because I permitted it, and I will not allow him to take credit for what is rightfully mine. He owes me for what has been lost. I have waited long enough to collect."

I'm in shock. All I can think about is how broken Rhys had felt — thinking he owed him his life, thinking he'd betrayed his friend. The truth is that Dimitri had tried to kill him — twice — and failed. He only didn't try a third time because he enjoyed that unspoken leverage; enjoyed having Rhys under his thumb.

"You're sick… you're… You're *repulsive*." I can barely speak. My voice is almost a whisper. "*You* should've died in that fire."

This time when he strikes me it knocks me to the ground. A bag of garbage breaks my fall, putrid waste spilling across the gravel when it tears. The smell is enough to make me gag, and I crawl weakly away from it as I cough.

"Get up," he hisses, wrenching me to my feet. The alley is spinning, and I feel fresh blood trickling down my chin. "You will not test me further, do you hear me?"

He drags me through the slim alleys behind the buildings by my arm, and I'm powerless to stop it. He knows I won't call for help even if I do see someone — his leverage over me is our joint secret. If I get the authorities involved I'm at risk of endangering myself right along with him. The only one who can help me is Julien, and he's well out of earshot. I'm grasping at anything to say — any way I can possibly deescalate this before he confronts Rhys — but I'm coming up short. Delia — does he hate her too? I'd heard him say he worried for her — was that a lie? Just like all the nice things he'd said about Rhys?

"Do you know what this will do to her? To Delia?"

"Cordelia has betrayed me time and time again," he spits, jerking my elbow. "But I allowed it — I regret my own weakness for her. She deserves to suffer now."

I don't understand how he can be so cruel. "How can you say that? After all you've been through together? Delia's only ever been your devoted friend."

He stops in his tracks, grabbing my sweater at the collar. "You know *nothing* of devotion, and neither does she." He's fuming, flecks of spit landing on my cheek. "I let her stop what might have been one of my greatest achievements — all because I loved her. I *worshipped* her. I gave her everything, but she discarded me without a second thought — first for the mere *memory* of that pitiful fool, and then for that horrid beast of a man."

His face twists at the mention of Julien, and I stumble on the brick when he forces me forward. My hip glances off the edge of a railing, tearing a hole in my sweater, but he doesn't slow. Did he just say he worshipped her? Has he been in love with her this whole time? Is this yet another thing no one picked up on? My head spins as I try to wrap it around what he just said. Delia would die if she knew how he referred to Vincent.

"That pitiful fool was your friend too. You said he was like a brother —"

"He was in my way."

His voice is cold, his upper lip curled. A shiver rolls through me, and I have to will my legs to keep moving. I'm starting to connect the dots, and I have to clench my fist as I swallow the bile in the back of my throat. Did he really admit what I think he did? I don't want to ask, but I have to. I have to be sure.

"You… You killed him, didn't you?"

"I did not have to." He pauses, checking the street before pulling me across it. "All it took was a few words. A whispered rumor to one of their crew. He was gone the very next day."

I'm in a bad dream. A nightmare. I feel dazed — I'd uncovered one horrible secret after another, and I now know I'd been terribly wrong about Dimitri. There's no reasoning to be done, nothing I can say that will change this course. He's dangerous and unhinged — more than I could've imagined. We're approaching my building, and what's on my mind now isn't what he's done. I'm terrified of what he might do next.

⁕⁕⁕⁕⁕⁕ FIFTY-TWO ⁕⁕⁕⁕⁕⁕

I hear raised voices from inside, and open the door to Rhys and Julien shouting frantically. He must've come back after I went missing. If we'd been on the main road he might've found me. Both their expressions go from relief to horror when they see me, my bloodied face, and Dimitri behind me, nudging me forward. They rush towards us and abruptly stop, just as I feel something sharp against my neck. I can't see it, but it definitely feels like a blade, and I now know that Dimitri had it somewhere in his long coat this whole time. I have my answer. *This* is what he's going to do next.

"Dimitri, *don't*!" Rhys looks like he's in shock. He shakily points to the desk. "I have it here — just *here*! Please — she's done nothing to you!"

Julien moves forward, and I gasp as the knife slices into my skin just a little. There's a faint tickling sensation rolling down my neck. It must've drawn blood.

"Julien, *STOP*!" Rhys shouts, panicked.

Julien halts, his face growing redder by the second. There's fire flashing in his eyes, both his fists clenched tightly.

"Please — just *take* it!" Rhys grabs a bound stack of papers from the desk and tosses them across the floor. They come undone and scatter at my feet. "It's all there, I —"

"Silence," Dimitri interrupts. "I have endured your voice for far too long — you will be quiet for once." He turns to Julien. "And *you* — sit."

Julien scowls, the muscles in his jaw working as he slowly drops into a chair near the table. Rhys is frozen in place, desperation in his dark eyes. His arms are at his sides, palms open in a silent plea.

"You thought you could deny me," Dimitri says. "But now look at you — crumbling under pressure. How easily you are molded. It is almost a shame I no longer have use for you."

I'm breathing shallowly in an effort to keep the blade away from the pulsing artery in my throat. I glance from Rhys to Julien, and he's staring straight at me. He's looking me up and down, from my face to my hip and back again, over and over. What is he doing?

"Please…" Rhys says quietly. "I don't understand…"

Julien continues his eye movements, and it suddenly it clicks into place. My hands are free, Dimitri's knife at my throat, my own knife in my pocket. He'd been adamant I keep it on me at all times, and had even shown me how to use it properly. He's reminding me it's there.

"You have always been too soft. Too weak. I was the fool to ever believe you had any sort of fortitude in the first place," Dimitri says. "I should have done it right. I should have watched you burn."

He guides me by my elbow to bend down, not moving his weapon from my throat. "Pick them up," he instructs, so I reach for the pages. I fumble with them as I slip my other hand into my pocket, closing my fingers around the switchblade. Once I have them all he forces me up, and begins pulling me towards the door. Rhys jerks forward and stops himself.

"Wait — what are you doing?"

"You owe me a debt," Dimitri says. "You have stolen much from me — things that cannot be replaced — so in return I mean to take away what you hold most dear. You should be grateful I do not make you watch. That shall be my very last allowance to you."

He continues to back me away, and a tear rolls down Rhys' cheek. My heart is in my throat, the knife pressed against it. *I* am the debt. The penance. The equalizer. He means to kill me.

I clench my teeth as I carefully flick the knife open, turning it so the blade is at the heel of my palm. I suck in my breath and jam my fist backwards as hard as I can, burying it to the hilt in his abdomen.

It startles him, and his blade slips from my neck. A hot line burns across my chest, and pain blooms below my clavicle. He's plunged it into my skin, and I feel the hard metal graze against bone as he sinks it deeper. I feel a burst of heat in the right side of my body when he pulls it out, and fall forward on my knees. Julien is already out of the chair. He tackles Dimitri, and his knife goes flying but he's still got mine. In a flash he pulls it from his side and drives it into Julien's hip.

Julien roars, and grips him by the front of his shirt, slamming him against the floor. Dull thuds turn to wet slaps as he hits him, only stopping when Dimitri's hands go limp. He slowly gets to his feet, breathing heavily, my knife still sticking out of his leg. The room begins to blur. My shoulder is on fire, a warm wet sensation filling my armpit. I feel Rhys' arms under me, and slump against him.

✶ ✶ ✶ ✶ ✶ ✶ FIFTY-THREE ✶ ✶ ✶ ✶ ✶ ✶

Something cold touches my face, so I hazily blink my eyes open. I'm in the bed and Delia's hovering over me. Her hair is pulled back and she's wearing a silky gray blouse, a faceted onyx gem shining between her collarbones. She looks like she's dressed for work. I look down and see white bandages covering my chest and shoulder. It hurts some, but mostly it feels stiff. I'm trying to piece together what happened. I dimly remember Rhys' panicked face, my blood on his shirt. Delia's tight lipped mouth. I remember she'd given me something for the pain, but I can't recall anything after that. It must've put me to sleep.

"Just cleaning you up a little," she says gently, wiping dried blood from my chin. My face isn't sore anymore, my split lip now a small scab. There's dried blood caked in the crease of my elbow, and it cracks into flakes when I move. "How are you feeling?"

"… Tired." It doesn't seem like I've been out for too long. The blurry harbor lights are visible through the rain streaked windows, but it's still daylight. "Can you… Can I sit up?"

She helps me inch back against the headboard, pulling the sheet over me. My sweater is gone, but I'm in one of my button up tanks, and they've cut off the left strap. Rhys appears over her shoulder, and she steps back so he can sit down next to me. There's a mixture of relief and worry in his eyes, and he silently takes my hand.

"How bad is it?" I ask. I recall the sensation of metal scraping on bone, and it sends a chill through me.

"He missed everything vital, blessedly," he says quietly. He shifts his eyes away, running his thumb over the top of my hand. "I should've stopped it. I should've… I'm so sorry."

I don't think he has anything to be sorry for. I don't really know what he could've done. There weren't any good options at the time. I hear a chair scrape back and Julien hobbles over. His face is drawn, and he gingerly sits on the edge of the bed, his leg extended. I feel terrible he'd been hurt. My wound is likely healing swiftly, but his is not.

"Julien… Your leg…"

"I'm fine," he says. "Delia fixed me up."

He smiles faintly to reassure me, but I'm not entirely convinced. I now know what it feels like to be stabbed. Wait — where is he? Is he still here?

"Where did he go? Where's Dimitri?"

Rhys' eyes shift behind me, and I inhale sharply. Is he standing there? I slowly turn my head and he's not, but I do see the lower half of his body. He's lying on the floor against the back wall, and there's a bandage on his torso. She must've patched him up too.

"It's all right," Delia says, noticing my alarm. "I gave him a sedative. He won't hurt you again."

I don't believe that for one second, nor do I believe he won't try to hurt one of *them*. They aren't yet fully aware of his true nature — they can't be. I don't think Delia would've been able to dress his wound if she knew what he'd done. My whole body is tensing, making my shoulder pulse. This can't wait. I have to tell them. No part of me wants to, but I have to. It feels so unfair that it's on me — that I have to be the one to confess instead of him. I don't even know how to begin.

"I have… There's something you should know. He's… Dimitri been lying to you."

"I'm aware," Rhys says quietly. "He's never let go of it — what I'd done to him. I just never thought he'd take it out on —"

"No. It wasn't your fault. That fire — you didn't start it. *He* did."

"What?" His brows knit. "No. Why would he have…"

"Because you stopped him from whatever he was doing with those patients. He *hates* you for it." He flinches, and I unsuccessfully try to swallow the lump in my throat. "He told me… He intended to trap you in there. He wanted you to *die* in that fire."

I can barely look at him. His face has crumpled, and he's clenching and unclenching his fists.

"But he... He *saved* me from it..."

"He didn't," I sniffle. I couldn't stop my tears even if I tried."You weren't supposed to get out. He pushed you as a last resort — he thought the fall would kill you. You heard him — he said he should've done it right and watched you burn. He's been using you ever since."

He rests his face in his hands, his elbows on his knees. I hate this. It's one of the most awful secrets I've ever had to utter, and it isn't even mine. What's worse is that I'm not done yet. Julien puts his hand on Rhys' shoulder, but he shrugs it away.

"I can't believe this," Delia says, watching Rhys get up and walk slowly towards the windows. She's angry, her arms folded. "I just... Of all the malicious, *sociopathic*..."

She's close enough to touch, so I gently grasp her sleeve. "Delia, sit down."

"What?" She sits carefully beside me. "Is there something more?"

I nod, and my chin trembles. All I want is to pull the blanket up over my head and disappear. Take her with me — take all three of them away to a place where none of these things ever happened.

"Vincent."

It's all I can get out, but it's enough to make her pale. I feel like my heart's about to cave in on itself.

"Did he..." She pauses, and for the first time ever I see fear in her eyes. "How do you know?"

"He told me. He said... He said all it took was a few words to one of those men and he was gone. He wanted to get rid of him because he was in love with you. Delia, he has been the whole time."

"No," she whimpers. She looks sick. "No... He *can't*... He..."

She covers her mouth and stumbles across the floor to the washroom, slamming the door behind her. Julien's face is red again, and he gets up stiffly and slowly limps after her. I hear a match being struck, and when I look up I see Rhys lighting a cigarette with trembling hands. My heart aches for both him and her, their pain and mine radiating from my center. I want to crawl out of my skin. The tape on this bandage is only making that feeling worse, so I carefully peel a little of it back, revealing the tip of a scarlet line in the middle of my chest. I continue to lift it — I know what he did to hurt them, but I need to see the extent of what he did to hurt me.

I wince as I pull the last strip away. The red line severs the ferns decorating my skin, and it connects to a purple splotch near my shoulder, the scabbing seam held together with neatly tied sutures. I press my lips together to stifle a sob, and lie back against the pillows. It could've been worse. I'll heal. Maybe if I keep repeating those things I'll start to believe them.

There's a commotion as the washroom door bursts open, and when I sit up I see Delia striding purposefully towards Dimitri. She kneels down and begins shaking him, and for a moment I'm afraid he'll wake up and grab her so I move to get to my feet. I stand up too fast, so I hold the edge of the headboard to keep myself upright as I exhale my relief. He can't touch her — they'd bound his hands to one of the exposed pipes on the wall. His dark coat is balled up beside him, and the blood on his shirt had dried into a stiff patch. His eyes open, and I'm aware of Rhys steadying my elbow as she leans down.

"Tell me why…Tell me *why*, you bastard! *I know it was you!*" Her voice is fierce and shaky, and her hair's come undone, spilling haphazardly over her shoulder. "How *could* you? How could you pretend all this time? Like it was nothing? Like *he* was nothing?!"

He whispers something I can't hear, and she suddenly slaps him, turning his face towards the wall with the force of it. She gets to her feet, and I see her red face, tears streaming down it. She wrenches her medical bag from the counter, its contents spilling when she slams it on the floor. She paws through them, plastic rustling and her nails scraping the concrete. Rhys takes a step forward when she picks up a small vial with a red top, her hands shaking as she plunges a syringe into it.

"Cordelia…" he says. "Cordelia — *don't*!"

She holds up the syringe, her lip trembling. I'm in suspended animation — what is she doing? Her swollen gray eyes move from Rhys to Julien, and her hand falls. The syringe drops to the floor as she wails, her mouth a square of anguish, and rolls away to rest against the corner of the cabinet. I hear Rhys let out his breath as Julien limps over to help her up. He gently scoops her into his arms as she clings to him, and Rhys moves behind him to her bag. He picks up another syringe and a different vial, and swiftly pulls a little liquid into it before plunging it into Dimitri's arm. His mouth is a thin line as he watches Dimitri's eyes begin to flutter closed. I'm realizing what he just gave Dimitri must be another sedative, but what she was about to do was far different.

"Why don't you take her home." He says quietly, sinking back on his heels. "He should be out for a while."

Silently I open the door so Julien can guide her through, and hear the soft rustle of plastic as Rhys gathers the medical supplies littering the floor. He sets the bag back on the counter and drops heavily into a chair, his head in his hands. I want him to comfort me — to hold me and tell me everything will be fine — but he might need it more than me right now. I touch his shoulder gently, and he responds by wrapping his arms around my waist, pressing his head against my stomach.

"What was that?" I ask, watching Dimitri's shirt move with his breaths. "What was she going to do?"

"Incapacitate him permanently," he says. "I understand why she wanted to, but it wouldn't change anything. The brief satisfaction isn't worth it."

"What's going to happen now? To him? He can't just stay there on the floor."

"I don't know," he sighs. "For now, this is where we are. They'll be back, and then we'll see."

✶ ✶ ✶ ✶ ✶ ✶ *FIFTY-FOUR* ✶ ✶ ✶ ✶ ✶ ✶

Julien returns sans Delia, and he looks like he's bathed, his wet blonde hair dark in its top knot. He shuts the door quietly, and Rhys calls to him without looking up.

"There's coffee on," he says. My sutures are out and he's rubbing salve on my wound, now a long pink scar.

"How is she?" I ask. I'm concerned that she's absent.

"Marginally improved. She slept a bit, which I think helped. She'll be by later. Said she had to make some calls."

"That should do for now," Rhys says, capping the jar. "If you'll excuse me, I'm going to wash up. Julien... would you mind keeping an eye on him?"

He'd given Dimitri another dose and he's presently asleep, facing the wall. Julien doesn't even glance in his direction.

"Yeah. Go on."

We sit silently at the table after he's closed the washroom door, rain tapping steadily on the skylight. Finally I get up to retrieve a box of papers and some loose tobacco to roll more cigarettes. We'd typically allot ourselves a certain amount for the day, but we'd mown through them quickly. Julien winces slightly when he stands to pour himself a refill.

"How's your leg?"

"It's not bad. The ointment's helping already," he says, replacing the carafe. His eyes move to my shoulder. "You're looking much better, which I'm happy to see."

"I didn't ever imagine I'd acquire any sort of battle wound," I sigh. "Maybe I can make up a better story for it."

He smiles faintly. "Just don't leave your part out. You're a little braver than I gave you credit for. Got him right when it counted."

"That was largely because of you. I'm glad you made me keep that knife on me."

"So am I," Julien says, watching me fasten the paper. He finally looks over his shoulder when Dimitri stirs, making sure he's still sedated. "You know… I never trusted him, if I'm being honest. Should've listened to my gut from the very start."

I wish I would've listened to mine too. That brief inkling — that moment I questioned his dynamic with Rhys. I'd second guessed it right out of my head, but then again I had no solid evidence to back it up. It's another mistake only made clear in hindsight. I'd mistaken him for a friend, and now I wish I hadn't. I set the cigarette down and start on another.

"Can't change that now," he says, turning back around. "The only thing good to come from knowing him is Delia."

I think about the overlapped circles making up all their relationships. I know how most of them are connected now, but I hadn't ever asked how Julien had come to know Delia. It doesn't make sense that it'd be through Dimitri. Maybe asking about her will give us a break from all this heaviness.

"How did you meet her?"

"Rhys," he says, smiling a little more. "He likes to credit himself with our relationship, and I guess it's mostly accurate. I met him after the incident with his and Dimitri's practice. He'd taken some time away — and distance. He moved clear across the continent. He was ready to go back and I was going with him, and he had a bunch of supplies he wanted to give to an old friend. Try and reconnect. It just so happened that friend was Delia." He sets his elbow on the table and leans his head against his fist, a dreamy look in his eyes. "I'll never forget the day we met. I was helping him carry boxes into her apartment, and I dropped one of them. Broken glass everywhere. Gods, I'd never heard a woman so beautiful curse so much. I think I fell in love that very moment."

I'm picturing it. Delia swearing as she bends to pick up broken glass. Julien towering above her, lovestruck.

"I couldn't get her out of my head. I was intent on

pursuing her, but Rhys warned me she might not be open to it. Broke my heart when I found out what she'd been through. It led us to find common ground almost right away though — had things we pushed down, couldn't deal with. We understood each other, and that understanding let us come to terms with a lot of things, and build a life together. It hasn't always been easy, but it's been worth it. I'm grateful every day that she chose to live, and chose me to share that life with."

I haven't ever heard him say something so sentimental. I knew he and Delia cared deeply for one another, but they never really talked about it. Getting a little peek at their beginning is sort of touching.

"Julien, that's… Awfully romantic."

He laughs softly. "Rhys doesn't hold the monopoly on romance. I like to think he's picked up a good bit of it from me."

Rhys eventually emerges from the washroom, and I take my turn in it. The minutes tick on as we wait for Delia, circling a loop of uncertainty. I already knew we couldn't treat this situation like normal people would — marching him in to the authorities is right out, so I didn't even bring it up. I'd asked again if they had an answer for the question of what to do about him, and they both seemed optimistic that Delia would return with one, but didn't elaborate. I have to assume there's something in the works that'll be explained when she arrives, and I'm hoping that happens sooner rather than later. Rhys said he can't give him any more sedatives, and it won't be much longer before the last one wears off.

I'm pacing beside the window when Delia opens the door. She's in fresh clothes, but her face is puffy and devoid of any makeup. She's clearly avoiding looking in Dimitri's direction, and sits down at the table with her back to him, looping the handle of her tote over her chair.

"When was the last dose?" She asks.

"A couple hours ago." Rhys says. "He should be coming out of it any minute now."

"Give him another."

"Delia, he's already well past the threshold —"

"*Give him another*," she says firmly. She stares at him, her bloodshot eyes watery. "Please."

I watch him take a deep breath, and he silently rises. Delia digs her silver case from her tote as Rhys extends Dimitri's unconsciousness, and when he's back at the table she clears her throat.

"Bear with me, here," she says, clamping a cigarette between her teeth. "I'm out of sorts, and I've just had a lot of information thrown at me. It took some doing, but I was able to get in touch with that former colleague from my days up north — the one who ran those drug trials I did dictation for."

"And?" Rhys sits forward. "Is she still connected?"

"She is, and she apparently has a direct line. I was fairly vague when I spoke with her, but she must've pleaded my case well, because I was contacted by an associate to the council. An actual *associate*. They've already sent a transport to collect him. It shouldn't be more than another hour or so."

"Gods," Rhys sighs, sinking back in the chair. "That's unbelievable. Thank you Delia, it seems you've saved the day."

"Not so fast," she says, smoke curling up from her nostrils. "I talked with the associate for a long time. He wanted details, of course, and he came back with a rather disturbing bit of news. Dimitri's been on the run from the council — for years on end. I hate to say you're lucky this came to a head before he roped you into collaborating with him again, but you are. If he had he surely would've tried to take you down with him."

His brows knit, and he folds his arms over his chest. "Why was he on the run?"

"It sounds like it was exactly what you tried to stop him from way back when, except worse. Experimentation without caution. Malpractice of an immeasurable sort. He'd vacate once it became noticeable, but he's left a trail of dead or permanently immobilized patients in his wake. He wasn't traveling on and off all these years because it was easier to practice. He was trying to avoid being caught."

"Fuck," Julien mumbles. "That whole thing with Sierra. The engagement was just another con — he was using her wasn't he? I *knew* something was off."

"That's exactly what that was," she says. "She was gullible enough to go along with it, too. Poor thing. No wonder she hated me. I can't even blame her for it."

Rhys picks up a cigarette just as Delia stubs hers out. "That's something else we should address. Do you think there will be an issue? With Sierra? It's a little worrisome now that he won't be around to keep a handle on it."

"She's better off anyway," Delia says. "Much better off. Regardless, it's out of our hands. When I said that associate wanted details I meant it, and that included anyone Dimitri was close with. I think they intend to follow up with her, and I'd much rather them deal with it. They're better equipped."

I've been sitting quietly, trying to absorb everything she'd laid out on the table, but I can't continue to remain silent. I have questions. I have so many questions.

"Can we back up for a second? What's this... Council?"

"A collective of others, like us," she says. "Elders, in a sense. They're sometimes able to... Handle situations our kind can't reveal publicly."

"And you're just *now* mentioning them?"

"Knowing they exist is irrelevant," Rhys says, tapping the ash from the cigarette. "No one's granted an audience unless you're someone of utmost importance, so the chances of you, me, or any of us ever coming in contact with them is slim to none. That is, unless you make a habit of performing despicable acts, it would seem. It's almost impossible to find out anything about them, so there's not much *to* mention. We don't even know where they're based."

"It's a miracle I was able to pull off what I did today," Delia says. "We're lucky I'm resourceful — *and* persistent." She pushes her chair back. "I should go. I directed them to meet me at the back stairwell, and they said they'd be punctual."

Julien stands up. "I'll wait with you."

＊＊＊＊＊＊ *FIFTY-FIVE* ＊＊＊＊＊＊

It's a little chilly near the water, but I'd warmed up since I started moving. Julien and I are slowly and silently jogging around the harbor, and I'm hoping it's the start to getting back to some semblance of normalcy. I had mistakenly thought that the heaviness in the air would be gone right along with Dimitri. It's been a few days since the anonymous dark suited men led him away but the weight remains, and I'm trying not to let it bury me. I was more than agreeable when Julien showed up to see if I wanted to take a quick run — I hadn't seen him or Delia since. I worried about his leg, but he assured me the ointment was working its magic, and it's evident by his easy gait that it is.

He's asked me how I'm doing, and I'd answered with a half truth. I don't hurt anymore. My wound is just a scar now, and I'm trying not to let it bother me but the memory it carries is still a little painful. The silvery line is a constant reminder of Dimitri's betrayal and I'd catch Rhys staring at it, though he'd glance away immediately. It leaves me wondering if he feels differently about me now. There's a tension between us — he's distant, and he won't look me in the eyes. It's crushing, but I keep telling myself he just needs time — that we *all* need time — and if I stay positive it'll get us there quicker. I'm not going to let this get the best of me.

Julien stops at the end of the last dock. Instead of turning around he lowers himself onto the edge, dangling his feet over the dark water. I sit down next to him and try not to make a face. The air by the docks always carries the scent of something stale and briny.

"It's gross," Julien smirks, noticing me wrinkle my nose. "Don't worry — I just want to sit for a moment. Been stuck inside too long."

"Has Delia gone back to work?"

He shakes his head slowly. There's a small scattering

of pebbles on the wooden planks, and he picks one up and tosses it into the water.

"She hasn't gotten out of bed for days. She won't talk to me about it either, which is abnormal." He picks up another rock and bounces it in his hand before throwing it. It seems we're having parallel experiences. Rhys barely says anything at all. "I know her, though. I know she feels responsible for what happened to Vincent — as if she could've stopped it had she seen through Dimitri. It opened a very old and deep wound for her."

I pick up one of the pebbles as he flings another. It's the color of bone, its smooth surface embedded with flecks of black. I sort of wish I'd have kept everything Dimitri told me to myself. I can't help but feel like I'm responsible for some of this pain.

"Do you think she'll talk to me?" I ask. It's a little daunting — I felt her hurt radiate through me when she screamed at Dimitri, and I know I'll absorb some of whatever she's feeling currently. If she's in a hole there's a fair chance I'll let it suck me in too, but I can't worry about how it might affect me. I want to be there for her if I can.

"I hate to put that on you. It's a big ask," he says. "But if you're willing, I'd appreciate it. She might be more open to talking about it with you. I think that's what she needs most. Just to talk about it."

"I *am* willing." I want to ask him if he'll return the favor, but I don't think I'm going to. If I say something's wrong between me and Rhys out loud it makes it real, and I don't want it to be real. I shove my hands in my pockets as I shiver. "I'll do it today, in fact. Let's go back — it's cold."

I'm still feeling a chill once I'm back in the apartment, even though I'd changed my clothes. I curl my fingers around the hot cup Rhys pours me in hopes the warmth will travel into the rest of my body. I watch him pull the collar of his shirt up to his nose, and he sighs as he begins unbuttoning it. He's been wearing it for three days in a row.

"How was your run?" He asks. His back is to me, the dark birds moving as he pulls a fresh shirt over his head.

"Cold, but otherwise fine. Julien seems to be moving about easier, but he's worried about Delia. I'm going over there in a bit to see how she is."

He turns around, his eyes catching on my shoulder before darting away. I pull my sweater up as he begins fitting cigarettes into his pocket.

"Getting out of here is probably a good idea," he says. "I'll come with you."

Julien gives me a half smile when he answers the door, and he looks happy to see Rhys behind me. I'm hoping them being in the same place will help. Julien's always good at lifting Rhys' mood. I leave them to the kitchen and wind through their apartment to the bedroom. It's dark, all the shades shut tight, and I can barely make out Delia's small form huddled under the patterned duvet. I crack one of the window shades, letting small slivers of light cascade across the blanket, and she stirs.

"Lynna?" Her voice is a whisper. "Is that you?"

"It's me."

She moves part of the covers back so I climb in next to her, and she rests her forehead against my arm. The air is thick with stale cigarette smoke and despair. It's weighing me down already, pressing me into the bed. It's hard seeing her like this — the most unstoppable person I know lying curled in the fetal position, her hair tangled and her face wet with tears. I don't know what to say to her. Should I say anything at all? I find her hand and fold it into mine, and she whimpers.

"I just... I feel so empty." Her voice is raspy, almost a whisper. "Gouged out. That bastard cried right along with me after Vincent was found. Gods... it makes me sick to recall. How he could look me in the eyes day after day is just... *Unfathomable*. Pretending he hadn't taken something from me. Pretending *he* wasn't the one who'd broken me. Encouraging me to move on with my life... And I *did*... And now I feel like *I'm* the one who's betrayed Vincent because I didn't know…"

She lets out a sob and buries her face in the pillow, but I don't let go of her hand. He emotions are rolling through me — pain, regret, loss — and they settle in the center of my chest, making it hard to breathe. I can't help but picture myself in her place, and imagining my life without Rhys sinks me deeper, my eyes welling as my breath catches. I'm on dangerous ground — if I'm not careful this will swallow me whole, too.

The strips of light from the slatted blinds inch slowly across the bed as I lie still beside her, her hand in mine. Finally she rolls over, stretching her arm to the silver cigarette case on her nightstand, the ashtray next to it overflowing. She sits up a little, clearing her throat as she lights a cigarette.

"The more I think back, the angrier I get," she says, exhaling a cloud. "I remember things that should've been obvious. The way he looked at me, or things he said in passing. The way he imitated Vincent, even. I thought it was because he respected him — admired him — but I think he was really trying to *become* him. Trying to take his place." She takes a long drag from the cigarette. "When he found out I was seeing Julien he told me it was too soon," she scoffs. "*Too soon*. It had been *years*. He had me questioning myself over it, even though he was the one telling me to move on in the first place."

She sniffles, tapping the cigarette over the ashtray. Shimmering tracks of tears roll down her cheeks, and she wipes them with her sleeve.

"I told myself I'd never let Vincent go, and I felt terrible when I started to," she says. "So I kept trotting out those memories, getting lost in the past, wishing things were different. It's only ever hurt me, and I know it hurts Julien even though he doesn't say it, so I've been trying to keep it to myself. Gods, none of this has ever been fair to him. That thought alone makes me feel so much worse. One day it'll finally be too much, and I won't even be able to blame him if he abandons me."

"I don't think he would — he loves you." I'm trying to reassure her, but maybe what I'm doing is reassuring myself. I can only imagine what it must be like to live alongside someone so haunted by the echoes of a love lost, sitting by and watching them slip back into it. I don't know how Julien does it. I think it would make me feel like I wasn't enough. Like I'd never be enough. "And I love you too. So does Rhys."

"I know," she sighs, squeezing my hand as she stubs out the cigarette. There's no more room in the ashtray, so she stamps it on the glass topped table instead. "And I feel terrible for behaving like this — the two of you have had an awful time of it and I haven't been there."

"You don't have to be the backbone of everything, you know. You're allowed to feel hurt, same as us."

A ghost of a smile flickers on her mouth. "I think I prefer being the backbone." She rubs her eyes, and slowly peels the blanket back, staring down at her wrinkled t-shirt. "This has to end. I've hit my expiration date on grief, and it'll only get worse if I continue to stretch it out. Let me wash up — a hot bath should make me more willing to rejoin the living."

Julien and Rhys are on opposite sofas in the living room, Rhys resting his head against the back and Julien with his feet up on the coffee table. Both look at me expectantly.

"She's out of bed. She's washing up now."

Julien gets up as I circle around the sofa, and mouths a 'thank you' when he passes. I don't want to be thanked — all I did was listen, and I know she'd do the same for me. I only hope my presence was what she needed at the time. I drop onto the sofa next to Rhys, exhausted. The conversation with Delia had drained me more than I thought. My heart flutters when he slides his arm around me — it's comforting. We'd barely touched in days. I sink against him and close my eyes for what I think is only a few minutes, but when I open them again I find myself fully lying down, my head in his lap. Delia is out of the bedroom and dressed, though her face is still bare, and she's curled up next to Julien. The three of them are talking quietly.

"Well there you are," Rhys says when I sit up. "Just in time, too. I was about to wake you."

"Sorry," I yawn. "I didn't realize how tired I was. What are you talking about?"

"Delia has made a suggestion, and I think I'm on board if you are."

"I think we could use a bit of an escape — a reset, if you will," Delia says. "Or at least, *I* could."

I sit up a little more. "Do you mean... Go somewhere?"

"Exactly that," she says. "I think a change of scenery might do some good. We were just discussing where."

I'm not opposed to it. Maybe a little time away will make everything feel new again. We can't seem to get back to the way things were as is.

"All right — I'm on board."

"Good," Rhys says. "I think I have an idea."

✶ ✶ ✶ ✶ ✶ ✶ *FIFTY-SIX* ✶ ✶ ✶ ✶ ✶ ✶

The wind cuts right through me, so I pull my jacket tighter. Rhys made note of the potential for colder weather, but I wasn't expecting it to be this drastic. I think I may have gotten too used to the mildly fluctuating climate of the city.

"Here," Rhys says, tossing a set of keys to Julien. "You're driving."

We've just finished loading our things into a rented car after departing the rail, and I'm praying whatever awaits us at the end of the winding mountain road is a place with heat and running water. I hadn't been given much detail except that the cabin belongs to Sergio, and he stays there a couple months out of the year. None of them had ever seen it before.

"Really?" Julien groans as he drops into the seat, Delia beside him. "You *had* to pick this car?"

"It was all they had left," Rhys says, frowning at the less than ample legroom in the backseat.

Julien rolls his eyes as he starts it, and the car jerks before stalling. He tries again with the same result, and Delia sighs loudly as she rubs her forehead. She looks both tired and annoyed. I peer over the seat as Julien takes a deep breath and shifts the car into gear, but it stalls again. I know what his problem is, but he looks so frustrated I'm a little hesitant to announce it.

"Julien… You're starting in third gear."

"Fuck," he mutters, moving the shifter into first. He takes his foot off the clutch too soon, and the car halts. His green eyes meet mine in the rearview. "I've only done this two or three times and it was *years* ago," He half laughs, shifting his eyes to Rhys. "*I'm* thinking we should make the person who rented this thing operate it."

"Don't look at me," Rhys says. "I'd really prefer not to spend the entirety of the trip in this parking lot, which is what we'll be doing if I'm tasked with it."

I'm a little surprised, and have to stop from laughing. "Really? *None* of you can drive? Have you lived under rocks your whole lives?"

It occurs to me that that might be the case. None of them own cars, and I'd never seen them behind the wheel at all. I almost do laugh when both Rhys and Julien defensively assure me they're more than capable when it comes to automatic vehicles, and I have to side with them in the fact that automatic is generally the standard format. Delia declares the opposite.

"It's unnecessary in the city. If I want to go somewhere I'll take a taxi or walk," she says pointedly. "I've never driven and I'm not about to start now, so one of you had better figure something out."

Julien's eyes are on me again in the rearview, and they're crinkling at the corners. "Fess up," he grins. "You can drive this, can't you? Don't make me embarrass myself again."

They're all looking at me, and I sort of regret opening my mouth. It had been a number of years since I'd driven anything at all, so there's a fair chance *I'll* be the one who's embarrassed. I'd done the same as Delia and relied heavily on the public transportation available in nearly every place I'd lived, but Julien isn't wrong. I'm pretty sure I can get us moving without much issue. My mentor had taught me, and I recall his wheezing dry laugh as I stalled his rusty car over and over on the roads surrounding his studio. He'd drilled that skill into me, and I'm hoping it stuck as well as tattooing had.

I open my door and brace myself against the wind, and we have a little parade around the car as we switch seats — Julien with me, and Delia with Rhys.

"Come on — cater to my ego and make it look less easy," Julien says over my shoulder as I shift into gear and the car rolls seamlessly forward. It jerks when I pull out of the parking lot, and he laughs when I frown. I hadn't done that on purpose.

I'm thankful the road is empty and the weather clear. I

wouldn't have been so willing had it been pouring rain. We climb the long road up the mountain through a forest of tall pines, the dark green landscape peppered with deciduous trees, their leaves turning beautiful shades of bright gold and orange. Rhys directs me onto a side road, and it becomes noticeably bumpier as we cross from pavement to gravel. After what feels like a long time the thick wall of trees opens to reveal our destination, and I gasp softly. It's barely a cabin in any sense of the word.

The enormous house sits overlooking the mountain pass, a shimmering lake below. The construction is modern instead of rustic — I was expecting a wooden A frame but this is asymmetrical, all smooth stone and glass and metal. The windowed walls connect to a wide wooden deck surrounded by several levels of granite outcroppings with steps in between. It's amazing. I've never seen anything like it in person. Once inside, I drop my bag in the entry as I survey the massive interior. It has a trace of what I imagined, but only a trace. Several walls are bisected logs, the furnishings all leather and chunky wood, and the mantel of the enormous fireplace is a large rough edged piece of stone. White fur throws are draped over the couches and decorate the floors, and a round wrought iron chandelier with what looks like a hundred bulbs hangs suspended from the highest part of the ceiling. I'm still not entirely clear on what Sergio does for a living, but he must be doing well. Delia must think the same, because she echoes my thought.

"This is hardly a cabin, Rhys," she says, dropping her tote by the kitchen island. The surface is a beautiful single slab of wood, and she runs her finger along a knot near the edge. "Sergio's doing better than he let on."

I pause next to her to admire the counter. "I can't believe you know someone with a house like this."

"It's one of many," Rhys says, carefully setting down a box next to the sink. "And while most of Sergio's properties are nice, this one is definitely something. I think he bought it from an architect."

Delia begins rummaging through the box he's brought in while he and Julien finish unloading the car, so I take our bags up to figure out where we'll be sleeping. It only gets more astonishing after I'm up the stairs — there are no less than five bedrooms, all with views of the lake. I choose one at the far end of the house, and immediately flop onto the bed. The bed, like every other piece of furniture in this place, is draped with a white fur throw. It's a bright room, the linens and walls both the same white, but the tigerwood headboard gives it a little warmth. There's a fireplace in here too — more irregular stone — and I'm already imagining the cozy flickering glow.

I let out a sigh, the covers rustling as I turn. It's almost too quiet here, and I don't know how I'll be able to sleep without the sounds of the city and the rain. Maybe I won't have to. The sun is setting, covering the room in a pink glow, but dark clouds are rolling low through the snowy mountaintops. There's a sliding glass door with a barrier railing, and when I open it I'm met with deliciously crisp air. It smells of fresh pine and impending precipitation, and the sloping hillside below is packed with lines of golden trees, their leaves falling like glitter with every gust of wind. It's so beautiful I momentarily forget why we're here in the first place. It seem Rhys had the right idea when he suggested it. I hear footsteps on the wood floor behind me, but I already know it's him before I turn around.

"Feels like it's getting colder. I'll be surprised if we don't wake up to snow falling," he says as he unearths a sweater from his bag. I watch longingly as he unbuttons his shirt to trade it for something warmer, and he offers me a small smile as he shrugs it over his shoulders. "Darling, close that door before you freeze. I can hear your teeth chattering."

I slide the glass closed, and he's already halfway through the door so I follow. It appears they haven't wasted any time. There's a fire going and Delia's parked herself on one of the large leather couches, wine in hand, while Julien's in a room right off the kitchen, opening and shutting cabinet doors.

"Interesting," he mumbles, discovering what looks like very expensive camera equipment. "Why he'd store that next to boxes of expired pasta is beyond me." He opens the one next to it, and inside is a hoard of scotch and whiskey bottles alongside an array of cut-glass decanters. His toothy grin appears. "Oh, *yes*. Rhys? Sergio said make ourselves at home, did he not?"

"He did," Rhys calls. He's adding more kindling to the fire, and embers flicker as he drops the last piece on. "Why?"

Julien doesn't answer. Instead he begins clanking through the bottles, so Rhys abandons the fire. Julien holds one up to show him, and his brows lift when he inspects the label.

"Heavens," he says. "Perhaps not this one. I don't want to wear out our welcome."

"Buzzkill," Julien mutters, elbowing him. He pulls the top from one of the decanters and inhales deeply. "This is good enough."

He begins pouring so I decide to follow suit, and help myself from the already open bottle on the counter. Delia motions for me to sit next to her beneath the throw blanket but I'm hesitant to have red wine next to anything white, and pause before sitting. She rolls her eyes as she watches me debate it, so I tell myself I'll be extra careful, and hope Sergio will forgive me if I ruin anything. We sit silently as the sky grows dark, listening to the crackle of the wood along with Julien and Rhys' quiet voices from the kitchen. Finally she speaks.

"I've wanted a fireplace for a long time, but there are none in our building," she says. "I hope we don't run out of firewood."

"I doubt we will," Julien says from behind me. I hadn't heard him come over. "The back wall outside is stacked high."

"Good," she says, leather creaking on the couch as she shifts. "I intend to sit here all evening."

Julien is standing behind the couch, and I'm getting the feeling he'd like to be a little closer to her. I finish what's in my glass and head into the kitchen to give him an opening, and linger until I see him sit down. Rhys is next to the windows so I join him, and we stand side by side watching the moon glow hazily behind the clouds. I want to lean against him but I'm hesitant — we'd barely been ourselves recently, and a gap had grown between us. I feel like we're standing on mirrored cliffs, and I don't know how to get to his side. His smiles are forced and when he does touch me it feels stiff. Unfamiliar. Is it me? Am I different to him somehow? Had we been irreparably damaged? I can barely ask myself those questions so I haven't asked him. I haven't said anything at all because I'm afraid of the answers.

"Look," he whispers. "It's snowing."

It is, the scant flakes swirling in the moonlight, white dust gathering on the windowsills. I hadn't seen snow in years. The city never falls to a temperature allowing it to form, and I'd mostly avoided living in places where it occurred. I'd forgotten how beautiful it is — it might even be worth the cold.

I turn to announce the snow to Julien and Delia, but it appears I'd made the right move. They're cuddled together beneath the throw — her head on his chest, and him softly running his fingers through her dark hair. I feel like we should give them some space, so I nudge his elbow. He takes my cue, and we circle around them to tiptoe up the stairs. Seeing them being affectionate is promising. If they can heal from this it gives me hope that we can too.

"We should have a fire in here then, shouldn't we?" He asks, stooping in front of the hearth. "Since they've taken over the one downstairs?"

I'd brought my now full wineglass with me, and cautiously set it on the nightstand away from the white linens.

"Definitely."

He places kindling on the grate as I lean back on my hands. The snow is coming down faster now, the white dots flitting silently in the dark. I can't see the lake anymore, just the steady glow of the moon high above the trees. The flames begin to crackle pleasantly, casting our shadows on the wall, and he sits down next to me on the edge of the bed. He smells like sultry smoke, petrichor, and a little bit of whiskey. It's only piling onto the ambiance already present. The snow, the fire, the fur — all of it is begging me to kiss him, so I gently press my hand against his fuzzy cheek and brush my lips to his. He responds, and my heart flutters when he shifts towards me, so I take that as an invitation and pull him down onto the soft throw. I want to feel his skin against mine — that warm radiance — so I tug at the hem of his sweater and he lets me lift it over his shoulders. I pull my own over my head, but when I reach for him he pauses. He stares somberly at it — at that silvern line crossing my chest — and shifts back to gaze into the fire.

I feel like I might burst into tears. He pulled away from me. He's *never* pulled away from me, and it hurts. We'd barely touched each other since it happened and it seems to center on my injury, like it's a wall we can't climb. I hitch the blanket up around my chest as I fight the tightness in my throat. It devastates me to think he can't see me anymore. Have I been obscured by this horrible snaking line carved into me? Is that what I've been reduced to? I sniffle loudly, and it breaks him out of his trance.

"Darling?"

The tears are coming and I can't stop them. I tried so hard to put on my brave face for everyone in an effort to get past this, but I can't pretend nothing's wrong anymore.

"I don't know what's happening," I whimper. "You're so different. You don't look at me the same, and you're so quiet all the time. It's this, isn't it?" I point to the offending mark, and his eyes shift to it then immediately drop to his lap. It only confirms my theory, and makes me feel worse.

"We haven't… We've barely touched, and we don't say more than a few words at a time to each other. I can't rid myself of this, Rhys. It's part of me now whether I want it to be or not, but I'm still *me* underneath it. This distance between us… It's *killing* me. You've pushed me away and I can't *bear* it!"

His face falls, and I cover my own with my hands as I sob. I feel like a cup filled with too much water, my emotions bubbling over the edge as it continues to overflow. The bed shifts as he folds me into his arms, and I hear his heart racing as he holds me tight against him.

"Gods," he says quietly. "I didn't… I *never* meant to make you feel this way. I'm sick at the thought of it." He rests his cheek against the top of my head, warmth from his body flowing into mine. "I've been letting it consume me — the guilt in knowing I've let you down even though I said I'd do everything to protect you. I *let him hurt* you, and he nearly took you from me. All out of my own blindness to what he was."

"I started to think you didn't want me anymore now that I have this," I sniffle. "Every time you look at it you have to look away."

He shifts back and gently brings his hand up to trace the raised line. My chin trembles as he locks eyes with me, and a tear spills over his cheek. He swallows hard, and when he speaks again his voice is low and gravelly.

"Don't ever think I'd love you less because of this," he says, static in his fingertips. "I love you more now than before. I've just… I've let my guilt cloud everything. I let it get in the way and now it's made things so much worse…"

I wrap my arms around him and he embraces me right back, threading his fingers through my hair. The gap between us has closed, the ravine filled in. My heart is full again knowing he doesn't feel any differently, and my body begins to relax as the tension drifts away. We lie quietly for a long time, arms still encircling each other, his heartbeat steady beneath my cheek.

"I don't know that I'll ever forgive myself," he says softly, breaking the silence.

"There's nothing to forgive. You did all you could — I know it, and I need you to know it too. Please — don't close yourself off from me like that. I can't help but think terrible things when you do."

"It pains me immensely to know you'd think them at all," he says wearily. "How I feel about you is something I don't ever want you to doubt."

I consider all he's said as we lie silently, warm flames flickering in the hearth. Maybe I'd been a little selfish, and let my own hurt get in the way. He's suffering just as much as I am, and I assumed I knew how he felt but what I should've done was ask. Instead I doubted him, and I doubted myself.

✶✶✶✶✶✶ FIFTY-SEVEN ✶✶✶✶✶✶

The sun came out and melted most of the snow, but I still have to sidestep the wet remnants on the deck. The wind had disappeared too, but it had blown most of the leaves from the yellow trees, leaving them bare with a carpeting of gold beneath them. I hear Rhys' laugh from inside, and the sound warms me almost as much as the sun. I'd left him and Julien to demolish the rest of the coffee so I could look over the lake, the day starting out brighter in every respect.

The fire was still burning when morning came, dim embers glowing in their ashen bed. I felt rested — it was the first time in nearly two weeks that I'd slept through the night. He looked less tired too, and there wasn't a trace of sadness in his eyes. Instead their corners were crinkled in their usual quiet amusement, and when I apologized for what I said he made it known that I didn't have anything to be sorry for. Warmth rolls through me as I recall the feeling of his lips on mine, moving down my neck onto that long scar — never stopping, never pausing once. I know I was partially at fault for the distance between us but it's gone now. We've found our way back to each other, and that familiar electric hum has been radiating through me all morning.

As I'm looking out over the water I notice a dock near the bottom of the slope, a figure sitting on the edge. I assumed she was still in bed but it's unmistakably Delia, her black hair shining in the sunlight. I step onto the pebbled path to walk down to her — she might want to be alone, but there's only one way to find out. If she does I'll know right away.

She turns when she hears my feet on the wooden planks, and I'm relieved to see her wearing both her makeup and a smile. She pats her hand on the dock so I sit down next to her, dangling my legs over the edge. The water is a deep cobalt in the center, small waves lapping the edge where it's clear and much greener in color. There's algae gently waving beneath the surface, along with the darting movements of small fish.

"Did you sleep all right?" I ask, and she nods.

"For the first time in a while, actually. And an appropriate amount — not too much." She squints out at the water, a smirk settling on her lips. "I have to assume you rested well. You two certainly didn't sleep in this morning."

How does she know we didn't sleep in? Did she *hear* us? The burning in my cheeks isn't from the sun, and she snickers when she notices my expression.

"Fun fact," she says. "Whoever built that house doesn't know a thing about privacy. You can hear everything *in* the damn place."

She definitely heard. That means Julien probably did too. I'm absolutely mortified.

"Delia, I am *so* sorry."

"Oh, it wasn't that bad," she laughs. "All right, it was a *little* bad, but it was also relieving. A good sign." I finally look at her, and her face is soft. "I didn't want to eavesdrop, but there wasn't much I could do about it. I heard some of your conversation from last night."

I'm not surprised she did. We weren't exactly speaking softly. I don't say anything, and she pats my hand gently.

"Honestly, it woke me up a little inside. I was so consumed with my own trauma that I hadn't realized the full extent of how difficult things were for you both. I know how much you care for each other, but we're all susceptible to getting lost along the way. Damaged goods, the lot of us."

I scoot closer until we're nearly touching. "You seem more like yourself right now, which I'm glad for. Julien was awfully cheery earlier so I gather things are better there too?"

"Worlds better," she says, gazing out over the water. "I had to accept that I could lose him too if I keep getting in my head, and I can bear the thought of that no more than I can bear the incidents of the past."

She leans back on her palms and turns her face towards the sky. Birds are flocking overhead, their cries echoing as they circle.

"I kept a part of Vincent alive through Dimitri," she says, brushing her hair out of her face. "But it's different now — it's tarnished — and maybe that's for the best. I can keep my memories, but I have to really let him go. I have to let it *all* go before it destroys everything good in my life. I know grief isn't linear, but I think I've finally hit my end point. I'm ready."

I pick at the splintery wooden dock as I listen. It's a profound moment for her, and I'm a little touched she's sharing it with me. I can feel the lightness emanating from her, some of that weight lifted, and it feels good. So much better than the heavy sorrow I felt in her bedroom. The birds circle once more, their mass forming an ever changing shape as they group and spread apart, and we watch as they disappear over the trees.

"We all have scars," she says, softly running her thumb over my shoulder. "But we have to learn to let them be just that, and not reopen them into fresh wounds."

She grasps my hand, so I squeeze it back. We sit for a while, the now warm wind blowing through our hair, carrying the scent of pine and musky water. I'm happy she's back to feeling more like herself again, and I am too. I feel cleansed by the snow and mountain air — my scar no longer an obstacle, my hurt melted away in the sunshine.

I hear pebbles crunching, and when I turn I see Rhys and Julien coming down the path. Delia waves and Rhys waves back, but Julien is busy kicking off his boots, his shirt halfway over his head. What is he doing? He flings his shirt to the ground and starts running towards us, his hair bouncing on his shoulders.

"No… Julien don't you *dare*!" She shouts, but he doesn't stop. We both duck as he dives over us into the water, the splash followed by an icy wave. He surfaces and tosses his hair out of his face.

"Holy *fuck* that's cold!" He laughs. He lunges at Delia's feet but she pulls them back. "Come on — get in!"

"Absolutely *not*!" She's trying to sound stern, but a smile is playing on her mouth. "I'm already soaked from that ridiculous maneuver!"

He flings water at her, and she laughs as she bats it away. He turns his grin to me, but I shake my head. It's far too cold. Julien rolls his eyes.

"No fun — the both of you! Rhys? You going to leave me hanging?"

I look up at him, watching him scratch behind his ear as he considers it. The gray in his hair is always more silvery in the light, and my heart does a little somersault when his crooked smile spreads across his face.

"This is lunacy," he laughs, dropping his shirt on the dock beside me. "I'm going to regret this, aren't I?"

"Let's go — race you to that buoy!" Julien shouts. He's swimming away already, and Rhys groans.

"Oh, that's hardly fair!" He's out of his boots and in the water in seconds, and both Delia and I shriek when he splashes us even more than Julien had. We both look like we've taken a dip now, but no part of me dislikes this. We watch in amusement as they glide through the water, and she laughs when Julien reaches the buoy first, raising his arms triumphantly.

"Look at that big idiot. Such a showoff."

Rhys has finally caught up and they're racing back now, keeping pace with each other. I didn't know either of them were such strong swimmers, and it's a little impressive to watch — Julien's muscled back skimming the surface next to Rhys' slim frame, both undeniably competent in the water. I hear her sigh dreamily, and when I glance over she's smirking, her gray eyes bright.

"You know," she says. "I have found, over the years, that you can think you've hit the peak for your capacity to love someone, then out of nowhere they'll do some dumb thing — some *stupid* thing like that — and you're right through that ceiling. You're head over heels all over again."

They're in the shallows now, and by the way Julien is splashing it's evident he's won the race back. Rhys is laughing, sinews flexing in his forearm as he slicks back his wet hair, and my heart tumbles when he flashes me a smile. I wonder if I'll ever hit my peak when it comes to loving him. Right now it feels limitless.

✳ ✳ ✳ ✳ ✳ ✳ FIFTY-EIGHT ✳ ✳ ✳ ✳ ✳ ✳

The bathtub is triangular, built into the corner of the all white washroom and surrounded by windows. I'm convinced there isn't a single spot in this place without a majestic view of the mountains. I lean against the side of the tub as I look down at the lake where we just were, the sparkling blue water tinged green at the edges, the dock still covered in wet footprints. We all reeked of pond after the visit to the lake, and had retreated to our separate corners of the house to rinse it away. The warm water feels — and smells — much nicer.

"Looks like we made it just in time," he says, squinting out at the sky. Dark clouds are dimming the sun, signaling more precipitation on the way. It doesn't seem like it'll snow again, but I'm all right with that. I prefer warmth and rain. He leans his elbow on the edge, head resting on his fist. The light outside has grown darker, but inside it's still bright, and so are we. The spark is back in his eyes, evidence that some of his weight has been lifted, and I'm thankful we've resumed our steady course. I have to believe it would've happened eventually had we stayed home, but I think this reset was just what we needed.

"I think you had the right idea to come here. This is the best day we've had in weeks."

"I agree, on all accounts," he says, hooking his foot around my calf. "Yesterday was terribly rough, but I think we've sufficiently turned it around."

We definitely have, but I still feel a little bad about it. I thought we knew each other inside and out, but it appears we're still learning. He smiles gently as he reaches for me, water sloshing when I fit myself into his lap.

"There's something I want to address," he says seriously. "In the future, I'll make an effort to be more open with you. I would never hurt you on purpose, but I can... Fold inward sometimes, and clearly it can make me a bit ignorant when it comes to how it's affecting you."

I sigh. "I should've been more open with you, too. I think I was just… Afraid to say anything. I was afraid I was right."

"And that's exactly what I'm getting at," he says. "I want you to tell me what's on your mind — always, and without fear. We have to talk to each other to survive together — that's the only way we'll know what's really going on. I'd like to say it'll never happen again, but despite my willingness to be conscious of these situations, I'm only human. If you ever feel like I've shut you out, please don't hesitate to say so. I promise I'll do my very best, and in return all I ask is that you trust me."

I think about what I assumed he was feeling versus what was actually happening, and how I could've avoided feeling like I did if I had done just that. Talked to him. Asked the questions. I shift my eyes to his chest and sweep my fingers across the rose I'd tattooed. I agree that communicating in times of distress is something we'll have to work on, but I don't think we have an issue with trust.

"I *do* trust you, though."

He covers my hand with his, pressing my fingers into the tattooed lines. "Trust that no matter what happens, nothing will diminish what I feel for you. Darling, I *love* you, and that'll never change."

I'd told him once that I'd never doubt him again, and I guess I haven't made good on that. I don't know that I can relinquish all doubt when it comes to how I feel about myself, but I think I can for how he feels about me. If he says never, he means it.

"I trust you. I promise."

He smiles — that enchanting crooked grin that makes my heart flutter — and softly presses his mouth to mine. Electricity buzzes between us as I thread my fingers through his hair, but I freeze when his hands start to slide up my thighs. I like where this is going, but I don't want a repeat of the morning. I cringe every time I think of it.

"Wait, stop!" I whisper, grasping his wrists. "Did you know these walls are absolutely paper thin?"

He looks a little bewildered. "Meaning?"

"Think about that for a second. I dislike having an audience, and I think the audience feels similar."

He stares at me blankly. I watch it slowly sink in and he raises his eyebrows.

"Oh dear. So they definitely heard —"

"*Everything.* Delia probably could've recounted it in detail. I've never been more embarrassed."

"Mmhmm." He's pressing his lips together, fighting the laughter I feel brewing in his chest. "Well," he whispers, his eyes landing on the knobs next to the edge of the tub. "We'll just have to employ a little cover noise, now won't we?"

He turns the dial, and suddenly the water's bubbling. Loudly. It's a jacuzzi tub and I hadn't even noticed. I can only imagine what they'll think when they hear it — the rumble of the jets accompanied by both of us laughing.

✶ ✶ ✶ ✶ ✶ ✶ FIFTY-NINE ✶ ✶ ✶ ✶ ✶ ✶

The dark skies have erupted into a thunderstorm, the familiarity adding another layer of comfort to this excursion. Delia was insistent on having another fire so here we are — camped out in front of the crackling flames, listening to Julien and Rhys carry on in the kitchen. They'd gotten into the forbidden scotch after all, figuring Sergio would forgive them eventually, and what started as a normal game of cards had escalated into a heated match. Delia shakes her head every time Julien slaps the counter, a half smile on her face. She feigns annoyance, but I know she likes his energy. She shifts on the blanket she'd spread out, rolling onto her elbow to turn the pages. One of the bedrooms had a desk, and on that desk she'd found a collection of Sergio's properties. I was stunned to see how many he has, and was equally interested in looking them over.

"Despite the allure of these magnificent places, I doubt I'd be able to function for long in one of them," she says, admiring a cantilevered structure jutting over a hillside. "Don't get me wrong — it's nice for the occasional retreat, but overall it's too quiet."

I have to agree with her there. I love the sounds of the city — the mechanical drone of the forced air system right outside our apartment windows, the humming tremble that accompanies the subway trains as they pass underground. I think my favorite might be the dim white noise of the cars on the highway, and I'd often crack the window so I could hear it better. She reaches for her wineglass, sipping before turning the page.

"Not to mention, desolate."

Something I also agree on. I like having everything at my fingertips. "Have you always lived in cities?"

"I have," she says. "I'd be no good in the countryside. It's all land — there's nothing to entertain me."

She looks fairly entertained at present. "You're doing well enough now."

"For a few days," she laughs. "Come on — have we met? I'm far too bourgeois to do this long term. If I get a hankering for something new I'd prefer to not have to travel an hour to get it. I'd likely spend *all* my time traveling."

I have to laugh. She probably would. The amount of shopping she does always struck me as a little excessive, but she works hard and is well paid as a healer, so if she wants to live in luxury I don't see why she should be denied it. I don't know if I'll ever stop being shocked by the amount I'd see her spend, but I have to chalk my reaction up to me living so minimally for most of my life — always worried about what I might need for my next move, waiting for that life I dreamed of to begin. It makes me a little ill sometimes when I think about what I'd put away for years on end, assuming I'd use it later. I never got to use it at all. It had burned up along with everything else.

"Speaking of something new," she says, the familiar twinkle in her eye. "Once we're settled at home you should let me take you out. That top is looking a little worse for wear." She nods at my sweater, my thumbs through the holes near the cuffs.

"I'm sure you don't need me as an excuse," I laugh. "Besides — I'm fairly certain I only slow you down."

"You *do* slow me down, but I prefer it," she says, turning the page. "It's not as fun by myself anymore. I like having my best friend with me, and I *love* making her try on things she'd never give a second glance."

Hearing her call me her best friend warms my heart in a way I haven't ever felt. I'd never had a *real* best friend before — at least, not one that I can recall. The friends I did manage to make over the years were more like acquaintances since I couldn't let them know the real me. More often than not they'd spook me if we did start getting close, and I'd either purposefully shut them out or disappear completely. I wanted to nurture those relationships but I couldn't, and I'm more than happy to nurture this one. Even though Delia came into my life by chance, she's not someone I have to settle for. She's the kind of person I might've run across in my old life and wished I could be close to — she's put together, effortlessly beautiful, devilishly smart — and the more I got to know her the more I loved the things that initially scared me about her. She's direct to a fault, but it never leaves me wondering what she really thinks, and I know now that beneath all that abrasiveness beats the soft heart of someone who cares deeply. She's also far beyond generous, and I worry sometimes that she might feel like I'm taking advantage of her graciousness. The only thing I have to offer is my presence, and I don't think it's worth much.

"What are you doing over there?" Julien calls. I watch him turn the bottle upside down as he pours the last of the vintage liquor into his glass. I hear Rhys clinking through the cabinet, probably in search of another. Sorry, Sergio. "Come play! It's fun. You'll like it."

"Oh, I don't think so," Delia laughs. "We're busy! Go back to your game!"

"You'll have to join in sooner or later," he grins. "We're running out of activities now that it's raining."

"Maybe in a bit," she says over her shoulder, and I laugh when she mouths the word 'no' to me.

She shifts closer and pours a little more wine in my glass before resuming her page turning. I hear the cards being shuffled as Julien and Rhys start up again, and sigh happily as I lean my head on my arms. I'm not thinking about the past anymore — about my scar, about Dimitri. I'm on the other side of it, cherishing the people I know will never betray me.

✶ ✶ ✶ ✶ ✶ ✶ SIXTY ✶ ✶ ✶ ✶ ✶ ✶

The trip home was a lot more animated, and I far preferred it to the long ride full of uncomfortable silence and masked emotional upheaval. I had a little apprehension about returning to the scene of the incident, but the retreat did just what it was supposed to, and I have a renewed sense of affection for everything we left. We'd been gone for only a few days, but somehow it feels like a month, and it's hard not to believe it hadn't been when I step into the greenhouse.

I'm amazed at the difference in growth. It's much less noticeable when I see it everyday, and I feel like now I can fully appreciate the budding flowers and new leaves. Zep had taken care of it while we were gone, much like he did when we went to the exposition, and I have to smile when I see the crossed out checklist we'd left. It's damp from the humidity, and there's a sprinkling of pipe tobacco next to it. I have no trouble imagining him up here, humming softly to himself as he wanders through the rows. I'm not sure what Rhys worked out with him in terms of compensation, since I'm sure he declined whatever it was, but I make a mental note to do something for him on my own besides thank him. I'll get the chance for that when we head down to the apothecary, which is the next item on today's itinerary. I want to walk around the studio to make sure everything's in place for when I go back to work. Well, when *we* go back to work. I'll no longer be doing it alone.

***

"Are you taking any time off when we get back?" Julien asks, leaning against the railing next to me. It's our last day in the mountains, and I'm standing on the deck watching the sun set. I'm trying to savor what's left of my time here, but I'm also ready to go home. Mostly to sleep in my own bed.

"I want to see how I feel, but I'd like to get back into a routine."

"Yeah, I think that's a good idea," he says, staring out over the tree line. The birds are circling and diving again, a small black cloud over the water. He kicks his boot against the railing, and soft thuds resonate through the wood. He looks a little pensive.

"You all right, Julien?"

He nods. "Yep. Just thinking about what I'm going to do next. I know you don't need me to go to work with you now that all that's over with, but... I could still go. You know, if you wanted."

Rhys had asked me if I meant to teach him, but Julien and I never formally discussed anything. I didn't really think about it at all. I just kept giving him exercises to do, and he kept doing them. It appears I have an actual decision to make, but I have a question for him first.

"That sort of depends. How far do you want to take this?"

"Honestly? I mean... The whole way to tattooing, if I can," he says, straightening a little. "What you've taught me so far... You have no idea what it's meant to me, and I can't thank you enough for taking the time to do that. This has given me something to work towards, so if you'll let me I'd really like to keep going."

There's cautious excitement in his voice. I love how much he wants this — it means he's serious. I was serious too — did I sound like this when I asked the old man to teach me? I don't remember asking him at all. I probably begged him since he was always so grumpy about it, as if I was putting him out. I don't feel put out at all by Julien. My instincts are telling me he'd do great at it, and I want to trust them. He'd been an incredible temporary student thus far, and from what I've seen he has the drive to work even harder if I push him a little, plus I'm realizing now that I don't want to be there without him. I'd gotten used to him working diligently beside me — asking questions, cracking jokes. I thought what I wanted was to work alone — I'd wished for that for *years* — but I don't think it is anymore. He's looking at me while he waits for an answer, but I'm watching the birds, their shifting shape turning to a speck in the distance. I hope I can do this. I hope I can give him what he needs, and I hope one day he'll be better at it than I am.

"It's only going to get more difficult, so you've got to be ready for that. You're not allowed to hate me for the amount of work I'm going to give you."

A smile flickers on his mouth. "Do you mean it? Really?"

I nod. "You have to be there every day that I am. Oh, and you can't give me too much shit if I'm running behind. If I'm going to mentor you, I reserve the right to —"

He startles me by wrapping me in a hug so forceful it lifts me off my feet. He's hugged me before, but never with this much intensity, and I have to laugh as I hug him back. This will be good for both of us, just like Rhys said. I know it will.

***

We hadn't talked about it more, but we have plenty of time for it and I'm glad we do. I'd had a rudimentary plan for teaching him drawing but I'll need a whole other one once he's ready to take additional steps. I think about it as I finish in the greenhouse and decide I might bounce my ideas off Rhys later on. I circle down the steps to see if he's ready to walk down, but when I open the door he's not alone. Julien and Delia are sitting at the kitchen table. We'd only just left them a few hours ago — why are they here? I cautiously take a step forward as I search their faces. They don't look upset, but something's off.

"What?" I ask. I'm frozen by the door.

"Hello darling," Rhys says. "Come and sit."

"I'm not sure I want to. Why do you all look like that?"

344

"Dimitri is dead," Delia says flatly. "We missed a few messages while we were away, and when I got back in contact with the associate he informed me that they'd deemed him too dangerous to be rehabilitated, and that he'd been taken care of."

I feel pinned to the floor. I don't know how to process this information. I'd never wished death on another — not really. I could think it for a moment — say it, imagine I wanted it — but I couldn't actively hope for someone's demise for more than a fleeting moment, even if they'd done something awful. Not even the scarred man's, and not even Dimitri's. How did they decide that? What deems someone worthy of execution? I wouldn't know. I can't even bring myself to kill a seedling.

"I don't know what to say." It's true. I don't.

"You don't need to say anything," Rhys says, pulling the chair out to invite me to sit. "It's done, it's over. There's nothing to do about it even if we wanted to."

I move towards the chair and hesitantly lower myself into it. "Then what more is there to talk about? You came here just for that?"

"Not… Quite," Delia says, fitting a cigarette between her lips. I'm nervous, and grow even more so during the time it takes her to light it. Finally she exhales. "That bit of news was actually secondary, but I thought I'd get it out of the way. What they really contacted me for was to extend an invitation. They want to speak with you. In person."

"Who does? That associate?"

"The council."

I sink back against the chair. The council? The actual council? The ones Rhys said we'd definitely never run into? Who *are* these people, and why do they want to talk to *me*? I must look as worried as I feel, because Rhys slides his hand into mine. I take a deep breath and exhale slowly.

"I'm sorry, I… In one breath you basically told me that they've done away with Dimitri, and now they want to see me. I'm sure you can see why I'm a little thrown."

"Your situation and Dimitri's are very different, obviously," Delia says. "What you are is extremely rare, and I think they're curious."

I forget about it sometimes. Just being one of them feels normal to me now, even though how I came into it is anything but. If I'm as rare as they say, I guess I can understand why I've garnered this sort of invitation. What I'd like is to say no, but it doesn't seem like this is the sort of thing you say no to.

"Where do I have to go — and when? Do I have to go alone?"

"We'll be going too," she says. "The associate asked to interview Rhys and I, and we agreed on the condition that we'd be able to accompany you. As for when, they suggested end of the month, and I'm supposed to be receiving details on where soon."

"We have some time, so let's just forget about it for now and get back to things here," Rhys says.

I'm not sure I'll be able to, and the look on his face tells me he's saying it to himself just as much as to me.

＊＊＊＊＊＊ SIXTY-ONE ＊＊＊＊＊＊

I pull the hotel curtain aside, revealing a glittering grid of streetlights far beneath my feet. This city is enormous — much bigger than the one we came from — and the pinpoints of light seem to go on endlessly. Streaks of pale green permeate the night sky, signaling dawn's arrival. I've been up half the night. I watched Rhys sleep for a while, the sheets moving with his breaths, but mostly I've been pacing by the window, far too anxious to rest. Today's the day I meet with the council.

Delia said they're curious about me, but despite my nerves, I might be more curious about them. The word 'council' conjures up an image of very old men with long beards, and I'd immediately imagined the scenario of our meeting. Them behind a long table and me in a chair before them, a spotlight shining on me as they pelt me with questions. Delia laughed when I told her, though she admitted she had no idea what to expect either. Both her and Rhys were astounded to find out the council was close to them all this time. One four-hour train ride close. They'd paid for both that and the hotel I'm currently pacing in, and the suspense is sort of driving me crazy. This whole thing is bizarre — secret councils, the supposed rarity of my existence, elders of their kind. I wonder what they'll ask me. I wonder if they'll let me ask anything myself. All I have are questions.

"Darling, come back to bed."

Rhys' voice startles me. I didn't realize he was awake. I pull the curtain shut and climb between the sterile smelling hotel sheets. The bed isn't comfortable, but he is, so I let myself relax into the warmth of his body and gentle petrichor scent of his skin.

"You haven't slept at all have you?" He asks sleepily, and I shake my head as I reposition myself. I've been lying here for only a few seconds and I'm already fighting the urge to get back up. He notices and pulls me closer. "Just lie here with me a little longer. Just a little longer."

Delia felt we should dress ourselves up in preparation for the meeting, and purses her lips when we step off the elevator. His shirt is pressed, but he's in his jeans with the tattered pockets, and my loose sweater has snags at the hem. She shakes her head at my leggings with the torn knees.

"Didn't care for what I picked out?"

I shrug. She'd picked out something similar to what she's wearing — tailored pants and a lace camisole tucked beneath a dark blazer — but it's still hanging on the back of the hotel door. I didn't care for it. I'd rather be comfortable and apparently so does Rhys, the pants and tie she'd suggested left in the same place as my outfit.

"Well, I tried," she laughs. "Let's go then — the car's already here."

"What's Julien going to do?" I half expected him to be here to see us off even though they'd instructed it just be the three of us, but it's early. He's probably still asleep. I thought the council might be interested to know him too given his history, but apparently not.

"I'm not extraordinary enough," he'd laughed when I asked about it. "That's literally the exact wording they used. Honestly, it's fine by me. I've spent enough time under a microscope, and I'd rather continue pretending there's nothing strange about me and go on with my life."

"He'll be fine," she says over her shoulder, her heels clacking on the tile as we cross the hotel lobby. "He already went out for a run."

I look for him as we roll through the streets in the back of a long black car, but I don't see him among the crowds of people on their daily commutes. The driver is silent, the only noises inside the car during the entire ride are the creak of leather seats and rapid click of the turn signal. He guides us through the maze of skyscrapers, and eventually steers us into an alley with a large slatted garage door, a metal box with a keypad attached. He punches a number into it and the door slowly rolls upward, revealing a sloping ramp descending below street level. We circle down the fluorescent lit cavern until he finally comes to a stop in front of an elevator. He opens our door without a word, so we take that as our cue to get out. After a few minutes the elevator door opens, and a tall woman wearing studious looking glasses and a dark pantsuit smiles, her blunt black bob shining.

"Welcome. I'm Bernadette, assistant to the council," she says, motioning for us to step onto the elevator. Her face is warm, and her husky voice is slow and a little soothing. "You must be Lynna."

She greets Delia and Rhys, and after we've filed in beside her she presses two buttons. The elevator hums as it moves upward, and the door opens to a room that looks fairly similar to the hotel lobby we'd come from, only it's four times the size. This building must be huge. Sunlight shines on the layered skyscrapers through the windows, the reflections casting long streaks of light along the floor. People are sitting among the clusters of furniture and grouped around what looks like a beverage station, all of them in identical looking white lab coats. The strong smell of coffee instantly makes me regret my decision not to sample any from the hotel earlier. A portly man in a dark suit is waiting outside the doors. His pleasant round face is all smiles, and he and Bernadette nod to each other.

"Rhys, Cordelia — this is Hamish. He will direct you to the waiting area."

They're separating us? My heart skips a beat, and Rhys puts his arm around me.

"No," Delia says. "The condition was that we'd be permitted to accompany Lynna."

"And you have," Bernadette says, still smiling. "The council wishes to speak only with Lynna for now. The associates are waiting for the two of you just through there, if you'll please follow Hamish."

Delia looks flustered, and neither she nor Rhys move an inch. His jaw is set and his fingers are starting to dig into my shoulder. Bernadette's smile doesn't waver.

"Please follow Hamish," she repeats. "Lynna will join you again once they're through."

Rhys' eyes meet mine, silently asking if I want to continue. I think I have to. We're too far into this to turn back. I nod and he squeezes my shoulder.

"Shall we?" Hamish asks. Delia huffs as she steps off, and I watch them follow Hamish as the doors slowly close. My heart is pounding now that I'm on my own, and it's so quiet in this elevator I can hear myself breathing.

"No need to be afraid," Bernadette says, noticing my nervousness. "Your arrival has been excitedly anticipated."

I'm afraid anyway, and try to distract myself by watching the floors tick by as we ascend. There are nearly a hundred buttons on the wall panel. We must be in one of the tallest buildings in this city. A secret council — right in the center of a sprawling metro? How does that work? Shouldn't they be in some sort of hidden compound in the middle of the woods somewhere?

"What is this place?" I ask.

"We are a highly prestigious medical research facility," Bernadette says, clasping her hands behind her. Her fingernails are shiny and clear, filed into smooth squares. "Our state-of-the-art institution handles various drug trials in addition to manufacturing. We have both a development laboratory and a hospital on site, in addition to a variety of other amenities."

She sounds like she's reading from a pamphlet. I wonder how many times she's repeated those sentences. What I want to ask next is what the council has to do with any of that, but the elevator stops before I can. The room is so different from the one Rhys and Delia disappeared into that I can hardly believe we're in the same building. It's the highest floor, the tops of the surrounding structures visible through tall arched stone windows. The walls are lined with glass enclosed shelves filled with thousands of books and labeled documents, a balcony walkway above with more shelves stretching the whole way to the ceiling. Long tables littered with files and more books line one side of the room in front of a row of glass windowed offices, the people inside standing to watch as I trail behind Bernadette. It's an odd contrast. Some of the books look to be very old, and there are worn leather armchairs resting on a weathered oriental rug with a frayed edge near the stone windows. The rest of the space is clean and corporate. She leads me through a glass door onto a large terrace — the building's rooftop. Enormous stone vessels bursting with plants flank the outside, and there's a water feature, a trickling stream cascading down a wall of dark stone into a black square pool with brightly colored fish shining in the bottom. The terrace is lined with a glass railing, more stone vessels spaced evenly along the perimeter. In the center are several pieces of furniture, where two men and a woman are seated around a low table, and they rise when we come to a stop in front of them. This is vastly different than the dark dungeon room I imagined I'd be interrogated in. They're different too, if they're who I assume they are.

They look old but not ancient, and are dressed more casually than Bernadette. The man closest to me is in new looking jeans and a black t-shirt, his bald head gleaming in the sunlight, a pair of thin oval glasses resting on his nose. The woman is small, her silver hair plaited neatly down her back. She's swimming in a long dress of floral print on a black background, enveloped in a long mustard colored cardigan. The third is a round man with a trim white beard in cream colored linen pants and a white buttoned shirt. All three are smiling, and all three have the same milky viridian green eyes as the vendor I'd met all those years ago. Their faces are warm, and their eyes don't carry the same intensity the vendor's had, but I'm still unnerved. Bernadette pulls a chair out for me to sit so I do — stiffly, my hands clasped in my lap.

"May I bring you something to drink?" Bernadette asks. "We have water, flavored or —"

"Coffee, perhaps?" The silver hair woman suggests. The word was on the tip of my tongue, but she's said it before I could. I nod to Bernadette, and she leaves me alone with them. They're staring at me like they're waiting for me to say something, and my throat is suddenly tight, my mouth dried up.

"Uhm… You're the… council?"

It's not my best effort, but it's all I can manage. My awkwardness is shining through like it tends to do when I'm nervous. They laugh softly, and the man with the glasses drapes his arm across the back of his chair.

"Not as impressive as you hoped, I imagine." He leans forward, extending his hand. "I'm Warmund, and this is Crane, and Fable. It's lovely to finally meet you, Lynna."

I try to control my trembling as I accept his handshake. I wish Delia and Rhys were here — I'd be more than happy to let them steer this meeting and sit on the sideline. Bernadette reappears with a cup for me, and I thank her before taking a long sip, grateful to have something to unglue my dry mouth. I clear my throat and set it on the table.

"What did you want to see me about?"

"First, I'd like to extend my sympathies," Fable says. She's eyeing the neck of my sweater, the tip of my scar visible. Her voice is soft and honeyed, and her creased face is pleasant. "We understand you were involved in an unfortunate incident, and are pleased to see you have recovered."

She's reminded me that they're the ones who probably decided what happened to Dimitri, and my nerves return. I can't help but wonder if this state-of-the-art facility also houses an execution chamber.

"What did you do with him? Was he… Executed? *Here*?"

"That is nothing to concern yourself with, my dear," Crane says. "Rest assured, he won't be a danger to you any longer." He pauses to sip from his own cup, and it clinks on the saucer when he sets it down. He sits back in his chair, resting his ankle across his knee.

"Now then," he says. "I suppose I'll get right down to it. We were hoping you'd indulge us with how you came to be involved with our kind. We have bits and pieces, but we'd like to hear it from you."

He's watching me, waiting. I feel like I'm supposed to give a speech I'm completely unprepared for. My eyes dart back and forth between them as I struggle to begin, and Warmund laughs quietly.

"It's all right. Take your time."

I take a deep breath and let it out slowly in an attempt to dissolve the tension in my shoulders. Where do I start? How much detail do they want? I decide to tell them about moving to the city, skipping over the part with the scarred man. When describe my relationship with Rhys, familiar heat licks at my face. I feel like I'm gushing about him to complete strangers, and I sort of am. Warmund and Crane's expressions remain unchanged, but Fable smiles.

"A love story," she says. "How wonderful. We're looking forward to meeting him, for a multitude of reasons. Please — go on."

I continue, explaining that I didn't know what he was until after my procedure, and Crane stops me.

"What led to it? The procedure?"

"I was having withdrawal, so they tried it to save me. I'd been taking Aeonia for years, but I stopped."

"So it *is* true," he says, sitting back. "How did you come to have it in your possession?"

I describe the vendor from the small market when I was living on the opposite coast. How mysterious he was, and how he had the same eyes they do. He asks me the quantity I purchased, and when I tell him he shakes his head.

"Seems we've been chasing a ghost," he says to Warmund. "From the sound of it there's nothing left to recover."

"Do you know him?" I ask.

"Not personally," Warmund answers. "He was once part of another council — long ago. He vanished along with a few priceless documents and a number of other valuable items. Aeonia was among them. It was the last of what was left from those who came before us."

Careful — it's very rare. It's derived from the blood of a long extinct civilization.

I can still hear the vendor's voice in my head. I thought he was being hyperbolic, spinning me a wild story to make a sale. Was he telling me the truth after all? I'm trying to fit the dizzying pieces of this puzzle together, and it's making it hard to string together a solid thought. Those who came before them — the civilization must be *related* to them then, which means they're not extinct at all. Is that why it worked — why Rhys' blood saved me? Because the compound in it is directly linked to the one in Aeonia? How did they not know that?

"The Aeonia… It's your bloodline, isn't it? Why can't it be created any longer if that's fact? Why are my friends who have extensive knowledge of these sorts of things so unaware of its origin?"

"You certainly have a lot of questions," Crane chuckles, fiddling with an undone button on his shirt. What he doesn't know is that I have more. Many more. "The history of Aeonia is not widely shared. Indeed, it is difficult to recreate exactly. We have attempted to do so repeatedly."

"But the blood… The compound in it… Isn't it the same? I was told those people were extinct, but if they're who you came from that can't be the case."

"Once our ancestors had intermingled with humans the potency was greatly reduced. None exist of that pure line now, so in a sense they *are* extinct."

Ancestors intermingling with humans? Pure lines? I

flash back to Rhys' comments on the origins of their kind — the split theories. Evolution versus the fantastical. The unexplainable jumps versus the biological evidence. I wish he was here to offer his two cents. My head is spinning. Can they connect the dots for me? Is it evolution that made him the way he is — they way they all are — or is it something else?

"Where did they come from? Your ancestors?" I ask tentatively. I can't believe these are the sorts of questions I'm asking. I wonder how many more of them I can get away with. "You speak as if they're somehow not of this earth."

"We're not entirely sure," Warmund says, and my heart skips a beat. They don't *know*? I thought he'd have a more direct answer, and it would let me know which side of the debate was factual. Before I can ask him to elaborate he redirects.

"You must understand that your survival of a procedure like this is remarkable," he says. "We have been able to instill longevity similar to ours through a host of inferior methods, but it is unprecedented that any assume our traits. We suspect your condition can be solely attributed to your use of Aeonia. Are we to understand correctly that you possess the accelerated healing capability?"

I'm struggling with the shift in conversation. I'm hung up on what he said about inferior methods and similar longevity. All I can think about is what they said about Julien. Isn't he extraordinary though? Isn't *all* of this extraordinary?

"Lynna?" He asks again. "The healing?"

"Oh — yes. Sorry."

"Can you describe you experience with it?"

"Well, I healed a broken leg in a few hours, and the stab wound was similar."

"Fantastic," Warmund beams. "Absolutely fantastic. Is there anything else you can do?"

Anything else? "What do you mean?"

"Our ancestors," Fable says. "There were some who

possessed other traits. Mental gifts. Almost all have been lost along the way."

Mental gifts? Does she mean the visions? I wouldn't call them gifts, but they were definitely not something I ever had before. They've all but faded now — I haven't had an episode in months. Did I have them because of some sort of trait I picked up?

"I'm not sure if it counts, but I did... *See* things, right after I was changed. I don't anymore, though."

"What did you see? Can you remember?" Warmund's sitting on the edge of his seat, his eyes boring into me. They're all looking at me with great interest now, and it's making me uncomfortable. I nod, and Crane snaps his fingers at Bernadette. She bends to listen as he whispers to her, and then she hastily makes her way inside.

"What time of day did the instances occur?" Warmund asks.

"Uhm... They were all over the place really, but I think mostly evening. I had dreams about them too."

"Primarily nocturnal," he nods. He shifts his eyes behind me, and I turn to see Bernadette rushing over with a stack of files, a ledger, and what looks like a recording device. She sets it down and presses the button. "This will need to be documented," he says. "Tell us what you saw — don't spare any detail."

Briefly I consider not telling them, since they hadn't even asked me if I want to be recorded. I'm too uneasy. I'd rather just get it over with. I'm keenly aware of Bernadette's hand flying over the ledger as I speak, and I try to slow my sentences but it's hard to focus on what she's doing all while describing what I'd seen and dreamed. Those burning bodies, metallic ruins, and that strange screaming infant.

"Do you know what they mean?" I ask once I've finished.

"We can't be certain," Warmund says. "The purpose of amassing this information is so we might be able to discern distinct meaning. This is why documentation was required."

"But how does that help if you don't know what they are?"

"There are others who have had visions," Fable says. "Much less clear than yours, though. Their meanings have been the subject of much question. Some believe they are a prophecy of sorts — events that have yet to come to pass. We believe they might be indicative of how our kind came to be here. How and why they arrived is still a mystery to us, and thusly remains a mystery to all."

She's answered the question we've been dancing around. They're leaning on the more fantastical side of things. I wonder what Rhys will have to say about it.

"So there were others? Like me? I thought I was supposed to be this rare thing."

"When I refer to 'others' I refer to ones before us, even," she says. "They were born with the gift. No one who has ever been altered has experienced what you have. Most do not even survive."

I'm pretty sure that's not true. There was another — he's why the idea for the formula that altered me even came about. I think of him a lot.

"But there was someone else besides me, wasn't there? He survived, and he had nightmares. I *know* I heard right."

"Survived indeed," Crane says. He stares at me pointedly for a moment, then leans forward and shuffles through the stack of files. He flips a few pages, reads, and licks his thumb before flipping a few more. Finally he stops. "Mmm — here we are. Trial eleven twenty six. Transformation subject is male, aged twenty four. Rejected second dose at midway point, forced restart after vital signs leveled. Another rejection, another restart. Subject stabilized, final dose administered. Seventeen days elapsed before subject regained consciousness. Post procedure notes… Experienced intense abdominal pain, severe headaches, loss of vision… Most of this isn't relevant." He turns the page. "Ah — here we are. Subject complained of hearing voices and experiencing regular night terrors. Refusal to sleep. Refusal of medication. Eventual suicide."

The file thwaps when he shuts it, and he drops it on the table. My throat makes a noise when I let out my breath — I hadn't realized I'd been holding it. I feel awful for that man. He was barely even that at twenty four. What I'd experienced was nothing in comparison.

"Perhaps now you see why we were so eager to meet you," Fable says.

I'm speechless. All I can do is nod. Bernadette begins gathering the files as the three of them stand, so I do too.

"Is… That it?" I ask. I'm ready for this to be over.

"You must excuse us," Warmund says. "We'll be following up with your counterparts, but it will be brief. In the meantime, Bernadette will bring you anything you wish. All you have to do is ask."

I stretch my legs once they're gone, hoping walking around will help clear the cluttered mess in my head. I lean on the glass railing, my stomach flip flopping as I peer over the edge at the buildings clustered around. I'm overwhelmed by the council, but I'm more overwhelmed by the idea that they might be something more than I thought. The possibility that they could actually be of an otherworldly race is unbelievable to consider, but I don't know what to believe anymore. I've experienced too many odd things to be confident in my ability to separate fact from fiction. Fantasy from reality. I sigh heavily, resting my chin on the edge of the glass. What will the reality of our lives look like after this?

They said they'd return shortly, but the minutes tick by with no sign of them. It's overcast and breezy, so I have hope that being abandoned to the elements won't leave me with any sort of peeling sunburn. At least I'm wearing long sleeves. I continue to stare out over the city, watching the ocean sparkle in the distance, the people on the sidewalks nothing more than small specks. Do those people down there have any idea what's hiding on the top floor of this building? Do they even give it a second glance when they pass? It makes me wonder how many things I've missed in my life. How many secrets kept secret because of my obliviousness.

Finally after nearly two hours I hear voices approaching. The council appears in the doorway, and Bernadette follows with a carafe of water with lemon slices and four glasses. I almost laugh. To someone looking in this might resemble a casual afternoon luncheon instead of the strangest meeting I've ever been a part of. It gets even more strange when a piece of paper is slid in front of me.

"What's this?" I ask as I scan it. It looks like... A legal document? For what?

"We trust that everything discussed here will remain confidential," Crane says. "Please give it a read. The others have already signed off."

My eyes move over the words. It's fairly vague, naming the facility and not them individually, but from what I can decipher it's saying I'm to keep anything discussed within these walls between only me and the three who know of this meeting. Good — it includes Julien. There's no way we could keep this from him even if we wanted to. When I near the end, I encounter something that gives me pause.

"It says 'penalty' but it's not specific. What does —"

"This is simply a formality," Warmund interrupts. "A redundant formality, given that what you are requires you to retain an air of secrecy to begin with, but we prefer to stress the importance by putting it in writing. Secrecy is what keeps you safe — what keeps *us* safe. We are here to help, not to harm, but we don't cater to those who take that importance lightly. You've experienced enough difficulty already. We'd hate to add to it."

My hand shakes as I pen my signature. I didn't need a warning to make me keep my mouth shut, but they've given me one. I don't intend to test it out. As I'm handing it back I hear Delia's voice, and spin around to see Bernadette with both her and Rhys in tow. *Finally*. He looks relieved to see me, and quickens his pace. I nearly fling myself into his arms when he reaches me, and hear Fable laugh softly.

"Well," she says, observing our embrace with interest. "I haven't sensed a connection like this one for some time. I can see now why you risked it all, Rhys."

Rhys looks like he doesn't know what to say, and I see redness creeping up the side of his neck as he awkwardly clears his throat. Delia is busied shaking Crane's hand, and Warmund rises, extending his own to Rhys.

"Yes, quite the pair, you two," Warmund says. "The tattooist and the alchemist. Rhys, Lynna, it was a pleasure, but I believe we've kept you long enough. We hope to hear from you forthwith in regards to our offer. Bernadette? Will you see them out, please?"

I'm trying to read anything on their faces as we follow Bernadette to the elevator. What did Warmund mean? What offer? I'm getting nothing — they've got polite smiles plastered on, and they keep them until we're back in the car.

"Bar," Delia says, rubbing her forehead. "I need to go to a bar right this instant."

"Agreed," Rhys sighs wearily. "We have a lot to discuss. Let's pick up Julien and get to it."

✳✳✳✳✳✳ SIXTY-TWO ✳✳✳✳✳✳

We find a quiet place around the corner from the hotel and settle into one of the booths, but once we have drinks in hand we sit in silence. Julien seems relieved to not have to entertain himself anymore, but it's clear he's a little annoyed that no one's talking. Both Delia and Rhys look a little dazed, and I'm feeling sort of similar. I don't know where to begin, so I spin my glass in a slow circle.

"I *knew* I was right," Delia says suddenly. She'd been staring into her drink, and the ash on her cigarette had burned almost the whole way to her fingers. She carefully deposits it in the ashtray before stubbing it out and immediately picking up another. "I knew there was a connection, but I never thought it went further."

"It's probably the only believable thing I've heard all day," Rhys says. "The components are difficult to dismiss. I like to think I would've discovered the link between our blood and the Aeonia on my own, but I was never afforded the opportunity. It was well out of circulation before I even began looking into it."

"What wasn't believable?" I ask. "Let me guess. It had to do with your potential origin?"

"Correct," he says. "It was a little disappointing, if I'm being honest. They made it a point to say their beliefs are purely speculative, but it's obvious they're weighted more on the farfetched side of things. I assume they inquired about whether or not you've acquired some sort of… 'lost trait', as they put it?"

"They did. They said your ancestors had mental gifts, but they didn't specify what. They were very excited about the visions, but I'm not sure they counted."

"They didn't specify because they don't exist," he says, draining half the whiskey in his glass. "I've never seen or heard of evidence to the contrary. I have the distinct feeling that those lost traits are simply a result of some sort of chemical imbalance that they didn't know how to categorize. Sure, there's plenty about what we are that doesn't fit neatly into a box, but there's a proper answer out there for each and every thing about us that isn't easily explainable. Answers that weren't invented just because."

This is why I wanted him there. I'm a little less skeptical than he is, but I like knowing the whys for his skepticism. He has reasons I never would've thought about. I wonder if he said any of this out loud to them. He must not have, given how courteous they were when we parted. Not to mention the fact that they'd offered something.

"What did you talk about in the interviews? What did Warmund mean when he said he'd offered something?"

"Yeah, I'd like to know a little more too," Julien says. "It appears you've been having wild conversations all day while I spent it watching the most boring television of my life."

"I'll give you the full rundown later," Delia says. "Right now my head hurts. I've never been interrogated like that, and in addition to there being about a million questions, they were *unbelievably* repetitive. We had to answer all over again when we were introduced to the council. They wanted to know *everything*. Our education, our skill sets — even our personal history. Apparently it was impressive enough to deem us worthy of joining their ranks. We've been offered positions."

They offered them *jobs*? I'm shocked, but only because I wasn't expecting it. Of course they'd offer them something. Delia is a gifted and dedicated healer, and Rhys is absolutely brilliant — it makes sense that the council would want to add them to their collection. I want to be excited for them. The mysterious council of elders has personally offered them something it would seem not many are afforded, but it'll change everything. My heart aches at the thought of leaving our home, and I can't even fathom the possibility that one might accept and not the other. The idea of splitting up is too much to comprehend.

"What are you going to do?" I'm trying to act casual, but the trepidation in my voice is obvious.

"Nothing right now," Delia says. "I'm too tired to weigh this out at present. They didn't give us a deadline, so we have plenty of time."

"That's about where I'm at, too," Rhys says.

I'm not convinced. It's as if I can see the wheels turning in his head already. It's an incredible opportunity — one he might never have again. I'm starting to feel just as tired as they look simply by thinking about it, so I rest my head on my elbow.

"Darling, you must be exhausted," he says. "I am too, but I at least slept last night. Let's get some rest. We'll be on our way home in the morning."

I don't rest at all that night. I do sleep on and off the entire way back, but it's not enough. By the time we make it to the apartment I'm so weary and wrung out I fall asleep fully clothed for the remainder of the day. I wake to the gentle sensation of him running his fingers through my hair, and when I blearily blink my eyes open he's sitting next to me in the bed, watching.

"You all right?" He asks. "You haven't said but a few words since we left the hotel, and you've been out cold the rest of the time. I was beginning to feel a bit concerned."

"I have a lot on my mind." Vague truth, but truth nonetheless. I'm happy to be home beneath the comfort of the rain pounding on the skylight, but at the same time it's hard to be here. All I can think about is that I might have to leave it — leave our calm and quiet home where we started our life together. I spent my past life doing just that — leaving everything behind — and all I want now is to stay in one place for once. A place that actually feels like home.

"I have a lot on mine too," he says. He grows quiet, and I sigh.

"That offer. It changes everything."

His hand slips into mine. "It changes everything and

nothing at all. I don't want you to worry. I'm perfectly happy going on as we have been. I promise."

I know he wouldn't say it if he doesn't mean it, but I also know he might feel two ways about it. I'm sure I'll find out which way will come out on top in time, but both worry me. Either choice has the potential to leave one of us unhappy, which means both of us will be.

★ ★ ★ ★ ★ ★ SIXTY-THREE ★ ★ ★ ★ ★ ★

My footfalls echo on the stone as I slice through the mist, willing them to go faster. I have to go *faster*. My muscles burn and my lungs feel like they're about to burst but I can't stop — he's catching up to me. He's right on my heels, but I can't let him catch me. If I can just give it all I've got for a few more yards I can make it to the rock wall.

Suddenly he's right beside me, the sound of his sharp breaths over my shoulder. He's caught up. We reach the wall and my feet pound louder on the wet pavement as I slow to a stop, and bend to catch my breath. He paces slowly beside me, wiping his sweaty face with the hem of his shirt. I was so close. Next time I race Julien I'm definitely going to win.

"I almost beat you," I pant, my hands on my knees. "Next go I'm leaving you in the dust for sure."

"I gave you a head start," he laughs. I roll my eyes, and he elbows me. "You *are* getting faster though. Wasn't as easy for me this time."

He leans against the wall, looking out over the ocean. Seagulls are hopping along the sand, chasing each other just like we'd been doing. I think Julien's insistence on a little competition each morning is his method of distracting me from the limbo we're in. It does take my mind off it for a time, but it's all I can think about once we stop — especially since we're back in the council city.

Only a week passed before they'd contacted Delia and Rhys again, inviting them to spend a few days shadowing their respective departments, likely in a further attempt to convince them. Both insisted they were on the fence, but I could tell how much they'd warmed up to the idea, and I could hear it in their voices as they weighed the pros and cons of relocating. Delia wouldn't have to work under an alias anymore, and she'd be far removed from the administrative issues and fluctuating schedule she frequently bemoaned. Rhys would have nearly infinite resources for any project he might want to pursue, and he wouldn't have to hide behind anything to do it. They hadn't confirmed, but I already knew our days in the rain were numbered. They were simply delaying the inevitable.

Julien sighs and turns back to the city, the tall council building visible near the center. Delia and Rhys are currently wrapping up their stint somewhere inside it, and we're to reconvene with them in a bar before we pack up to leave. They'd spent the last portion of this trip in long meetings with the staff, and undergoing a series of demonstrations to back up their skills. It resulted in them arriving at the hotel in the evenings with weary faces, but they were both incredibly upbeat. They were being tested, and they were passing every one with flying colors. We'll find out the final results today — they'll have official placement offers, I'm sure, and I'll finally know what my future holds.

Instead of camping out in our rooms, Julien and I spent most of this trip walking the city end to end in an attempt to get the lay of the land — peering in shop windows, admiring houses on well-to-do streets, wandering up the sandy coastline. I don't hate it here, but I'm not sure if I'd be able to love it the same, even though it rained on and off throughout our stay. My heart is still hundreds of miles away, embedded in the walls of my studio and our comfortable dark home, and the idea of transplanting it is more difficult than I thought. My life began there. The real life I'd daydreamed about for such a long time. I knew we'd have to leave eventually but that time always seemed so far in the distance, and now it's looming on the horizon. Julien waxed optimistic and encouraged me to keep an open mind in between distracting me with activities, and I had to appreciate his efforts. He'd be uprooting himself too, and our futures are linked now — I know he wants the outcome to be positive no matter what the decision is.

"Should we skip coffee and go straight back to clean up?" He asks, adjusting his knot of sweaty hair. "We might need to build in some extra time — I'm only mostly sure I know where we're meeting them."

I give the ocean a last look, feeling the wind on my face. I have to admit — the salty breeze is kind of nice.

"I'm not skipping coffee," I laugh. "We'll find it."

They already have drinks waiting for us when we finally arrive at the bar — late, and damp. It started to rain right before we set out, and we had to stop to pick up a new umbrella. Julien had misplaced the one we'd been using.

"Oh, look who's the one running behind now," Rhys jokes when Julien slides into the booth next to Delia. "Let me guess — the rain kept you?"

"No." Julien grins. "It was her fault. She lost the umbrella."

"I don't believe that for one second," Delia laughs.

Both of them look cheerful, their smiles bright, and it leads me to believe things had gone very well. I want to be happy for them since it feels wrong to not, but I'm having a hard time with it.

"Well?" Julien asks, watching her reapply her lipstick. "What's the verdict? Did they narrow it down?"

She smacks her lips and drops the lipstick in her tote. I can tell she's trying to downplay how excited she is, but the smirk is creeping onto her mouth anyway. "They did. They want me on the board after I get acclimated. That means I have a shot at one of the top positions right off the bat. Can you believe it?"

"Delia! That's amazing!" He says, and she giggles when he wraps her in his arms. "I'm so proud of you!"

"What about you?" I ask Rhys, watching him tap his cigarette on the table.

"Well, it'd be a bit different from running the apothecary — I'll say that," he says, smiling slightly. "Nothing as prestigious as top healer."

Delia reaches over and smacks his arm. "Don't be so

modest! They've offered him a lead spot in their development sector — it doesn't go much higher!"

He shrugs, his crooked smile growing. I'm both surprised and not at the same time. I never questioned his competence. "Rhys... That's incredible. I mean, really."

"It seems they recognize talent when they see it," Julien says, raising his glass. "Cheers, and congratulations to both of you!"

I keep fairly quiet for the remainder of the time we spend at the bar. I couldn't get a word in if I wanted to — they're too busy excitedly rehashing their final meeting and fawning over the amenities that will accompany their new spaces. I don't want to ruin it for them. It's their decision to make, not mine, and the look on his face is telling me it's the right one. I'll have to accept it. Once we're back at the hotel to prepare to leave I go right to packing after shutting the curtains so I can't see the city. All I want to do is go home and enjoy what little of it I have left. As I'm stuffing clothes into my bag he sinks down onto the edge of the bed.

"I think we need to have a conversation," he says. "Now that I have all the pieces, we should talk about this in depth before deciding."

I zip up the bag. "What's there to decide? I pretty much knew this trial period was just a formality before we even got here."

"Nothing's been set in stone."

"But it's obvious how much you're looking forward to it. I already know you'll love it."

"While there are plenty of positive factors, there are things I'm not exactly keen on," he says. "I admit I'm not jumping for joy over the idea of giving up the apothecary, and I'm honestly a little devastated we wouldn't have the greenhouse anymore." He pats the spot next to him, inviting me to sit. "Not to mention something very important — what this means for *you*. You'll have to restart your business all over again. It's not exactly wonderful for you, now is it?"

I sigh as I sink down next to him. Sure, it'll be a headache to uproot the studio, but I've done it before, and I have everything I need now in addition to enough saved to front rent for a new place on my own. It's not really an obstacle like it once was.

"I'm not worried about the studio — I'll figure that out. What's important is that this opportunity could give you so much more than you could have back home."

"It could be more — a great deal more," he says. "But regardless of the logistics of what a career change like this could mean for me, there's the issue of how you feel. I know you have concerns — they're all over your face."

I do have concerns, and all of them are centered around what this might mean for *us*. I'd been continuously reassuring myself that shaking up our lives won't change us — won't change our connection or how he feels about me — but it still eats at me and I feel terrible for it. He'd made it abundantly clear that nothing would alter his feelings and I'd promised to trust him, didn't I? Why am I so hesitant over something as simple as a change in location? I'd wanted change for so long, and I got it — my life changed drastically for the better when I met him. What's to say this new change won't bring similarly wonderful things — for *both* of us? Is it because I got what I wanted so now all I want is to press pause? Lock us in place?

"Listen," he says when I don't respond, his dark eyes soft. "This is *our* future we're talking about, so we have to make this decision together. It's about *our* happiness in the life we're building — not just mine."

Our happiness. Our life. Together. I'm starting to realize that while I thought I was thinking about how this change might affect *us*, I was really just thinking about how it would affect *me*. I thought I was keeping an open mind, but I was stewing silently, wallowing in selfishness. I can't demand to keep things exactly the same because I've grown attached to that sameness, that stability I've anchored to the steady routine of our life. I do trust him, and that means I have to trust that we'll be the same no matter where we land. I refuse to deny him the possibility of improving so much for himself when all he's ever done was think of me and what I wanted most. He's doing it even now — asking me to weigh in, making sure *I'm* sure. All I'm doing is sulking when I should be celebrating him.

"Lynna? Please say something. I need to know if —"

"I'm sorry."

His brows knit. "Sorry? For what?"

"For not saying something really important out loud." I press my palm against his fuzzy cheek, and he smiles softly as he leans into it. "I am *endlessly* proud of you. I had no doubt the council would see your worth, because I see it every single day. You deserve this, and if it'll make you happy, it'll make me happy."

He looks like he might cry. "Darling —"

"No — I mean it," I interrupt. "I'd never want you to miss out on something so incredible. I don't ever want to hold you back. I want you to follow every dream you ever had, and I want to be there to cheer you on. Us supporting each other — that's what makes a good life, that's what I want for me and you. I was afraid to leave our home because I thought it would mean we wouldn't be us without it, but that's not true. My home isn't a place anymore — *you're* my home. Our life belongs wherever we —"

This time it's him who cuts me off, his mouth on mine as he presses me against the stiff hotel sheets. I know I'm making the right decision. I can let go of that fear and pull up that anchor of stability — we'll still be attached to it.

✴ ✴ ✴ ✴ ✴ ✴ *SIXTY-FOUR* ✴ ✴ ✴ ✴ ✴ ✴

My last day in the studio is bittersweet. It feels like an end and a beginning all at once.

Most everything's in boxes — the books, the prints, the inventory — and the apothecary shelves are empty next door, cardboard squares stacked along the wall. Zep left a little while ago after saying a mildly tearful goodbye — I think I'll miss him more than he'll miss the apothecary. I never met any of his family, but from what Rhys said it seemed like he was looking forward to spending more time with them, and I was glad to know he wouldn't be alone with nothing to do. We only have a few days left before the big move, and I'm hoping I get at least one or two more clients before I close the door behind me for the last time. Julien had a lot of packing to do at home so I encouraged him to stay and work on it, and leave me to what's left here. I wanted to experience these final moments the same as I did when I entered this city. Alone.

I have a lot on my mind, which is mostly the cause of my want for solitude. I feel homesick already and we haven't even left, and the more boxes that accumulate in the apartment the more real it becomes. I meant what I said to Rhys in that hotel room — about what I want for our life, and about where my home is — but saying it and facing it head on are two different things. I was determined to let go, but he'd said something unexpected when we returned, and it seemed like he was having some trouble doing that himself. He wasn't ready to part with the apartment, so he decided to retain ownership of the club and keep it on the back burner, just in case things in the council city don't pan out. It surprised me, but I was comforted by the idea of it being there, our memories cemented in the walls, a piece of us lingering behind. The studio and the apothecary would have to go, and there's already a sign in the front window listing them for lease. He said it would be a better option than selling, and they belong to him not me, so I trust that whatever he wants to do with them will be the right thing. I have to trust that everything we're doing is the right thing.

I sink down onto my stool, and let it drift across the floor as I consider the time I spent in this city. I have a lot of memories here, and though the bad ones are sharp pieces that still hurt on occasion, I'm thankful the good outweigh them by a landslide. Leaving the familiarity of the first place that really felt like home is daunting, but I've been consoling myself by imagining all the new memories we'll make. We'll have a new apartment, I'm determined to find a new studio — better than this one, if possible — and I know there's a million hidden things to discover in that enormous city. Briefly I think of the woman I'd met on the train when I arrived here. I'm getting my beach. I wonder if she ever got hers.

The doorknob clicks as it turns, and there's a small knock on the window. I'd forgotten to unlock it. When I swing it open there's a man standing outside, and I smile when I immediately recognize the tattoo on his arm. Black roses.

"No kidding," he smiles, opening his arms for a hug. It's the client I'd tattooed nearly two years ago. The one who gave me the business card. Seth. "I've never stopped in here so I thought I'd check it out — I didn't expect to find *you*!"

I pat him on the shoulder before releasing him. "You caught me just in time. It's my last day — we're moving."

"Oh, no way," he says, glancing at the sign in the window. "Well, if this is my last chance I'd better seize it. Got an hour or two for an old client? Or at least a few minutes to catch up?"

What a fitting end to my time here. A gift of irony from the universe. "Always."

Leaving people like him behind is always the worst part of moving, so I'm glad he'll be the last I inscribe. He decides on a peony next to the roses, and fills me in on what he's been up to in between winces. I like hearing updates about his life, and especially that things are going well for him. When we near the end he asks me a question, and it catches me off guard. He'd been quiet a while, his eyes closed as I work in a tender spot near his elbow, and I'd completely zoned in on the flower.

"Did you ever end up going?"

I stop the machine. "Where?"

"To that club? I'm pretty sure I gave you a card last I saw you."

The club. Did I ever. "I can't believe you remember that. I did. Do you still go?"

"Not really," he says. "The guy I've been seeing isn't keen on that type of music. I think I might be able to get him to compromise. Eventually."

I laugh quietly. "Compromise is key."

"Try telling *him* that," he laughs. "Well? What did you think? Did you have a good time for once?"

I have to pause to consider my words before they come spilling out of me, so I take a moment to wipe the smears of ink from his arm before resuming. I want to tell him that the simple act of handing me a business card in an effort to cheer me up created a domino effect that impacted my entire future. I want to tell him that he inadvertently pointed me in the direction of all the things I'd been dreaming of — an end to my loneliness, cherished friendships, and the sort of love I never thought I'd ever get. I want to confide in him about the unbelievable thing I'd become, the dramatic events I'd endured, the bright possibilities awaiting us in the new city. I want to tell him all of it — hug him all over again and thank him — but I can't.

"I had such a good time I became a regular, if you can believe it."

He looks pleased. "See? I *knew* you'd like it."

I'd given him a little truth, but it doesn't feel like enough. He deserves more. I stop the machine again and look up at him.

"Seth, I have to thank you. Giving me that card... It changed my life. Definitely for the better."

He grins. "That's amazing! I'm glad to hear it. Talk about life changing — did you happen upon that bartender that works upstairs on the weekend? If you didn't, you should swing by before you leave. He makes a killer cocktail, and he's an absolute *joy* to talk to."

I can't keep the smile from my face as I finish the last petal, lingering on the word.

Joy.

It's an accurate summation of what I found in this city.

I'm ready to see how much more awaits in the next.

SCINTILLA

CHIMERA
Part Two

Scintilla | sɪnˈtɪlə |

(n.) a tiny, brilliant flash or spark

Change cities. Leave the past behind.

Lynna's no stranger to starting over, only now there's a degree of excitement. She's about to embrace the unknown future in a beautiful city – about to build a new life with the man she adores. Her dream has come true and then some. Surely more will follow.

But what if the past follows?
What if that dream becomes a waking nightmare?
And worse – what if it's all in your head?

ACKNOWLEDGEMENTS

To my amazing mother, Jan Bowman. Not only did she instill a love of reading in me from my earliest years, she's also been an incredible source of encouragement and support in all aspects of my life. She read multiple drafts of the manuscript (even the awful first one!) and provided a vast amount of insight — and grammatical corrections (which I know made her cringe, as she was my high school English instructor). I love you so much, Mum. I couldn't have done this or life without you.

To Pete Larkin — my longtime friend, talented coworker, purveyor of Starbucks, partner in crime, and biggest Rhys and Lynna stan. Thank you for reading every single draft and writing exercise, for listening to my endless chatter about this project, and thank you the most for believing in me. Always.

To my Kyklops Tattoo family — Derrick Porter, Jeff Sotace, Evan Gealy, Jess Scutella, Trevor Howells. I couldn't have done this without your love and inspiration, and I wouldn't be where I am without your support. I love you all more than I can ever convey.

To Peter Buck and crew of Elsewhen Press — thank you for taking a chance on me and for being an absolute joy to work with while making my publishing dream come true.

To Julianne Ingles of Guts Publishing for her invaluable coaching and support. I am a better writer because of you.

To my wonderful friends who agreed to give my draft a first read: Mark Smeltz, Nicole Lee, Jess Scutella, and Jon Orr.

To the Industrialist Hotel of Pittsburgh, where I spent hours upon hours holed up in a corner room overlooking the city. Thank you for being my second home for writing.

To nearly twenty years of clients, many of whom have become dear friends. There are little pieces of so many of you embedded in this story. Thank you for your trust, and for letting me become part of you just as you've become part of me.

Elsewhen Press

delivering outstanding new talents in speculative fiction

Visit the Elsewhen Press website at elsewhen.press for the latest information on all of our titles, authors and events; to read our blog; find out where to buy our books and ebooks; or to place an order.

Sign up for the Elsewhen Press InFlight Newsletter at elsewhen.press/newsletter

Urban fantasy by Tej Turner

The Janus Cycle

The Janus Cycle can best be described as gritty, surreal, urban fantasy. The over-arching story revolves around a nightclub called Janus, which is not merely a location but virtually a character in its own right. On the surface it appears to be a subcultural hub where the strange and disillusioned who feel alienated and oppressed by society escape to be free from convention; but underneath that façade is a surreal space in time where the very foundations of reality are twisted and distorted. But the special unique vibe of Janus is hijacked by a bandwagon of people who choose to conform to alternative lifestyles simply because it has become fashionable to be 'different', and this causes many of its original occupants to feel lost and disenchanted. We see the story of Janus unfold through the eyes of eight narrators, each with their own perspective and their own personal journey. A story in which the nightclub itself goes on a journey. But throughout, one character, a strange girl, briefly appears and reappears warning the narrators that their individual journeys are going to collide in a cataclysmic event. Is she just another one of the nightclub's denizens, a cynical mischief-maker out to create havoc or a time-traveller trying to prevent an impending disaster?

ISBN: 9781908168566 (epub, kindle) / 9781908168467 (224pp paperback)
Visit bit.ly/JanusCycle

Dinnusos Rises

The vibe has soured somewhat after a violent clash in the Janus nightclub a few months ago, and since then Neal has opened a new establishment called 'Dinnusos'. Located on a derelict and forgotten side of town, it is not the sort of place you stumble upon by accident, but over time it enchants people, and soon becomes a nucleus for urban bohemians and a refuge for the city's lost souls. Rumour has it that it was once a grand hotel, many years ago, but no one is quite sure. Whilst mingling in the bar downstairs you might find yourself in the company of poets, dreamers, outsiders, and all manner of misfits and rebels. And if you're daring enough to explore its ghostly halls, there's a whole labyrinth of rooms on the upper floors to get lost in...

Now it seems that not just Neal's clientele, but the entire population of the city, begin to go crazy when beings, once thought mythological, enter the mortal realm to stir chaos as they sow the seeds of militancy.

Eight characters. Most of them friends, some of them strangers. Each with their own story to tell. All of them destined to cross paths in a surreal sequence of events which will change them forever.

ISBN: 9781911409137 (epub, kindle) / 9781911409038 (280pp paperback)
visit bit.ly/DinnusosRises

King Street Run

V. R. Ling

To Thomas, archaeology was time travel... little did he know how literal that would turn out to be.

King Street Run is a satirical fantasy thriller set among the iconic buildings of contemporary Cambridge.

Thomas Wharton, an archaeology graduate, becomes drawn into the problems of a series of anachronistic characters who exist in the fractions of a second behind our own time. These characters turn out to be personi cations of the Cambridge Colleges; they have the amalgamated foibles, history, and temperament of their Fellows and students and, together with Thomas, must enter into a race against time to prevent their world being destroyed by an unknown assailant.

At the age of six V.R. Ling (Victoria) watched the TV adaptation of *The Hitchhiker's Guide To The Galaxy* and it sparked a life-long love for science fiction and fantasy (she therefore considers the first five years of her life to have been a waste). Science and fiction have separately shaped her life; the science part came in the form of a degree in archaeology, a Masters in biological anthropology, and then a PhD in biological anthropology from King's College, Cambridge. On the fiction front, Victoria is influenced by the likes of H.G Wells, Jules Verne, M.R James, Charles Dickens, Wilkie Collins, and many others. Victoria by name, Victorian by nature. She is a huge animal lover, vegan, loves sixties music, adores classic *Doctor Who*, and has an antique book collection that smells as good as it looks.

ISBN: 9781915304513 (epub, kindle) / 97819153041414 (304pp paperback)

Visit bit.ly/KingStreetRun

ABOUT ERIN HOSFIELD

Erin has been an artist since she was able to hold a brush, and collected her BA in Fine Art from California University with the intent of becoming a painter. After falling in love with tattooing she decided to chase that dream instead, and made it a reality in 2006.

Outside her day job, that is very much a dream job, she likes to overextend herself by means of a variety of time consuming endeavors. She's an amateur herbalist, candlemaker, miniaturist, playlist curator, landscape painter, video game enthusiast, and most recently – novelist. Between those pursuits, she can be found having an anxiety attack from too much caffeine at her home in Pittsburgh, which she shares with her partner and two grouchy canines.